T0157432

FRAUGHT

WITH

HAZARD

FRAUGHT
WITH
HAZARD

The Heroic Saga of Shipwrecked
Armada Survivors in Ireland

Paul Hemenway Altrocchi
and Julia Cooley Altrocchi

FRAUGHT WITH HAZARD
THE HEROIC SAGA OF SHIPWRECKED
ARMADA SURVIVORS IN IRELAND

Copyright © 2015 Paul Hemenway Altrocchi.

All rights reserved. No part of this book may be used or reproduced by any means, graphic, electronic, or mechanical, including photocopying, recording, taping or by any information storage retrieval system without the written permission of the publisher except in the case of brief quotations embodied in critical articles and reviews.

Certain characters in this work are historical figures, and certain events portrayed did take place. However, this is a work of fiction. All of the other characters, names, and events as well as all places, incidents, organizations, and dialogue in this novel are either the products of the author's imagination or are used fictitiously. If there are only a few historical figures or actual events in the novel, the disclaimer could name them: For example: "Edwin Stanton and Salmon Chase are historical figures..." or "The King and Queen of Burma were actually exiled by the British in 1885." The rest of the disclaimer would follow: However, this is a work of fiction. All of the other characters, names, and events as well as all places, incidents, organizations, and dialogue in this novel are either are the products of the author's imagination or are used fictitiously.

iUniverse books may be ordered through booksellers or by contacting:

iUniverse
1663 Liberty Drive
Bloomington, IN 47403
www.iuniverse.com
1-800-Authors (1-800-288-4677)

Because of the dynamic nature of the Internet, any web addresses or links contained in this book may have changed since publication and may no longer be valid. The views expressed in this work are solely those of the author and do not necessarily reflect the views of the publisher, and the publisher hereby disclaims any responsibility for them.

Any people depicted in stock imagery provided by Thinkstock are models, and such images are being used for illustrative purposes only.
Certain stock imagery © Thinkstock.

ISBN: 978-1-4917-6679-8 (sc)
ISBN: 978-1-4917-6681-1 (hc)
ISBN: 978-1-4917-6680-4 (e)
Library of Congress Control Number: 2015906878

Print information available on the last page.

iUniverse rev. date: 05/18/2015

DEDICATION

To my daughter, Cate,
for suggesting and happily enriching
my retirement in Hawaii and for uplifting
the quality of my Golden Years' scribblings.

Contents

CHAPTER 1

Spain and God: A Holy Partnership?
(July 1588)

Captain Francisco de Cuellar paced the deck of the galleon *San Pedro* as the Armada neared the shores of England. Like an animal on the prowl, he used every one of his senses trying to surmise the intentions of his adversary. Somewhere on that dark sea Admiral Charles Howard, Commander of the English fleet, was deploying his ships to destroy the Armada before it could land troops to conquer England and restore Catholicism, the only True Religion. What was their unholy, anti-Godly plan?

Francisco was too alive in mind and body not to utilize all of his perceptive powers. As an Armada Captain he felt it his duty to interpret all clues provided by the enemy, both obvious and subtle, even though he knew it was the job of the Spanish Fleet Admiral, the Duke of Medina Sidonia, to read English minds and formulate tactics. Francisco was more than a little concerned, however, that Sidonia had no prior naval experience nor did the seasoned Army General, Francisco de Bovadilla, who commanded the invasion troops aboard.

As the wind quieted down, the Armada slowly emerged into a quieter sea, silvered by moonlight breaking through sprinting clouds. He noted the clutch of enemy ships' lanterns to the northeast bobbing up and down, first swarming to the southeast, now heading back towards the Cornish coast. *What are they up to?*

Francisco's eyes penetrated the darkness as he processed observations shouted down from the crow's nest. *What would I do if I were Sir Francis Drake, England's brilliant naval strategist? Surely his counsel prevails in conferences on board Admiral Howard's command ship because of his notable success against the Spanish, not only in the New World but also in Spain. I'd do the unexpected*, thought Francisco. *Are those lanterned ships merely decoys?*

Francisco used the intermittent splotches of moonlight to study the sea. He was uncertain whether the tiny black butterflies he seemed to visualize, hardly detectable against the dark waves far to the south and southeast, were phantoms or actual ships. An uncomfortable feeling spread across his chest. His sixth sense convinced him that those were unlighted Drake-led English ships moving sinisterly around the Armada to attack from the rear. *I must send a message to Medina Sidonia even though he may regard it as an intrusionary impertinence.*

Francisco immediately sent a pinnace to the fleet's command ship, the *San Martin*. The pinnace soon returned with a blunt "Dispatch received." The envoy reported that General Bovadilla, who at sea had virtually equal power to that of the naval Commander-in-Chief, had commented with contempt, "The English sneaking up on us from the rear? *Fantasia! Fantasia!* Can Captain Cuellar not see the lights of the English Armada to the north? When he has more experience in battle he will learn to trust his eyesight more than his presumptive imaginings!"

In two hours the night brightened towards day, clearly revealing the butterflies, now white-winged, to the rear of the Spaniards. It was indeed Drake's squadron, while Admiral Howard's group of ships beat along the southern English coast, always keeping the upwind weather gauge.

Medina Sidonia ran up the *San Martin's* Holy Standard and gave flag signals for his fleet to remain close together in their defensive, tightly packed, crescent formation. The Armada's curved shape looked like a huge bird of prey with the galleon *San Martin* and four galleasses being the head. The wings of fighting and supply ships fanned out on either side for a width of seven miles.

Francisco felt confident that Medina Sidonia would follow his King's orders and avoid sea battles with the English navy. Sidonia had more than

10,000 army personnel on his Armada ships but a successful invasion of England required the additional 16,000 battle-hardened troops of the Duke of Parma awaiting in the Netherlands. King Philip had repeatedly emphasized to his military leaders that the Armada must *not* engage English ships. The Armada *must* remain intact to achieve its primary duty of convoying and protecting the invasion force as it crossed the Channel, entered the Thames River estuary and landed its army, the best in the world, on English soil for a quick victory.

Francisco silently cursed the Armada leadership, particularly Sidonia's complete lack of naval knowledge and strategy. Francisco knew that the Duke had begged his King not to name him the Armada's Commander because of that very inexperience. King Philip, heavily bound by Spanish tradition, had insisted on appointing the leading noble of the realm so all would respect him.

As English Admiral Howard ran up the blood-red fighting flag from his mainmast, a small English pinnace, the *Defiance*, sailed close to one of the Biscayan vessels and fired a broadside as a defiant gesture of contempt. Rather than returning fire, Medina Sidonia ordered shipboard musicians to play stirring, fight-for-God religious music—*Regi Perennis Gloriae, Salve Regina* and other inspiring hymns. Francisco wondered if Sidonia, who was deeply religious, thought of his Spanish ships as floating churches rather than powerful fighting machines.

Soon Drake began an attack upon Portugal's *San Juan*, sailing up rapidly in his smaller *Revenge* and, at a distance of a few yards, pouring cannonballs into her and then sailing away before the unwieldy *Spanish* galleon could maneuver her guns. Admiral Sidonia immediately ordered raising of the battle flags. Combat began in earnest.

Francisco had heard on the docks of Lisbon that under the direction of experienced Captain John Hawkins, the English Admiralty and their naval architects had for years been building a modern fleet of smaller, sleeker, faster fighting ships to accord with a new English naval strategy—never come within "push of pike" of the enemy ships, never grapple and board them—tactics which had been time-honored methods of war at sea since the eras of ancient Greeks and Romans.

Naval battles henceforth would be a combat of ships, not of army soldiers on decks slippery with blood. Always stay upwind of the enemy,

3

dart in and out of the enemy battle line, turn quickly into the wind or tack at angles impossible for the top-heavy, lumbering galleons and galleasses of the Armada.

Francisco had also heard that English gun designers were building guns with purer iron content and better-built gun carriages for more rapid and accurate firing. English guns could be made ready in a minute or two for reloading and firing their quick broadsides by highly-trained gun crews. Spanish gunners, by contrast, could only re-fire their cannons, locked into heavy unwieldy gun mounts, after thirty to sixty minutes or even longer. Francisco knew that their own gunners, from all over the Spanish Empire including Italy, Sicily and Sardinia, often had no training at all. Spanish Admirals had such limited ammunition that they didn't allow target practice in the months the Armada lay in harbor in Lisbon. Now they faced an entirely new kind of battle.

Many Spanish cannons were made of inferior grades of iron full of air bubbles. Such cannons often exploded after a few shots, killing their gun crews. Many cannonballs burst in the air long before reaching their targets. Cannonballs usually missed the rapidly-moving English ships by such a wide margin that sometimes the Spanish could hear loud laughter from English crews.

Francisco was concerned that English ships were all captained by highly experienced men such as Drake and Hawkins who had years of familiarity with the winds, currents and tides of the English Channel. The faster, more adroit English ships were sailing in under the castles of the galleons and galleasses, delivering shots on one side then darting around to the other side to deliver another broadside and flicking away like porpoises playing games against slowly-moving whales.

The *San Pedro* soon found itself, as Francisco wanted, in the midst of the fighting, but the Spaniards were totally unprepared for the English quick-attack-and-run tactics. The sulfurous smoke made it hard to get the big picture except when gusts of wind cleared the air. Gradually Francisco became aware that Portugal's *San Juan*, under the leadership of second-in-command Admiral Juan Martinez de Recalde, was the continuing target of Drake, Hawkins and Frobisher. Medina Sidonia, now coming up alongside, ordered the *San Pedro* and several other fighting ships to follow him to rescue the *San Juan*.

Francisco's ship came nearer and nearer to the cannon blasts surrounding the *San Juan*. Then there was sudden silence on the sea. The wounded *San Juan* stood alone. Drake and his comrades had slipped the leash of battle to attack in another unexpected quarter, keeping the Spanish fleet off-balance, never in the right strategic place. The *San Juan* sailed into the protective embrace of the *San Martin*, *San Pedro* and two other Spanish galleons.

It was clear to Francisco that the English ships were experimenting with various tactics, seeing which were more effective against the top-heavy, poorly-maneuverable Spanish ships led by captains who had little or no experience with naval warfare.

Clever tactics for heretics, thought Francisco, *keeping the Armada constantly on the defensive, completely neutralizing hundreds of years of Spanish battle experience with grappling and boarding. Were the English actually the ones with new modern ideas and strategies, including religious? If so, who should be regarded as heretics? Is it possible that the status quo, old guard Spanish leaders, who tenaciously grip outmoded ideas like hawks clutching their taloned prey, are the real heretics by steadfastly refusing to change either their worldly or other-worldly concepts?*

Francisco wondered how ordinary Spanish naval seamen and army recruits could regard their Armada as a serious military venture when each officer took several gentlemen friends and "retainers" along with them. All the gentlemen officers and guests brought servants. Francisco invited no one to accompany him but he knew that Prince Ascoli had brought thirty-nine servants and Don Alonso Martinez de Leyva thirty-six. Commander Medina Sidonia brought a retinue of twenty-two noblemen and forty servants. Several Spanish officers even brought their wives, as if they were all going on a holiday picnic.

Francisco thought about the tons of weight these extra guests added, and the tons of extra food necessary and the confused thinking which allowed such inefficient practices.

Francisco reflected on the useless carnage when a single cannonball struck decks crowded not only with useless personnel but with hundreds of troops ready to board the enemy's ships in a battle guided by English non-grappling strategy. When the trim English ships sailed past the hulking Spanish galleons, their culverins sprayed the upper decks with anti- personnel metal fragments while gunners manning the cannons on decks below waited until the Spanish ships were heeled over somewhat to the opposite side so they could aim their cannonballs below the water line. The logic of such focused tactics was impressive.

Francisco had heard from his veteran navy seamen that the English would have no army troops aboard or any servants or noble guests. They kept decks open for maximal efficiency of the crew in carrying out essential sailing and battle tasks. No wonder the English fleet was so superior, not merely in ship design.

Francisco shook his head as if trying to eject these dangerous thoughts and facts from his brain. He knew he had a general openness of mind and wondered whether anyone else in the Armada allowed such contrary ideas to breach the traditional Spanish military mind-set. *But I must keep these thoughts to myself in an epoch dominated by the Spanish Inquisition. It is not prudent to disagree either with religious orthodoxy or any military or political decisions guided by an absolute monarch.*

Drake and his comrades soon returned and concentrated on Pedro Valdes' *Rosario* which had become temporarily detached from her Andalusian consorts. Captain Valdes, trying to get away from multiple fusillades, had crashed his ship into the *Santa Caterina,* causing the *Rosario's* bowsprit to fall into the sea. Drake concentrated on the rest of the *Rosario's* rigging.

Suddenly a powerful explosion shook the sea and roiled the waters as the *Rosario's* stored powder kegs exploded. The eruption spewed sailors, soldiers, masts and rigging high into the air like a volcanic eruption and then splattered them into the devouring deep. Francisco saw the terrible blast. *If destiny demands*, he thought, *I and my ship will sink into the blue-black depths but only if I can take Drake with me. God put him into my hands, I pray thee.*

Valdes made the signal of distress with his flags. Francisco sailed the *San Pedro* towards the *Rosario*. He was almost within shouting distance, his battle soul afire, when Medina Sidonia's flagship signaled "Disengage. Head eastward at once."

Francisco couldn't believe the message. Was the Admiral abandoning the *Rosario* to its fate? Hard to swallow and obey. Francisco fired a defiant but distant salvo at the swiftly-moving *Revenge* of Drake as it closed in.

A cloud of battle smoke blew Francisco's way, dropping yellow-brown sulfur veils over the *San Pedro*, preventing him from watching the further tragic demise of the gallant *Rosario*, now in the hands of *El Draque*, whom Francisco knew had perfected his piratical tactics stealing gold and jewels from King Philip's treasure ships in the Caribbean and along the coasts of Spanish America.

The *San Pedro's* twenty-six year-old Captain Francisco de Cuellar bowed his head and said a brief prayer. He was a pious Catholic, totally loyal to his devout, divinely-inspired king, but he had an analytical mind and wanted to justify his captainship by improving his ship's battle performance. Francisco crossed himself as he stared into the twilight of an embarrassing first day of battle, wondering what God, Fortune and Sir Francis Drake had in store for him. Would the war last longer than the few weeks King Philip had promised?

Francisco tried to suppress any negative thoughts about their first battle with the English but he didn't succeed. King Philip had convinced him that conquering heretic England and getting rid of Queen Elizabeth were heavenly missions carried out with God's approval. *Is it possible that King Philip and Spain are wrong? Could their invasion of England be ill-advised?*

Vignettes of his small family castle in Cuellar passed through Francisco's mind. *Will my aging mother still be alive when I return? How long will I be absent from my passionate bride, Zabella? Will her feelings towards me change if I am gone from home more than a few months?*

CHAPTER 2

Onwards Into the Future
(April 1588)

Three months before the Armada's first unsavory battle with England's navy off the coast of Cornwall, the mouth-watering scent of lamb roasting on a spit lured Francisco and his best friend, Sebastian, into the brick-lined kitchen of Francisco's castle in the town of Cuellar in north central Spain. Francisco's freshly-minted bride, Zabella, and his mother, Doña Anna, were almost finished preparing the farewell feast.

From the cellar rack Zabella selected a bottle of ten-year-old red wine from the family vineyards. She greeted her husband with a tight embrace and extended a warm hand to Sebastian. "Welcome, brave military adventurers. Sebastian, I have heard a great deal about you, *con mucho gusto*. Welcome to Cuellar! Now let us celebrate as we send you both on your noble venture plied with such affectionate memories that you will return to us quickly and victoriously."

The table was set under the grape arbor in the castle's small courtyard. The late morning meal was both festive and poignant. Francisco and Sebastian were leaving that day to join the Armada in the Spanish invasion of England. The lively courtyard conversation was tinted with somber seriousness. At meal's end Zabella and Doña Anna cleared the table and began packing food for the men's trip to Lisbon. Francisco and Sebastian sipped fortified *vino de Jerez*, Spanish sherry, and then decided to take a walk through town.

"I can see that you are happy," Sebastian said, "but tell me, what do you really know about Zabella? Do you mind if I ask?"

"Not at all, old friend." Francisco explained to Sebastian that Zabella had felt out of place on her family's small farm in rural southern Spain so she moved to Salamanca at the age of seventeen. She worked as a waitress at a Basque restaurant for three years and then became the restaurant's lead dancer. She next decided she wanted to try her hand at business. She talked the restaurant owner into allowing her to open a satellite Basque restaurant in Cuellar with her as manager and half-owner.

Francisco continued. "Three months after she opened *The Shepherd,* we met and rapidly fell in love. Her restaurant is already successful and is especially crowded on Friday and Saturday nights when Zabella expertly performs old Spanish folk dances with castanets."

They walked down the cobblestone street past pigeons pecking at invisible seeds as Francisco pointed out the landmarks. From time to time they glanced back at the small hilltop castle which overlooked the surrounding agricultural valleys. The castle had been built by an ancestor of Francisco in the 1300s supported by several hundred acres of vineyards, olive groves, wheat, oats, onions and beets along with pastures for sheep and cattle.

"I'm sorry you couldn't make the wedding, Sebastian, but I'm very glad you could meet Zabella and my mother before we join the Armada."

"They are both most attractive and gracious ladies but why did such a conservative fellow decide to marry Zabella after only a few weeks' acquaintance? Why not just get engaged?"

"She makes me feel whole following many years adrift after leaving the university where you tried to lure me into all kinds of depravity. Zabella is vibrant, exuberant, spontaneous and has none of the haughtiness and false airs of wealthy girls which I find so distasteful. I feel blessed."

"It's a shame you've only had a few days with her as your wife before we head off to help fulfill King Philip's divine mission."

Sebastian and Francisco had become close friends in 1578 in their first year at the University of Salamanca, Spain's oldest university, founded in 1218. After three years, Francisco became frustrated with his studies, quit and joined Philip II's navy. Soon thereafter, the king decided to expand his Empire and his grip on world trade by annexing Portugal, which he justified because his mother, Isabella, had been a Portuguese Princess.

When the main Portuguese island of the Azores, Terceira, refused to recognize Philip as its King, Spain's navy invaded the Azores. In the ensuing humiliating battle, the Spanish navy was roundly defeated. Francisco was wounded in the arm but distinguished himself. Two years later he was First Mate on a galleon which helped conquer the Azores. After his father died, Francisco resigned from the navy to return to Cuellar to manage the family estate.

In January 1588 two events occurred almost simultaneously— Francisco met and promptly fell in love with Zabella and he was called back to duty by King Philip. He was given three months to get his estate in order and then report as Captain of the galleon, *San Pedro*. At age twenty-six he was the youngest Armada Captain. He believed fervently in his King's self-appointed mission to enfold Protestant England back into the Vatican's loving embrace.

Despite his mother's gentle suggestions to wait and let the relationship with Zabella blossom and solidify over time, Francisco was not to be deterred and the marriage had occurred a week before.

Sebastian, meanwhile, graduated with a BA and MA after six years of study and many romantic flings. He took two years off to travel around Europe but, at his father's urging, he returned to Salamanca for a Ph.D. in Religious Studies. Francisco knew that Sebastian, during his first year, had become progressively more disillusioned with Catholic fanaticism, the Inquisition and burnings-at-the-stake. He finally withdrew and joined the army. He arrived in Cuellar a week after Francisco's marriage, on the day they had to leave to join the *Felicisima Armada*, the Most Fortunate Fleet, in its glorious quest to conquer England.

They walked back to the castle where Sebastian enthusiastically thanked Doña Anna and Zabella for their hospitality and told Francisco, "I will go on ahead and wait for you so you will have privacy to take your leave."

"Thank you, my friend. Would you walk both horses to the San Basilio town gate? I don't want to look like El Cid dramatically riding out to battle!"

Francisco hugged his tearful mother and began walking arm in arm with Zabella down the cobbled streets towards his proud destiny. He looked at his wife with ardor pulsing through his body. She was not a classical beauty but was alluring and pretty. He adored her seductive smile, stunning figure, energetic personality and passionate love-making. Above her low-cut, white flowered blouse her thin neck was encircled by his wedding present—a necklace of deep blue sapphires on a sterling silver chain.

Que atractiva! Que pasión! thought Francisco. How lucky to have found such a happy and enthusiastic wife, especially one with no experience with men despite her age of twenty-five. She had confessed that she had kissed two or three men in Salamanca but had never allowed them to be alone with her, following the advice of her devoutly religious mother. Many times during the past week she had told Francisco that being with him made her very glad she had waited.

Francisco promised he would return triumphantly home in time for the fall harvest. As Francisco and his bride walked towards the main town gate, they were surrounded by a bevy of children who followed him as closely as the children of Hamelin had tailed the Pied Piper.

The children were very fond of him. He often came down to Cathedral Square in late afternoon, sat on the church steps and sang songs to the accompaniment of his *vihuela* with its six pairs of gut strings. He preferred its softer sweeter sounds to those produced by his *guitarra*. Sometimes he gathered the group at the town's San Basilio gate with its two defensive towers, one square and one round. He sang about Durindal, the great sword of Roldan, which changed into a Spanish knight; about the battles of Rey Don Rodrigo, last King of the Goths; about the Moors during their more than 700 year occupation of Spain; and about gypsies whose encampments in the plain of Segovia he had often visited. He told the children stories of his battles in the Azores and tales of the Court at Madrid where he had worked when his father was Treasurer to the King.

"Sing us a song, Don Francisco!" they begged. "Tell us stories!"

"Today, *niños,* I depart to do God's work for our king. I shall tell you all about my adventures when I return! Here is your reward for seeing me off!" He passed them handfuls of sugar cakes made by Doña Anna and they twittered like excited sparrows.

As they trudged away, Zabella heaved an audible sigh of relief and then asked, "Will you indeed be back soon, *amante mio?*" She looked at his handsome face, radiating energy and good humor. He was tall with features more Celtic than Latin, with dark blue eyes under thick black eyebrows, a somewhat pointed chin and wide lips.

"Can you doubt it? The greatest Armada in history is waiting in Lisbon and the greatest army in the world is assembled in Flanders under the Duke of Parma. We will slaughter them. Then we will sail home with English treasure in Spanish chests! I will bring you fancy clothes and sparkling jewels, my darling. God oversees our heroic task!"

"I believe you, my noble husband," said Zabella as she kissed him fervently.

They had come to the church square in the center of town. Dom Pedro, the priest whom Francisco had known all his life, hurried over.

"Ah, my boy, God be with you and may our Blessed Lady of Henar, protectress of Cuellar and of all its people, keep you safe. I have no doubt you will return a hero!"

From around the plaza, townspeople called out, *"Adios. Adios, Don Francisco!"* and shouted wishes for *"buena fortuna"* and *"salvo retorno."* Francisco smiled and waved.

As they walked towards the town gate hand in hand, the Segovian plain stretched before Francisco and Zabella. Paired oxen were plowing red earth in the cool sunshine of early April. He took a deep breath, relishing the smell of freshly turned, moist soil. Almond trees tipped with red buds stood behind starkly leafless, gnarly grapevines. Two shepherds and their dogs were tending large flocks of sheep. In the distance beyond the silver windings of the Eresma and Clamores Rivers were the beautiful snow-capped Guadarrama mountains.

These scenic landscapes of Cuellar and its environs were deeply imprinted on Francisco's soul. He squeezed Zabella's hand and said, "How lovely Spain is and how beautiful you are!"

Zabella looked up and smiled broadly. They walked through the double-towered gateway where Sebastian waited with the two horses which were cropping grass between cobblestones.

Sebastian de Carvajal was of short stature with a classic handsome Spanish look, his face darkened by Moorish admixture. Below wide shoulders his toned torso thinned to a narrow waist. His face was oval with sharp cheek bones, a long aquiline nose and full lips. His dark brown eyes twinkled with irony and mirth. His black hair curled along a smooth olive forehead.

"Watch over this handsome warrior, Francisco," said Zabella. "He will leave a trail of swooning girls from here to London!"

Francisco embraced Zabella, kissed her tenderly and watched her start back towards the castle. *"Adios, mi amor!* I shall return soon!" he shouted.

She turned, threw him a kiss and waved. As her red skirt swayed into the distance, the two men returned to the city gate. They mounted their horses and rode past Francisco's vineyards and fields, reaching a place which gave the last clear glimpse of the hill of Cuellar. On the high castle battlement the miniature figure of Doña Anna was visible. Francisco waved his black velvet cap with its white plume.

"Anda! Hacia adelante!" cried out Sebastian. "Onwards into the future!" He cracked his riding-whip close to Francisco's knee, sending both horses galloping down the southwest road towards Salamanca, Alcantara and Lisbon where, on the broad waters of the Tagus River estuary, the greatest gathering of ships in history rested peacefully on calm waters, its sailors and soldiers supremely confident in their destiny.

CHAPTER 3

Divinely Inspired Mission
(July 1588)

As the early dawn began to hue the scattered clouds, Francisco de Cuellar stood at the prow of the *San Pedro* wondering how and why the powerful Armada had been so humiliated in their first battle against the English navy the day before. He stood straight, befitting a confidant Captain in the world's most powerful navy . . . or was it? *Could yesterday be just a series of unlucky coincidences,* he wondered, *or was it a foreshadowing of disastrous future events?*

As a pious Catholic he was eager to help King Philip and God punish Queen Elizabeth's England for repudiating Catholicism. Once the Armada had defeated or bypassed the English navy, England was protected mostly by civilians armed only with farm implements. It should be an easy conquest in just a few days or weeks. Most of England's regular army was helping the Dutch free themselves from Spanish Catholic colonialism in the Netherlands.

In this gentlest of seasons for ocean weather—the summer—the Armada had already encountered several gales since leaving Lisbon on May 20, 1588. Among the 131 crewmen and 141 soldiers on board the *San Pedro*, there was already spreading discontent about rotted food, foul drinking water and crowded conditions.

Flashing through his mind like vivid frescoes, Francisco kept rekindling scenes since he had ridden from Cuellar Castle on that early April day three months before. He visualized the Armada moored on the Tagus, looking so invincible as Lisbon's Archbishop blessed the Holy Venture while standing on the deck of the fleet's flagship underneath its majestic banner with a crucified Christ on one side and a gigantic Madonna on the other. He remembered Lisbon's Holy Nuns presenting sacred relics to all ship captains to guarantee the Armada's success. Then came the up-anchor and away, martial and hymnal music ringing out from every ship: *"O Gloriosa Domina, Excelsa Supra Sidera . . . Gloria a Dios en las Alturas . . . Ave Virgo Sanctissima."* How could chests not swell with pride and certainty of victory?

In the lead of the Armada was the mighty 2000 ton galleon, *San Martin*, under command of the 39 year-old Duke of Medina Sidonia, owner the largest agricultural estates in Spain and inheritor of the oldest dukedom in the country.

Francisco had been made aware that the Duke disliked military people, hated war, got seasick easily and tried his best to talk King Philip out of making him overall Armada commander. He was chosen only for his high social position after the first Commander, the Marquis de Santa Cruz, the most respected military leader in Spain, unexpectedly died a few weeks before the Armada was scheduled to sail. The Duke knew nothing about war at sea but the King wouldn't change his mind.

In the Parade of Ships on the Tagus, next came the Squadron of Portugal, with Francisco's best friend, soldier-sergeant Sebastian, aboard its primary ship, the galleon *San Marcos*. Then followed the great squadron of Castile, including Francisco's own galleon *San Pedro* and one of several ships in the Armada named *San Juan*. Most Armada ships had sails dramatically emblazoned with a blood-red cross on a white background, or the reverse. Francisco recalled how the *San Pedro's* blue-and-gold banner of the Madonna took the wind so impressively over the horse head prow, the ancient symbol of the town of Cuellar.

Next came the four huge galleasses of the squadron of Naples—the *San Lorenzo, Zuñiga, Girona* and *Napolitana*. These were so bulky, slow and unwieldy that they often had to be propelled by a tier of oars on each side with four or five rowers per oar. Rather than the slaves used in Roman warships, Spanish oarsmen were conscripted criminals who could shorten their sentences by volunteering as oarsmen in time of war.

The Armada sailed majestically past the lovely villas, gardens and flowering orchards of Lisbon's elite suburbs with sunlight falling warm and golden in a seemingly Holy benediction. Then the endless parade of ships sailed out of the broad Tagus estuary into the Atlantic, turning north on pleasant summer breezes towards inevitable victory. Almost immediately, however, came an unseasonal shift of wind striking sails with full fury from the north, driving the poorly maneuverable ships many miles south to Cape Espichel.

As the Armada slowly struggled north over succeeding days, many seamen became sick from the food. The eleven million pounds of Armada biscuits were barely edible, some made from flour poisoned with lye by the Portuguese, presumably as revenge for Spain's invasion and quick conquering of their country based solely upon King Philip's omnivorous appetite for power and wealth. The Portuguese had enjoyed their independence since 1143 and were proud of their blossoming culture and worldly expansion, especially to Africa and South America. Francisco had been told many times by Portuguese seamen how the concept of being a colony of Spain again was absolute anathema to most Portuguese citizens.

Francisco thought further about the Armada's "bad luck." Much of the 600,000 pounds of pork and similar amounts of beef and fish, despite liberal sprinkling with salt, had rotted in hastily constructed barrels made of green untempered oak. The cheese was moldy and stinking. Many of the 11,000 barrels of fresh water, sitting for weeks on the warm docks of Lisbon, had become contaminated because the wood was not properly seasoned.

Most of these problems were caused by Sir Francis Drake's audacious attack on Cadiz and nearby ports of Spain and Portugal in April of 1587, destroying 1700 tons of seasoned oak barrels and staves. This necessitated manufacturing thousands of casks with green wood, preventing the natural expansion of dry seasoned wood which ensured their intactness. This caused internal contamination and rotting, ruining a significant proportion of the Armada's food and water supplies which had to be thrown into the sea. The meager diet of Armada personnel now consisted mainly of beans, rice, chick peas, weevil-infested biscuits, dried fruit and barrels of cheap acidic wine which evolved more towards vinegar every day.

Francisco found it difficult to believe that sixty-one year-old King Philip did not assign invasion planning to military professionals. Francisco had been informed by court insiders that the king spent most of his time ensconced in his new Palace of Escorial twenty-eight miles northwest of Madrid, almost monk-like in his asceticism, brooding and planning alone, refusing any input from his court advisers in Madrid and issuing orders himself after consultation with God.

Francisco, as Captain of the *San Pedro*, tried his best to instill good cheer in his men and emphasize the holy quest of their mission but it already was an uphill struggle with daily exposure to foul food and unusually stormy weather. Many crewmen became too sick and weak to man the yards. Dark looks and dark hearts became increasingly commonplace.

The Armada finally reached Cape Prior on the northern Atlantic coast of Spain but mighty adverse winds out of the northwest scattered the fleet. Most ships eventually were able to re-join the Armada in the harbor of Corunna but valuable summer invasion-time was being lost. Admiral Medina Sidonia wrote to King Philip advising him to abandon the exploit because the inauspicious beginning, especially the weather, could mean that God had forsaken them. The King, however, sitting in his cold, bleak office reached by a secret door behind the altar of Escorial Chapel, ordered the expedition to proceed as planned and confidently predicted that God would always work His miracles to bail them out.

Many disagreed with the King's logic including his nephew, Alexander Farnese, Duke of Parma, Spain's Army Commander in the Netherlands for ten years. Regarded as the finest Army leader in Europe, he had been battling English troops for three years and had been able to defeat them only in small skirmishes. Larger battles usually ended in a stalemate. Francisco had heard that Parma had a high regard for English generals and was against the entire concept of invading England, fearing that he would lose his crack troops in a useless cause. He had warned his uncle that "God will eventually tire of working miracles for us."

Feverish repair work on leaking ships and wind-battered masts and sails was carried out in Corunna's harbor by day and torch-lighted night. On July 22, 1588, the Armada finally sailed under a fair wind from the south. When new storms arose, with winds almost always from the north, many of the ultra-religious Catholic crew also began to wonder whose side God was on.

The sun was breaking through the clouds and seemed to shine directly upon the flagship *San Martin*. As the banner of Christ and the Virgin unfurled in the strong wind, trumpets on every ship sounded the call to morning Mass. Every man went down on his knees. Philip had ordered that morning prayers and evening Angelus were obligatory. This was a Holy Mission of God. A Dominican friar, Father Antonio, presided as the men intoned: "0h great God, Sovereign Lord of Heaven and Earth, Thy will be done . . . Holy Mary, Mother of God, pray for us now on our Sanctified Mission."

Francisco welcomed the oncoming conflict as a young giant might welcome the prospect of tossing a pygmy over his shoulder. After all, Spain had the mightiest army and navy in the world. *Despite yesterday's clashes, how could some of my men fear Captain Drake, a common pirate-thief, the eldest of twelve sons of a farmer?*

After morning prayers, Francisco stood on the deck and spoke to his men: "Here we are, comrades, on one of the greatest adventures Spaniards have ever had the glorious privilege to engage in . . ." A deck-hand coughed derisively and spat into the sea.

"It will be clear sailing from now on," continued Francisco, "and a quick victory despite yesterday's unpleasant encounters with our enemy. God and our Lady of Henar are with us. Here is a special token the holy nuns of Lisbon gave me as a sacred relic to bring us good fortune." He put his hand to his neck and drew out a thick gold chain with a gold and glass locket attached.

"Here in this locket is part of a finger bone of St. Lawrence, Patron Saint of King Philip." He handed it to Father Antonio. "Bless us with it, Father, if you will."

Padre Antonio passed among the ranks of soldiers, sailors and noblemen gathered on deck, waving the locket and intoning the sainted blessing. Negative utterings could be heard. One sailor said, "If that Devil Drake attacks us again, spitting fire as he did yesterday, that could be the end of us."

"The end of us?" cried Francisco in a booming voice. Having noted this little group of malcontents gathered below the mainmast, he had walked quickly into their midst. "Anyone who talks about Drake like a scared rabbit will do double duty. What's your name, sailor?"

"Leon Perez of Avila, Sir."

"Leon? A lion, indeed! Straighten out your mane, let out a roar and get to work, Lion. For your comments, I'm sending you down to the bilge to relieve one of the pump men. As for Drake, he's just another man like you and me, not a devil or dragon. He's just a lucky risk-taker with bravado."

Back on the prow Francisco inhaled the surrounding fog, relishing the smell of the alluring mist and silently praying that God would grant him the opportunity to send Drake and his *Revenge* to the bottom of the sea to keep his rendezvous with Neptune.

Deep in his heart, however, for one of the few times in his life, Francisco harbored pessimistic feelings about King Philip's divinely inspired mission. *What was divine about conquering and killing people for believing in a somewhat different religion? Why was Spain being led by an eccentric loner who lived like a monk communing in solitude with God, remote from common Armada sailors and soldiers who were putting their lives in jeopardy to invade a country they knew nothing about?*

Listening to the wailing of petrels in the dense fog, Francisco thought that these English Channel seabirds seemed to agree with his moody mental meanderings.

CHAPTER 4

The *Felicisima Armada* Attacks
(August 2, 1588)

The Spanish Armada sailed slowly in its tight bird-of-prey formation eastward along the coast of France towards Calais and its rendezvous with Parma's army. The wind was from the northeast, allowing the Armada to have the weather gauge for the first time. Admiral Medina Sidonia immediately ordered an attack on the English navy. The great Spanish ships slowly turned around and, with the northeast wind at their backs, sailed down the channel towards their adversaries.

Francisco gazed at the waves and shook his head. *How can our admiral so easily violate the fundamental strategic order of our king never to directly engage the English ships in battle, thus putting in jeopardy the basic mission of the Armada which is to convoy our invasion troops?*

The Armada's drums sounded and her soldiers shouted as the two navies came closer. Every Armada ship had selected its target. Its massed forward line was steady, assured, mighty. *La Regazona*, a huge galleass, advanced upon Admiral Howard's ship, the *Ark Royal*. *La Regazona's* thirty cannon thundered but most cannonballs widely missed their target or exploded in the air. General Martin de Bertendona had marshaled his soldiers on the boarding deck, ready to leap across to the *Ark Royal* as soon as secure grappling was accomplished.

Figure 1. Map of Europe at the time of the Spanish Armada's planned invasion of England in 1588.

Francisco's *San Pedro* eased towards Drake's *Revenge*. Confusion was evident on Spanish ships with so many troops crowding the decks. Army and Navy officers often gave simultaneous conflicting orders. The *Ark Royal* and the *Revenge* came closer through the rifting smoke.

Then an unseen but mighty ghost intervened. The wind veered in from the south. The sails of the Spanish Armada fluttered and whipped and the ships slowed. The English fleet quickly adapted and sailed northward around the Armada. Francisco observed that Drake preferred to initiate strategy rather than respond to it. The Armada tried to tack but the high, castled ships were so unwieldy that they could not sail closer to the wind than at right angles.

There was now a cluster of Spanish fighting vessels around the *Triumph*. Sidonia signaled Francisco to accompany him as he advanced upon Frobisher's ship. The splendid *San Martin* moved ahead, with the *San Pedro* following, all pennons flying. Several swift English ships came to rescue the *Triumph*. Cannons thundered and the water churned with the splash of Spanish cannonballs falling short. The Spanish ships, their decks red with blood, swayed under the impact of English cannonballs, their masts splintered. Sailors and soldiers fell like toys. Most of the English ships were completely intact as they sailed swiftly past the bulky Armada ships, unleashing their devastating cascades of cannonballs at close range.

The *San Pedro* began to receive fire. Its cannons boomed back but its inexperienced gunners missed badly. Francisco saw a line of his men bowled over by a cannonball and the deck washed with streams of blood. Father Antonio was there in a moment with his cross and last rites.

There was a sudden shivering of the *San Pedro* from a volley of cannonballs delivered from the opposite direction. Francisco rushed to the other side. There, sailing past in all her trim sleekness, was Fleet Commander Howard's *Ark Royal*, his Queen's lion-and-unicorn standard with her motto of *Semper Eadem*, "Always the Same," flung in time-defying words, her bright red cross of St. George and her Tudor lion pennons flying from the mainmast. Francisco knew that Admiral Howard was a widely-respected diplomat and cousin of Queen Elizabeth and that he always chose his captains based solely on their naval experience and expertise.

"Blast her, blast her!" shouted Francisco but the *San Pedro's* shots fell short as the *Ark Royal* rushed on to Frobisher's rescue. The *San Juan, Florencia, San Cristobal, San Pedro* and the Armada's flagship, the *San Martin*, kept firing as the sea was lashed into a white fury. The sounds of cannon, straining rigging, pounding of drums, squealing of trumpets, shouts of the officers and screams and groans of the dying overwhelmed the air.

The *San Pedro* was leaking badly and one mast had been struck. Francisco sent more pump men below. Using their very successful tactic of darting in close and blasting away at point blank range, then speeding away, the English ships remained almost unscathed. In a great rift in the sulfur smoke, Francisco and his soldiers and sailors watched as the *Ark Royal* sent a blast through the *San Martin's* rigging, folding the Holy Standard of Christ upon the mast like the head of a crucified Christ leaning on his chest.

A groan went up from Francisco's ship and many men crossed themselves. The event seemed symbolic, like a stroke of doom against the magnificent ships of the *Grande y Felicisima Armada*. Francisco felt physically crushed but he rallied his spirit and cried out, *"Coraje. Anda! Anda, Santiago,"* giving the favorite war cry of officers to instill courage in their men to go on the attack, using the name of St. James, the apostle of Christ who was patron saint of Spain.

Now Francisco was everywhere on deck shouting orders and encouragement. But Sidonia's *San Martin* was crowding back upon him. Howard and Drake were pounding it and now two other ships were bearing down on the *San Pedro*. Thunderous cannons and smaller culverins smashed into his ship at a rate ten times faster than the Spanish cannons fired.

At the end of fifteen minutes there were many holes in the hulls of the *San Martin* and *San Pedro* and none in English hulls. The doom of death was descending on the squadrons of Castile and Portugal and the great flagship of the Spanish Armada. Cold black wings of defeat seemed to be pressing their ships downward into the sea. Not far away was *El Draque* feinting, pivoting and completely preventing traditional Spanish grappling strategy.

Trying hard to rise above the tragic panoramic ocean scene of ignominious defeat orchestrated by the immensely clever strategist, Sir Francis Drake, Francisco looked up into the sky, crossed himself and said quietly, "God, give me the power, opportunity and righteousness to blast that clever wizard out of the sea."

Suddenly the British cannonading ceased. Through the shreds of sulfur vapor, Francisco saw the English ships tacking away to the northwest. A signal-gun sounded from Sidonia's ship. The *San Pedro* and other heavy Spanish galleons made the agonizingly slow circle back into their defensive crescent formation, leaving the sea-fields of defeat. It was now late afternoon. In silence the dejected Spaniards gathered around the mainmast of Francisco's *San Pedro* and lifted their tired voices in the obligatory *Ave Maria*. Following mass, the chanting burial ceremony for dead comrades was conducted by the two friars, with seventeen cocooned bodies slanted into the sea.

The music had scarcely faded on the yellowish, smoky afternoon air when a pinnace was seen moving away from the Spanish Admiral's flagship towards the *San Pedro*. Captain Cuellar ordered his men to draw up in formation on deck. The rope ladder was let down and up came a messenger with the standard of Medina Sidonia and a rolled parchment. He was followed by a heavy-set individual in red doublet and hose, black jerkin and black cloak who carried over his shoulder, blade down, an axe. No one failed to recognize the official fleet hangman.

The bearer handed the parchment to Francisco. The document was signed by Admiral Sidonia and was brutally blunt. It declared that hereafter the captain of any ship which left its assigned place in the line and order of battle would be hanged without appeal or parley. Francisco wondered whether the Admiral was already seeking scapegoats to cover his own ineptitude.

The message bearer handed the Captain a small oblong of paper on which was written: "Admiral the Duke of Medina Sidonia's order of August 2,1588, fifth hour, received by . . ." and requested Captain Francisco to sign it. He did, with strong strokes, as anger erupted within him.

How could battles be won if formations and alignments must be so stringently kept in the fury of battle? What if he had Drake lined up for powerful cannon blasts? Should he abandon his temporary advantage just to stay in line, as at a sixth grade dancing lesson? Good Lord! Did dedicated Spaniards fight best when under threat of death from their own inexperienced, amateurish leaders?

Francisco concluded that Army Commander Francisco Bovadilla must have played a lead role in this battle absurdity and that, except for Spanish tradition, it was completely illogical for Bovadilla to have any power of command whatsoever in a naval battle. He walked briskly back to the *San Pedro's* prow, feeling deeply the pervasive bitterness of failure. *It is becoming dramatically clear,* thought Francisco, *that the Armada is not going to achieve its divine mission unless God Himself intervenes with a well-timed miracle or two.*

CHAPTER 5

Fiery Panic

(August 7, 1588)

A day at sea in a galleon is not a silent experience. Ships create their own world of noises. Timbers creak and groan endlessly with different tones and rhythms, made louder by the fulcrum power of too-high, too-heavy Spanish masts constantly swaying from side to side. Sails of different sizes flap, hum and sing as the wind frequently changes in speed and direction. Broad prows don't slash cleanly through the turbulent sea but cause dull thuds echoing through the ship.

Seagulls, shearwaters and petrels screech insolently or add haunting cries to a ship's oceanic cacophony. Groans of the wounded add a low-pitched resonance, as does the grumble of malcontents, their numbers increased by foul food and the sting of defeat.

August third was a day of comparative quiet. The British remained in view, always keeping to windward. The Armada pulled out of their defensive crescent formation and proceeded onwards towards Calais in four majestic columns with a width of five ships led by the flagship *San Martin*.

On August fourth the battered *San Luis*, consort of Medina Sidonia's flagship, had become partially detached from the Spanish fleet. Several English ships including the *Victory*, *Ark Royal* and *Golden Lion* sailed rapidly and closed around her. But Medina Sidonia quickly moved to protect her in his *San Martin*, along with Oquendo in the *San Salvador*, Francisco in the *San Pedro* and several other galleons. There was a fierce fight for five hours. Francisco couldn't understand why Sidonia was again defying his King's order never to engage the English ships in battle. The different rate of firing of the two fleets was evident to all, as was the markedly better marksmanship and effectiveness of English weaponry.

Francisco had heard scuttlebutt that the English spent two years improving their gunpowder, making it more chemically stable, durable and resistant to dampness. Spanish powder was notoriously unreliable but no one in Spain had the technical knowledge to correct the problem. Since King Philip did not intend to do combat with the English Navy, it had not been a priority.

Due to the different emphasis by the two countries in ship design, quality of armaments and training, not a single English hull had yet been pierced whereas there were now hundreds of holes in Spanish ships. The *San Martin* was badly damaged and the *San Pedro* was so peppered that Francisco temporarily withdrew her from battle to make repairs. Its cannonballs, when they occasionally found their target, had bounced off the English ships like children's pebbles against a turtle shell.

Francisco's zeal, courage and motivation were at their highest peak but what could he do with such inferior equipment and outmoded tactics born in a long-ago century?

That night the sea became calmer. Only two Armada ships—the *Rosario* and a supply ship—had so far been lost out of the full fleet of 130 ships but a cloud of gloom hung over the Armada. In the dawn light Francisco saw a humpback whale spouting on the surface, then diving and waving its black and white tail flukes at a distance of only fifty yards. The vignette diverted Francisco's mind. Knowing from his years in the navy that whales were seen only rarely in the English Channel, he briefly wondered, *Who is more off-course in its mental compass, the whale or King Philip?*

Francisco's mind wandered and he recalled that Catholicism had been overthrown in England by Queen Elizabeth's father, Henry VIII, triggered by anger at Pope Clement VII for not granting him a divorce from his Catholic Spanish wife, Catherine of Aragon, so he could marry the beauteous Anne Boleyn.

During the morning a more favorable following breeze blew intermittently from the southwest and the Armada was able to sail slowly towards Calais, one of the few English Channel ports deep enough to allow harbor for the large Spanish ships. Now they needed to lick their wounds and repair damage in the safety of a defensible harbor. As Sidonia approached the French coast, he sent out message-bearing pinnaces to the Duke of Parma who was supposed to be waiting at nearby Dunkirk with his troops and barges. On the windy morning of Saturday, August sixth, the Armada anchored at Calais. Only fifty miles north around the loop of the Forelands lay the entrance to the Thames, the Armada's pathway to London. The wounded Spanish ships spent the day repairing damage.

The next morning the closely-packed Armada ships rode at anchor, their brightly-painted hulls simmering in the sunlight. The English navy was clearly visible outside the harbor. Francisco noted that English pinnaces were gathering around the *Ark Royal*, apparently bringing officers for a council of war with Admiral Sir Charles Howard.

Spanish pinnaces returned to the *San Martin* with bitterly disappointing messages from the Duke of Parma who reported that, due to unforeseen circumstances, his land force was still at Bruges, not Dunkirk, and would not be ready for at least two weeks. There had also been delays in constructing the necessary troop barges. Francisco wondered how much of this was intentional.

In the afternoon Francisco watched Drake's squadron move to its usual position exactly to windward of the Armada, to the west of Calais. *What new trickery was he scheming?* Sidonia advised his fleet to be wary of a possible fireship attack. In the forefront of Spanish minds was the devastatingly successful attack of two fireships on the Spanish army at Antwerp three years before. Both English fireships smashed into the main bridge of Antwerp, the massive explosion killing 800 of Parma's troops in their camp next to the bridge.

Francisco gave himself no moments for sleep that night. He was alert in every nerve as he tried to think like *El Draque*. He assigned more lookouts on all three masts while he paced the decks, peering into the darkness in all directions. At midnight a new wind straight from the west started just as the tide began moving in towards the Armada. Francisco was certain that the canny English would use this tide against them.

His eyes strained, trying to penetrate the darkness and the minds of his enemy. Fire was the grimmest hazard for wooden ships, almost their entire construction being of flammable material—timber, canvas, cordage, tar and barrels of oil for lamps.

Black clouds began piling up over the waning moon. Francisco prayed for rain which would delay any fireship tactic. To the west, he could just make out faintly visible tiny sparkles of ships' lanterns. As Francisco stood at the *San Pedro's* prow, he noted the force of wind steadily increasing. There was a portent in the air which had texture, prickling his skin.

Suddenly a line of small flashes of fire brighter than lanterns appeared from the direction of Drake's squadron. The flames enlarged quickly and began moving forward. The flames rose into columns of billowing red smoke which silhouetted the masts and ships of the Spanish fleet. *My God*, thought Francisco, counting them—*eight fire ships! Was the Armada doomed?*

Admiral Sidonia fired his signal guns and flashed his lantern signals to pull anchors and sail away. He had previously sent a strongly-worded command to all Armada captains that under *no* circumstances were they to cut anchor cables rather than pulling them up, reminding them that anchors were also vital in their secondary use in maneuvering and stabilizing ships when sailing in turbulent seas, which they were experiencing almost daily.

Francisco immediately shouted the order to pull up his two anchors. His sailors panicked and yelled their protest: "We must axe the cables! There's no time to haul them up!" Francisco stood over his men and firmly commanded them to pull up the anchors properly by their thick hemp cables.

The fires of the advancing fireships were leaping higher and higher, driven ever closer by the wind. Spanish guard-ships were able to grapple the two outside fireships and pull them away but the remaining six headed straight for the closely-packed Armada.

Francisco always was calm and clear-headed in an emergency. He quickly steered his ship towards nearby Gravelines at the mouth of the Aa river, 15 miles south of Dunkirk. There was widespread panic in the Spanish fleet, however, with so many young crews and inept captains. Against the Admiral's orders, most ordered a hacking of anchor ropes.

There was pandemonium among the Armada's ships, all trying to get away at once. The mass of ships, with inexperienced naval crews now driven by fear and frenzy, began crashing into each other, smashing hulls and rudders. The six fireships did not strike a single Spanish ship, remarkably steered by wind and currents right through the mêlée to strand on the harbor beaches, their fires fizzling out harmlessly. None had been loaded with explosives.

Francisco's *San Pedro* was close to the Admiral's *San Martin*. Both ships maneuvered steadily through the chaos, the cool thinking of the Admiral and Captain allowing them to weave through the crowd of Spanish ships, now in complete disarray. The Armada drifted and fled in wild tangles towards Gravelines and Dunkirk. Francisco looked upwards and thought: *God, why are You allowing the Devil's whelps to prevail once again?*

Francisco gazed with frustrated but growing esteem towards the distant English fleet. No wonder Drake triggered such fear in his adversaries and respect in his peers. Francisco shook his head in wonderment at the superior skills, seamanship and tactics of Drake and his much smaller English fleet. The thought briefly flitted through his mind: *Since Queen Elizabeth has claimed for thirty years that she rules by Divine Right . . . is it possible that the English are the ones who are actually divinely-inspired? Would an all-seeing God align Himself with such an inept fleet as the Spanish Armada?*

CHAPTER 6

Hazardous Shoals

(August 8-10, 1588)

At three in the morning Admiral Sidonia fired a signal for his ships to gather around his flagship and drop anchor but few of his ships were within range or had anchors. Two hours later the sun rose and showed the *San Martin* almost deserted. Only six vessels were anchored around her—the *San Marcos*, the *San Juan de Castile*, the *San Pedro* and three other galleons.

In the distance towards the harbor of Calais the hulk of the magnificent galleass *San Lorenzo* of Naples could be distinguished. During the night's confusion it had collided with the *San Juan* of Sicily, losing its rudder, many of its oars and its mainmast. Now the heretics, including Admiral Howard, were gathering around the doomed ship seeking surrender and loot.

Sidonia gave the signal to sail towards the scattered Armada of 129 ships which were now regrouping to the eastward. Francisco saw that it was Drake's *Revenge* leading the attack on the six Spanish galleons, its red St. George's crosses and bright pennons brilliant in the early morning light. Almost alongside came Hawkins, with Frobisher and Fenner to the right, Winter and Seymour to the left. Most of the English captains were of humble origin but had long experience at sea and knew how to work together in coordinated attacks.

"This is our opportunity," shouted Francisco. "Aim well, my men. *El Draque* is just as mortal as we are." Francisco marveled as Drake came gliding smoothly towards them over the ruffled waves like a flying fish.

The *San Pedro* cannoneers were ready with ball and fuse, the crew with grappling hooks, soldiers with primed muskets. Every gentleman volunteer, whose way had been paved with money and gifts to be a witness at this historic event, stood at the ready, sword in hand.

Sidonia's *San Martin* began firing its cannons and the *San Pedro* quickly followed but almost all of the cannonballs missed their target. Drake held his fire until he was close to, and exactly even with, the *San Martin* and then delivered his broadside. The *San Martin* trembled and swayed as most cannonballs struck their mark. She and the *San Pedro* replied with their cannon but most shots weren't even close to the rapidly moving target. Now the *San Pedro* received the full blast of Fenner, and the *San Marcos* took the broadside of Hawkins.

The English cannonballs and shot did far greater damage as the English ships slipped past almost untouched, like enchanted demons. A number of Spanish cannons exploded, killing their crews. Many Spanish cannonballs were too small for the bore, went wobbling down the barrel and left the gun mouth at unpredictable angles. Other balls, cast poorly of an inferior grade of iron, exploded in flight. Not a single English hull was pierced while many new holes appeared in Spanish hulls, some dangerously near the water line.

Francisco watched Drake sail into the lines of the now-arrived, main Spanish fleet which had moved steadily towards the engagement. Hawkins, Frobisher and Fenner concentrated on Sidonia's flagship and its inept guardships. The swift English fighting ships passed repeatedly, delivering their thunderous broadsides accurately. Drake was like a sly fox darting from under the very paws of larger but slower hunting hounds. Francisco felt as if the Spanish ships were stuck in the quagmire of their own thinking, trapped in the sticky muck of a slow-motion nightmare.

The *San Pedro* rocked and resounded from the broadsides. Men fell at their posts all over the ship—cannoneers, sailors from the rigging and particularly army troops crowded together on the open decks. Ship sides were splintered and holed, sails torn, supply casks split open. A red flood of blood slimed across the decks and drained over the side.

Hugh de Moncada, Admiral of the four galleasses from Naples, after a futile half-hour's stand on the *San Lorenzo*, fell mortally wounded with shrapnel in his head.

All of the English ships were now engaged in this mighty battle of August eighth off of Gravelines, France, a port close to the northeastern limit of the English Channel near the North Sea.

Francisco could see that the English strategy now was to concentrate their firepower serially, attacking detached or disabled warships and defenseless supply ships.

The *San Pedro's* sails were shredded, its hull full of holes. In the rifts of battle smoke Sidonia saw the listing hulls of the *San Felipe* and *San Mateo* surrounded by the enemy. The *San Martin* changed direction to give assistance. The *San Pedro* slowly followed. Now Don Alonso de Leyva on the *Rata Coronado* and Oquendo on the *San Salvador* sailed in to give battle.

Francisco moved his ship towards the wounded *San Felipe*. He sailed past the *Maria de Begona* and saw her decks piled with dead. Blood poured out of her scuppers. How long could such an uneven battle be maintained? Francisco's supply of cannonballs was giving out. As the *San Pedro* sailed towards the cluster of ships, Francisco sighted the *Revenge* working her way into a gap between the *San Mateo* and *Maria de Begona*. He followed Drake into the opening.

"Come on, men, let's get him!" Francisco shouted. The *San Pedro* delivered a bow cannon blast into the stern of the *Revenge* which ripped apart Drake's red dragon banner. A great shout went up from Francisco's crew to salute this special moment of symbolism. The actual harm done to the *Revenge*, however, was negligible. As usual, Drake slipped out quickly and was gone.

By three o'clock in the afternoon, the *San Martin* and *San Pedro* and fourteen other Armada ships were fighting almost alone in a small sea-space, receiving the major attention of the English fleet. The wind was picking up and the sea becoming increasingly rough, swinging the already leaking and damaged top-heavy Spanish ships violently from side to side, straining the seams.

The gun smoke blew away and the whole scene became a brilliant panoramic painting. Four hundred yards away the *Maria San Juan* of the squadron of Guipúzcoa played out her death role. Her rigging gone, her sides splintered, she slowly tipped, keeled over and went to the bottom, taking a hundred and forty Spanish souls into the cold sea.

The water was rising in Francisco's ship in spite of the pump-men's desperate work. "If it is Thy will, oh God, we shall try to sink heroically," exclaimed Francisco as he looked at the dramatic scene of large whitened waves, heaving ships and sulfured orange fire streaking from English guns. The *San Pedro* seemed to settle as if she were going to her doom.

Francisco gave orders: "Cease fire. It is time to pray. He knelt on the deck as his men sank to their knees. In a strong firm voice Francisco prayed aloud, using the hymnal words: *O Reina del Cielo, O Madre Divina, Oye nuestras voces, Olamente y benigna . . ."*

A sudden silence fell over the sea. All English firing had ceased. The English fleet was withdrawing. Francisco rose quickly from his knees. He shook his head in wonderment as he watched the English sail away. *Could they be nearly out of ammunition, as we are?*

"Milagro! A miracle!" he cried. "To the pumps again, my men. We shall yet be saved. Caulkers, work hard; patchers, plug those holes. Sailors begin to mend the rigging. The Lord and Our Lady are with us after all. We shall yet recover, and yes, we shall fight another day for the glory of Spain. We shall save our ship by our faith and hard work. *Anda, Santiago, Anda!"*

All night the wind blew from the northwest, pushing the battered Armada ships east along the northern coast of France. Lanterns burned all night as caulkers, patchers, pumpers and sailors worked incessantly on the *San Pedro.* Friars moved among the wounded offering encouragement and prayers. Captain Francisco worked around the clock.

A gray cloudy morning revealed a grim situation. The *San Pedro* was alone. Sidonia's *San Martin* and seven other ships were a mile to the west. Drake was upwind towards the English coast intermittently harassing the seriously wounded Armada. Admiral Sidonia attempted to rescue the men from the damaged *San Felipe* and *San Mateo* but had to give up because of rough seas.

To the southeast lay the deadly banks of Zeeland towards which the winds were persistently pushing the stricken Spanish ships. They were now so close that the crew of the *San Pedro* could see breakers overfolding on the shoals with their rolling burden of sand. Death on the Dutch sand bars now seemed certain. Sounding lines showed a depth of six fathoms—only thirty-six feet. Francisco called determinedly for more and more work as if to defy the might of wind and water.

Some of his men cursed, some prayed. Most responded to their Captain's energetic spirit but it all seemed of no avail against the powerful forces of nature. A half hour later the depth was five fathoms. Francisco began to realize that only a Higher Authority could save them. He ordered the *Ave Maria* sung at the mainmast. The men knelt and sang, *Ave Maria, gratia plena . . . Sancta Maria, Mater Dei . . . Ora pro nobis peccatoribus . . .* The friar moved among them giving final absolution.

Vignettes of the hilltop town of Cuellar flashed through Francisco's mind—the apricots-in-the-sun feel of his wife's ardent young body, the musk of her tumbled hair, the vehemence of her physical responsiveness. He thought of his mother, the deep quiet love in her brown eyes, her soft voice and cherishing mannerisms. Scenes passed before his eyes of the tawny Segovian valley and snowy mountain backdrop, of life in the family castle, its armory and historic chambers, its great circular stairway, its galleried courtyard and grape arbor.

Had not this very fleet been declared invincible by priests, nuns, Church and State? Had not the King assured all captains that no power on earth could overcome the *Felicisima Armada,* the Most Fortunate Fleet? Francisco called for the Dominican Friar. "Antonio, my thoughts have been wandering. Why has the Lord deserted us? Could our cause against Protestants be wrong? Are such people really evil just because they have modified somewhat the Catholic religion?"

"We will talk later in depth, Captain. Your thoughts are not blasphemous." As Father Antonio walked briskly away to tend to the dying, Francisco rose from his knees to supervise his ship to its end, come what may. The sandbars were looming closer, closer. The reverberating low-pitched thunder of waves on the shoals could be heard and felt. He ordered another sounding—four fathoms.

The men crowded the rails in silent awe at the spectacle of nature's power luring their ship inevitably towards its final destiny. Then the sails began to flap. A shout came from a sailor in the rigging, "The wind is changing! God be praised!" As if moved by the hands of ministering angels, the wind was indeed shifting suddenly around from northwest to southeast. The Captain quickly gave orders to the crew, turning the ship away from the sandbars.

Crewmen's caps came off and they cheered as one. Some men even danced a few steps of the *corranto* as the ships began moving away from the death-dealing shoals of Zeeland towards the deeper waters of the English Channel.

CHAPTER 7

The Hangman Cometh
(August 10-13, 1588)

After the unexpected rescue from the shoals, Spanish spirits rose again. The crew was still hard at work patching holes and mending the rigging and sails. The wounded lined every deck. All wondered whether the repair work would be sufficient to allow the ship to withstand any new storms in this most stormy summer in living memory.

The milder wind was taking them east by north along the Belgian and Dutch coasts, away from Parma's supposed 16,000 troops and invasion barges. At the scant evening meal Francisco ordered the opening of two casks of *Valdepenas de La Mancha* red wine to boost his men's morale.

On August eleventh, Sidonia summoned his chief fleet officers for a war council on board the *San Martin*. Afterwards, pinnaces were sent with orders to all Armada ships to abandon invasion plans and head into the North Sea to the sixtieth parallel, sail around Scotland and the Hebrides and west into the Atlantic to fifteen degrees longitude, then make the southward turn towards Spain. They were instructed to give Ireland a wide berth because of its perilous, poorly-charted coast.

The message bearer who brought orders to Francisco was a Segovian well known to him who gave him a few extra items of information. "Francisco, several ranking officers disagreed strongly with the Admiral. The King's bastard son, Don Alonso de Leyva, said that Sidonia was making all of them appear like a pack of cowards. Captain Oquendo told Sidonia that such spineless behavior would haunt all of them for the rest of their lives."

"Who else spoke their mind in opposition," asked Francisco.

"Vice Admiral Juan de Recalde warned strongly that many of the Armada ships were too battered and full of holes to make it safely around northern Scotland and would stand a strong chance of shipwrecking on those coasts or on the treacherous west coast of Ireland."

"Didn't anyone side with Sidonia?"

"Yes, General Bovadilla said that heading back down the Channel would be the most hazardous choice of all and that trying to hole up in Norway or Sweden for repairs was too uncertain. He predicted that the stormiest weather in half a century couldn't possibly continue."

Francisco commented, "Admiral Sidonia's plan was obviously Bovadilla's." Francisco soon learned from a pinnace messenger that Sidonia, needing scapegoats, had ordered court martial of all captains who, against specific orders, had cut their cables the night of the fire ship scare in Calais.

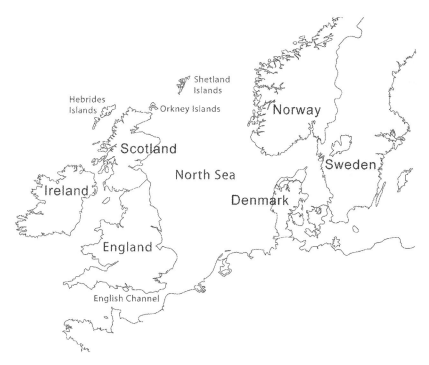

Figure 2. The North Sea and nearby countries.

Francisco could not believe that Sidonia was ordering total abandonment of the King's Grand Project. *What kind of a sparrow-hearted leader is he? We should renew our spiritual energy, repair our ships and then turn suddenly, catch the English fleet off-guard and sink them.* The taste of wormwood was in Francisco's mouth, the lead weight of despair in his belly.

The *San Martin* turned directly north, heading straight into the North Sea, with the safety of Scandinavia to starboard. The rest of the Spanish ships turned to follow while the English fleet lingered five miles behind, making no effort to engage.

By August 13, 1588, the Spanish Armada was strung out over a distance of fifteen miles. The *San Martin,* fighting headwinds from the Arctic, reached the fifty-sixth parallel off the Firth of Forth. At this point, Admiral Charles Howard's English fleet stopped its pursuit, turned around and, with a strong following wind, quickly made its way towards home ports.

Francisco watched the victorious English vessels grow smaller until they were toy ships on the great blue expanse. He was deeply concerned about Artic gales and hazardous crags of the Shetlands, Orkneys, Hebrides and western coast of Ireland. There were terrible enemies, too, within ships—illness from scanty and often polluted food; wounded men in mortal peril from infections. Every ship was a floating hospital and charnel house.

Francisco could hear Drake's laughter over Spain's ineptitude. *El Draque's victory is well-earned,* he thought. *I envy his tactical brilliance and superb implementation. Easy for us to make excuses but, from every aspect, we deserved to lose. Vanished victory, vanished hope.*

Enough of gloomy thinking. Time to get back to work. The Admiral's *San Martin* was just ahead. Francisco hailed his sailing master, a dour weather-beaten old fellow from Malaga. "I must get some sleep. My thinking is foggy. I have had very little sleep in the past ten nights. Take over for me and continue making repairs as rapidly as feasible. Then catch up with the *San Martin.*"

Francisco was in deep sleep for five hours. Then there was a pounding on his cabin door. "Captain, Captain Cuellar!" With great difficulty he roused from sleep and went to the door. A message-bearer said "Urgent dispatch" and handed him a tied parchment. Francisco unrolled the document and found a written message from General Bovadilla, now in temporary command. It ordered Captain Cuellar to come aboard the *San Martin* at once.

Francisco put on his cuirass and formal helmet, girded his sword-belt, went to the ship's rail and down the ladder to the waiting tender. When the two had seated themselves, Francisco asked the messenger if he knew the cause of this summons.

"Can you not guess?"

"No. Perhaps you can enlighten me. I have been asleep."

"There is talk on board the Admiral's ship of two captains who dared defy orders and presumed to lead the fleet ahead of the *San Martin*, a severe insult to the Commander. General Bovadilla is beside himself with rage and says the two captains shall hang for it."

"Hang for it?" Francisco exclaimed in astonishment. "Hang? Almighty God! I did not give orders to pull ahead of the *San Martin*!" He then thought, *I must summon extreme clarity of thought to meet this completely unjust threat to my survival. I must develop strategy to counter the arrogant Bovadilla's accusations with dignity.* He knew that Bovadilla had recently demoted twenty captains for cutting cables. The looming crisis overcame his weariness and began to illuminate his thinking.

Francisco's tender reached the *San Martin* just before the one bearing Cristobal de Avila arrived. As Francisco came on deck, he was received by two military guards and asked to deliver up his sword. The red blush of shame spread over his face and he protested.

"The sword will be restored to you," said one of the guards, "if you are found guiltless."

Cristobal de Avila, an elderly gentleman with a kindly face, gray hair and erect carriage, came up the ladder looking bewildered. Francisco stepped forward and clasped Don Cristobal warmly by the hand. "Courage, my friend. Mention everything you have done during your long career in the King's service."

"Thank you, Francisco. All courage to you, too, in this unexpected and completely undeserved trial. Let us have faith."

The two accused were now conducted into the small council room next to the ship's chapel where General Bovadilla sat at the head of the table in full army regalia, a purple plume in his crested helmet and the Order of Calatrava, with its cross and red lilies, glittering on his shining corselet. Also at the table were five military officers and two velvet-caped noblemen, among whom Francisco was happy to recognize his old friend from Madrid, Don Valerio de Valente. Behind Bovadilla stood an assistant and a secretary. Candles were in sconces along the wall illuminating eyes at strange angles, giving sinister expressions to their faces. The air in the small council chamber was heavy with the smell of leather, oiled metal, tainted breath and unbathed bodies.

Bovadilla cast an arrogant look through both defendants. He was handsome with a long upward-curling moustache over thin lips, a sharp nose, piercing dark brown eyes and thick black eyebrows. There was that blend of strength and weakness in his face which often indicates a willful compensation-by-cruelty to make up for faulty character.

"Step forward, Captain Cuellar."

Francisco moved closer to the table. He stood straight, all six feet of him.

"Captain Cuellar, you received written orders from our Admiral, the Duke of Medina Sidonia, instructing the fleet to follow him into the North Sea?"

"Yes, honored Commander, I received them."

"Yet your ship did not follow him. You took it upon yourself to precede him."

"Respected Commander, I retired to my room for a nap after ten days with almost no sleep. I placed the sailing master in charge with instructions to carry on with necessary repairs and then catch up with the *San Martin*. I have no idea why or how our ship got ahead of your ship while I was asleep for five hours. There was certainly no intention to disobey orders."

"What you say matters not a jot. What you think matters less than a jot. What you did is extremely dangerous in a time of war and is a capital offense. You should be hanged immediately but our Commander is giving you a chance to state your case, which is more than you deserve."

"How dangerous, Commander? The English fleet had disappeared over the horizon. My main obligation was to get the *San Pedro* rapidly repaired to make it ready for northern seas. I needed to get myself in better shape. Sleepless humans are not optimally effective in war or peace."

"Insubordination on land or sea, Captain, is very hazardous." A repetitive nervous twitch of Bovadilla's chin deprived him of his austere ferociousness.

"Yes, Honorable Commander, but this was not intentional insubordination. My sailing master had important repair duties to oversee, including dangerous holes near the water line. I'm sure the ship got ahead of the *San Martin* before he realized it. I, myself, have been a more than loyal officer. I served as a First Mate at Terceira where you were Army Commander. I was promoted for my war-time conduct at that time. On the night of the fire ships, the *San Pedro* was one of the few to pull up anchor, not cut cables, and the first to follow the Admiral out to sea."

"Is this true?" asked Bovadilla of Don Diego Flores who sat on his right.

"Yes, I believe it is true," answered Don Diego.

"It is true, indeed," echoed Don Valerio de Valente.

"This good record might partially offset the later crime," responded Bovadilla, "but" . . . he looked searchingly through Francisco again with a haughty air, the flicker of candles dancing like glowworms in his eyes. He paused for a few seconds, Francisco feeling as if he were being held suspended on the prongs of Fate over a hot fire . . . "it is questionable. We will send you to the *San Marcos*, the galleon of Judge Advocate Don Martin de Aranda, for his capital opinion. For our part, we deprive you herewith of your Captaincy and appoint in your place Hernan Gomez de Tortoles as Captain of the *San Pedro*. Your sword will be handed over to him."

With a feeling of plunging into the dark, cold sea-depths, Francisco remained quiet. He had never heard of Tortoles but was relieved by the transfer of authority to the Judge Advocate rather than remaining in the clutches of an evil, arbitrary, insecure dictator without scruples who was clearly trying to relieve his guilt for the Armada's defeat.

Bovadilla turned to his Secretary: "Write a note summarizing what transpired here and give it to the messenger who will accompany Don Francisco de Cuellar to the *San Marcos*. Now step forward, Don Cristobal de Avila. You likewise received the Admiral's orders?"

"Yes, honorable Commander, but I needed sea space in which to repair my badly damaged vessel. The *Santa Barbara* was filling with water and in danger of sinking. So I ran a bit ahead . . ."

"So you ran ahead on your own authority?"

"On the authority of emergency conditions, honorable Commander . . . a life-and-death matter for my ship and my men."

"A life-and death matter, indeed, as you will find," responded Bovadilla coldly.

Don Cristobal's face flushed and he said loudly: "Death for gaining a little sea-room in which to repair a badly-damaged ship? Death in a fleet already decimated by death? Life is what we need more of in this fleet." And, under his breath, he added, "Life and victory."

The coal of Bovadilla's eyes burst into flame. He angrily stood up and exclaimed, "Don Cristobal de Avila, heretofore Captain of the galleon *Santa Barbara*, I order you, without remand or appeal, to be instantly hanged from the yardarm of a pinnace. You will be borne, thus hanging, through all the fleet. Secretary, write the order and have it taken to the Admiral to sign."

Francisco immediately said, "Commander, I beg you! Captain Avila has given far more service to Spain than I have—splendid years in the Indies, Oran, Lepanto, Terceira. Let him plead, too, before the Judge Advocate. I beseech you, let the decision be made in a Court of Law."

The old gentleman cut in, exclaiming: "Take care, Francisco! The taste of blood is in the shark's mouth!"

Bovadilla rose, unsheathed his sword and brought it down full-blade upon the table, jarring out of their sockets two candles which dusked themselves on the table. "At once!" he cried. "Take these men away, Don Cristobal to the hangman, waiting only for the Admiral's signature, and you," turning to Francisco, "I have a mind to . . ."

Francisco's soul plunged. Bovadilla, lips and moustache curling, paused . . . then said, "Take him at once to the Judge Advocate before I change my mind. The paper! Let me see it!"

The decree came back from Medina Sidonia duly signed. Bovadilla gave it a quick look and signed his name with an anger-twisted scrawl. Francisco found his heart beating like a cornered boar. The guards on either side of him guided him brusquely out the door. Don Cristobal was already out on deck, ready to go over the side.

"God go with you!" cried Francisco. "You have given superb service to your country and Spain is in great debt to you."

"God bless you, my friend. I will die content. May you be saved by an even-handed Judge from this disgraceful abuse of power. We are just scapegoats for the ignominious failure of our ill-led Armada." One of the guards kicked him in the shins and the hangman shoved him to the rail. "If you live, Francisco, take my love to my dear ones at Avila." Then he disappeared over the side.

"God go with you, too, Francisco." It was Don Valerio de Valente who stood by Francisco and warmly clasped his hand as his guards released him to board the pinnace.

Ex-Captain Cuellar watched the little boat carrying Don Cristobal to his doom while his own tender crossed to the *San Marcos*. It seemed to Francisco as if he had swallowed the whole sea, so salty was the taste in his mouth, his gullet, the runnels of his belly, the channels of his thoughts. He knew that Don Cristobal had a devoted wife in the walled town of Avila in Castile, four sons, two daughters and a bevy of grandchildren. He was not commanded to participate in the Armada; he had volunteered. After the mission was over, he had planned to retire.

The pinnace reached the *San Marcos*. Only at this moment did it occur to Francisco that Sebastian was on this ship. As for the Judge, he did not know what kind of approach should be made to this new life-and-death arbiter. He suddenly felt very tired, as if he had been pulling at oars for many hours. *Am I capable of further effort in this contrived and biased process? No matter what I say, will my effort prove fruitless? Am I just a pawn in a pre-decided military chess game?*

The smell of wet ropes greeted him as he climbed the ladder of the *San Marcos*, a ship 260 tons larger than the *San Pedro* with almost twice as large a complement of men. Sebastian was waiting at the rail in a crowd of onlookers.

"Amigo!" exclaimed Francisco.

"Amigo!" said Sebastian, quickly adding, *"Buena, buena fortuna!"*

Francisco was taken to a small room below deck where he was made to wait while the Judge and his staff were given an oral summary. At last he was conducted to a small room provided with chairs, table, lanterns and candles. There were three men at the table, two with quill pens.

His first look at Judge Martin de Aranda was reassuring. He had a gray beard and sideburns, blue eyes and the expression of a calm, deliberate and fair man. The Judge invited Francisco to be seated at the end of the table and said: "I will hear your view of the case, Captain Cuellar."

Francisco gave a brief resume of his past services to Spain and stated his case.

"I must scrutinize your recent conduct at sea, Captain Cuellar. Did the *San Pedro* advance ahead of the *San Martin* in a straight line or at an angle?"

"To give an exact answer my sailing master should be summoned, for I was asleep in my cabin. In retrospect, I suspect the angle was about thirty degrees."

"To the best of your knowledge, how far ahead of the *San Martin* in the actual line of advance did the *San Pedro* go?" The Judge Advocate began to draw a sketch on a sheet of paper.

"Honorable Judge Advocate, I fear to make a wrong estimate lest I be thought to err on the side of self-exculpation. She may have been one league ahead."

The Judge turned to the messenger standing at the doorway. "Go fetch the man who was on watch on the *San Pedro's* mainmast from the fourteenth to the sixteenth hour."

After thirty minutes the sailor of the mainmast was brought in. The Judge began. "You were on mainmast watch from the fourteenth to the sixteenth hour?"

"Yes, Sir."

"Did you note the *San Pedro* pulling ahead at about the fourteenth hour?"

"Yes, Sir."

"At what angle was she bearing?"

"At about thirty degrees, Sir."

"How far out would you say she went at an angle?"

"About a league, Sir."

"How far ahead of the prow of the *San Martin* would you say she went?"

"She was no more than half a league ahead at any time." At this moment there was a commotion outside, a murmur, then the rising sound of voices protesting.

"No! No! Impossible! What are we coming to? God's blood. No! No!"

"Find out what the trouble is!" ordered Aranda.

The Judge's assistant went out, returning a minute later with a shocked expression. "There is a pinnace loitering below, from the yardarm of which hangs the body of Captain Cristobal de Avila, convicted of the capital offense of sailing his ship ahead of the Commander's. The pinnace is going the rounds of the fleet. The men are stirred up, Sir."

The Judge's face paled. He rose and addressed Francisco.

"I am satisfied with your report and with that of the man on watch. I do not find it necessary to call in any other witness. In our judgment the error was unintentional and the case is hereby dropped. Since General Bovadilla has deprived you of your Captaincy, I shall give you quarters on this ship. Don Francisco de Cuellar, you are welcome as our guest."

Francisco was too overcome to do more than bow his head and quietly say, "*Gracias infinitas, Honorabile.* I appreciate your sense of justice and the evident nobility of your character."

The room emptied quickly. All were eager to see the death pinnace. Sebastian was waiting outside the door. He put his arm around Francisco's shoulder.

"How did it go, Francisco *mio?*"

"Released to life, *amigo*, and the Judge Advocate gives me quarters on this ship."

"God, in whom I sometimes almost believe, be thanked!" They embraced and walked to the railing.

The setting sun crimsoned the white hair and drooping figure of Don Cristobal de Avila hanging from the pinnace yardarm as it slowly made its rounds of the Armada conveying its grim message.

CHAPTER 8

Stormy North Sea Welcome

(August 1588)

Admiral Sidonia resumed direct command immediately upon the execution of Don Cristobal. Now he ordered all rations reduced. To lighten the ships, Sidonia ordered that all horses and mules be cast overboard—the horses which, bridled with silver and gold, caparisoned with silks and velvets, were to have borne the triumphant Spanish cavaliers through the streets of London as in a gilded Roman Triumph. The mules were to pull the artillery.

Being an aristocrat, Sidonia had no understanding of the needs of lower classes. It never occurred to him that his seamen and soldiers desperately needed fresh meat in their diet. Tons of potential meat were thus cast into the sea, to the anger of the disheartened sailors and soldiers.

Now the seas began to mount. The Admiral signaled all ships to stay together but the cannons boomed in vain, going unheeded for unanticipated human reasons. The public exposing of Don Cristobal's hanging body was the last straw. English cannons, repetitive defeats, huge waves, inimical winds, hunger, fever and dysentery did not tear asunder the unity of the God-inspired Armada. The gruesome exhibition of the martyred body of the respected and popular Captain had been the final crushing blow to Spanish esprit on all levels.

Francisco watched ship after ship fall behind the now-disrespected Commander. A hundred ships went their own way and disappeared over the horizon with such esteemed leaders as Don Alonso de Leyva, Martin de Bertendona and Miguel de Oquendo. Ex-Captain Francisco de Cuellar, with no official duties to perform, requested assignment to any necessary tasks to help make the ship as seaworthy as possible for the dangerous journey which lay ahead.

There was an increasing amount of illness on board, made worse by under-nutrition, fatigue from overwork and lack of sleep, and the depression of defeat. Francisco tried to lift the morale of his shipmates with his good cheer, his stories and his songs. One of the *San Marcos* musicians loaned him a *guitarra*. Either alone or with Sebastian he sang love songs, folk songs, battle songs and gypsy songs, including "The ballad of Conde Claros," *"En la Ciudad de Toledo"* and the song of the three Moorish girls of Jaen—Axa, Fatima and Marién. Those strong enough often joined in. It was clear to Francisco that their medicine of song was superior in its effects than any treatment from the ship's doctor, especially if blood-letting was involved which could quickly propel a seriously ill patient to the brink of dying.

Francisco's recent close brush with death from the malevolent Bovadilla had made him more aware of life's potential brevity. He now more intensely appreciated the wonder of human senses—watching the ocean's shifting colors, the sails billowing towards home, the interesting faces of three hundred men reflecting hope, resignation or despondency. What a privilege to be able to hear the waves roaring, the sails singing, the rigging humming.

Francisco refused to dwell on the miserable conditions on board. Water could not be used for bathing or washing clothes. Body smells added to those of festering wounds were at times almost overwhelming; there was little circulation of air through lower decks even in heavy winds.

Nobody talked more about home than Donel O'Conner, son of a western Irish chief known as O'Connor Sligo. Donel, only eighteen years old and gripped by wanderlust, had shipped out as an ordinary seaman from Ireland, spent time in Spain, then signed on to the Armada for sheer adventure. Like many who lived in Ireland's seacoast towns frequented by Spanish merchants, he spoke a mongrel Spanish. He and Francisco often discussed the merits of their respective countries while Sebastian leaned against the rail and laughed at them for being such provincial louts.

Donel had become good friends with Sebastian and Francisco and the three got together, whenever completion of their tasks permitted, for chit chat about any topic. "Ah," said Donel one day as the three stood together on deck, "we must soon be rounding the heads of Scotland, and shortly after, you'll be smelling the lovely green fields of Ireland." Along with his quick laugh, Donel had blue eyes, curling dark hair, honest simplicities and a broad smile which made him immensely likeable.

"Is Ireland really as green as they say?" asked Sebastian.

"Green as heaven and as beautiful," answered Donel enthusiastically.

"The town of Cuellar is gold and purple now," said Francisco.

"And the grapes and girls are no doubt ripe for plucking," added Sebastian.

"Wouldn't you give anything for a jug of beer brought to your table by a lusty, large-breasted colleen?" asked Donel.

"The thought had occurred to me," said Francisco, thinking of Zabella.

"What a fiendish invention is the sea. A world of water and not a single drop fit to put down the throat of a dying dog. The Devil is a clever fellow," said Sebastian laughing.

"Shh!" said Francisco. "Are you aware that a friar on board could turn you over to the Inquisition for such remarks? You wouldn't act so cocky while burning at the stake!"

Sebastian's remarks in the past had opened up disturbing conflicts in Francisco's own thinking. Cracks of doubt which had started as a student at Salamanca had fissured significantly in the recent life and death dramas during which God had seemed to desert the Armada. "You're not really a henchman of Satan, Sebastian," said Francisco. "Your heart is good but your faith needs mending. Don't you believe in God at all?"

"Of course I do. Who can look at the stars and not believe in God?"

"I have done some thinking about these matters, Sebastian, as we used to discuss at Salamanca. I confess that doubts have sometimes come swarming around me recently like stormy petrels diving over a school of small fish."

"God created the world, including Ireland," said Donel, smiling. "That I know. His angels are everywhere over its lush fields and hills. You can hear them singing in the woods below Ben Bulben and along Cummeen Strand on blessed Sligo Bay where I would love to be right now."

"Keep your faith, lad," said Sebastian, "especially since we may not get safely home. I'm ready whatever happens. My heaven is as big as the universe."

"You may find, *amigo mio*," suggested Francisco, "that your heaven and mine are the same."

"Oh, no! You mean I may have to tolerate you in the afterlife as well? That's what I would call true suffering." Sebastian laughed heartily.

"Endless philosophizing, without an adequate supply of beer, can get wearisome," said Francisco, smiling. "It's getting damn cold out here. Let's get below deck." They headed down as the North Sea began to declare itself. Drifting squalls of rain spattered across the deck and windy gusts began to sing dolefully in the rigging, like Homeric sirens trying to lure sailors to their doom.

A powerful storm from the southwest, brewed in the ocean's cauldron, drove the Armada north over increasingly mountainous waves. The sound of the wind rose to a shriek. In succeeding days there was increasing mortality in the undernourished and wounded soldiers, sailors and noblemen. Canvas-wrapped bodies on deck, waiting to be tipped into the sea, were daily spectacles. The bitter cold of northern seas penetrated the bones of the living.

By the twentieth of August most of the scattered fleet had made the turn westward between the Shetlands and Orkneys north of Scotland. Although supplies were badly needed, there was little hope of successfully reaching any safe harbor and most ships no longer had anchors. The *San Marcos*, pounded by wind and wave, began to leak at the seams.

A few carpenters and caulkers kept working and trained others to take their places when they became weak from exhaustion. Among these substitute workers were most of the silk-and-velvet noblemen, who acquitted themselves well and, without exception, volunteered for any task.

Late one afternoon the three friends, briefly off duty, climbed the stairs to have a look at the sea. There was a clearing yellow streak in the sky. Half a league in front and to the right they could see the silhouette of a sister ship, the 350 ton *San Bernardo* of the Portuguese squadron.

"Good God but she's low in the water," exclaimed Sebastian.

"She's sinking," said Francisco.

"Just as we are, inch by inch," added Donel.

"Don't despair," exclaimed Francisco. "We're keeping even with the sea. We'll come through, Donel, so you can see your dear old Sligo again."

"God bring me to Ireland! Cast me, even as a piece of driftwood on my beautiful home shore, dear Mother Mary, and I'll bless you forever!"

"Look!" cried Francisco.

The heavy prow of the *San Bernardo* dipped into the sea, hesitated, then the stern went up and the ship slipped silently beneath the waves.

"Can't we rush forward to pick up those poor devils?" shouted Donel.

"They won't last long in this cold and unforgiving sea," said Sebastian, "and, as the Irish believe, the sea requires its due. Those who interfere with God's will by effecting ocean rescues are often punished themselves. Better for them to die quickly."

Francisco and Donel crossed themselves. "God have mercy on their souls," murmured Donel, "and on ours. Oh God, I don't want to die at such a young age without having tasted more of the beauties of life, including relishing the joys of a loving colleen." Francisco put an arm around him but said nothing.

In twenty minutes the *San Marcos* came abreast of the *San Bernardo's* sinking place. A few pieces of timber and an overturned small boat were riding the waves but not a single human being, dead or alive, could be seen.

CHAPTER 9

Treacherous Coast

(September 1588)

A few days later, Fair Isle, a small inhabited island, was spotted through a rift in the fog, located midway between the Orkneys and Shetlands. Juan Gómez de Medina, Captain of *El Gran Grifón,* flagship of a supply squadron, headed his ship directly for the island and wedged it among the rocks. Francisco, Donel and others on the *San Marcos* watched with fascination but the distance was too great to see how many men successfully made it to *terra firma*.

On September 16, land was again sighted—Creane Island, off Scotland. There had been talk through the ship of the possibility of reaching safely one of the northern ports of Scotland. Many on the *San Marcos* besieged the Captain and begged him to bring the ship to harbor.

"If the wind dies down a little we might make a try for it. Be patient."

The wind, however, increased, howling its defiance at human hopes. The seas rose to meet the sky and the *San Marcos* mounted and fell like a child's toy. In heavy seas, their wobbling tall masts continued to pry apart the already-weakened seams. The crew wondered how much battering the ship could take as it was driven westward beyond the line of the Hebrides.

"We're nearing Ireland! I can smell it," exclaimed Donel one afternoon a few days later.

"Hah, are you delirious or just in love with your Irish fantasies?" asked Sebastian, smiling.

Tears came into Donel's green eyes. "When we get back to Spain, I'm going to quit the Armada immediately. I've had enough of adventure for quite awhile, thank you. It's time for me to pursue a peaceful life on the good green land of Ireland and find me a cozy lassie."

"Even with all its impressive wounds, Donel, our ship might surprise us and get us back to Spain intact," said Francisco. "We're supposed to avoid Ireland and its treacherous coast. I don't want to follow the sea any more either. I'll be quite happy to retire to my own hilltop and raise crops, animals and children in peace."

"Tell me more about your wife, Francisco," said Donel. "She's beautiful, I'm sure."

"Yes, and getting more so every day I'm at sea. Hazel eyes with flecks of green and flames all through her. Oh, to be grappling and boarding her at this very moment!"

"We Spanish haven't been very good at grappling recently," said Sebastian. "Do you think Zabella will be faithful to you during this long haul away from home?"

"Sebastian, I should cut your heart out! Of course! My Zabella is a loyal small town girl and she loves me!"

"Almost no girl, *amigo,* is faithful when her husband is away. I believe in the sea's cruelty, the beauty of our planet, the courage of man and the joyful and often untapped zest of pretty women. About their steadfastness *in absentia,* I have strong doubts."

As Francisco reached to throttle him, Sebastian danced playfully out of range.

Three days later Francisco watched Donel come up on deck in the very early morning. The sea was rolling less violently. A light mist enveloped the ship, just beginning to clear in the vague warmth of dawn. As the sun rose, the gray-white mist took on a silver-gold opalescence. Donel seemed to be studying the mist carefully. Then he suddenly shouted, "Land, Francisco, land! Those shadows in the mist are Ireland!" He gripped the rail, tears pouring down his cheeks.

"My God, I think Donel is right. It must be Ireland!" exclaimed Francisco to Sebastian who had joined them. "Where are we, Donel? Can you recognize anything?"

"Dear God, I think it's my own dear Sligo! That flat-topped shape is Ben Bulben, which is part of the Dartry Mountains in County Sligo where the noble Princess Grainne and the humble warrior, Diarmuid, nurtured their forbidden love in ancient times. And that's Knocknarea Mountain with Queen Maeve's great cairn atop it and there's the blessed Cumeen. God, put strength into me! I want to jump overboard and swim for home!"

"Hold him tightly, Francisco," said Sebastian. "I think he may actually try it."

The three stood at the railing while the unwieldy ship moved inexorably towards Ireland, helpless to fight the waves and wind from the northwest. Ben Bulben rose against the gray-blue sky and the great crescent beach of Sligo Bay opened out before them.

The top deck was packed with men, some of whom extended their arms towards the land as if to bring it closer. As the *San Marcos* neared the little island of Inishmurray, she slowed and dropped anchor between it and Streedagh Point. Shortly the supply hulk *Falcon Blanco* and the galleon *San Juan* of Castile came into view and, with anchor cables still intact, dropped anchor about 200 yards away on either side of the *San Marcos*. The Captain of the *San Marcos* told all on deck that they would wait for a smoothing of waves before sending pinnaces to shore to collect fresh water.

For four days the three galleons rocked strongly at anchor, the waves too rough to lower any boats. In these damp green hills of Ireland would be many springs of cool clear water. Every throat was parched and wrinkled from weeks of warm bitter wine, the last supply of potable water having been consumed a week before. To the thirsty men, the situation created torments of the mythological Tantalus who so offended Greek gods that he was condemned to an eternity of thirst and hunger. Whenever he reached desperately for water or food, it was pulled slowly away from him by invisible forces.

"See the peat smoke rising from those distant cottages?" said Donel. "At those hearths are cooking sweet golden oat cakes and pots of rabbit stew with gobbets of turnips and carrots and pearl-white onions floating in them. There are pitchers of cool buttermilk on all the tables. My own home isn't far away."

More than once Donel strained in the arms of his friends who watched him closely and constantly. Two sick sailors did leap into the sea, one from the *Falcon Blanco* and one from the *San Juan*. Both quickly disappeared.

On the fourth day the ship leaned more heavily with each long swell coming in from the Atlantic, foretelling a new storm working its way eastward towards the three anchored ships. Just before dawn on the fifth night, the sky piled up blue-black clouds. Thunder and lightning began. Violet and bright blue fiery luminosity danced through the rigging—Saint Elmo's fire, named after the Italian Patron Saint of Sailors, which could bring either good or bad luck.

The ocean became steadily fiercer and the three ships rode on mounting waves, pulling harder and harder at the thick hemp of their anchor cables. By dawn the rain stopped but the skies were still gray. The wind increased and the ships lurched and wallowed. The anchors dragged and the thick rope anchor cables began to shred.

The *San Juan* of Castile was the first to tear loose and move inexorably towards shore, driven by powerful waves and wind. Now it was every man for himself as the ocean beckoned to all. Some on the *San Juan* were trying to tear up planking from the deck, some were rolling barrels to the rail, some were jumping overboard, some were being washed over the rails. It was evident that most couldn't swim and quickly sank. Many who had sought a last refuge in the high rigging were hurled into the air like flailing marionettes as the ship rocked violently from side to side.

"We may be next," cried Francisco to Donel. "Find some wood!" The *San Marcos* began to heave and strain in a last mortal agony. "We won't break loose from our anchor cable," cried Donel urgently. "We can't break loose! The Good Lord couldn't be so cruel as to bring me to Sligo's very shore and then destroy my ship, my friends and me!"

Francisco grabbed the railing just before a mountainous wave swept over the *San Marcos* and her cable severed. There was a roar of water in Francisco's ears but he managed to hold on.

The decks had been swept clean of people except for the very few who had been able to take hold of an immoveable object. Sebastian and Donel were gone. Francisco could see men and wreckage floating like kelp on the writhing sea.

Francisco's clear thinking in emergencies asserted itself. He noted the high roof of the captain's cabin and thought he might be able to cling to its curved, ornamental railing. The *San Marcos* climbed the next oncoming wave. During the moment when the ship rode in the trough, Francisco ran to the ladder and climbed to the top of the stern cabin's roof. He looked back to the forecastle roof now beginning to dip into the sea. Those who had taken refuge on the prow jumped in, most of them quietly, some with a shriek of "God have mercy!" Many floated out on barrels or chairs. One Spanish nobleman threw off his drenched velvet cloak, lifted a heavy gold chain from his neck, threw it into the sea and jumped in.

Francisco saw that Judge Advocate Martin de Aranda was now standing below him, motionless, holding on to a rung of the steps, head down, apparently praying. "Your Honor! Your Honor!" shouted Francisco over the cacophony of sound. "Give me your hand."

Aranda shook his head, gestured negatively and bowed his head again. Francisco, feeling that he owed his life to Aranda's benevolence, was eager to save him. He seized the judge by the shoulder. "Come, *Honorifico*! Up here on the roof!" Aranda reluctantly climbed the stairs where he and Francisco clung to the railing's gilt and green wooden frieze.

The ship was now about a hundred and fifty yards from shore. The scene revealed an unexpected horror. Francisco saw clusters of men on the beach stripping bodies of the half-drowned Spaniards of all their clothes, then bludgeoning them to death. When Spanish chests rolled in, the Irishmen smashed them open while the rest danced around the chests with a primitive glee.

"I'll take my death from the sea rather than from those brutal savages," said Aranda. "I would like to see my family again but God apparently doesn't want us to live."

"Oh, no, *Honorifico*. We have already lived longer than most on our ship. Who are we to say that God does not intend us to live?"

"If you get back to Spain, Francisco, please go to Saragossa and tell my wife how much I loved her and that I will await her in a better place."

Another huge wave crashed over the ship and bore them into the sea. Francisco looked about for something to which he and the Judge Advocate might cling. The wooden cover of a hatchway came within reach and he grasped it. "Come, your Honor, it will hold the two of us!"

The Judge Advocate shook his head. Francisco urged again: "You gave me back my life. Let me help you keep yours. Come!" He dragged the Judge towards him and the two got aboard the unsteady platform which was as big as a good-sized tabletop. It went under the water with their weight, then rose. Immediately another wave immersed them. Francisco was twisted when a heavy piece of wood crushed his legs against the cover, reddening the water. In pain, he gripped the floating lid tightly.

Thirty feet away the Judge was trying to keep his head above water but couldn't. A large wave came over him and he disappeared. Francisco knew that the Judge, like most Spanish nobles on board, had sewn heavy gold ducats into his clothing and now was paying the ultimate price for his earthly love of gold.

The same oncoming wave bore Francisco under the surface. Pictures of life in Spain churned in his mind like little quoins of twisting kaleidoscopic glass—brief vignettes of riding oxcarts into golden valleys as a child, of his father and mother singing in church, of fishing in the river Eresma, of dancing at grape festivals, of rollicking with gypsy children, of holding Zabella in a passionate embrace, of waving goodbye to his mother . . . *adios . . . adios.*

Francisco's legs ached, his nostrils and throat were full of sea water. He had difficulty holding the wooden hatch cover. The powers of wind and wave were overwhelming him and he began to see the inevitability of dark death. Then he was flung against something hard and resistant which knocked the breath out of him . . . he was on solid sand, alive despite his inability to swim.

He climbed up on shore to get away from the pounding waves. He rolled over onto his back and looked up. Two Irishmen stood over him with grim faces and blood-stained shillelaghs—their walking sticks which served as killing clubs, sometimes with lead poured into the handles. They bent over, looked at him closely, then kicked him over onto his stomach. They shook their heads and moved on. Francisco turned on his side, and, as he did so, noted that his shirt, vest and breeches were red with blood. This explained his narrow escape from being clubbed to death; his bloody clothes weren't worth stealing.

Some fifty yards off a large group of Irishmen were gathered around some bright bales of cloth and a chest that had just washed in. They were yelling and pushing in their eagerness to scavenge. The small gold chain with the precious relic of St. Lawrence given to him by the nuns at Lisbon was still under his shirt and the pouch of coins paid out at as Captain's wages at Corunna was still attached to his belt, so he would be a lucrative find.

He cautiously began to inspect the slopes rising from the beach. The low banks were sliced by paths, with clumps of heavy beach grass and scrub under which a man might be able to dig and hide himself until the pitying twilight came. Inch by inch Francisco clawed the sand and hunched himself along the beach by his elbows, his painful bleeding legs dragging behind him. He hoped a Spanish chest would hold enough loot to keep the greedy Irish distracted.

When he finally reached vegetation he took hold of a clump of sword grass, cutting the palms of his hands as he did so. He hoisted himself up, cluster by cluster. He made a curve of his body, skewed himself around a bush and looked back towards the thunderous, merciless surf.

The beach was awash with corpses and living men surrounded by savages. One Spaniard was standing quite listlessly while the Irish stripped him. Another was kneeling with hands raised in entreaty. Jackets and doublets were taken off both men, rosaries and chains pulled off along with their shirts. Then the standing Spaniard and the one still so earnestly imploring for his life were both bashed over the head with shillelaghs and they keeled over onto the sand.

The sun beamed through low-lying clouds and over the wave-scalloped horizon, creating a stunning saffron backdrop. The little black figures on the beach looked like puppets enacting a carnival tragedy of death. *Surely this gruesome panorama is not actually happening,* thought Francisco. *I must have struck my head and am imagining this entire macabre scene.*

CHAPTER 10

Grim Hibernian Reality

(September 1588)

Francisco scooped a little hollow under a bush into which he might sink deeper out of sight. His legs were bleeding, especially the right lower leg which had a long gash down its side. He realized the pain was greater than a superficial gash but he couldn't detect evidence of a fracture. His bush was about thirty feet from the widest path down the bank. Twilight was descending which might protect him from discerning eyes and menacing clubs.

As night came on, however, the scudding clouds parted intermittently and yielded luminous patches of moonlight. In one of these patches Francisco became aware of what looked like a hummock of kelp on the sand below him which seemed to be getting closer. He soon realized this must be a Spaniard who had draped himself in kelp. When the crawler finally drew near, Francisco lent him a hand and pulled him up. "From what ship are you?"

"The . . . *San Juan* . . . of Castile," he said slowly and hesitatingly. "Thank God . . . for a living Spaniard . . . on this . . . shore of death."

Francisco saw that, beneath the kelp, the man was stark naked and his head was bloody. The Spaniard lay panting for a few moments in the darkness, intermittently illuminated by moonlight. How could you tell from a man's body what sort of a man he was, from what category of life, to what place or rank of achievement he belonged? If one could see a man's face, one might read some personal history written in the facial lines or expressions, etched by past happenstance. Speech and voice yielded clues. This man articulated with a hint of Madrid. No wrappings of status remained.

Francisco let his companion rest while he watched the pathways in both directions. He sat up for a better view. As he watched, every sense acute, he became aware of a file of shadows moving swiftly down the broad path from the slope summit. Some sentience that was sub-olfactory gave him a subtle clue. It was a file of wolves. He shuddered. When the wolves had reached the beach he ventured a question: "Are you from Madrid?"

There was a pause and a faint affirmation. "At the Court of his Majesty perhaps?"

"Yes."

"Perchance you knew my father, the Treasurer of King Philip, Francisco Gutierrez de Cuellar? He went back to his native town of Cuellar to end his days and died seven years ago."

"Yes . . . I knew him . . . A good man. Shall we ever . . . do you think . . . get back to Madrid?"

"God willing, I think we shall. And you, *Señor*, who are you?"

"I am . . . *el Conde de* . . . the Count of . . ." Then there was silence.

Francisco laid a hand on the body and shook him but there was no sign of life. Even after all the horrors he'd been through, he was strangely affected. Tears gathered in his eyes. The moon, in a great space between clouds, shone on the beach where he could make out black blocks of tossed lumber and wreckage, the pale flesh of stripped Spaniards and the silhouettes of a few horses and men. Wolves appeared as black, low-slung prowling shadows. He said a brief prayer for the count.

He hunched quietly down again under the bush, closed his eyes and fell asleep. He was later awakened by a spraying of sand over his arms. Two bareheaded Irishmen, arrested in their headlong flight down the hill, had stopped by the bush and were looking down at him. One was an old man with white hair. The other was younger and black-haired. Scythes were hanging over their shoulders. *Here goes my head sliced off like the top of a carrot,*" Francisco thought.

The older man stooped down to look at him, saw his stained clothes and bloody leg, shook his head and said something in a strange language, not English. Francisco had learned some English in his time at the Court of Madrid. He realized it must be the old Irish language, Gaelic.

The old man looked at Francisco's companion and felt the body. The younger man stalked down the hill. To Francisco's surprise, the older man pulled up some dry ferns and scythed some grass from the upper slope, returned and drooped them over Francisco's bare legs.

"*Gratias, gratias,*" said Francisco, using the Latin which the old man might recognize from Catholic masses or church schools, "*Maria, Mater Sanctissima, te benedicat.*"

The old man nodded. Then he tugged at Francisco's shirt and pointed up over the bluff to the left. He gestured again with an arm to indicate a turn to the left. Then he put both palms upward in the attitude of praying, then clasped and shook his two hands in the gesture of friendliness.

"*Templum Dei?*" asked Francisco. A temple of the Gods? He got no response.

"*Monasterium?*" said Francisco. The old man nodded his head up and down delightedly.

"*Gratias! Deus te benedicat,*" said Francisco.

"*Benedicat. Benedicat,*" echoed the old man. He shook Francisco's hand, then, grinning, he hurried off down the dune, his scythe gleaming silvery in the moonlight.

There are good folk in Ireland, after all, thought Francisco. *If I can find the monastery, perhaps the monks will help me survive.* He started to crawl up the bank but almost immediately heard the voices of men and thudding of hooves. Crawling back quickly to his bush, he curled up tightly under it. A cavalcade of armored Englishmen, perhaps a hundred, came riding over the bank and pounded past him.

Glad still to be alive when they had gone past, Francisco began crawling up the dunes. At the top of the bank he took hold of a willow branch and pulled himself slowly to his feet. He began to limp, seeking the left turn the old man had indicated. He limped for perhaps a mile and a half in the intermittent moonlight. He hoped to encounter a stream. His throat was dry as leather. The short trees seemed to be thinning out. He could see traces of the dove-wing gray of dawn.

Now there was a well-beaten path to the left. After a half mile he came out on a high grassy plateau with the faintly roaring sea far below. Two hundred yards ahead of him he could see dark outlines of a ruined abbey, its towers jagged against the pink sky of dawn. As he approached, he noted shattered windows with broken glass lying beneath. Where were the monks who had so recently lodged here? Killed? In hiding?

A small oblong chapel stood detached to the right of the Abbey. Francisco moved to the front of it. There was no longer a door. He peered in with a quick look. He moved inside, trying to adjust his sight to the dark interior. There were triple-arched windows on either side from which the glass had been pushed out. There were life-sized statues underneath the window ledges.

Then, as his eyes adapted, he suddenly realized that the statues were actually six naked men on each side, hanging by the neck from the iron bars of the windows. He gasped. By the cut of their beards and hair and cast of their features, they were unmistakably Spanish. They were his fellow countrymen, unfortunates from the beach who had been able to reach what they considered safe sanctuary. Then they were captured, stripped and murdered by whom, the English or the Irish?

He looked closely at every face, recognizing only one—that of an officer from the *San Juan* whom he had seen in the company of Don Enriquez in Lisbon. Poor fellows. They had managed to roll in alive from the wreck of the *San Juan* and reach this bitter hill. Francisco knelt on the chapel floor and his words poured out:

"Oh, Mary of Henar, where were you when these men were so pitilessly killed in a holy chapel? Have mercy on their souls, divine mother of Jesus, and give them peace."

Francisco sat down to gather his thoughts in silence. *The whole Irish countryside and treacherous sea below represent death. How they all had longed for safe solid land and it had only brought inglorious slaughter by gluttonous bloodthirsty savages.* He prayed again in a quiet voice:

"Oh, Lord, there are very few survivors of these shipwrecks. All we wish for is to get back to our beloved soil of Spain. For me, I only want to return to my town of Cuellar where all that is beautiful awaits my coming. If I am never to see home again, please give me a quick death now."

For a moment he seemed to be lifted up to the rafters of the little chapel so that he looked down on his body lying on the cold stone floor.

Could it be he, Francisco de Cuellar, lying encircled by hanging bodies and praying for death, he who had been so full of life and vigor, so full of faith in himself, in God, and in the Holy Enterprise of the Armada when he had sailed out of Lisbon less than three months before?

Now he felt as if he were futilely fighting off the black encirclement of death. *If death is waiting everywhere, is there any point in resisting what seems inevitable?* His mind went briefly silent, then he concluded that life was an incessant war against death and, no matter what the odds, he must rekindle his zest for living. *If God is testing me, He is certainly creating formidable barriers to the continuation of life.* Out of sheer fatigue he fell asleep.

Francisco awoke a few hours later, crawled a few paces to the west wall just beyond the row of dangling bodies and slowly stood up. He walked painfully out of the chapel thinking that whatever horror comes, he must strengthen his soul to meet the challenges.

In the early light of morning he took a path beside the ruined Abbey along the top of the wooded bluff. He soon came upon what had been the monks' vegetable garden. It had been crisscrossed with the hooves of many horses and most of the vegetables had been uprooted, meaning that the hanging of the twelve shipwreck survivors had been carried out by the English.

Francisco found two radish roots but eating them upset his stomach. His legs were hurting, especially the deeply wounded right lower leg, but he kept walking, driven by the whip of the will to live. *Which direction shall I walk,* he wondered. *There is death everywhere. To the left is the ocean shore with local knaves doing their dance of death around corpses and treasure chests. On the right is hostile countryside in which, now and then, one might find a kindly soul.*

He weighed all possibilities and decided to return to the beach which might be empty of murderers by now. Perhaps a chest of biscuits or bottles of wine may have been overlooked or neglected by those hunting for silver, gold and gems.

Francisco started limping slowly back towards the beach. When he spotted two people coming along the path he hid behind a bush. Voices came to him on strange sustained high notes. They were not speaking, they were wailing. It was like the unearthly sounds made by ships' sails in a storm, as if elemental spirits were conversing in haunting incantation. It was the primeval sound of keening, the ancient sound of sorrow.

Soon Francisco could make out words. Two pitiful Spaniards were addressing and entreating the entire Holy Pantheon: *"Jesu! Maria! Ay de mi! Sant Antonio! San Francesco!* Oh God, Holy Father, with Thy divine mercy protect us in this merciless land!"

As they came even with his bush, Francisco stood up and said in Spanish, *"Buenos dias, amigos!* God be with you!" Both men were stark naked. One had a large crimson-matted wound on his head, the other a hunched-up shoulder with a large bruise.

"Come off the path into the thicket with me. We've got to decide how to preserve ourselves in this God-damned country. From which ship?" asked Francisco.

"The *Falcon Blanco*," answered Garcia, the one with the hurt shoulder. "We are soldiers. We threw off all our armor and jumped into the sea. With God's good grace, we came ashore safely with about a hundred others from the ship. It was midnight. The shore was alive with plunderers."

"I was there. I'm from the *San Marcos*. What happened to you after that?"

"There was a crowd of about a hundred English soldiers who had ridden down on horseback from their garrison. They were brutes. They bashed and clouted with abandon. If any Spaniards were still alive they were jumped on with nailed boots or just wantonly clubbed, or they dragged men by their beards and cut off their parts and held them up in the moonlight."

"Good God, what beasts. But we must remember that we are invaders who came to kill and destroy people and their religion. How did you happen to escape?"

"By pretending death after we were clouted and kicked. When this troop of bastards began looking for plunder farther down the beach we crawled up the bluff unnoticed."

"We can't go on in such small numbers," answered Francisco. "I suggest we go back to the shore, forage for food and collect any other living Spaniards. Not all Irish have bad hearts. Perhaps a few of us could get through to a port where we can find a ship heading back to Spain."

"Very well. You lead," said Diego, the one with the wounded head.

The three stumbled towards the beach in silence. In an hour they came to the brink of the bluff above the shore. There were no living persons in sight, only hundreds of naked white corpses, pieces of timber, wooden chests hacked open, and pieces of masts riding the sand incongruously. They inched carefully down to the beach. Scavenging crows and seagulls were everywhere. The wolves had gone.

Francisco was limping towards a metal box of the kind used to hold ships' biscuits. He stepped aside to avoid a naked body which was lying on its back, with one eye staring into the unseen daylight. The other had been pecked out. Something about the cheekbones and ragged black hair caused Francisco to stop abruptly. He bent over the body.

"Donel! My God, Donel!"

Great sobs poured out as his body shook. He remembered the figure he had seen at twilight on his knees, pleading for his life. *That must have been poor Donel, who had finally reached his own shore, only a few miles from home. He had begged the Irish marauders in Gaelic for his life but lost it because he was on a Spanish invasion ship. What a cruel fate.*

Francisco wept unashamedly until he heard the two Spaniards calling. They were bending over a body and crying out, "*El Capitan! El pobre Capitan.*"

Francisco pulled himself up and stumbled across the sand. There lay Don Diego Enriquez, the little hunchback, the beloved Captain of the great *San Juan*. His clothes had been taken and the crooked body which he had carried through life with such dignity of demeanor looked so plain when stripped of his shining personality. Francisco felt an urgent desire to give him a decent burial.

"We must bury the Captain at once," said Francisco firmly. "And we must bury my Irish friend, Donel."

"But why?" asked Garcia. "We can't go around burying all the bodies on the beach! It is more important to hunt for food to keep ourselves from becoming corpses too!"

"At night the wolves come down and feed on the bodies. We must save Captain Enriquez and my friend from such desecration. If you will not help me, I will do it alone."

As Francisco started to drag Don Enriquez's body across the sand, Diego and Garcia helped him. Together they hauled both bodies up to the line of dune grasses, then knelt down and began to scoop deep trenches out of the sand with their bare hands. Francisco began to wonder where Sebastian might be, whether he had been cast up dead on this same beach or whether, with all his vigor and shrewdness, he might have been able to make his escape.

Francisco was bending over to scoop out more sand when a big hand lifted him up by his doublet. He looked up. Four Irishmen surrounded the three gravediggers. The unwanted visitors pointed to the trench as much as to say, "What are you doing, hiding treasure?"

Francisco pointed to the two corpses, then made the sign of the cross to signify that they were trying to give the poor men a decent burial.

Now the big fellow began unbuttoning the two remaining buttons of Francisco's doublet and drew it down roughly over Francisco's thighs and buttocks. For a moment some of Francisco's old fighting spirit returned and he resisted. The Irishman kicked him over into the sand, accentuating the pain in his legs. His trousers were roughly stripped off and his boots removed.

Recovering his breath, Francisco tried a few words in Latin hoping that some of the meaning would get through. It didn't, so on a whim he spoke in Spanish. "You are Catholic. I am Catholic. For the love of Mary, the mother of God, why do you treat us like this?"

For answer, the Irishman took hold of Francisco's linen shirt to tear it off but the oldest man in the group spoke suddenly and authoritatively in Gaelic and the man let go. Then in slowly spoken, heavily accented but understandable Spanish, he addressed Francisco: "You are right. You have asked mercy of Mary, the mother of God. I, as a chief, give you mercy."

"God bless you." Then it occurred to him to say, "One of those we are burying, a dear friend, is the son of one of the chieftains here. Perhaps you know him, Chief O'Connor Sligo."

A terrible transformation came over the older man. For the first time he took notice of the two bodies. A cry came from him as he knelt beside Donel. He poured out wild words and his hands went over Donel's head and face and body. After a time, O'Conner stood up and said:

"You were his friend. Tell me about him. He went off for adventure two years ago out of Sligo harbor and we've not heard from him since."

Francisco told all he knew, ending with, "He loved you well, Chief O'Conner, and he loved his home. He longed more than anything on

God's earth to get safely back to Ireland. When he set foot on his own shore, someone bashed him on the head despite his pleas for mercy."

"We'll never know whether the killer was English or Irish. The Lord works in strange ways."

"He does indeed," said Francisco quietly, deciding not to mention that it was Irishmen who had killed Donel.

"If you can get to my village," said O'Conner, "there will be some rags of clothes and some food for you. We don't have much anymore. You probably wonder why we take your clothes. Yours are made by professionals, ours are simple and homespun. And you shall have your doublet and boots back right now. We will do anything we can for Donel's friend, even though you are invaders."

"God bless you. How is it that some of you are so kind and some just want to kill us?"

"We're all quite poor here and we've been treated so brutally that part of us has become savage, as the English have always claimed. Forgive us."

"Is there any hope of our getting back to Spain?"

"There are powerful Irish chieftains in the north still holding out successfully against the English. The very first man to help you on the way will be my friend, Sir Brian na Murtha 0'Rourke—0'Rourke of the Ramparts. I'll have one of my sons show you the way while my other two sons and I carry our dear Donel home for burial."

Francisco's clothes and shoes were restored. Then O'Connor took off his cloak, the body of Donel was laid inside it and, after hand-shaking between O'Connor Sligo and the three Spaniards, Donel's family carried him up the hill. The son who remained behind helped to lay Don Enriquez in his grave and to heap sand over him. Then he led the way up the beach for a short distance and took a path up the dune into the woods. Where another path branched to the right, the Irishman stopped, motioned forward with his hand, and said, "O'Rourke. O'Rourke."

Francisco took his hand and pumped it gratefully and their guide walked away. As the day wore on, Francisco's limping became worse and he often had to stop and sit down for a few minutes of rest. So he suggested that his two companions go ahead. They agreed.

Francisco picked up a piece of straight branch for a crutch and began to limp along the path. Three ravens rose from a nearby tree, seeming to mock him with their raucous cawing. Francisco, however, interpreted their strident sounds as urging him onwards. He enjoyed the harsh calls and audacity of certain birds like ravens, crows and jays. When the ravens stopped on a nearby branch, seeming to wait for him, he smiled and picked up his stride with renewed energy. *One can't be overly choosy about friendships in Ireland*, he thought.

CHAPTER 11

Thatched Hut and Velvet Gown

(September 1588)

After walking about a mile, Francisco caught sight of some limpid blue-black clusters of bilberries clinging to a bush. He tore off the fruit and fisted it into his mouth as ancestors of his might have done a hundred thousand years before. His clothes became splotched with purple but who cares? To his dismay, his hungry stomach ejected the first handful. More slowly, then, he ate the berries that were left, setting in motion pangs of hunger which had been lying dormant—a situation his forebears well knew. Complete starvation eliminates feelings of hunger within a day; eating little bits of food intermittently leads to frequent feelings of hunger.

He limped forward. Surely these woods would offer further edible opportunities. Every bird that crossed his path appeared to him as a winged morsel of meat. He realized that he could bring himself to eat animal flesh raw, untouched by fire. *How fast we descend to the habits of Early Man,* he thought, *when our fortunes decline.*

He visualized the quiet vine arbor in his castle courtyard heavy with grapes. He imaged himself sitting there, breaking a loaf of bread and watching the graceful movements of his mother as she set before him a flask of Legrono just drawn up from a ledge in the courtyard well. *It is time for me to become a homebody. No more ships. No more oceans. No more glimpses of hell. I feel completely suction-cupped by the tentacles of historical destiny, helpless to exert my individual will and lead a life of peace. Enough of life's dramas.*

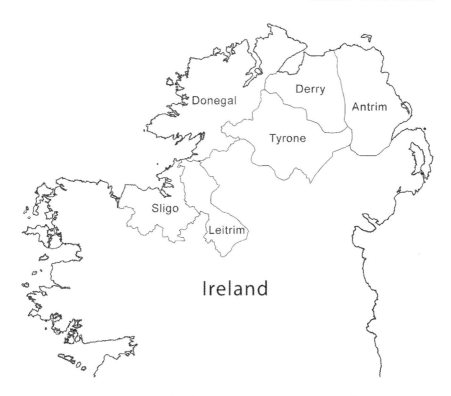

Figure 3. Counties of Ireland relevant to Francisco's quest for survival.

When he had limped on for another quarter mile, he thought he heard at last the sound of water strumming over stones. The water sound grew louder, like a spoon tinkling in a Murano glass. How many months had it been since he had tasted cool fresh water? He left the path and stumbled forward, landing on his knees at the edge of a little pool where water splashing over rocks was singing its love song. He extended himself on the ground and drank slowly but eagerly. The water had the tannic taste of peat but it was cool and he couldn't get enough.

When he sat back at last, he noticed the bright green leaves and crystal stems of a patch of watercress growing along the other side of the narrow stream. He leaned across, plucked a handful and devoured it down to its roots along with some hazel nuts from a nearby bush. At last the hollows of his stomach were filled with a few ounces of food, his throat was no longer cracked with thirst and a faint hope emerged that he might, step by cautious step, be able to get out alive from this Irish hell.

A linnet sang joyously on a nearby bush, reminding Francisco why it melodious warbling notes made it a popular caged bird. He admired its bluish head, the red patch on its forehead and its russet-brown back, happy that he could once again simply appreciate a bird's beauty and no longer consider it a piece of flying meat.

Francisco lay back and rested a few moments listening to nature's quiet symphony, then walked back to the path. He began to notice more details of the scenery—the flame-colors of spindle trees and alders, the sun-reflecting leaves and berries of wild holly, the small white Scots rose with its bright red hips in full roundness in these late September days, and now and then a burst of bright purple foxglove. For a few moments he was almost happy alone with such beauty, briefly suspending his prism of pain and adversity.

He passed into a place where trees were sparse. The land sloped down to a small valley set with a dozen thatched huts. On a hill a mile away stood a gray castle. In the far distance the great flat mountain that poor Donel had called Ben Bulben appeared as a shaded cube against the sky.

Francisco had scarcely drawn breath to take in the scene when a yelping and yowling began behind him and two enormous Irish wolfhounds jumped towards him. They were followed by an old man, two younger men and a young girl. While the dogs barked and leaped around him, one of the younger men cried out in crude Spanish:

"Surrender, Spanish bastard!" Whisking a hunting knife from his belt he made a lunge towards Francisco. For a moment Francisco defended himself with his walking stick but the aggressive Irishman made a slash across the already-wounded outside of his right leg. The blow doubled him up and he fell to the ground. Just as the Irishman was about to deliver another slash, the girl cried out in Gaelic and brought her hand down hard on the knife-wielding wrist. The Irishman, wrenching free, looked at her with blazing anger. The old man said something. Now the third man, to Francisco's amazement, exclaimed in French, "Yes, what's the use?"

Francisco, his right leg now spilling blood, remarked wearily, also in French, "With me limping on my stick, he could certainly see that I couldn't do battle. Why are these Irish so pugnacious and brutal?"

The girl had the simple prettiness of youth with curling blue-black hair, a ruddy complexion and eyes as blue as a Moorish mosaic. The girl said something to Francisco in Gaelic and laid a hand on his bleeding right leg. The violent young Irishman broke out into rough words directed at the girl. The old man motioned to the two other men to be off. The knife-wielder departed with a grunt and ugly look, the other with a frown. The two dogs loped after them.

Francisco put out a hand to the old man and spoke his church Latin, "*Gratias. Dominus te benedicat.*"

"*Amen,*" said the old man. He then put a hand on Francisco's doublet and started to pull it down from Francisco's shoulders.

"*Non. Non. Furtum! Furtum!* (Thievery!)," exclaimed Francisco.

The old man signaled to the girl. Together they stripped off Francisco's doublet and shirt. Francisco resisted, crying out in Spanish:

"You will not take all that lies between me and the weather!" It was of no use. The old man was strong and the girl was a young lioness. The shirt came off and the man immediately exclaimed "*Per Jesum!*" The girl began to dance with glee. For there exposed against Francisco's naked chest was the St. Lawrence relic and his pearl and silver rosary.

The old man held Francisco's two arms while the girl, smiling, lifted the two chains from Francisco's neck and put them around her own.

"*Rosarium! Rosarium!*" shrieked the girl happily.

At the sound of the girl's joyous outcries the two younger men came into the clearing again with the dogs. They arrived in time to help with a searching of Francisco's clothes for further treasure. They quickly discovered the pouch of coins fastened to the inside of his doublet's waistband. The gold crown pieces were turned out into avid palms causing a jig of joy by the girl. The old man said something in Gaelic which the speaker of French translated for Francisco's benefit, "He says you must be a rich nobleman and should be held for ransom."

"I am of ancient Spanish heritage but am not rich," replied Francisco in French. "I am only a ship's officer. The coins are the pay given to me by the Commander of the fleet at Corunna four months ago. I had hoped to use it along the way to help me get back to Spain. You have left me with nothing except my life and a bleeding leg."

The girl reached out towards him and whispered some Gaelic words softly into his ear which he interpreted as a brief moment of compassion. The girl helped him back into his shirt and put her arm around his shoulder.

She directed the man who spoke French to support him on the other side and they helped him walk slowly down the slope towards the village.

"Where do you come from in Spain?" asked the man.

"From Cuellar, near Segovia. And you?"

"From Paris. I fought with French volunteers at Terceira and was taken prisoner by Don Alvaro de Bazan. A gallant gentleman. He spared my life. I bear good will to Spaniards."

"How do you happen to be here in this God-forsaken country?"

"Ah, for adventure! To see the world and taste the vivacious, unspoiled Irish girls."

They led him down the hill towards a simple straw-thatched hut. It was a dwelling of the most primitive kind without windows or chimney. It had soft leather for a door, woven twigs, straw and mud for walls, tree branches for support, rushes on the dirt floor and a fire-pit in the center.

The girl helped Francisco lie down on the floor near the fire and placed beneath his head a sack of heather tops and leaves. Then she removed her blouse, becoming naked above the waist. She threw the blouse over his legs and covered it with rushes. *So much for native medical lore,* thought Francisco, *but at least she seems to care.*

The girl leaned over him, allowing her large breasts and his own gold chain and medal of Saint Lawrence to rub over his chest. It was as if she were trying to impart to him her own primeval healing powers in combination with those of a Catholic saint. *What a strange combination of savagery and kindness these people display,* he thought as he fell asleep.

In the gray of morning Francisco was awakened by quiet laughter and low-pitched groans. He was able to make out two slowly moving mounded figures on a nearby pallet of straw in the rhythmic embrace of love—the colleen and her French lover. Francisco wondered whether the world would ever again grant him such a happy digression from life's turmoils.

A few minutes later, after some urgent grunts and sighs, the two disentangled themselves. The girl walked over to Francisco and spoke to him. By her intonation he guessed she was asking how he felt. He answered in Latin that he felt much better. She then asked in Gaelic whether he was hungry, pointing to her mouth.

He rubbed his stomach and made the sign of zero. She laughed, added wood to the fire, heated a pot of water placed directly into the side of the fire and prepared an oaten porridge. Francisco knew that oats had been introduced into Ireland several thousand years ago because they survived better than wheat in a rainy climate. She then fetched a crock of buttermilk. He sat up and moved to the edge of the fire to enjoy his Irish breakfast in warmth.

The three men stood and drank buttermilk from cups carved from the trunks of small trees. They had just set the mugs down when there was a hubbub of loud voices and the barking of dogs at the end of the village encampment. The girl rushed to the door, then shouted at the Frenchman. "She says to lie against the far edge of the room," he interpreted, "and pretend to be sleeping. Don't say a word. It's the English probably hunting for Spaniards. She'll do the talking. She has, as you have seen for yourself, a way with men," he added with a wink.

The girl just had time to slip the chain from her neck and drop it into the ashes at the side of the fire-pit when two of Sir Richard Bingham's men from their posting at the neighboring castle darkened the doorway. Both carried long halberds, a favorite English weapon consisting of a long pole with an axe blade and long spike on one end. They pushed aside the cowhide and came in.

"Good morning, Miss. We've orders from her Majesty, the Queen, to round up all Spaniards. Have you got any here?"

One man started towards Francisco but the girl quickly intercepted him, put one arm through his, brushed his elbow against her breast and said, "Leave now and come back tonight if you want to learn more about Irish culture." She gave him a glance to melt a flint stone.

The man boomed a laugh and said to his companion, "Hear that, James? I think she means it. She wants to see both of us here this evening."

"I'd rather satisfy my battle-axe but I'm game for tonight. Let's go."

Francisco breathed a sigh of relief. He wondered how many times he would face the scythe of death before he arrived back home. He now said in French to the Frenchman, "Please tell your young lady that I thank her. She has twice saved my life. If I get safely back to Spain, what can I send to her? I have nothing left to give her now except my trousers."

The Frenchman spoke slow Gaelic to the girl, then translated her reply back into French.

"She wants a fine velvet gown. I wonder what she would do here in this simple village wearing a velvet gown. It would probably soon be torn off by men."

Francisco narrowed his eyes speculatively as he looked at the girl, picturing her in such a gown. "*Monsieur,*" he declared, "if one could send her to a hairdresser and dress her nicely, I believe she would compare well with any ballroom beauties in your Paris or my Madrid."

"Yes, Caitlyn is pretty or I wouldn't have loitered here. But women are all vain cats, from Patagonia to Paris."

"Ask her what color velvet she would like."

"Her favorite color is red. All women want to wear the color of courtesans because all women are courtesans at heart."

"Except most nuns," answered Francisco, "and my own mother and wife."

"Even nuns in my experience," rejoined the Frenchman. "As for your mother, I suppose you can trust her, but a wife never! The more trustworthy a wife seems, the less trustworthy she is when her husband is away."

Francisco felt his face reddening. "Most Frenchmen take the fruit of female bodies without respect for their immortal souls!"

Far from being offended, the Frenchman laughed.

After his bowl of porridge and another mug of buttermilk, Francisco knew he had to leave. He must put distance between himself and Bingham's Spaniard-slaughtering troops. He now brought up the subject of his best possible chances for escape to the north. With the Frenchman translating, the old man gave his advice, guiding Francisco to the leather doorway.

"Avoid that nearby castle like the plague. It's full of Governor Richard Bingham's men. They've stolen four thousand head of cattle out of this country, murdered many a fine Irish chieftain and recently many Spanish."

"I know," answered Francisco. "Chief O'Conner has already warned me about them."

"Well, then, you see those hills rising near Ben Bulben, some with high summits? Beyond them lives one of the greatest chiefs in Ireland, Sir Brian 0'Rourke. He detests the Queen of England with a poisonous loathing. He will shelter all Spaniards who come his way. He'll show you the way to Donegal which is full of English-haters like Mac Sweeneys, O'Donnells and O'Neills. Up there on the north coast in Donegal, Derry and Antrim there'll be ships of the chiefs going every small while to the coast of Scotland."

"Any other advice?"

"You must keep away from the wide path to Donegal, my boy, for that is the road the English follow along the coast. Keep to the little paths that skirt the foot of Ben Bulben. Tell any friendly folk you meet you'll be wanting to go to Lake Melvin and the Castle of Rossclogher. Tell them Granddaddy Teighe Keohan of Glenade is a good friend and sent you with his blessing."

"*Gracias, Señor* Teighe, for the directions. May I get my own shirt back?"

"Yes, but not your cloak. We need it more than you do."

Caitlyn went to the corner and brought out some oat bread which she gave to Francisco. He kissed her unwashed hand and thanked her for saving his life. She murmured something in return.

The Frenchman translated: "Caitlyn says not to forget her red velvet gown."

CHAPTER 12

Irish Venison and Segovian Wine
(September 1588)

The dogs that had barked Francisco into the village now barked him out. When the path curved into the woods, he turned for a final look at the tiny hamlet. Caitlyn was waving with a piece of white cloth. As he limped into the woods, a song thrush, soon to depart for warmer climes, saluted him with its flute-like whistles.

Caitlyn's a pretty girl, he thought, *but can't in any way compare to my Zabella. I wonder if Zabella is thinking about me right now, perhaps imagining me riding splendidly through the streets of conquered London. How her heart would grieve if she knew I was a shipwrecked vagrant roaming through the Irish countryside in constant danger of my life.*

Francisco's right leg was quite painful, made much worse by the malicious knife cut by Caitlyn's brother but the wound didn't seem infected. It wasn't leaking pus and didn't have a foul smell. Despite the sturdy walking stick which he had made from a branch, walking was slow. A new injury required rest in order to heal. The skin on his left leg was intact but there was widespread black and blueness from the crush injury he had sustained during the shipwreck. There was considerable swelling of both ankles and feet.

Although Francisco had a high tolerance for pain, he was constantly aware of a throbbing curtain of hurt between him and the world, made worse by the necessity to keep walking in order to survive. Being barefoot increased the challenge, his tender feet aware of every pebble and irregularity. The weather was cold and damply penetrating, especially at night. He wondered whether he would ever feel warm again.

Francisco stopped often to lean against trees. He worried about human enemies walking down the path looking for victims of their intrinsic wrath. He soon came upon a six foot wide stream, one of the many coursing down from Ben Bulben, lined by watercress and mint. Although past their prime, they were edible and he knew that he needed vegetables in his diet in order to heal properly. He crawled along on his knees, plucking and munching. His mind made a comparison to Nebuchadnezzar II, 6th century BC biblical King of Babylon, who built the magnificent Hanging Gardens of Babylon but went insane and stooped in his madness to eat grass.

Francisco had the ability to look down at any scene from above. The recent sharply dramatic experiences, being closely brushed by death in so many different forms, had led him to consider more deeply the meaning of Life, God and religion. He sat down and leaned against a large oak tree. It occurred to him that, until recently, his life pattern had fit together like pieces of stained glass in the great windows of Segovia's Cathedral, recently completed after more than fifty years of building. Now the apparent abandonment of the Spanish Armada by God and the usually merciful Madonna of Henar had strengthened his latent doubts.

What if Sebastian were right? What if God consisted only of a vast web of Spirit flickering through the universe like the Pleiades which shimmered high over ships' masts on November nights—remote, shapeless, faceless, heedless. Man must work out his own fate among storms, wild beasts and killer-humans, hate prevailing far too often, as Sebastian had suggested.

Francisco seemed to be in a detached state, wondering what would happen next to this unfortunate hobbling creature who was a confident Armada ship captain in a previous life. A squirrel chattered, as if scolding him for his lugubriousness.

God forgive me, he thought, as he crossed himself from old habit. *Jesus suffered the hatred and cruelty of his fellow men, the loneliness of Golgotha, the torture of the cross. Why should I, so insignificant a man, not suffer more? The priests keep telling us it is man's glory to suffer.*

He tried to maintain a steady slow pace, now and then pausing to eat a few bilberries and drink from streams. He never knelt for water without being thankful, remembering the endless seas of salt and hundreds of barrels of slimy polluted water on his ship which had to be thrown overboard. The path gradually emerged into the open among occasional thickets of heather, with moors and peat bogs spreading to the left and the steep slopes of Ben Bulben rising on the right. He thought of Donel who would have been happy to guide him around Ben Bulben, talking cheerily all the way. *Why had life been so unkind to him despite all his innocence?*

Limping on his stick, he looked like a man three times his age. He planned to conceal himself for the night as soon as he sighted houses or people. He came around the huge trunk of an oak and saw a simple hut. No dog barked, no horse was tethered outside. He moved cautiously, peeking around the half-open door which was made of small branches roped together with strands of grass. Lying fast asleep on the floor was a boy of about fifteen with a club and a book beside him. It was a beautiful book bound in brown velvet with a gold clasp and gold filigree work in the center, presumably a book in a protective chest recently cast up by the sea.

The boy, though poorly clothed, was of such a gentle appearance that Francisco decided to talk to him. He spoke quietly the Latin greeting, "*Salve.*"

The boy bounded to his feet in alarm, then stooped quickly for his bludgeon.

"*Non! Non! Amigo. Amicus. Ami.* Friend," said Francisco, trying all the languages he knew.

The boy made a quick shoulder shrug of not understanding. Francisco smiled and decided to try Latin again. "*Hic liber in lingua Latina?*"

"*Sic. Anglicus tu?*"

"*Non, non. Avertat Deus! Non Anglicus. Hispanicus. Amicus.* (No, no. God forbid! I am not English. I am Spanish and a friend.)"

Figure 4. Locations of Francisco's early trials and adventures in Ireland.

"Amicus!" exclaimed the boy. Transferring the club to his left hand, he held out his right. The two carried on an awkward, short-sentenced conversation in Latin. Francisco learned that the boy, his father and two brothers were all that was left of a family of seven children belonging to a branch of the Mac Carthy clan that had once lived in a castle at Mullaghmore, a strategic point overlooking Donegal Bay. The English had seized the castle after a strong fight in which half the family had been killed. The Mac Carthy survivors had taken shelter with the monks of Staad Abbey for an entire winter and there the boy, Morven Mac Carthy, had studied, learned some Latin and decided to become a priest. When the English burned the Abbey, the surviving monks and the Mac Carthys had scattered.

The father and his three surviving sons had been living in this hidden place for a month, watching movements of the English and planning to join eventually with the rest of their clan to recover their castle. Morven had been ordered to remain behind today to guard the hut and other treasures and bring home the four cows from pasture after sunset while his father and older brothers had gone to the shore for more treasure hunting.

Several days before, said the boy, all four of them had seen the Spanish ships founder while they had been down at the beach gathering carrageen, sea-kale, samphire and lovage roots for food. They had managed to pick up a Spanish chest before anyone else could seize it.

Francisco reached for the book. On the inside cover he found, in a small swirling hand, the name of Father Domenico of the *San Marcos*. The chest, then, probably had contained vestments, gold and silver chalices, and crucifixes of the Catholic service. *Were such objects really of value to someone in a simple hut in the wilderness?*

Francisco now made a gesture to his mouth and across his belly, querying whether there was any food. Immediately Gaelic hospitality rose to the level of action. The boy went out, returning shortly with an earthenware jar of buttermilk, a few samphire plants, a cup of brambleberries and some Spanish biscuits with their telltale weevil tracks. Hungry as he was, Francisco gently said "no" to the old sea biscuits which recalled such unpleasant memories.

To his surprise he was enjoying the taste of buttermilk more and more and knew it was helping to heal his wounded body. The samphire, too, after he had become used to its somewhat metallic and briny taste, slid pleasingly into the empty hollows of his stomach. As evening began to shadow the glen, Francisco was overcome with drowsiness. Morven placed a few dried oak leaves, ferns, twigs and two cubes of peat on the coals. Soon a small fire lighted the gloom. Francisco, basking in the warmth, went to sleep.

Two hours later, Francisco was awakened by the barking of dogs and loud voices. He got up and stood in a dark corner, leaning with both hands on his walking stick. Morven stirred the fire and, by its light, Francisco saw the branch door pushed aside by a big brown-bearded man in goatskin jacket, long pants tied at the ankle and a blue cloak held with a silver clasp. He entered, followed by two younger men, one with black hair, one with red. They were fine-looking men. He wondered, however, what darkness might lie in their hearts, instilled by their own life difficulties.

The father spoke to Morven in Gaelic as his sons set down two wooden boxes, one of which Francisco recognized as a container of dried tunny fish, the other as holding bottles of wine.

Immediately the father discovered Francisco and pointed to him in his dark corner. Morven went into a long explanation. Then the father walked towards Francisco, held out his hand and said, *"Amicus."* He led Francisco into the center of the room and the two brothers shook his hand. The father gave orders and a log table was quickly set, upon which were placed biscuit, carrageen, smoked venison and, finally, one of the bottles of wine which they opened with belt knives. The father gestured towards Francisco and made a remark which Morven translated as "This is all in your honor, *Señor*! We bring out the King of Spain's daughter—his wine!"

Mac Carthy went into a corner and brought five large mollusk shells which he placed upon the table and filled with wine. Francisco asked permission to look at the bottle. It was wine of Segovia but not from his vineyards. "From the vineyards of my own province. *A su gusto!*"

The father gave a brief toast. "We are sorry for the tragedy which brought us this wine but may the same seas bear you safely home soon."

Francisco gave his reply to the toast by Morven's father, "May you never know what it is like to be shipwrecked, which implies abandonment by God but if that day comes, may you meet men as friendly and hospitable as the Mac Carthys."

One of the brothers, feeling wine-emboldened, slapped Francisco on the back and placed a hefty cutting of deer haunch before him. The Mac Carthys ate hastily and the meal was over quickly, without further talking. Then Francisco was given a special straw bed while the others stretched out in various corners of the hut with their big cloaks serving as blankets.

As he lay down for sleep, Francisco listened to an owl hooting and thought, *I have almost nothing left, just a thin shirt and trousers. Not a ducat or anything of value, not even the strength of my once able body. Nearby are the fragmented remnants of Spain's great Armada lying starkly along the Irish coast and the disintegrating bodies of my friends and associates drifting in the rough sea and lying in the cold Irish sand. Yet here I am alive with men of good will under a roof and next to a warm fire, having just consumed a delicious meal of venison and fine Segovian wine. Strange world.*

CHAPTER 13

Fern Frond Fashion

(September 1588)

The next morning Francisco awoke to the sound of angry voices and spattering rain. The two older brothers were quarreling over division of their beach plunder. The hut shook with their fisticuffs until they took their quarrel outside into the mud.

No food was brought out since they ate only one meal a day. "What will you be doing on this rainy day," asked Francisco of Morven.

"We don't pay much attention to rain. It begins raining in the fall and rains almost every day in winter. We go about our usual activities. We hunt as we used to with bow and arrow so we don't give away our position. Thus we save precious powder and ammunition to use against the English. They first conquered us for no reason four hundred years ago but they keep re-invading us, always finding an excuse to do so."

The boy went on to describe how they netted birds, trapped hare or went down to the sea to fish and gather sea laces and kale. They plucked purple melic grass for mending the ropes of nets. They gathered honey, herbs, berries and nuts. They made candles of reeds and butter or spent time sharpening their knives with flint. They milked their cows and set the milk to sour for buttermilk. If there was extra time, he read his book. There was plenty to do in this country of God.

Francisco wanted to rest his leg longer but decided it was time to be moving on to O'Rourke country with the hope of finding a ship sailing for Scotland. So, after considerable talk with the father and muddy brothers, Francisco's plans began to take shape. Mac Carthy decided to put Francisco and Morven on two of the nags and let Morven accompany the traveler part way. The horses were brought from their hiding place in the woods. There were strong handshakes and exchanges of farewell in Gaelic and Latin. Then Morven helped Francisco mount his horse. Morven himself mounted the Irish way, beginning with holding the nag's left ear.

The two started off through dripping woods. Where the leaves had packed down, the going was not difficult but where the swollen streams rushing down from the Dartry Mountains intercepted the path, riding was not easy. When the way led out into the open at the edge of peat bogs, they might sink in mud up to the horses' hocks.

By early afternoon the rain let up. The path emerged from the woods and skirted a low mountain spur with peat bogs on the left and solid ground on the right covered with green and brown bracken and furze. Morven, as guide, was riding ahead. Presently he reined his horse and inclined his head. "What is it?" asked Francisco in Latin.

Morven put his index finger to his lips. Francisco could hear the faint sound of horses' hooves growing rapidly louder. In a moment were added the brittle sound of clanking harness metal, voices and louder thudding.

"Spain, Spain, we have to hide!" cried Morven in so sudden and terrified a voice that the skin of both horses rippled from mane to tall. "The Sassenachs! The Sassenachs are coming!"

Francisco knew the Saxon word meant marauding Saxons most likely in the form of Governor Bingham's soldiers. Francisco dug his heels into the flanks of his horse and began riding up a steep incline with many sharp flinty stones. Twice his animal came to its knees on the slippery rocky slope and Francisco almost fell backwards.

The Sassenachs were getting close, the thuddings very loud. There was a cleft between two outcrops. Francisco prodded his horse which again stumbled, striking sparks from the stones but, with Francisco's urging, leaped up and into the narrow cleft, Morven following. They now had to remain still and hope the Saxons wouldn't see them in the shadows.

"Lean backward and grab the tail to keep it from flicking," said Francisco. "The slightest motion could betray us."

The thudding and voices raced past below. Francisco and Morven dismounted and led the slipping, sliding animals down the slope again.

"*Via pericolosa*," said Morven.

"Life in almost every aspect is dangerous for Spaniards these days." The boy smiled at his new friend. They two rode down the hill and found a decent path that ran for two miles before skirting the edges of a peat bog, then changed direction into a forest. They were moving steadily when they began hearing a deep splashing and soon rode into a forest glade flanked by a waterfall. They were horrified to see twenty horses and about thirty men standing or kneeling on the bank to drink. They were Irishmen of the rougher sort, gathered in a band for illicit deeds.

Morven and Francisco drew up their horses and tried to turn but four of the men rushed at them and seized the bridles. Morven lashed out with his riding-stick and cried out some words in Gaelic that made the four men step back. Now all the rest gathered around. Morven spoke in a loud voice. Francisco could make out only the words "Mac Carthy . . . O'Rourke . . . *Espain*."

The leader of the band, a tall fellow with dour blue-black eyes and long scraggly black bangs of hair over his forehead, questioned Morven further and motioned his gang away. One of the original four, however, made an emphatic remark and pointed at Francisco. Immediately the four men dragged Francisco from his horse.

Francisco lashed out with his own riding-stick even more furiously than Morven. It was of no use. One of the men wrested the stick out of his hand and the others began to punch and kick him about the shoulders, arms and legs, cruel blows that doubled him up, brought exclamations of "*Jesu!*" and "*Madonna!*" and at last laid him flat on the ground.

That he, the once sturdy Captain Francisco de Cuellar, should be flattened by these brigands! His body suffered but his pride suffered more. One Irishman was bending over him now to strip him of his shirt, while two others knelt on the ground to take off his pants, reducing him quickly to nakedness. It was hard for Francisco to believe they would stoop so low just to get a better-made shirt and pair of linen trousers. Didn't thieves have some rules of decency? How could one not call these people savages?

As the group began to remount, somebody kicked him hard on the right thigh. There were receding shouts, laughter, thudding of hooves, then only the sound of falling water. Morven was bending over him. The boy's face was distorted with anger and there were tears in his eyes. "Ah, *vivas, vivas,*" he said.

Francisco weakly responded in Latin, "Yes, I am alive. Praise be to God. I hope they are proud of themselves for vanquishing and thrashing one so weak and defenseless."

Morven ripped a piece of cloth from his own trouser leg, dipped it in the stream and began to wash off the blood from Francisco's right lower leg where his wound had reopened. Then he helped Francisco slowly to his feet. He was able to walk slowly, limping heavily. Morven took the goatskin jacket from his own shoulders and tried to put it around Francisco's shoulders but Francisco, sure that it was the only one that Morven possessed, refused to take it.

"No. No. God bless you, my boy. O'Rourke will outfit me, I feel sure. How long will it take me to get to his place?"

"You're about eight miles from Lough Gill after you've gone 'round the Dartry mountains and the Leitrim hills. You turn right, follow a footpath along the lake and you'll come to O'Rourke's castle situated on the shore. But now we have to do something about your nakedness. Let's gather you a fine packet of ferns. This is the last fern glade you'll find on the way. The wind won't whistle on you quite so sorely if you can protect yourself with a few fronds of the bracken."

Morven took the knife from his belt and, proceeding along the stream, cut the tallest and heaviest ferns. Francisco limped behind, doing the best he could with his bare hands.

"Let's make you a garment," said Morven. "I've seen poor Irish, driven out of their flaming homes and stripped of all their goods, wearing such fern outfits many times. You need something to protect you from the wind and cold. Your skin is already all goose-prickled."

Morven found some young willow trees and cut narrow strips of bark with his knife. He tied together the larger fern fronds, laying them over the front and back of Francisco's body, fastening them around the chest and waist with withes and dropping a skirt of ferns around him. Then he stood off and surveyed his work, not knowing whether to laugh or cry.

Francisco decided the issue. For the first time since he had joked with Donel and Sebastian on board the *San Marcos*, Francisco let out a big hearty laugh.

Morven laughed, too, but briefly. He asked in Latin whether Francisco was all right for his journey. Francisco recognized that Morven was one of the more sensitive Gaels, unusually sympathetic for one so young, traits of which the best priests are made. Francisco, refreshed by the moment of mirth, answered, "Yes, forward to conquer castles and any local dragons! God bless you, my boy. May you be able to finish your studies in Rome itself some day. You will be in my prayers."

"And you in mine, *Señor*. God guide you through all dangers and back to your own Spain!"

Morven mounted his horse and rode away, leading Francisco's horse and attempting to hide his tears. Francisco paused for a moment to contemplate the compelling contrast between Morven's kindness and the gang's savagery. Then the fern-garmented, limping Stone Age man began walking haltingly towards Lough Gill, leaning heavily on his walking stick.

CHAPTER 14

Stragglers in Peril

(October 1588)

Francisco was eager to get as near to friendly country as possible before dark. Animals and birds, not alarmed by his slow limping pace, paid their respects—rabbits, a badger, squirrels, two does and several crows. The smaller bird species had already flown south to their winter homes in tropical climes. The path emerged from the woods onto cold soggy ground. By the green shimmering streamers of the northern lights he was able to see clusters of boulders ahead.

Coming nearer, what had seemed boulders were straw huts by the side of a lake. He hoped to find an unoccupied storage hut. He could hear snoring as he passed several houses. Then he came upon a smaller cabin with an open doorway. He peered inside and could just make out sheaves of oats stacked against the wall with several mounds of sheaves on the floor.

Suddenly there was an animal gasp as a mound moved and sat up, wild-eyed and covered with shreds of straw. Then another creature elbowed himself up and another. The six eyes gleamed, the three mouths gaped. Francisco stood transfixed. The Spanish expression for "Holy Madonna!" escaped him.

"May God be with us!" exclaimed one of the sitters in good Castilian.

"Heaven be praised, you're Spaniards!" exclaimed Francisco.

"You are not a demon then? Isn't that a tail behind you?"

"Only a frond sticking out of my fern outfit. Who are you?" asked Francisco as he sat down.

The three Spaniards told him how they had beached at Streedagh Point with twenty others, had been stripped naked but escaped bludgeoning because just then a Spanish chest had been discovered. They made their way up the dunes. Near an Abbey thirteen of them had been captured. The others, including themselves, escaped into the woods. Eleven had found one another again and had journeyed until today when a troop of Sassenachs jumped them in the open country, killing eight. "God directed the three of us here."

"We must all be of good courage," said Francisco, "for God and the Holy Virgin surely intend that we shall live. There are friendly Catholics three or four leagues away in the village of Chief O'Rourke. Tomorrow we will go there. You have not yet told me the name of your ship or your own names."

"We are Sergeant Fernando Castro, Enrico Perez and Ricardo Torres, soldiers of the *San Marcos*."

"Good Lord! My fellow shipmates, I am Francisco de Cuellar."

"Ah, Don Francisco! *Capitano!* We thought you were dead, swallowed by the waves. Thanks be to God that you were able to escape the beach-massacre!"

Francisco well remembered Sergeant Castro but was vague in his recollection of the other two. No doubt they knew him from his songs and guitar on the stormy decks.

"Shall we ever get back to Spain, Don Francisco?" asked Enrico.

"We shall survive, God willing. We shall see our beloved Spain again and all those dear to us," said Francisco, as much to cheer himself as his shipmates.

"Were it not blasphemy," whispered Enrico, "I would rather see Spain again than the gates of heaven embroidered with gold!"

"I think God would forgive you your wish," said Francisco. "I often pray to God that I may return to my home on the little hilltop near Segovia where my new wife awaits me. I think of her far more frequently than my Lady of Henar. Now we need to rest so we can garner our strength for the journey ahead. At daybreak we must find Lake Gill and walk along it until we find O'Rourke's castle and his supposedly friendly people."

Now Francisco asked the question he longed to ask but was afraid of the answer. "By any chance did any of you happen to see, alive or dead, my friend Sebastian de Carvajal?"

"Yes!" said Fernando. "Sebastian was with us at the Abbey and got captured."

"Then he must have escaped," replied Francisco, "because there were only twelve hanged Spaniards at the Abbey and Sebastian wasn't one of them. I looked at all their faces. Sebastian's the kind of man whom Fortune falls in love with, the kind She rescues against all logic."

Francisco felt happy and exuberant that his best friend could be alive.

The men were awakened at dawn by voices. Between stems of straw Francisco could see through the open doorway a dog and three tall figures in the pale dawn light. Two carried pitchforks. One of the men said something in Gaelic, then stepped through the doorway. The other two moved away with the dog. The man who entered held in his right hand a double-axed halberd.

All four men under the straw lay absolutely still. *Death by halberd is not a pleasant way to die,* Francisco thought. *Surely the sound of our beating hearts can be heard by this armed stranger.* The man looked at the clumped straw. Then he muttered something unintelligible and walked out.

After a minute Francisco got up the courage to crawl and look out the door. There were about thirty workers in the field and at least two guards with halberds watching for Sassenachs. Their own hut was clearly visible so there was no possibility of escape by daylight and no going out to find water or food. They must wait for nightfall.

"Would you rather die by halberd or pitchfork?" asked Enrico.

"Neither, thank you," said Ricardo.

"Would to God," exclaimed Sergeant Fernando, "that I had my sword. I could take on at least five of those pitchfork men and silence their hostility permanently!"

"Yes," added Francisco, "if I had my former strength I'd teach those two halberdsmen a lesson or two! But the Good Lord has seen fit to take away our clothes, our weapons and our strength, leaving us barely with our souls."

By noon the sun had warmed the cabin and the men were thirsty. Ricardo began to murmur, "I can't stand it. The oat dust is in my throat, choking me. I must crawl out to find water."

"Hold on, Ricardo," urged Francisco. "It's only a few more hours 'til sundown."

"I've got to go!" cried Ricardo emphatically. "My tongue's like a clapper in a rusty bell." He dived towards the door but just as quickly he turned and crawled back, for voices could be heard approaching. The four men quickly lay down and covered themselves with straw. A half dozen Irish, after hot work in the fields, sat down outside the door and began loudly gulping buttermilk.

One of the Irishmen then walked in and threw himself down for a nap on a scattering of oat stalks near the door. A few minutes later, there was a loud sneeze from the straw where Ricardo lay. It was a tense moment but the Irishman kept on snoring.

Francisco was too primed for danger to be able to sleep. After an hour he heard shouts and barking of dogs. A man ran into the hut, slapped the prongs of his pitchfork against the belly of the sleeping Irishman and they ran out the door. Francisco limped to the door and could see the dogs and a group of men chasing someone.

The four Spaniards immediately agreed that this was the moment to make their own escape. They quickly began crawling the seventy-five yards to the woods. Fernando was the first to reach cover. He stood up, looked towards the group of field workers and, in a low voice, said, "Take care! They're facing this way again. Get flat!"

Ricardo in panic rose from his knees and ran to the woods. Fernando, sure that Ricardo had betrayed them, caught up with him, called him a fool and struck a blow to his face. Ricardo fell to the ground. Francisco crawled slowly with a pained expression on his face as he made it into the trees.

Francisco, now feeling his usual calmness in an emergency, told the three they had to keep moving and try to find water. A few minutes later a small splashing sound reached their ears and shortly they came upon a stream. Ricardo plunged, landed next to the bank and started gulping.

The rest knelt down and drank more slowly. They tore mint and watercress from the banks. Ricardo was seen to pick off a fat white slug from a root and pop it into his mouth.

Francisco took charge. "Fernando, you are in better condition than the rest of us. While we rest, look around for berries or nuts. The light won't last long."

Fernando's quest brought only a handful of bilberries which Francisco carefully divided, berry by berry, among the four. "Now then, we should be moving on as long as twilight lasts."

The four men, naked except for the fern apron still clinging to Francisco, started shuffling through the trees and bushes. Presently the thicket opened out into meadows overgrown with gorse. Darkness had already descended when Fernando noticed firefly-like lights in the distance.

The small lights multiplied as they came closer. Candles and peat fires were visible through windows of the village. Two dogs began to bark. Francisco cried out in Latin as he beat on the nearest door, "Please help us, in the name of God."

A tall Irishman came to the door, peered out at the strange naked group and beckoned them to enter.

CHAPTER 15

Castle of Disappointment

(October 1588)

It was good fortune for the four garmentless men to have entered the house of Niall Mac Sweeney, an Irishman of goodwill towards Spaniards, the head man of this small village which lay at the outskirts of O'Rourke country. He quickly distributed Francisco's companions among other houses and kept Francisco in his own household with his wife, two daughters and three sons.

Francisco's leg wound elicited the women's pity. They began to wash his legs with warm water and prepare and apply poultices using mistletoe, St. John's wort and other plants. In the morning when Francisco's companions came to the door, the women refused to allow him to continue his journey, declaring emphatically that he must rest his leg and allow their traditional remedies to help the healing process.

Francisco's condition forced him to agree and he said goodbye to his three former shipmates. It was good to be cared for by gentle-handed women, to lie by the low-burning peat fire and be covered by a warm blanket. The Mac Sweeney women were tall, blue-eyed, classic Celts with broad smiles. Their tender attentions to his wounds sent Francisco's emotions again to his young wife. He always pictured Zabella in one of two situations. First, he felt the wild physical presence of her warm body like a peach in the sun, quivering on a bough shaken by the arm of desire. Then he saw her as an image of the Madonna, paneled in sunlight against a blue sky, sitting beside his mother under the grape arbor in his castle courtyard. Only rarely did he wonder whether he was idealizing someone he hardly knew.

Francisco often closed his eyes, pretending to doze while the Mac Sweeney family pursued their tasks around him, the mother cooking oat cakes on a flat iron griddle, the daughters weaving fern and rush mats and fiber ropes, the father and sons mending their fishnets or spreading out the Irish moss called carrageen to dry outside the hut. They boiled it to use as a medicine for colds and also fed the gluey seaweed to their cattle.

After three days Francisco was up exercising his legs again. Both were still painful and swollen, especially the right, but they looked and felt better. Although Mac Sweeney and his family pleaded with him to stay, he was determined to move on towards O'Rourke's castle. They were able to provide him only with a woven rush cape and a ragged cloth to wrap about his loins. He walked out of the hut with friendly gestures and kisses blown from his palm Spanish fashion.

He found a walking stick. Soon he was again in open bracken and furze country. He walked slowly, knowing that the right knee was insecure and could buckle at any time. He finally saw in the distance, against a lavender hill, the gray bulk of a towered castle.

As he proceeded over the rolling heath he saw once again that it was much more than merely a traversable space. It was filled with color spread by Nature for his visual enrichment. *How often humans fail to drink in the beauty of their environment,* he thought. *Here for my Epicurean delight is a carpet of color featuring the rose of bell-heather, the brown-yellow of dwarf gorse, the blue-purple of devil's bit and the brilliance of innumerable small red and orange plants, a mixture of the final flowers of summer with the changing colors of fall. Being alive, perceiving, wasn't that a fundamental joy of life and the human spirit? I must never take living for granted again.*

Now Francisco hopped along a little more rapidly, more like a wounded dog than a mutilated toad. He approached the wooded shore of Lake Gill and turned right along the wooded shore towards the castle. He could see that it had been gnawed by war, including cannon fire. As he got closer he saw figures huddled around the castle gate—men sitting, crawling and walking like the damned in some earthly Purgatory. Spaniards they must be, debased to nakedness by greedy natives who stole their very clothes because the stitching was better.

Francisco crossed limpingly over the bridge and dry moat past the guards who brusquely motioned him across. A few sorry figures stirred themselves, waved weakly and uttered words of greeting. Fernando and Enrico came forward to meet him. Francisco was out of breath and could only say, "Any hope?" as he rested his right arm for support on Fernando's scrawny shoulder.

"Not much."

Discomfort corkscrewed through Francisco's belly. There apparently was little to be optimistic about in this great castle of hope to which they had looked forward for so many days.

"O'Rourke is away," explained Fernando, "and while most of his people here tolerate us and allow us to stay, there is nothing for us to eat, nothing to keep us warm and no promise of help of any sort when O'Rourke returns. Many of the people here were probably kind once but the cruelty and harassment by England's occupation army for many years has wiped out their basic goodness."

"Ricardo?"

"No longer with us. The energy of life deserted him."

Cynicism curled Francisco's lip. *Why trust the Madonna of Henar any longer? She has forsaken the forsaken.* Old wasps of spiritual doubt began to swarm through his mind.

"How about cattle?" asked Francisco.

"Stolen. O'Rourke has gone on a retaliatory foray."

"I think we should assemble all our fellow-Spaniards and begin to organize, talk and share ideas. How many Spaniards are here?"

"About seventy."

"Seventy are stronger than three."

"You have my respect, Don Francisco," said Fernando. "You're smart and you're brave. Many a man with festering wounds would have given up long ago."

Francisco now hobbled across to where the largest group of Spaniards was sitting, lying and leaning against the castle wall in the thin October sunlight. The faces of all the Spaniards were leathery, haggard, and grimy, their eyes looking out from hollow recesses and their lips stiffened into grimness. Fernando and Enrico assembled the other available Spaniards.

Just as Francisco was getting ready to speak to the group, five burly Irishmen came out of the gate with big shillelaghs and began to swing them threateningly. The Spaniards shuffled, crawled and tumbled away. Two of the slowest-moving Spaniards were struck. Francisco escaped only by humping along at top speed. By way of punishment for the forbidden assemblage, no Spaniard was taken into the castle enclosure that night. The naked men slept against the walls in little trenches scraped by hand. Sometimes two or three would bundle together, cold limbs against cold limbs in the frigid night. Faint curved curtains of the Aurora Borealis cast dim light on these haggard remnants of the invincible and Most Fortunate Armada.

In the morning Francisco, who had slept very little because of the cold fall temperature and hard ground, suggested to Fernando and Enrico that the three of them go begging for food from the houses inside the walls. It seemed a last resource. If they were beaten with sticks, they would suffer together.

So Francisco in his fern-wrap and loincloth, the other two naked, passed through the just-opened gate shortly after dawn. The old fellow on guard started to set his pike across their way, then nodded slowly and let them go through.

The walls of the castle enclosed an area about three hundred feet in diameter. Small huts were set against the interior walls, some built of stones, others of clay or mud and wattle. The daily movement of people had just begun. The first group they encountered consisted of women carrying crude clay jugs for filling at the lake. Francisco approached the women, pointed to his mouth and made a chewing motion with a querying look.

The women smiled and the oldest of them turned to a younger woman and seemed to give an order. The younger woman set her jug on the ground and, motioning the Spaniards to follow her, went to one of the better looking stone huts. She disappeared inside and was gone for only a few moments. Returning, she gave each of the three Spaniards a dry old oat cake. Francisco detected the crumb-furrowed look of weevil paths but it was food and he was ready to eat not only flour beetles but hairy caterpillars. The girl carried over her arm potential clothing consisting of two sacks and an old greasy blanket which, after observing Francisco's gashed leg, she presented to him, handing the two sacks to Fernando and Enrico. Francisco took her hand and kissed it.

The women then motioned them to follow as they looked for more food from their neighbors. They hobbled after the women, pursued by curious children. A few threw small stones at the Spaniards until the oldest woman turned on them with a strong Gaelic tirade. Her expression and gestures and the impressive appearance of her head, which was bound in a turban of dirty linen, suggested Cassandra on a rampage. Francisco was impressed. Here indeed was a friend. The children disappeared like mice into crannies.

Now they heard sounds of voices and commotion back at the gate. All four women set down their jugs in the dust and ran towards the gate where men in dark blue and green Irish cloaks marched in. Two wounded Irishmen were carried in makeshift litters and eight others had blood-soaked bandaged heads, legs, and arms—the wounded from O'Rourke's foray. The four women of the jugs were leaning close to one of the litters. The older woman who had befriended the Spaniards was stroking a bandaged head and speaking in a high tone of grief.

Now Francisco could make out a few words shrilled out by nearby Spaniards who had clustered around the returning foray warriors.

"*Don Alonso! La Girona! La Girona!* Keelybegs! Keelybegs!"

Francisco moved closer and took the nearest Spaniard by the shoulder. He was repeating these words over and over mechanically in a dry cracked voice.

"What is it?" demanded Francisco, shaking the dazed Spaniard by the shoulders.

"Keely-begs, Keely-begs."

Francisco moved to the next Spaniard, a younger man. "What are they saying? What is it?"

"One of the Irishmen speaks Spanish well. He brings news from Sligo that Don Alonso de Leyva is in the harbor of Killybegs with the galleass *Girona*. He has room for Spanish survivors after the ship gets some repairs. God is with us! God is with us!"

"How far is Killybegs?"

"Fifteen miles to the north as the crow flies, according to these Irishmen."

"And as we must walk?" asked Francisco.

"About forty miles."

Francisco tried to imagine forty miles on foot with his painful legs. He turned to Fernando and Enrico over whose faces the muscles, so recently immobilized with weariness, were now working with excitement. "Would that we had wings of seagulls to fly to Killybegs. Many of us will drop by the pathside but it's worth trying. God will help us!"

Francisco now raised his voice and addressed the Spaniards around him. "All those who want to try for Killybegs must beg bread or oat cakes or anything edible, then meet at the gate in an hour and we'll start together. I'll try to explain to the Irish leaders what we're doing so that perhaps they may give us a little farewell gift of food for our journey. Where's the Irishman who speaks Spanish?"

It took fifteen minutes of precious time to find this man. He had already been taken into his little house against the castle walls and was being cared for by his womenfolk. Francisco explained the new situation to him. The man sent a messenger to bring the Chief's father and other leaders from the castle.

When they arrived at the wounded man's bedside, Francisco was able, through the Spanish-speaking Irishman, to explain that the most fit Spaniards were leaving for Donegal Bay and Killybegs harbor. Would it be possible to give them some oat cakes, bread or any recently-caught trout from the lake as a parting gift to save them from death by starvation on the way?

The matter was briefly discussed, the women adding words of urgency. Although the village had little enough food for itself, they would try to scrape up a few provisions. Within minutes the women and a few of the men from the castle appeared with garments, small packages of oat cakes and a few jugs of buttermilk. About fifty Spaniards gathered to receive these farewell gifts. The rest lay about on the ground too ill to move.

O'Rourke's father gave them a square of green and black cloth that his son always wore and said: "Show this and say that Brian O'Rourke gave it to you." Then, with a stick, he traced their route in the dirt.

The weary but newly energized Spaniards walked slowly toward the gateway exchanging blessings and farewells. They raised their scrawny arms in gestures of gratitude and spoke words in Spanish and in Latin thanking their castle hosts—*adios, benedicte, laus Deo* and *alleluia*. Francisco, Enrico and Fernando stepped aside and let them pass. Francisco saw them as a pathetic group of undernourished bodies and souls plodding wearily but optimistically toward the Purgatory of Hope.

CHAPTER 16

Trudging Towards Salvation

(October 1588)

As Francisco limped towards the gate he paused to bend over the most stricken of the Spaniards who were too weak to walk to the *Girona*. He pulled a few oat cakes from his sack to distribute among them. Fernando did the same and the gesture was imitated by a few others but Enrico declared:

"You're good men but fools. We need every scrap of food if any of us are to get through to the ships. Food for the strongest, not the weakest, is the law of survival."

"But not the law of God," murmured Francisco.

Enrico now quickened his steps and moved ahead of the group. Francisco couldn't help feeling discouraged about this early and obvious "me first" declaration. He didn't say anything but an acrid taste came into his mouth as if he had just licked a copper bell.

"I'm surprised at Enrico," Francisco said. "You're a different breed, Fernando. In fact, you go too far the other way, the kindlier way. If I begin to slow down I want it clearly understood that you're to move ahead with the faster ones. Promise me that you will."

Fernando smiled. "I'll try to adhere to your wishes but time will tell."

For the initial several miles through bog and heath, Francisco's steps were quickened by hope and he forgot his legs. At Kinlough, five miles from O'Rourke's castle, the group was met by staring villagers. Then several young bullies stepped forward and yanked Francisco's sack from him. Francisco, insecure on his legs, lost his balance and fell to the ground. He had the presence of mind to show the square of green and black cloth and to repeat the name of 0'Rourke several times. This had a subduing effect on the villagers who talked the bullies into leaving. Francisco now found that his limping and pain were increasing.

"Go on, Fernando. I can't keep up. I'll walk slowly and if the ship is under repair long enough at Killybegs, I'll make it. If not, I'll head for Mac Clancy's castle on Lake Melvin which should be only a few miles to the north."

"It's almost nightfall, Francisco. I'll help you walk until dark. Then we'll rest for the night and perhaps you'll feel better in the morning." Fernando crutched his arm under Francisco's and helped him along but a more common remark, as the rest of the company hobbled past them, was "Come on, *compañeros*, move faster!"

Francisco and Fernando finally reached one of the streams that pour down into the head of Lake Melvin. An oak trunk had been laid across the rivulet from bank to bank making a difficult crossing for one with precarious legs. The time had come when he must no longer delay his friend.

"Fernando, I'm leaving you. I'm heading for Mac Clancy's castle. I'll rest up and join you in a few days. You must leave me."

"I should stay with you but I will heed your orders, Captain." Fernando put his arms around Francisco and clasped him tightly. Francisco watched as Fernando walked rapidly across the oak trunk. At the end of the log he turned, waved, then picked his way through the furze bushes and bracken of the heath, disappearing into the undergrowth.

A vast emptiness came over Francisco. His right leg began to tremble so he sat down on the stream bank to rest. Now alone in the Irish wilderness, he wondered what Fate had in store for him.

The rippling, quietly moving stream in the lovely forest setting gave Francisco a feeling of temporary peace. *How can so much beauty and sorrow co-exist in such close approximation? Should I pray or is my destiny entirely up to me?* He rolled onto his side, coiled himself under the blanket given to him at the castle and fell asleep.

The sun was high in the sky peering through gray clouds when Francisco awoke. He stiffly crawled to the stream, drank water and ate a few watercress. Then he crawled slowly over the oak log, painfully got to his feet and moved along a bog path. Here and there his feet sank into the muck. Once he sank deeper but, using his crutch-stick, he was able to latch into the tangles of bog myrtle and pull himself free with a loud sucking sound. Soon he realized that he was lost. There should be a way to Lake Melvin somewhere here. It began to rain. Francisco wondered whether Nature was trying to dissolve him. He moved slowly, bent over against the rain like an old man although he was only twenty-seven.

He heard voices. A woman wrapped in a large black blanket came alongside, touched him and said something in Gaelic in a voice unmistakably compassionate. Francisco looked up. There were two women and two men with peat spades over their shoulders. The woman who had touched him opened out her blanket and spread it around Francisco, taking him literally under her wing. He could only speak the word, *"Gratia! Gratia,"* hoping that the *"Gratia Dei"* of their Catholic services was sufficiently well known. The woman smiled. Slowly she helped Francisco walk until they were among thatched cottages at the other end of the bog.

Francisco was taken into a warm cottage where an elderly man sat by a peat fire. The woman wet a cloth from water in a warm pot next to the fire and washed Francisco's muddy legs. They had him lie down on a rush mat in front of the hearth and covered him with a dry blanket. Now Francisco watched while his benefactress set a pot over the fire. She had a motherly face, apple-red cheeks, brown eyes and a mouth which seemed to have been shaped by laughter. In a few moments she was giving him hot beef broth and oat cakes.

Francisco sipped the broth and tried to explain his plans. *"Keely-begs, barco, España,"* and he pointed north. He had decided to make a try for Killybegs and *La Girona* rather than head towards Rossclogher Castle and MacClancy at Lake Melvin. The woman and her husband nodded. The woman laid her hand on Francisco's leg and shook her head sidewise. Francisco began shaking his head affirmatively and the woman again gave her head the sidewise motion, then, struck with the humor of all this head-play, burst into a hearty laugh. Francisco felt too tired to laugh but he smiled. *How long it has been since I have enjoyed fully-felt laughter!* The disappearance of Sebastian had signaled the end of light-hearted, happy humor.

The rain was beating relentlessly against the wooden door and window shutters of the house. *How warm it is inside and how cold I have been for so long*, thought Francisco. *Shelter is taken for granted until one doesn't have it.* As he drifted off to sleep he envisioned the galleass of hope on the other side of the wet green hills. His sleep was a restless one with jumbled apparitions of men drowning, giants coming down to beaches with bludgeons as big as trees, of death and burials, of pain and endless fatigue and legs churning hopelessly in mucky swamps.

Francisco awoke suddenly, frightened by his nightmares. The peat fire was only a small red glow and there was heavy snoring in the room. Francisco tried to untangle the alarming cobwebs of recent sleep. Had he slept for an entire afternoon and evening? A cricket rubbed his forewings together, chirping in the thatch. A crow cawed more quietly than usual; *is he showing his pleasure that the rain has stopped?* The darkness of the room imperceptibly silvered into dawn. He was sweating and his throat was sore but Francisco knew he must start walking.

The family stirred and got up from their pallets and mats. Francisco rose slowly to his knees, then his feet, while his hostess was busy at the fire. When she turned and saw him standing, she made vehement gestures of protest. Francisco wagged his head and pointed to the cottage door, then away to the north but he had trouble even standing. His hostess helped him sit down on a bench beside a crude table and she set a bowl of oat porridge before him.

He had little appetite but forced himself to empty the bowl. He got up to go. Noting his determination, his hosts made no further protests. As he departed they gave him a large piece of woolen cloth that once had been a saddle blanket. It smelled horsey but would add warmth to the blanket given to him at Castle O'Rourke He thanked them enthusiastically. The immense difference created by any garment is only truly appreciated by those forced to go naked in public.

His host stood at the door and precisely gestured the way he should take north if he decided to try to make it to Killybegs. Francisco clasped the hands of his host and hostess, bowed to the grandfather and moved slowly off into a misty dawn, once again amazed at the close proximity in Ireland of kindness and killing.

His right leg was painful and unstable and he was able to move only very slowly. He still had a sore throat and probably a fever but the strong pull towards Killybegs and its ship of rescue drove him onwards. He fell several times and it took two hours to reach the wider road his host had indicated was the direction towards the coast. At last he saw a cluster of cottages. He felt hot and thirsty, was coughing and knew he wasn't thinking clearly. These people would give him water . . . or would they set their dogs on him and beat him with sticks?

He stumbled forward and fell on the dirt road. He tried to rise but couldn't, as if ship's cables glued him to the ground. He felt sweaty and weak. He could see the Madonna being carried away on a galleon, her blue garments blending with the color of the sea . . . disappearing . . .

He became aware that he was being lifted, then set down on a hard surface that presently moved with a jogging, creaking motion, rocking him to sleep. Many hours later he awoke. He was lying in a real bed in the house of a merchant of the village of Bundoran, to which he had been carried in the cart of a farmer who found him lying on the road. The merchant had called in a local medical practitioner. The merchant, having done business at Sligo and Donegal with Spanish traders, knew enough Spanish so that he and Francisco could converse.

The country doctor told him he had been taught to bleed patients with fevers but had become skeptical of the practice. He prescribed special plants in combination with food and rest and got much better results. He treated Francisco's leg wounds with hot cloths followed by a salve. To Francisco's query as to how soon he would be able to travel northward, the doctor's reply was, "In two or three days if all goes well. Be a patient patient."

He was informed that Killybegs was only twelve miles northwest across the water. He still could reach that harbor of hope if the *Girona* were delayed for any reason.

He consumed all the restorative food that the merchant's servant brought him. He rested and slept. His youth and strength and vitality gradually flowed back into his weary body. The fever and sore throat disappeared in thirty-six hours. The right leg improved. The merchant gave him a servant's outfit of blue trousers and warm blue wool jacket. He kept his two blankets for nighttime use and for protection against rain. Francisco thanked the merchant and the doctor, apologizing that he possessed no token of tangible gratitude and suggested that God would reward them.

It was a beautiful pale blue October day. There was a new joy and feeling of optimism as he stepped out of the house. He had only walked a few steps when he heard the bee-murmuring sound of excited people and saw the villagers running down a path through the dunes. He decided to follow in the crowd's direction.

As he arrived at the edge of a dune above the beach he looked out over Donegal Bay and there, not six miles off, was the large galleass *Girona*, pride of the Armada. Her hull, driven by long red oars and white sails, glistened in the morning sun as it headed towards Spain and freedom.

Francisco stood in his own silent world as he watched the *Girona* moving slowly out of the bay without him. He was happy for those on the ship but once again he felt the anguish of a marooned sailor on an uninhabited island watching a vessel of possible rescue sailing farther and farther toward the horizon.

When will God and Life stop challenging me? It seems like a constant chess match from which I rarely emerge the winner. Am I doomed by God to permanent wandering in a foreign land? Francisco recalled Homer's Odysseus who suffered so many calamities on land and sea before coming home twenty years later to his faithful wife, Penelope. *Am I destined to be a Spanish Odysseus? Like Penelope, is Zabella loyally fending off potential suitors? I wonder.*

CHAPTER 17

Bellows and Fangs

(October 1588)

As Francisco gazed at the disappearing ship, he decided to pay homage to the ancient Celtic tradition of warriors who spent their last moments laughing at the irony of life as they lay bleeding to death on the battlefield. So he began to laugh, quietly at first then louder, which soon pulled him out of his temporary inward-thinking self-pity.

When the proud galleass had become a small speck, he walked slowly back to town but noted a new bounce of optimism in his limping step. He reached the house of his host, the merchant, and knocked on the door.

"Ah, my friend," said the merchant, "I am so sorry. It was your ship, was it not, that was leaving? But I have a new suggestion."

"Pray tell me," said Francisco, smiling.

"You have become more Gaelic in a short time, Francisco, smiling at your own bad luck! It will do wonders for you! Now listen to me. It is useless to try to board a ship out of Sligo or Galway or any of these western ports. It was only by the help and protection of the powerful Mac Sweeney that the *Girona's* Captain Fabricio Spinola and his guest, the outranking Captain, Don Alonso de Leyva, were able to repair and re-outfit the ship. I have word that the English are watching all ports even more closely than before."

The merchant continued, "My advice is that you go from here to the powerful Mac Clancy who has many friends in the north. Those ports are still in strong Irish hands. Ballycastle of the great Sorley Boy Mac Donnell is about a hundred miles to the northeast. Only twenty miles across the water from Ballycastle lies Kintyre, Scotland. From friendly Scotland there are many ships going south to France, Belgium, Netherlands and Spain."

"Thank you," replied Francisco with new enthusiasm. "I'll follow your advice and try to smile my way through any barriers. Whatever happens, I'll remember your kindness like a beacon of light in this dark and difficult time."

Once more he clasped the merchant's hand and limped off. The good doctor's poultices seemed to be benefiting his legs. He could walk better. Killybegs being out of the picture, he headed southeast toward Mac Clancy's castle and potential contacts with northern Irish chiefs.

After four hours of limping, he saw a middle-aged man briskly approaching, heading north. Francisco noted that he was clean-shaven, neatly dressed and that his face was intelligent. The expression of his light blue eyes and plump mouth was affable. Francisco worried that his Spanish origin would be easily discernible because of his swarthy skin, the triangular shape of his face and his brown deep-set eyes, deeper than ever now in his hunger-scooped orbits.

On coming even with Francisco, the man raised his hand almost in a benedictional gesture. He looked searchingly at Francisco and immediately said, "*De España tu?*"

"*Sic. De España*," answered Francisco.

"*Benedicte. Ego sum pretus.*"

A priest. A feeling of relief swept over Francisco.

The priest laid his hand on Francisco's arm and, in crisp Latin, said: "What ship were you on? Where are you headed? How may I help you?"

Francisco told his story briefly in good Latin. Then the priest pulled some hazelnuts from a pouch at his belt and gave them to Francisco, saying: "I'm sorry I can't accompany you to Mac Clancy's castle but I'm on my way to some parishioners on Lough Erne who need me sorely. I must work in secret and dress as a layman. The English are forever tracking us down and breaking up our little Catholic parishes. But we manage, we manage. When they destroy our churches, we worship at God's first altar—stones of the field."

Francisco's voice broke as he answered. "Confess me, father. I've been darkly discouraged many times in recent months. I've felt the Holy Madonna and her blessed Son deserting me and have had dark thoughts. I have failed in my prayers and rosaries."

The priest listened to details of his journey since the shipwreck, then pronounced:

"You've been sorely tried, my son. I know that God forgives you. May He, in all His mercy, bring you safely back to the harbor of your home. You seem truly repentant. And now, to reach Mac Clancy's castle, follow this path south for about three miles, then, when you come to a crosspath, bear east towards Lake Melvin and, on an island close to the shore of the lake, you will see the castle. There will be boatmen to carry you over."

"Thank you, father. I will follow your directions."

As he continued to walk southeast, Francisco began to contemplate all that had transpired in recent days. When he came out of his reverie he realized that he was seeing none of the landmarks mentioned by the priest. He must have missed the path to Mac Clancy's castle.

A moment later a figure entered from a side path. He was a squat Irishman with trousers tied at the ankles and a patchwork armless jacket made of scraps of various kinds of leather roughly sewn together revealing very muscular, dirty arms. Similar sewn leather scraps encased his feet. Long hair came down over shaggy eyebrows and he had erratic eyes, one of which looked inward towards his nose, the other staring at Francisco.

"*Castillo, castellum* . . . Castle Mac Clancy?" asked Francisco, trying three languages in rapid succession and pointing first in one direction, then another, his eyebrows lifted in query.

"Mac Clancy? Mac Clancy?" repeated the man gutturally. At last a light broke in the forward-looking eye. "Ah-h-h, Maglana, Maglana!"

"*Si, sic.*"

The man clutched Francisco's upper arm and moved his fingers along it, feeling his muscles. "Ah-h-h," muttered the fellow again, deep in the caverns of his throat. "Ah-h-h!" He held Francisco's arm and began to lead him back along the side-path from which he had emerged.

"*Per questa via?* This way?" asked Francisco.

He tugged Francisco more strongly. Francisco now pulled back and, pointing down the path, queried again: "Maglana? Maglana?"

"Maglana!" repeated the gruff man who now seized Francisco's arm in an iron grip and led him along the path along little streams into deeper groves. A vague fear began to creep over Francisco that his companion's too firm grip connoted evil intent. He tried to draw it away. The stranger jerked the arm forward forcefully.

After almost a mile the glen opened out into a clearing with a small stream and cabin made of wattle and mud-daub and a three-sided structure, open at the front, in which stood a forge with smoldering peat. Also visible were bellows, a blacksmith's hammer and various metal products, many of a military nature—shields, swords, spears, battle-axes—as well as horseshoes, knives, scythes, sickles and turf spades.

To a tree between the forge and the house was tied a mastiff who leaped wildly, clawed the air and opened its jaws as if to yelp but never emitted a sound. The animal was like some chimerical creature as it continued to leap soundlessly into the air. Francisco's flesh crawled. It was all too apparent that he had been taken captive.

Now Francisco's self-appointed guide let go of his arm and uttered a strange animal yell on a rising note, dipping quickly into a deep guttural. Out of the house came an ugly woman with greenish eyes, several teeth missing, black hair falling over her face and shoulders, and wearing a soiled green-black skirt and cape.

The man uttered rapid words in Gaelic. The woman then felt the muscles of both of Francisco's arms and nodded her head. She re-entered the house and came back with some oatcakes which she held out to Francisco with filthy hands. He took the cakes and made a bow to the uncomely creature. The two watched him eat the cakes to the last morsel.

Francisco pointed to his mouth and tilted his head backwards. The old woman nodded and brought him a rusty metal cup. He walked to the stream and quenched his thirst. The ugly Irishman again seized him by the arm, conducted him to the forge, pointed to the bellows and with easily understandable gestures ordered him to start working. Before beginning his forced labor, Francisco asked again, "Castle Maglana? Where is it?" sweeping his arm around the glen.

For answer the blacksmith took a strap that hung from a hook and whipped Francisco across his shoulders so fiercely that he fell forward into the black dirt. Francisco looked up into the threatening face of the blacksmith and to the large hand that held the strap. He picked himself up and went to work at the bellows, resting as much of his weight as possible on his left leg.

As he worked, his mind worked, too. He must bide his time, obey orders, toil hard and study the habits of the blacksmith and his wife. He must await the arrival of others who might come to collect the blacksmith's products. He wondered whether this man was Mac Clancy's armorer. He would analyze his situation closely and wait for the opportune moment to escape.

Until the sun went down, Francisco kept the bellows blowing, supplying the fire with peat from a large oblong pile behind him. The smith was making battle-axes that day and after fingering the battle-keen blade he often had Francisco feel the slaughterous edge. Francisco got the message. He also realized that underneath the forge bully's brute strength, crude demeanor and tyrannical behavior was an excellent craftsman.

At twilight the smith made a horizontal gesture with his two arms to indicate that work was over. As the two men passed the chained dog, the animal leaped high into the air and bit ferociously at Francisco. The blacksmith quieted the animal with a few tugs on the rope that throttled him into obedience. Then he placed his two blackened hands on the animal's cheeks, drew back the mastiff's lips and displayed the dog's sharp fangs, giving Francisco a good look.

Francisco's body wasn't used to such hard physical labor and he was bone-weary. He expected no more than an oat cake or two for supper but the blacksmith clearly demanded abundant food, presumably from Mac Clancy, in return for his hard work and skill. There were four boiled rabbits for supper, one for Francisco, two for the blacksmith and one for his wife. There was a thick bowl of oat porridge for each and a pitcher of beer poured from a barrel. For dessert they ate honey spread over sliced blackberries and apples.

Francisco made sounds of appreciation and rubbed his bulging stomach with momentary pleasure. For the first time, gleams that were not malicious came into the eyes of the blacksmith and his wife and they actually smiled. As he lay down to sleep, Francisco thought, *They must regard me as a collegial co-worker! I know that many people think of life as a succession of anecdotes but this is getting ridiculous. Who will ever believe my increasingly bizarre experiences in Ireland?*

Every morning after a breakfast of buttermilk cooled in the stream and oat cakes with butter and honey, Francisco walked to the forge with his captor. In spite of the hard, repetitive tasks, he found the arm exercise invigorating. He even smiled occasionally, shaking his head in disbelief at his farcical situation. He kept his mind focused on potential means of escape.

The blacksmith and his wife kept him under constant surveillance. At night he slept on the sod floor with his wounded right leg chained to a post. His captors sometimes awakened him with their brief noisy sexual conjunctions but otherwise he slept well and deeply, covered by a warm woolen blanket. By day he was continually with the blacksmith and his mastiff.

On the fifth day he had a brief upspring of hope when he heard voices in the glen and caught sight of three horsemen. Before going out to welcome his visitors, the smith came up from behind Francisco, stooped and shackled his right ankle to the anvil with a locked chain. The blacksmith carried armloads of weaponry and other implements to the three horsemen who strapped them to their horses. In exchange the blacksmith was handed a number of food sacks.

Francisco wondered how much of his life he would spend in this Glen of the Devil? How could he escape? Would murder be necessary? What trickery to equal Odysseus' deception of the blind Cyclops, Polyphemus, would be required?

When the blacksmith sauntered back to the forge, Francisco pointed to his ankle and couldn't help doubling his fists at his captor. The blacksmith laughed as he took a knife from his belt and, waving it at Francisco's throat, drew it swiftly through the air with a decapitating gesture. He laughed again as Francisco quickly undoubled his fists and the smith unlocked his shackle.

Is it really possible that I, Francisco de Cuellar, able Armada ship captain, am now a lowly slave working for an ogre in a remote Irish glen?

On the eighth day the smith was intently bent over the blade of a dirk, beating it to a fine edge. Francisco saw walking towards them the priest who had treated him so kindly recently. Before the smith was aware of a third presence, the priest reached them.

"*Pater! Pater! Salvate me!*" shouted Francisco. "*Hic sum captivus, infelicisimus captivus!*"

"You are not here of your own free will working for a wage?" he asked Francisco in Latin.

"No, father! No! I have been kidnapped and enslaved here under dire threat of death!"

The priest turned upon the smith with lightning in his eyes and delivered a tongue-lashing in Gaelic which made the muscular blacksmith lower his head. The priest turned to Francisco and said, "I am going to Mac Clancy's castle. I will have an escort sent to you soon. I have told the smith that he will be severely punished by man and God if any harm comes to you in the meantime. I will now go into the house and confess these sinful creatures."

Francisco could see, through the hut doorway, the figures of the couple kneeling before the priest. He visualized his life since leaving Lisbon as alternating calm and storm. Just when he began to experience the comfortable tranquility of temporary deliverance he was hurled against rocks of torment. What did it all mean? *Are these earthly hazards, including almost daily threats of death, designed to test and strengthen my currently tormented soul? Is Sebastian right? Is there no purpose to it all, no meaning, no individual value in life?*

In the late October sunlight Francisco, now released from anvil servitude, smiled as he looked at the situation around him. How could he transform such strange interludes into a positive force? As Horace put into memorable words, life provided opportunities to seize the moment. *Carpe diem.* Francisco firmly decided that he was tired of being a flaccid fluttering leaf blown passively by the forceful, fickle winds of Fate.

CHAPTER 18

Irish Eyes

(November 1588)

Three days passed during which the blacksmith and his wife stretched their ugly mouths in unaccustomed smiles and fed Francisco as if he had been Maglana himself. When Francisco offered to help at the forge half of each day to divert himself from the tedium, the smith accepted. It was now early November 1588, only four months since the *Felicisima Armada* had sailed so confidently from Lisbon. It seemed much longer.

At noon on the third day three horsemen rode into the glen with an extra horse. One was a Spanish nobleman, Don Antonio de Ulloa, fifty years old, from the *San Juan* of Castile. Francisco rejoiced talking with him, discovering that he was a man of great knowledge. Francisco learned that there were nine Spaniards at Mac Clancy's castle, all well-treated.

The horsemen gave Francisco a goatskin jacket, blue woolen pants, a knife with leather sheath, a pair of leather boots and a long saffron-colored cloak. *I feel almost human*, he thought.

Francisco took cynical delight in shaking the hands of his enslavers, receiving in return pats on the back delivered with dirty palms and grimy smiles. Then he mounted his horse and started off with his escorts, riding along a road which traversed the villages of Glenade, Largydonnell and Kinlough. Half a mile south of Kinlough the foursome turned northeast along the trail which Francisco had missed. Presently they rode into shallow swamps. Here they dismounted and walked along a concealed, twisting path. Large flat stones had been artfully laid in the shallow water. Thus the way to Mac Clancy's Castle was kept secret from enemies, with hooves and feet leaving no trace. The going was slow and careful.

It was late afternoon when they arrived on the shores of Lake Melvin, known for its four islands of Inisheher, Inishmean, Inishtemple and Inishkeen. Mac Clancy's small but splendid castle six stories high rose from an un-named island a hundred and fifty yards from shore. Strengthened by a base of huge cut blocks of stone, the circular castle occupied the entire small island. The castle walls closely abutted the island's shore except for one indentation for boats to land. The shore's margin sloped rapidly into deep water. The castle had the usual slits for viewing and defense, with iron-grilled windows on higher levels. A green pennon flew from the castle top.

The shore itself was reedy for thirty yards, beyond which was a settlement of huts, a church, barns and enclosures for cattle and horses. A number of armed guards patrolled the area, primarily as protection from raids by predatory gangs of Irishmen. Several boats were drawn up to the bank where a narrow waterway had been cleared of reeds.

Francisco was rowed to the castle, landing at the small pebbled embayment. The only entrance to the castle was through a three-foot-thick hinged stone door on the second floor, the same thickness as the wall. The door was opened once a day with steel winches, reached by wooden stairs which dropped down. When the door was closed each evening the only access was by rope ladders let down from the castle parapet in the manner of ancient ascents into the famed Irish Round Towers.

Narrow stone stairs wound down into the first story assembly hall. Here a husky fellow with long flowing red hair was standing in red wool trousers, goatskin jacket and long red cloak. Fastening his cloak was an immense gold brooch which must have come down from old Irish kings. He was talking with his battle-axe men, some of whom were professional mercenary soldiers known as gallowglasses, wearing shining metal corselets and helmets. Now and then he turned to three tall stalwart young men, also wearing bright cloaks and gold brooches, who were his sons.

A number of women were moving about wearing dark cloaks over dark gowns, with white linen coifs coiled around their heads. Some wore silken mantles and golden bangles.

It was clear at a glance that, in spite of his ancient Irish name of Mac Finnodaha, there was in Chief Murtagh Mac Clancy considerable intermixture from long-past Viking incursions. He looked more Scandinavian than Irish. Two wolfhounds stood at his side.

"*Benvenutus ad Castellum Maglana!*" welcomed Mac Clancy in Latin in a strong voice, extending a hand, the back of which was matted with reddish-gold hair. He gave Francisco's skeletal hand a hearty crunch. Francisco answered him in Latin:

"Thank you, Chief Mac Clancy. To come to your great castle after all the misadventures on sea and land with which God has seen fit to challenge us, is like arriving at the gates of Paradise."

The deep note of a horn sounded through the castle. One of the Irishman took him by the arm and, pointing at his mouth, indicated it was time to eat. Francisco was guided upstairs into a large stone-walled room with a sizeable blackened fireplace on one side. There were long rows of crossed pikes and battle-axes hooked along the walls. At the end of the room was the head table, behind which on the wall was a big round shield carrying Mac Clancy's insignia. Rough log tables and wooden benches had been set up at right angles to the chief's table.

The Spaniard who had accompanied Francisco on horseback from the blacksmith's forge, Don Antonio Ulloa, now caught sight of Francisco, made his way to him and led him to his own table. Francisco was about to sit down when Don Antonio tugged at his elbow and said:

"Not yet, Francisco. There are two old Irish rituals we go through every night for which we remain standing. That man on Mac Clancy's right is Fergal Bhaird. He's like a combination of priest and old Druid bard. Even Mac Clancy pays close attention when Fergal speaks, as if he were the living embodiment of the wisdom of Ancient Celts.

Bhaird shone out luminously, lighted by torches held in the hands of two young men who stood behind him. His hair was silver-white, his white beard was braided and his face had finely-cut features. His nose was long and narrow, his lips thin. His eyes were sea-bright blue under thick white eyebrows. He wore a heavy green robe with fringed hem and sleeves, caught up at the left shoulder with a magnificent old Irish gold brooch. An Irish harp leaned against the wall behind him next to two elegant wolfhounds sitting on their haunches.

Everyone in the hall now became still. In a loud voice Mac Clancy boomed, "Fergal Bhaird, pronounce, if you will, the blessing on our bread."

Two servants set large baskets of bread and oat cakes on the table in front of the bard. In a chanting voice he spoke Gaelic words which Don Antonio interpreted:

"Our Lady of the Field, change these golden crops of God into the health of our bodies and souls that we may give glory to the Source. Amen."

"Our Lady of the Field. Did you note that?" asked Don Antonio. "Ceres, Demeter. As old as man's crops. Interesting, isn't it?"

"Not our Blessed Lady, then?"

"Same thing. Demeter, Goddess of Harvests, was a Sacred Lady to the Greeks."

"Where did you acquire such scholarly knowledge?"

"Oh, I studied for many years at Salamanca," said Don Antonio, "then for two years in Paris. Everything ancient interests me."

"I studied at Salamanca, too," said Francisco.

"Fellow student, I salute you! Now we can sit down."

Francisco began to observe the assemblage. The Chief's three sons sat near their father, the oldest on his left, the two others beside the bard who was placed on the Chief's right. There were several older men at the head table along with the armed chief of security. Three gallowglasses stood behind Mac Clancy's chair holding large battle-axes. At the far right of the table was Mac Clancy's wife. She was fair-haired with delicate features, the lustrous rolls of her hair appearing under a dazzling white coif. Her tunic was also white, partially covered by a green silk mantle. A large gold torque was clasped around her neck.

A girl sitting on her left had her eyes locked on Francisco. When their eyes met, she gave him a captivating smile. She was stunningly lovely with the classical beauty of a Greek statue. She looked to be in her mid-twenties with flaming red hair tumbling in curls down to her shoulders and gleaming green eyes glowing like emeralds. Her cloak of dark crimson was held with a green-gemmed brooch.

The head table made a regal portrait worthy of Leonardo da Vinci. They were by far the handsomest people Francisco had seen in Ireland. He leaned over and asked Don Antonio who the lady was who was sitting next to Mac Clancy's wife.

"That is Chief Mac Clancy's unmarried youngest sister. Her name is Alana."

"Alana. What a lovely name. What does it mean in Gaelic?"

"One who is beautiful, peaceful and harmonious."

"Her eyes are spellbinding and her smile would melt stone. Why isn't she married?"

"Mac Clancy has tried to marry her off several times but she has refused. She says that only she will choose her husband and that she will know immediately when their lives intersect. If that never happens, she will remain happily single and will be content with her books."

"Books?"

"Since early childhood she has been fascinated with learning. At her insistence she has been tutored by priests in languages and history and has surrounded herself with books. She doesn't speak Spanish but speaks Latin, Italian and French. She is most charming."

When all the company had seated themselves, Ferghal Bhaird took the two torches presented to him by two young servitors. Then, using high-pitched incantational cadence, he spoke Gaelic words in a lilting voice which Don Antonio translated for Francisco:

"Since the Sun has gone down behind the hills, let the fire-sparks be lighted to His glory on our hearth, on our tables, in our hearts. God, Sovereign Light and Source of Life, bless the seeds of the Sun here in our fields, in our bodies and our souls. Of Thee the flame, to Thee the flame."

Don Antonio whispered into Francisco's ear, "Sun Worship."

"Sun worship? Like the ancient Gaels?"

"Yes. I think it's Celtic sun worship, now Christianized. Look what he's doing now."

Fergal Bhaird set one torch to a taper on the table, then swiftly strode to the hearth and set the other torch to the branches piled inside. Then the servants took the torches from him and lighted the sconces along the wall. The tapers on the tables had been lit before the call to dinner.

Now both men and women servants passed baskets of bread, hunks of meat from the great roasts of beef at the Chief's table and crocks of beer. At the end of the meal, wooden platters with honeyed pastries and nuts were passed around by the coifed women.

After dessert Mac Clancy rose from his place at the head table, drew his knife from his belt and clanged the shield behind him to command attention in the old ritual manner of the ancient sagas. Then he laid his right hand on the bard's shoulder and requested him to sing.

The bard rose, grabbed his silver harp and began tuning it. Francisco glanced towards Alana. She was gazing at him. Both smiled. A strange feeling went through him.

Don Antonio turned towards Francisco and said, "Now the bard may sing the praises of Mac Clancy and his ancestors from Niall of the Hy Niall down through the sons of Mac Flancha of the Red Face to our Mac Clancy. Or he may sing of the beauty of Lake Melvin and its wooded islands, or of the coasts of Donegal or of some ancient heroism. You will be able to imagine from his mellow intonations, the rhythm of his fingers and the retort of the strings what he is describing. You will find it quite beautiful as it begins to affect you."

The bard paused a moment, his blue eyes seeming to intensify in color as his thoughts deepened. Then, strumming his hand across the silver wires, he began chanting a song in Gaelic with a melancholy cadence and a dip at the end like the rolling of a gentle wave:

> The sea rides white tonight.
> It bears us a strange booty,
> Turning over and under the purple wave;
> Not the green hair of the mermaids,
> Nor the mooned pebbles,
> Nor shiny driftwood from the Isles of Aran,
> Nor the storm-plucked feathers of gulls,
> Nor the death-bellied herring,
> Nor shell nor the shell's heart, the pearl.
> The sea rides white tonight,
> Bearing a strange booty;
> Pouring treasure from yellow hills far away,

Silver and gold from the hills of Spain,
Casks of the sweet blood of earth,
The vintage of Spain;
Bolts of cloth like a dripping rainbow,
Banners and pennons from the tall ships
And the great timbers
And sweet carved women of the helms;
And people . . .
People sleeping in the folded waves,
Soldiers and seamen and captains
And priests of Rome,
And eminent Spanish nobles.
It yields us the dead.
The sea rides white tonight.
It swirls us a strange booty,
Turning over and under the purple wave,
Bearing us the living trawled from nets of death.
It brings us our brothers of Spain!

Francisco found himself very moved by the words of this newly-created song as translated for him by Don Antonio; still more by the haunting melody which prickled the surface of his skin and fingered the roots of his hair with a beat similar to primitive magic ceremonies. It was as if he were carried along by words and music into the earliest human resonances, into gatherings in caverns and among trees, assemblages in which pagan gods were lured to join the conclaves of ancient man.

When Don Antonio had translated the last line into his ear, scarcely realizing what he was doing but deeply moved, Francisco rose from his place and, lifting his flagon of beer, gave a resounding toast in Latin:

"Here's to this illustrious bard, Fingal Bhaird, this great leader, Chief Murtagh Mac Clancy, their beautiful ladies and clansmen—our new friends. We are all the creation of God and we Spanish are deeply honored to sit at your tables and share these wonderful moments with you."

His voice, so rarely used during the long and difficult days since the shipwreck, rang out deep and clear. Mac Clancy rose and translated the toast into Gaelic in a loud mellow voice. The whole assemblage rose to their feet, lifted their flagons, looked towards Francisco, shouted something that sounded like "*Spagna Aboo!*" and drained their beer mugs.

"It means 'Hail to Spain!'" translated Don Antonio. "You did well. There seems to be a great deal of friendly feeling in this hall. We need it!"

Now Chief Mac Clancy gave an order to his servants who shortly returned with flasks of wine and filled the empty flagons. Although the flasks were unmarked, Francisco recognized the red wine of Tarragona. He relished the rich taste while thinking of his beloved Spain.

After supper, tables were pushed back and the company, joined presently by the women, sat close about the fire on benches or rushes on the floor. The bard sat beside the fire on a stool and sang paeans about Mac Clancy and his ancestors, his harp strings often rippling into sequences of ascending and descending notes called the *sruith-mor.* He also sang battle songs that were fierce lampoons against the Sassenachs in the tradition of Druid satires that were supposed to traverse the air and destroy their enemies. The assembled group often added their voices in natural harmony.

On two occasions as Francisco inhaled and relished the entrancing atmosphere, he noted that Alana had her penetrating eyes still fixed on him, not shifting a scintilla when his gaze met hers except that she quickly embroidered her beautiful face with a subtle but enchanting smile. *My God, what a creature,* he thought. *Have I ever seen anyone so beautiful?* He had difficulty moving his eyes away, as if they were bound by invisible silken spider threads. Unusual new emotions stirred within him.

At last Chief Mac Clancy gave a bow of his head, a word of praise to the bard and made a gesture to signify that it was time for dismissal of the company. Everyone quieted while the bard sang an end-of-evening song:

> The wind is whistling over the bogs tonight.
> Under its combing fingers
> The waters of Lough Melvin ripple and rise,
> The yellow grasses on the moors tremble,
> The gray wolves' hair rustles in the moonlight,
> The marsh birds murmur in the sedges
> And draw close the sleeves of their wings.
> The sun is asleep
> And color has gone from the world.

It is well to rest in the darkness
When shadows cover the manifold brilliance.
Dream well in the black-honeyed beehive of sleep
And waken again
In the undarkening glory of our painted dawn.
Breathe in the flame of our Sun,
The source of Life and the world's beauty.

The remarkable evening, so different from his experience, affected Francisco with unusual fervor. He couldn't stop thinking about Alana, her bewitching eyes, her charismatic smile and the powerful pull between them.

CHAPTER 19

Palm Reading

(November 1588)

The next day Francisco found that men and women who spoke Latin or a few words of Spanish stopped to talk with him. Gaunt and bony though Francisco had become, his eyes still sparkled brightly with a roguish gallantry which delighted the women. The deep masculine timbre of his voice added to his appeal and his injuries elicited feminine sympathies.

On the fourth night of Francisco's stay there was an abrupt change of castle atmosphere. A horseman had arrived in the late afternoon and a stir of excitement swirled through the castle. Francisco learned that some of Caffar O'Donnell's cattle had "strayed" onto Mac Clancy's fertile pastures at the head of Lake Melvin, a favorite habit of O'Donnell when pasturage of his own was running short. Therefore, this evening Mac Clancy and his men were planning a foray to ascertain the truth. The Irish way to deal with such intrusions was to preempt the cattle and convince them to change their clan allegiance.

Any Spaniard who wanted to join the foray was urged to do so. Only the Chief and nine or ten others would ride horses. The rest would run on foot. It was a favorite sport of the fighting and clannish Irish. Pugnacity was not only an Irish pastime but they argued that small forays were designed to prevent later bigger battles with greater loss of life.

Supper was served an hour earlier and a new dish was added to the menu. In the kitchen hearth, servants turned on spits the carcasses of animals to which, when served at table, some of the hair still clung. "Are they sheep or deer?" Francisco asked Don Antonio.

"Wolves, my friend, wolves. An old Irish custom when there is a pending foray."

"Wolves?" Although the smell of sizzling wolf was intriguing, Francisco could get down only a few morsels even with abundant beer. Each foray Irishman cut the meat off with his own knife and ate it as ravenously as ancient Scythians who were neighbors of the Celts long ago on the shores of the Black Sea.

Chief Mac Clancy called in a loud voice for a song from Fingal Bhaird. He stood very straight, plucked the strings with vigor and the words of his song rang out with a strong and sturdy marching rhythm. The name of "Maglana" echoed again and again.

"He's naming all the mighty ancestors of Mac Clancy, the fighting ones," explained Don Antonio. "It's a call to battle."

"Yes, I guessed that. I'm even beginning to pick up a few of the words. I must try to learn some Gaelic like you, Don Antonio, though I could never hope to equal your linguistic facility."

"Listen. The bard's reaching a climax and the bagpipers are about to join in."

Four bagpipers appeared at the far end of the dining hall. Flagons were filled and there was a crescendo of excitement. Mac Clancy waved a mighty hand to and fro as the music of the bagpipes joined the harp and song of Fingal Bhaird. Soon the whole room was filled with the motion of swinging bodies. Then the Chief cried out the call to battle, "*Farrah! Farrah!*"

"Maglana! Maglana!" sang the bard in a lusty voice. "He is the crown of the mighty O'Neills, the honored tribe of Ith. He is the Cuchulainn of cattle raids, the hero of a thousand forays, the battlefield giant of Donegal!"

The whole company of men arose and shouted, "*Farrah! Farrah! Maglana aboo! Aboo!*"

Mac Clancy turned and struck the shield behind him with his sword. Everyone rushed out of the hall shouting over and over, "Mac Clancy, lead us on to victory! *Farrah! Farrah! Maglana aboo! Aboo!*" The men ran to the castle gate which was now opened for the foray. They climbed down the lowered wooden stairs into boats and disappeared into the night.

Mainly women were left in the dining hall with a few serving boys clearing off tables, plus Francisco, four fellow-Spaniards and three elderly men. A servant put new logs on the fire. The tables were pushed back and the older women seated themselves on benches, the younger on floor-rushes. The Chief's wife and sister sat together on a bench close to the fire, the light and shade of the flickering flame playing on their lovely faces.

There was laughter among the women for a few minutes, then the Chief's wife called upon an old man to tell a story. Although Francisco could not understand it because Don Antonio had gone on the foray, he was fascinated by the lilting cadences. It was neither song nor poetry yet there was a lyrical rhythm with an appealing undulating quality. *These Irish are conjurors with voice,* thought Francisco. *It is as if they had listened for centuries to the melodies of birds, the stone-splashed music of streams, the murmur of leaves in the wind and to fairy sounds from their hiding places in forests, hills and lakes.*

Francisco was immersed in his thoughts when he heard his name. "Don Francisco de Cuellar, *Señor!*" It was Shauna, wife of the Chief.

He looked up.

"What can you do, Francisco," she said in Latin, "to entertain us? Can you sing us a song of Spain? Or tell us stories of your adventures? Or some old Moorish tale?"

He responded in Latin, "Thank you, my lady, for the gracious suggestions. Would that I were a gifted entertainer but to sing a song I would need my Spanish guitar, now a part of the ocean's flotsam. As for my adventures, they do not make a pretty after-dinner tale." He was stalling for time as he searched his mind for a courteous way out of this invitational dilemma. He felt naked without his *vihuela*. He quickly looked at the red-haired Alana and caught a nod of encouragement.

A thought darted from a crevice in Francisco's mind. He remembered his skill at fortune telling, an art he had learned as a boy at summer gypsy encampments in the valleys near Cuellar. It was a talent he had honed in his student days at Salamanca and during his summers at the Royal Court in Madrid. His proficiency consisted not only in interpreting the various branching lines, interruptions, mounds, valleys, crosses and stars in hands, upon which the gypsies had set down signs of meaning as determinate as those in astrology. Most subtly of all, he had become adept in analyzing the hand as a whole, seeing its light and shadows and feeling the totality of its meaning as well as feeling invisible vibrations from the mind and spirit of the person being analyzed, a rare ability. Even the gypsies had been impressed with his sensitivity. They had warned him to avoid over-dramatization.

"I can tell fortunes by the gypsy art, *Señora* Mac Clancy, if you deem it appropriate." There was a murmur of delight from the women around the fire when the Lady Mac Clancy repeated Francisco's proposal in Gaelic.

"Ah, *Señor*, how pleasant! That will indeed be interesting and fun for us. Please begin by telling mine and please call me Shauna."

Francisco rose from his place on the rushes and, kneeling in front of Mac Clancy's wife, took her hand gently in his and said, "*Permissum, Shauna?*" to which the lady answered "*Sic.*" He took Shauna's right hand and cupped it in his own. It was very soft and transmitted a glow of warmth. He felt it slowly and carefully before opening it quietly, trying to sense its meaning.

"Ah, *manus formosa et pulcher*," he said, "so fair a hand, with virtue and kindness and good deeds written across it."

"And good fortune, too?" she asked.

A shadow seemed to pass between Francisco's face and hers. There was a small mound of disaster sitting midway between the Mound of Venus and the lifeline but he said, "'Tis a long life with a shadow or two across the path but not many. Your three strong sons will carry on your family for many generations." The lady Mac Clancy smiled happily.

"And will I have many joyful years with my lord, the Chief?"

"One's hand only indicates the owner's life story," Shauna, "not someone else's. I do sense problems eventually, however, from foreign invaders and times of hardship hiding in the hills."

"My Lord is a strong man," she replied. "He will never succumb to the foul English."

"In the meantime I see many happy days spent with your husband here in the castle on the lake. Many a day of tasking and laughter, many a night of banqueting and romance."

"Thank you, Don Francisco. And my sister-in-law's hand? Alana, show him your hand."

Alana's hand suffused him with unfamiliar emotions. He quickly read its gypsy signs that it was a happy and promising hand but he was initially flustered for words. "Ah, *beata manus, felicisima*. A most happy and beautiful hand, as is the owner," he said.

"With love in it?" asked the twenty-five year-old Alana, smiling radiantly.

Francisco was puzzled by what he saw in her future but he clearly saw the past and present. "Yes, I see many eligible men riding to Castle Mac Clancy to ask you for your hand in marriage, even quite recently."

"True, true!" exclaimed Alana. "Dennis 0'Reilly, son of Hugh, rode from Tullymongan Hill only three months ago to ask me to marry him. Several others have preceded him since I was seventeen years-old. You see through the mist of time to things as they were and are, Don Francisco, but what about the future? That should be easy . . . I am not a complicated person."

Don Francisco smiled and studied the hand further. "I see other fine men coming. They ride from east and west but you bring sadness to these suitors. You have high standards and crave a perfect fit with your soul. You will not allow anyone to force your choice, even your brother."

"From which direction will my successful suitor come?"

"Let me see if the hand conveys that future to me." He was enthralled by the stunning beauty of her face and her flowing red hair cascading to her shoulders. He felt the power of her eyes and smile. He tried hard to focus and truly sense the meaning of all clues. Tracing the hand's lines gently with the middle and index fingers of his right hand, he studied it carefully, trying also to sense emanations from herself. There was a distinct star on the mound of Venus with its rays extending farther to the left than the right but the other signs conflicted. Interpretation failed him.

"I am having trouble reading the signs, my Lady, but your fate appears to lie neither in the west nor east. There are initial problems between you and your loved one despite powerful feelings of attraction. He comes to you through unusual circumstances. Your course together is rocky in the beginning. Eventually I see you two coming together beyond the borders of Ireland, looking out towards golden sunsets and then starting a new life in a far-off place across the seas."

Francisco began to sense more than the mere lines in her hand. "I see you and him and your child or children climbing aboard a large ship and sailing to a distant land, perhaps a large island, exotic and beautiful. From there the seeds of Mac Clancys will flower over the broad earth."

"How lovely," replied Alana. "It sounds just like *Tir na nOg*, in Irish mythology a Land of Eternal Youth and Happiness."

Francisco released her hand and realized that he was sweating profusely. It had required special effort and extra concentration to read Alana and her palm correctly and remain candid.

Alana brought Francisco's hand to her cheek and held it there with her head bowed for several seconds. Then she released it, clapped her own hands together and laughed. "Those are exciting predictions, Francisco, and they appeal to me. They are quite consistent with my own dreamy imaginings. You have made me very happy. Thank you."

"Now tell my fortune, Don Francisco!" "Mine!" said another. Cries came from all quarters now as the women surrounded him. It reminded Francisco of the children of Cuellar gathered around him for stories and song. Mac Clancy's wife now spoke authoritatively over the clamoring voices and told the ladies it was time to disperse and give Francisco a rest.

"It is time for the evening to end," she said to Francisco in Latin. "I can see that telling fortunes is not an easy task. Your mind seemed to be transported to another place when you were reading Alana's hand. Your face became red, you started sweating and you began to breathe harder. Now you look exhausted. You provided us with good and extraordinary entertainment. We may soon call upon you again. You are good at what you do, Don Francisco, and you impressed me with your effort and honesty."

CHAPTER 20

A Time To Stand

(November 1588)

All the next day Francisco knew no peace. The castle women and even some of the men besieged him to tell their fortunes. At first he complied, regarding the enterprise as a pleasant occupation to while away the hours. Then he decided to turn palm reading to his advantage. So he told the group that he would only read the palms of three individuals per day and after each reading, that person had to give him a one hour lesson in Gaelic in whatever manner they chose.

At sunset Mac Clancy and his men rode into the village opposite the castle, followed later by those on foot with thirty cattle lumbering along beside them. There were no wounds and no deaths. There was much lively talking when the foray victors reached the castle. Don Antonio told Francisco that the two O'Donnell lookouts had been clubbed unconscious at the beginning. The rest of O'Donnell's men had been drinking and slept through the raid. The thirty cattle, grazing illegally on Mac Clancy's land, had been subtly influenced to join Mac Clancy's herds.

The evening banquet was loud and raucous, featuring two roasted steers and plentiful beer. Mac Clancy told his own impressive version of the exploit followed by Fingal Bhaird's dramatic rendering in song.

Embroidering of stories seemed to be an intrinsic Irish trait accomplished by linguistic artistry, merry twinkles in the eyes and abundant beer.

When Francisco mentioned that too many people wanted their fortunes told, Mac Clancy quoted a Roman adage, "He who makes a success of something must suffer the consequences. You are a fortunate man! Who complains about dozens of women asking for one's personal attention?" His giant laughter rang out against the castle walls.

Francisco turned away with a gracious bow, once again smiling to himself that he, Francisco de Cuellar with an ancient proud Spanish lineage, was now a popular gypsy fortune teller in Ireland. A laughing devil seemed to dance in Francisco's Puppet Show of Life but it was better than being torn to pieces by wolves on the shores of Streedagh Bay.

After Sunday's mass at the shoreside church, Mac Clancy was no longer laughing. One of his spies had ridden in, his horse covered with sweat despite the chilly early November day. He reported that General Fitzwilliam, England's military commander in Ireland, had started marching from Dublin with seventeen hundred men in search of stray Spaniards and their Irish hosts. Having heard that Mac Clancy was sheltering several Armada survivors, he had turned his line of march towards the castle and was only two days away.

Mac Clancy responded to the crisis with logical strategy. He gave orders for the departure of all his people and their cattle and sheep to the mountains despite the early winter weather. Then he took a boat to the castle, summoned all the household and told them they must get ready for departure within an hour. Such a large contingent of Sassenach troops could only be fought with allies and that took time. He gave his orders firmly but quietly. He now he turned to Francisco.

"How about you and your Spanish contingent, Francisco? Where will you be going? Our meager conditions in the hills are not designed for guests."

Francisco asked for a few minutes to think. He climbed to the parapet where two older guards paced the circular walkway on top of the castle. He looked out at the lovely view of Lake Melvln with two of its mint-green islands visible over its blue-gray waters. He looked down at himself from above, knowing that he was about to make a life and death decision. *Isn't it finally time to become truly active participants in our own destiny? Wasn't the whole Armada mission imbued with noble Spanish virtues and heroic ideals which we have not been given any real opportunity to express?*

As if struck by lightning he suddenly realized that here was the perfect situation for a heroic decision. There was no other choice. He walked down the circular stone staircase and confronted his nine fellow Spaniards.

"Men, we have nowhere to go and few options. It is time to stop fleeing and hiding. We must grasp this opportunity to show our Spanish virtue and courage. Our lives in recent weeks in this country haven't been worth a *peseta*. We have been bludgeoned, stripped naked, kicked, knifed and humiliated. Like the three hundred Spartans at Thermopylae in 480 BC, at times in life one must take a strong stand, no matter what the odds. That time is now.

"We courageous few must stay and defend this castle against the 1700 soldiers of the English army who are determined to slaughter us. The island site and castle design are ideal for defense. The English can come no nearer with their artillery than the solid ground next to the village almost two hundred yards away. Unless they brought their heaviest weapons, and the speed of their march suggests otherwise, most of their shots won't even reach us. The water around the castle is deep and any approaching boats are perfect targets for our weapons. We certainly have nothing to lose except our lives which have been in daily jeopardy since the shipwrecks.

"Let's succeed or die right here, a band of brothers infused with pride and self-respect which have been almost completely absent from our lives since we departed so confidently from Lisbon. United by blood, we shall be remembered in death from this day forward or, if we survive, we shall carry our heads proudly throughout our lives and feel pity for those who could not share our brief moment of bravery here in Ireland."

As Francisco spoke, he could feel Spanish fighting valor flowing back into his mind, heart and spirit and into those of his comrades. Don Antonio was the first to shout the traditional battle cry, "*Anda, Santiago! Anda!*" Then every Spaniard took up the cry honoring their patron Saint James, "*Anda, Santiago! Anda!*"

Francisco walked down to Mac Clancy who was busy helping his people into boats. "With your permission, Sir, we choose to stay and defend your castle against the English!"

MacClancy's eyes widened. After a few moments of silence, he put his hand on Francisco's shoulder and exclaimed, "Magnificent idea! I approve absolutely! We will supply you!"

As soon as the household had made the last boat journey to shore, Mac Clancy had his men bring whatever weapons and ammunition they had— only six crossbows and six muskets. Long-term provisions in the castle storerooms were sufficient for ten men for six months, including barrels of beer. A dozen boatloads of large stones and boulders were gathered, rowed to the castle and taken to the castle-top to hurl down upon the enemy if a landing were attempted.

Then Mac Clancy took a Holy Bible bound in silver and velvet and had each Spaniard swear upon it that he would under no circumstances abandon or surrender the castle to the enemy for any reason other than death. The rite concluded, Mac Clancy got into his boat, waved at the Spaniards and shouted, "*Farrah! Farrah! Anda! Anda! Aboo, aboo.*"

Two mornings later, as Francisco stood on the parapet awaiting the English onslaught, he reflected upon famous historical battles of the few against the many, most of which ended in death for the few. He briefly wondered why he had suggested this desperate strategy of ten against seventeen hundred. *Am I just tired of being pushed around by the stormy vicissitudes of life? Why would anyone accept such impossible odds? Am I trying to prove that I and my fellow shipwreck survivors are invincible warriors like Odysseus outside the walls of Troy? Yes. Fate has presented us with a magnificent opportunity which must not be missed.*

An image flashed across his mind of the first time he glimpsed Alana's extraordinary beauty, enthralling smile and spellbinding emerald eyes. *I wonder what role she played in my unexpected decision? I didn't even say goodbye to her.*

He now saw black figures moving where solid ground ended near the Point. The English had arrived. He felt serenely confidant that he and his comrades could emerge triumphant. If he was wrong, he didn't mind facing death. He was a professional military man and he had made the correct military decision. The thought energized him. He watched the Sassenachs swarm like a colony of well-trained ants on the shore.

The English began to raise their hundreds of tents, shouting defiance and raising their fists at the castle as they did so. In the late afternoon sun, Francisco saw the English building two gibbets which stood menacingly against the orange-yellow sky.

A small boat now put out with the lion flag of England at the helm and a trumpeter standing in the prow with the white flag of truce fluttering from it. The boat came within thirty yards of the castle. The trumpeter blew a proud set of notes and the man with him cried out in Spanish:

"Futile men of Spain holding Mac Clancy's castle, we call on you to surrender! Your defensive stand is beyond preposterous!"

So their spies had been active. Francisco shouted, "Mac Clancy's friends never surrender."

"Foolhardy Spaniards, you are doomed! Give up! We hold Don Graniello de Swasso and Don Valerio de Valente as captives. They will be hanged before nightfall unless you surrender. You cannot possibly hold out against two thousand English soldiers. Lay down your arms honorably! Your lives will be spared, we promise you!"

Fat chance of that, thought Francisco. "We value well the lives of Don Graniello and Don Valerio but we are soldiers and our job is to hold Castle Mac Clancy against all besiegers."

"That is your resolve?"

"Yes, until the several hundred of us are piled in heaps around the castle wall."

"Several hundred? What a foolish lie. There are only ten of you. If your decision is to die we shall be accommodating, you foul invaders of our land." The trumpeter blew quick-spurting notes which cast derision over the castle walls. The boat rowed back to the promontory.

So the English had capable local spies. Francisco knew that the fate of the two Spaniards had already been decided. He was equally sure that, had he surrendered, the gibbets would have hung the ten castle-defenders as well. The Irish he had encountered knew well that the English "word of honor" was worthless.

The Spaniards watched as the translator conveyed Captain Francisco's answer to a group of helmeted officers on shore. The two Spaniards were promptly conducted under the gibbets. They seemed to be wearing their rich Spanish velvet capes. There was a trumpet signal. The capes were snatched from their shoulders and they were revealed in the final indignity of nakedness. No priest was there to render final comfort. The two men were stood up on wooden chairs, the nooses were adjusted and the chairs pulled away. The swinging Spaniards jerked for a few ultimate seconds, then hung still against the sunset. Francisco lowered his head and crossed himself.

The next day the English began setting up their field cannons which were fortunately of small caliber. As Francisco had predicted, they had left their heavy artillery behind. Most of their shots fell short, causing only small splashes part way to the castle. Stones on the castle walls were hit twice and fragments flew but no significant damage was done.

Did the Sassenachs have a large enough supply of vessels to attack from several directions at once? With such vertical castle walls, Francisco felt confidant that their boulders, six muskets and six crossbows would suffice in the short term.

The English spent six days trying to set up a closer bombardment from the promontory but the swampy shore proved a formidable deterrent. They decided to attack with musketry-men in twenty medium-sized boats. Francisco told his men to lie low, not to show themselves or return any shots. The boats stopped seventy-five yards from the castle but their musket balls had no impact. No attempt was made to approach closer. They were probing the Spanish defensive strategy.

The next night two sets of three boats each, tied together, came close up under the walls, expecting to escape detection. One of the Spanish guards, however, heard the splash of an oar which triggered a downpour of boulders upon the assailants. All six boats overturned as the men panicked and leaped off. Most of the soldiers couldn't swim and drowned. A few began the swim back to the village. One who made it to the entrance embayment of the castle was discovered at dawn and dispatched with a musket ball.

Now the Spaniards observed greater boat-building activity on shore. The English also inaugurated constant harassment, by day and night, with the approach of small flotillas of musketmen and archers using long bows. The Spaniards kept out of sight, allowing the enemy boats to come close enough for a few shots from wall-slits by the best Spanish marksmen. Several English soldiers were hit. The defenders used ammunition only when necessary.

Since there was a constant acceleration of enemy harassments and every day the approach of larger flotillas, Francisco wondered how long he and his men could sustain the siege. Obviously their tactical options were limited. Two of his men were already beginning to counsel yielding the castle and escaping along the bog path into the countryside. Francisco spoke strongly against the disgrace of such a strategy:

"We have promised our generous host Mac Clancy to hold this castle until the end and hold it we will. Our own honor and the honor of Spain demand it. Let us agree that the word 'surrender' is not in our vocabulary."

"Then we are doomed," said one of the men.

"We've been doomed ever since we allowed the English to out-tactic us, out-sail us and out-shoot us at sea. Then our inept leadership told us to head north instead of back through the channel directly home," declared Francisco. "But fight we shall and live we shall until the last whisper of breath is ousted from our bodies! Heaven willing, we shall all see Spain again! Seventeen hundred English have made not one iota of progress against us. Their ammunition and provisions are dwindling and soon they will ignominiously depart, to our Glory. The Irish bards will sing our song for generations to come! We shall become part of Irish Legend!"

Don Antonio patted Francisco on the back. No further dissent was heard.

On the sixteenth day of the siege the Spaniards watched a flotilla of makeshift boats and fifty small rafts made of logs lashed together being pushed from shore. There were six rafts much larger than the rest and upon these several culverins and demi-cannon were being loaded.

"That doesn't look good," murmured one of the Spaniards.

"Don't be so sure," rejoined Francisco. "We have every advantage of position. The Irish castle-builders outdid themselves with ingenuity and I'd rather have you Spaniards on my side than all the English culverins arrayed against us. We are better soldiers with far greater determination and courage. We will only be defeated if we become defeatist."

When he saw two men praying, Francisco was reminded that he had been forgetting prayer. He now said, "Praying to God is not being defeatist. Let us all pray silently in our own way."

The flotilla moved slowly. A little wind had sprung up and was rocking the boats. As the wind grew stronger, the guns shifted position and required holding by the troops. Stronger gusts now blew across Lake Melvin with the chill of winter on its draught. The waters began to roil. The raftsmen's paddles made little progress against the force of wind and roughening waves.

Voices shouting loud orders carried over the water. Now midway to the castle, the English struggled against the worsening weather. Culverins tipped off rafts and plunged to the bottom. Boats overturned and men drowned. Half of the flotilla barely made it back to shore.

Finally, thought Francisco, *Nature has turned its powers against the English rather than the Spanish. Have God and Mary of Henar finally heard our prayers?*

From the parapet Francisco inhaled the wind and held his head triumphantly high for the first time since sailing from Lisbon. He left one guard and told the others to come with him. They walked briskly down the castle stairs into the dining hall where they lighted a large hearth fire and drank Spanish wine which Mac Clancy had provided for any special occasion. They briefly congratulated each other but otherwise sat silently, smiling wearily as they sipped their wine, absorbing the penetrating heat and watching the dancing flames happily celebrate their victory.

The wind became stronger and colder, all night whistling and moaning around the castle. Then came snow in a blinding white whirl. By morning there was a foot of wet snow over Rossclogher Promontory and over the English tents, many of which had collapsed under the weight.

By afternoon the Sassenach tents were down and only the snow remained. The English had decamped.

CHAPTER 21

Join Our Clan

(November 1588)

Looking down from the castle walls it was hard to believe that the promontory of Rossclogher had recently been the assembly area for a large Sassenach attacking force and their artillery. The garmenting snow had covered up all evidence of an English army. Had seventeen hundred English soldiers really been defeated by ten underweight, recently clothesless shipwreck survivors or was it only a figment of their imagination, enhanced by wine and beer?

For four days they were total masters of Mac Clancy's castle with no worries, plenty of provisions, abundant wood to burn in the great fireplace and an ample supply of beer. They decided not to consume any more of Mac Clancy's Spanish wine. Then Mac Clancy and his people, well advised by their lookouts of the Sassenach departure, came down from the hills. Great was the rejoicing and back-slapping praise of the Spaniards. Everyone was jubilant and emotional over the unexpected result.

"You are forever my brothers!" declared Mac Clancy. "You are now members of Clan Mac Clancy with all the privileges! What I have is yours! You deserve it! Your victory enriches our collective souls."

They sat at head table with Mac Clancy and drank his homemade beer and Spanish wine and ate the choicest portions of roast boar, beef and mutton, sometimes served with white thorn honey. Fergal the Bard created dramatic songs about the Spanish heroes of Castle Mac Clancy with no need for embellishment. He referred to Tara, Emain Macha and Temora in the ancient days of mighty heroes and the Red Branch Knights and Ossian, the ancient mythic king.

On the second night of rejoicing, Francisco wore a blue velvet Spanish cloak tied at the waist with a silver chain that Mac Clancy had ordered two of his beach plunderers to bring forth. Sitting next to Francisco, Mac Clancy put a hand on his shoulder and said:

"My brother, I would make the bonds closer between us. I have considered well and I give you the high honor of wedding my sister, Alana."

Francisco, for an instant, was struck dumb but then he replied: "I can think of no higher honor, Chief Mac Clancy. No women in all Ireland are more beautiful in the extreme or more enchanting than your wife and sister. But I already have a wife of my own, eagerly awaiting my return to Spain. Happy though I am here and though you have been magnificently hospitable, I crave deeply to return to my own country. We now earnestly beg your help in getting us to the friendly northeast country and in securing safe places on board ship to Scotland."

A dark shadow passed over Mac Clancy's face. "This is not good, brother. We urgently request you to reconsider. The Church will set aside your marriage. I can easily arrange that through our local priests. Stay with us, marry my sister and enter the Mac Clancy clan in ties of blood. One day this castle shall be yours. There are castles in Dartry which I shall give to my sons but this castle you have saved shall be yours and Alana's. My sons have already agreed."

"My lord . . ."

Mac Clancy held up his hand in front of Francisco. "My honored guest. You need time to consider such a life-changing offer. You shall have it. In one month it will be Christmas. You will see how splendid and festive Mac Clancy's castle can be. You shall have that month to get to know my sister and then give me your answer. In the meantime you are part of our family."

The next day Francisco was besieged by people of the castle urging him to cast his lot with Mac Clancy. They reminded him that English soldiers were constantly scouring the countryside for stray Spaniards. They recently marched all captured Spaniards to the Queen's Deputy in Dublin, the fierce Bingham, who selected a few redeemable nobles to convey to Queen Elizabeth in London and lined up all the rest and shot them.

Francisco smiled and told everyone that he was very content and joyful at Mac Clancy's castle. He needed time alone but was only able to escape from the crowds in late afternoon just before twilight. It was bitter cold with the wind still howling. He wrapped himself in a dark Irish cloak and walked out of the fire-warmed hall up the courtyard stairs to the parapet.

The cloudy evening afterglow was a pale reddish-orange. Mac Clancy had paid him the highest compliment a man can give but Francisco didn't like to be forced into anything, especially a bigamous marriage. *Should I get to know Alana better and give our togetherness a chance? How can I? I am married in the eyes of God and Zabella hasn't done anything wrong.*

He gazed out at the peninsula covered in snow, still lending oblivion to recent human presence. *Is all of life so transient that its memory-traces can be wiped out by a mere change of weather? Life at the castle is a stimulating and happy respite from earthly turmoil. Why not spend another month in this joyous environment?*

He looked out at the distant Sperrin Hills. *If human beings could only be as benign as the landscapes God made for them. What screaming battles with axe, spear and sword those pleasant hills must have witnessed for thousands of years! What men with malignant hearts are lurking there still, ready to kill any Spaniard trying to escape towards freedom and home? What is the wisest decision for me and my nine Spanish comrades? How can I optimize our future?*

Francisco was ready to return downstairs when he felt another presence. He wheeled about. There was a slight figure near him wrapped concealingly, head to foot, in a dark woolen blanket. A feminine hand pulled a fold of the mantle away and Alana showed herself.

"I know you are troubled, Don Francisco," she said. "You do not wish to offend my brother and me. I know that the desire is strong upon you to leave our castle."

"True, my lady," he said. He took her hand and laid a kiss upon it which made him tingle. "I esteem you well and find your beauty and demeanor beyond description. I hold your brother in the highest regard and he has been wonderful to us. But I am a Spaniard. My heart and the shape of me, body and soul, were formed in Spain. My King, my wife, my mother and all my duties are in Spain. I feel it is to Spain that I must return even if I have to crawl and float on a log the entire way."

"I come to tell you that my brother, who finds you most fascinating, admirable and honorable, intends to keep you and your Spanish friends here always. He respects you immensely, as I do. He believes letting you go from the castle into the midst of all the wolves around us would be like letting caged birds be torn to pieces by wild hawks. He plans to keep you brave Spaniards, who have so gallantly defended his castle, for his personal guard. He regards it his duty to protect you from imminent harm as you protected his castle. He wants you to fall in love with me and doesn't want to let you go—ever."

"Never let us go?" asked Francisco.

"Let me tell you my wishes and see if we can come to an agreement. I have been waiting many years for the right man to come into my life. I think you may be he. I have felt it deep within me since the first time I saw you in the castle. You noted it, too, I could tell. When our eyes caught the other's, neither of us could move them away. We were both transfixed by a strange and wonderful power. Do you admit it, Francisco?"

"I didn't understand it then but yes, I agree. My heart beats differently when I am with you. Your enthralling smile and inner harmony quite undo me."

"Your character and demeanor do the same to me. I don't know what love is but I think I am beginning to feel love for you. It is a marvelous feeling—so new to me, so wondrous. Can't we both let it happen to see where it goes?"

"What are your wishes for us, Alana?"

"I would like you to stay a month longer. Let me plan our time together and then you will participate in our Christmas festivities. I have some ideas to allow our interaction and feelings to evolve. Let Time and God lead us wherever they will, two happy souls on a joint life adventure."

"Sounds excellent but what happens thereafter?"

"In the long term, Francisco, I want only what you want. I intend to fall in love only once. If I don't find myself in love with you, I will want you to leave so I may continue my quest. I dearly want marriage and children. If you are indeed my one true love, I will always think of you first. If you wish to leave, I will help you. My brother is a formidable adversary and may do everything in his power to prevent your departure. He is very serious when he says you are now his blood brother and a member of the Mac Clancy Clan for life."

"Alana, you are a stunningly beautiful person who quite takes my breath away and creates unfamiliar feelings within me. How can I refuse a month with you?"

"I don't want you to refuse. The thought of being with you excites my mind and my heart. I honestly believe, after all you have been through in recent months, that it would help your body and soul to stay here peacefully with me for a month to gain strength and clarity both physical and mental. I will look after you and bring you peace, whatever you decide."

Coming close to him she put her head on his chest and whispered, "Do you really believe it would be difficult to stay?" She placed her hand gently on his arm.

"How I wish I were totally free and not conflicted with the tug of obligations," he answered as he stooped and kissed her hand, feeling once again a compelling attractive force. "Your suggested solution is sage beyond your years and sounds wonderful to me. As your gallant knight, my honored Lady, I eagerly pick up your glove and accept your exciting challenge."

CHAPTER 22

Giving Love A Chance

(November-December 1588)

The next morning was clear and sunny. Alana, two servants and Francisco left the castle by boat for the village where her servants picked up supplies. Alana walked with Francisco to the stable where they chose horses. They rode on the submerged, twisty flat-rock trail through two hundred yards of watery bogs full of shrubs, then along a path through a forest with well-spaced trees. After three miles they emerged into a lovely glade with a tall, narrow waterfall spilling into an emerald pool garlanded by ferns. Low wooded hills formed the backdrop. The stream from the pool meandered quietly through the grassy clearing.

The glade was surrounded by stately leafless oaks and hawthorns. Near the stream, thirty feet from the forest, were two log cabins separated by a covered walkway. The rear dwelling contained a cooking area with fireplace, large iron pots for heating water and doing laundry, stacks of wood along the walls, a storage area for provisions and a general usage area including two chairs, two mattresses and warm blankets for servants. The front dwelling was larger with a stone hearth at one end, a table with two chairs, two rush-filled mattresses leaning against the wall, a tub for bathing, a stack of woolen blankets and paintings of local landscapes on the walls. A red deer stag's head with impressive antlers was mounted over the door.

"This is our hideaway," said Alana. "At my request my brother built these simple cabins for me as a present for my eighteenth birthday. I discovered the glade quite by accident from the hill above when I was a child doing a bird-walk with my servants. It's my favorite place in the world, far from earthly disquiet. I come here often, even in winter. I promised my brother that I would never sneak off alone, so I always come with my two favorite servants, Patrick and Riona. They are your age of twenty-seven but have been married for nine years. They have been inseparable since they were six years-old. They love this place as much as I do."

"How often will we come here?" asked Francisco.

"We will stay from one to several days at a time depending on the weather, our mood and our harmony. If heavy snow occurs we will probably choose to stay at the castle until the storm passes but we shall let our spontaneity rule the day. I told Patrick and Riona that the purpose of our time together was to see whether we could fall in love and might want to get married some day. They are completely discrete and trustworthy and will stay in the background."

"Sounds wonderful. What will we do every day?"

"I have many ideas and I want yours. I speak French and Italian but not Spanish. I think we should spend half of each day talking Gaelic and half speaking Spanish. My brother found some books in Spanish in a chest on the beach. We will bring those and I will bring some in Gaelic."

"Can you locate a guitar for me?" asked Francisco.

"By all means and I will bring some of my painting equipment. I am hoping for complete naturalness with each other without any constraints," added Alana. "That is who I am when I am here. Is that possible for you? I hope I don't shock you!"

"The concept appeals to me immensely but I'm afraid I have some inhibitions to overcome. I have spent so much of my life with restrictions and barriers that I can't think of anything more pleasant than being with you unboundaried. I will do my very best to let go and be myself."

The next day was clear with a gentle breeze. After exchanging language lessons Alana said, "It's time to enjoy our somewhat chilly sunshine. Patrick and Riona have made a small private quadrangle outside in the grass near the creek, lined by a two foot wall of firewood to shield us from the wind. Let's go there now."

They walked hand in hand to their wood-lined sanctuary near the waterfall. "All right, Francisco, it's time to be natural!" Alana turned away, took off her clothes and wrapped a towel around her waist. She walked slowly over to Francisco, kissed him on the cheek, ran to the pool, dropped the towel and jumped in.

She hopped out after less than a minute. "Wow! Cold but refreshing!" I've been doing that a few times each winter since I was a child. She faced Francisco completely naked and then slowly put the towel back around her waist. "Are you shocked yet?"

"You look supremely beautiful and I love your happy comfort zone but give me a little time to gather my courage! I had a long cold swim recently, not of my own choosing—a bit traumatic for a non-swimmer." He sat down inside the protected area.

Alana walked to the quadrangle and stood over him. She had beautiful breasts of moderate size with an uptilt at the ends and erect nipples from the cold water. Francisco was fascinated that she seemed so completely at ease.

"Why are you staring at my breasts, Francisco? Don't you like them?"

"Of course I do. They, and you, look marvelous. I have never been with a naked lady outside in the sun and it quite captivates me. Am I really the first man to be with you like this?"

She sat down and took his hand in hers. "No other man has ever seen me naked or touched me but I feel very comfortable with you."

"I love your naturalness and I feel some of my bashfulness attenuating."

"I'm glad you realize how relaxed we are with each other even though we have known each other for such a short time. Since my brother built this retreat for me five years ago I spend most of my time here bare-breasted except on the coldest days. It makes me feel more at-one with nature. In summer I often walk around the glade quite naked. Patrick and Riona also do so."

She lay down on her back in the warm grass, pulled him down next to her and soon went to sleep. Francisco removed his clothes except for his loincloth and absorbed the warm sun, nicely protected from the quiet breeze by the firewood wall. He looked down on the scene from above and shook his head in wonderment after so many horrendous happenings.

When Francisco awoke an hour later he leaned up on his elbows and was astounded at Alana's beauty, her flaming red hair draped over her shoulders, flowing down between her breasts.

Alana awoke, smiled and said, "I think you like what you see."

"It's not only that, Alana, but also your total uninhibited joy in this lovely remote setting. You are kindling rare feelings within me which I'm not sure I have experienced before."

"Likewise, my dear. I have kissed two of my suitors on the cheek out of a sense of courtesy but have shared nothing with them. With you I feel no barriers whatsoever which quite amazes me! Have we really known each other only a few days?" She let out a gentle rippling laugh.

"Even your laughter includes a Gaelic lilt, Alana! Did Irish faeries put you together to bewitch and enchant me?"

"I have actually heard faeries speak to me in this glen, more as a child than as an adult but I do believe in them. Sometimes the little people say charming things to me and sometimes they make impish, humorous comments which make me laugh out loud."

"Why not believe in faeries?" answered Francisco. "It's a beguiling part of Irish culture."

"Now it's time for some oak cakes, honey and buttermilk," said Alana. "Then, even without a guitar, you're going to sing Spanish songs to me . . . slowly, so I can try to distinguish one word from another. Now let's walk arm in arm to our simple wilderness cabin." A pair of rabbits sitting by the stream watched them, then lowered their heads to eat plants next to the stream.

They spent two or three days at a time in their cabin, alternating with a day and night at the castle. Each day at the glen they tried to do something new. Alana painted landscapes and took him on nature walks around the glade. He surprised her with his knowledge of birds. She impressed him by identifying every call from the winter contingent of birds. They both knew something of plants. They talked alternately in Gaelic and Spanish, only rarely in Latin.

He gave her guitar lessons. She began to walk around the cabin wearing nothing above the waist. So did Francisco. Sometimes on the warmer days they would sit by the stream silently holding hands for minutes at a time, drinking in the beauties of nature, listening to woodpeckers tapping or watching an occasional doe come to the glade to eat leaves on small bushes next to the forest. They loved taking afternoon naps holding hands in their wind-protected sanctuary.

"I can tell when you are thinking of me," said Alana. "You used to spend some of your quiet time worrying. Now you are just sending nice thoughts my way. You seem peaceful and content, so different than when you first arrived."

One cooler day, wearing a sweater and cloak, she painted while sitting next to the stream in her chair. He tried to make sense out of an Irish Bible which had Gaelic in one column and Latin in the adjacent column . . . slow but interesting and he became absorbed in the complex Gaelic words and expressions. Alana made much more rapid progress with her Spanish because of her fluency in Latin, Italian and French. He tried to paint but barely progressed beyond childhood squiggles. He preferred to watch her paint, amazed how she would start with the antlers of a red deer and then paint the animal from within outwards instead of painting an outline of the animal first. He thought she had more talent than she realized and frequently complimented her.

Often when it was gray and chilly they took insect walks, spending long minutes watching ants or stream inhabitants like water striders. On sunny days they took brief dips in the emerald pool, followed by sunning in their enclosure or sitting next to the stream with their feet playing in the chilly water.

Whenever they left the castle for a sojourn in the glen, three of the chief's professional warriors accompanied them carrying fresh supplies, including steaks of red deer, Ireland's finest meat, containers of home-made beer and a few bottles of Spanish wine from the beaches. In the adjacent cabin Patrick and Riona cooked fine dinners of venison or beef and Irish oat bread which Alana and Francisco enjoyed at their table close to the crackling fire. They slept next to each other on the mattresses, covered by warm woolen blankets. They touched each other but, by mutual agreement, did not proceed further.

Alana had explained her viewpoint during their first visit to the glen. "It is not fair to you and Zabella to tempt you with anything more. I know that you want to remain true to her. I have a strong desire to remain a virgin until I am sure I have met the man of my dreams. Although I have waited many years to make love to a man and eagerly look forward to the experience, each of us must be sure of our feelings before we take that romantic step. To me it does mean a commitment but I don't expect you to feel the same. We can certainly wander and caress and be gentle and loving with each other, which is all new and wonderful for me. I can't imagine, now or in the future, feeling so natural with anyone else. I do hope we can remain strong and resist temptation."

"That is indeed my desire," replied Francisco, "but if my feelings towards you grow, which I anticipate, and we spend so much time together, I may find you increasingly difficult to resist."

One day when they came in from sitting next to the waterfall pool on a cool windy day, the wooden tub was in front of the fire full of hot water. "Come, Francisco, it's time for your Lady of the Glade to give you a soapy Irish bath. Take off your clothes for your loving companion. They both undressed and Francisco was about to sit in the tub when she said, "No, I want you standing. I want to learn more about men and how they function."

Starting with his neck and shoulders, she slowly washed him with a soapy cloth moving tantalizingly over his whole body except the middle. Then she dropped the cloth and concentrated there with her soapy hands. He quickly became aroused. "Are you sure you want to continue this?" he asked. "You are stunningly beautiful and I deeply care for you. I am helpless if you choose to proceed."

"This is what I want to see and feel," she said. "I've waited endless years and I am in love with you. Yes, I desire to do this right now! Tell me how it works and what to do next while you remain standing in the tub."

He showed her what to do and was overwhelmed with her alternating gentleness and vigor. Her skill made him more and more excited until he exploded with an intensely pleasurable release. He was breathing rapidly and his legs trembled. Alana waited a few moments, breathing deeply herself, then said, "Thank you, Francisco, for allowing me that lovely intimacy. I wanted to see more precisely how babies are made. It seemed totally normal between us, everything, as if we belonged to each other. Was it the same for you? I have never been so exhilarated, just feeling your rising excitement and being able to participate as your loving partner."

"Your spontaneous joy continues to amaze me, Alana. My excitement was uncontrollable and I loved watching you concentrate on your exhilarating new adventure."

"While I was loving you, another method occurred to me which I would like to try, perhaps day after tomorrow. Would that be all right? This is an exciting privilege for me, almost like participating in the origin of life in the Garden of Eden."

"Why not tomorrow?"

"Because that is the time for you to bathe me and see what responsiveness you can bring forth from a naive, inexperienced colleen! Shauna tells me that the acme of excitement can keep on happening time after time in a woman and can be quite wonderful."

Thus did Alana and Francisco grow closer in their peaceful wilderness hideaway as time grew shorter and shorter for their togetherness. Both marveled as their feelings progressed and their harmony evolved into something special. Alana was amazed when Francisco told her that their amazing interaction was new for him also. "You didn't experience such harmony with Zabella?" she asked.

"I thought she was the love of my life but it is increasingly clear that I was lonely and became infatuated. She actually told me this herself and urged me not to insist on marriage before I left on the Armada. The more I am away the more I realize she was right. I built her up in my imagination. My imminent departure for war clearly blunted my judgment. Actually I hardly know her. Every time I tried to talk seriously with her, she would distract me with amorous activities, without meaningful preliminaries or any real love between us. There was no meeting of the minds and I realize now that she is almost a complete stranger to me."

They continued their glade retreats, with brief trips back to the castle until only a final weekend remained. After a contented day of language lessons, painting, a long walk and napping in their sanctuary, they were sitting in front of the hearth silently watching the fire's fluctuating flames and sipping *Chacoli*, a sparkling dry white wine from Basque country, when Francisco said:

"As you know, Alana, this month has been fantastic, the happiest of my life, and I am quite sure I am in love for the first time. You make me tingle all over whenever I think of you. I am constantly perfused with the most wonderful feelings towards you. How we restrained our passion for each other is difficult for me to believe. I think King Philip should award me a medallion for heroic self-control which allowed me to succeed in a more difficult task than the arduous sufferings of Hercules in his twelve Labors!"

"I have waited many days for you to tell me that, Francisco. I have felt similarly for the past three weeks. You are the man I have sought since I was seventeen when my brother began to push me towards marriage. I now feel that you are my one true love. I also know that you, being an honorable gentleman, have made the decision, despite your new love for me, to return to Zabella and that you feel you must leave within a few days."

"How remarkable that you guessed that, since we never discussed it. Although I love you beyond my wildest expectations, I do have to return to my marital commitments in Cuellar. I regard myself as a moral Catholic and I must honor my promises. Can you forgive me?"

"There is nothing to forgive. That was our agreement. Your decision in no way destroys my love. Of course I am envious but I honor your decision. It only enhances my love and respect for you. Now, however, I have one final request before we leave our idyllic retreat. I have already asked Patrick and Riona to leave us alone for a few hours because we wanted completely private time. Please get one of the mattresses and place it front of the fire. Then we will both take off our clothes. We will hold hands and continue sipping our Spanish wine until the mood overwhelms us."

"And then?" asked Francisco, breathing more rapidly.

"Since we have now declared our love for each other and have behaved so honorably for so long in restraining our passion, my faerie consultants have happily dissolved all barriers between us and are urging us to join in ecstatic harmony. I want us to make beautiful love together, forever embroidering this exquisite glade and our hearts with indelible memories, no matter what Life's tribulations have in store for us."

CHAPTER 23

Rural Irish Christmas

(December 1588)

The Christmas festivities began on the twenty-fourth of December when the clans gathered at the shore village, arriving by horseback and on foot. Guest of honor Chief Brian O'Rourke, his wife and his retinue rode up from his castle of Dromahaire on Lough Gill, sixteen miles to the southwest. Francisco decided not to mention his brief and humiliating visit to O'Rourke's castle and, fortunately, O'Rourke did not recognize him because Francisco's clothing and physical appearance had changed so significantly in recent weeks.

There were scattered clouds and a cold wind was blowing from the north. A large grassy space between the village and the edge of the swamp was used for the holiday games and contests. The crowds stood about wearing their woolen cloaks or goatskin jackets with some of the women wrapped in woolen blankets. All enthusiastically watched and yelled and filled their wooden cups with beer from barrels. There were wrestling matches between large Irishmen clad only in loin cloths, reminiscent of those early Celtic heroes who went naked into battle. There were running and jumping events, contests between men wading through bogs on stilts and men with balance poles seeing who could remain longest on rolling logs in the cold lake.

A touch of blood was introduced when a pack of greyhounds competed for hares released across the open sward. The crescendo of contests continued as a target of a stuffed man was hung from a crossboard set between two poles. The figure was clothed in a white ruffled shirt, black trunks and black boots. A piece of metal four inches square, a quintain, had been attached to the forehead.

"This is Governor Richard Bingham of Connaught!" cried Mac Clancy. "Hit him between the eyes. The metal must ring! A fat pig to the man who best cleaves Bingham's skull!" This event, with participants attacking it with swords while galloping past, featured the prowess of Mac Clancy's and O'Rourke's gallowglasses. The competition was very popular and a great roar greeted every clang of metal, representing the symbolic death of the abhorred English tyrant who was trying hard to obliterate Irish people and culture.

One could feel the bristle of hatred everywhere against the Sassenachs. Francisco, standing in the crowd, could feel the dark tension and he thought, *Why can't the English leave the Irish and their beautiful Gaelic culture alone rather than trigger endless hatred by constant invasions and cruelty? But where in these Irish celebrations is the Christmas emphasis on love and the miracle of the Christ Child? This seems a strange way to honor such sanctity.*

There was a sudden interruption by new loud shouts. A farmer's cart was dragged by six Irishmen into the open space. In it stood the stuffed figure of a woman dressed in a red silk gown and a purple velvet cape, with countless strings of beads made of wild berries and hips of wild roses looped around her neck. Her hair was made of orange-dyed ropes and in it were loops of beads and a crown of hammered tin.

"Queen Jezebel! Elizabeth the Queen!" The cries rang out in Gaelic and Latin, all accompanied by the hiss of hate. When the wagon reached the center of the grassy space, Brian O'Rourke dashed forward on his horse and speared the figure out of the cart to the ground, accompanied by a great roar from the crowd.

Four of O'Rourke's clan now pushed the empty wagon out of the way while the other two men attached the Queen's cloth body with long ropes to the tail of O'Rourke's horse. There were yells of scornful laughter. Now O'Rourke lashed his horse forward and dragged the Queen across the grassy space. He then galloped back, dismounted and thrust his sword into the Queen's body, eliciting another tumultuous roar.

Now Mac Clancy lined up his mercenaries around the stuffed regal figure. The first blow was his by right and he chopped her head off. Then every armed man took his turn. The Queen was hacked to bits. Francisco realized that this loathing for England and its Queen was fully justified. The English had been killing the Irish and treating them like stupid savages for four centuries merely because they were mostly herders, peasant tillers of an infertile soil, poor and spoke a strange ancient language.

At last Francisco could feel an ebbing of the tide of hate. The gentle sound of singing could be heard. Six monks with lighted torches came chanting through the village. Behind them four monks carried a platform with a statue of the Madonna painted in blue, white and gold, wearing a crown of gold-painted wood and a necklace of colored shells. Behind her walked four more monks bearing a wooden cradle containing a painted wooden Christ child. The Irish were deeply moved by this procession, kneeling as it passed. They bowed their heads and crossed themselves.

Francisco and his fellow Spaniards joined the procession to the little church. The statues were set up on either side of the altar. Rush tapers, burning brightly, were placed before them. A special evening mass was conducted with singing accompanied by a single flute.

When mass was over, Mac Clancy's provisioners distributed sheep and cattle to the villagers for their Christmas Eve feast. Then he ferried O'Rourke, his lady, his chief of gallowglasses and his bard over to the Mac Clancy castle. The rest of O'Rourke's important men followed, along with castle inhabitants.

The smell of roasting beef and mutton permeated the dining hall. Large plates of honey cakes were on every table. The powerful, specially-fermented and distilled wheat drink, *uisge*, known in Ireland since the 1100s, was served along with copious beer and mead.

Fingal Bhaird sang a Praise Song of O'Rourke. Mac Clancy and O'Rourke clapped their flagons together with a clang, sloshing beer down the sides. At that moment Alana's and Francisco's eyes met and each gave the other a slight head movement.

They met at the parapet. In honor of Christmas celebrations no guards were present. Francisco gave Alana a brief but enthusiastic kiss and kept his arm around her. They looked out silently at a nearly full moon over Lake Melvin, two of its shadowed islands in the distance, with sparkling fires and revelry at the village. After a few moments he said, "My comrades and I must be leaving soon, Alana. Come what may, I am so glad I decided to stay the extra month. You are forever tapestried within every fiber of my loving heart."

"So you are within mine, my dearest. With a fervent mind and soul I feel certain neither of us will ever regret our beautiful, enchanted time together."

After a prolonged kiss, Alana walked slowly to the staircase while Francisco gazed at the moon, deeply reflecting on the remarkable twists and turns of Life.

CHAPTER 24

Escape

(December 1588)

With Alana's help, Francisco and his Spanish comrades made their plans. Eight were physically well enough for an escape but only five decided to attempt the hazardous scheme against Mac Clancy's wishes—Francisco; Don Antonio, who was sure he could keep up with the younger men; Pedro Petri, a half-Spanish, half-Italian master of cavalry who could talk of nothing but Florence, his childhood home; and Marco and Zorco, the two Spanish soldiers.

The escape-planners counted on the castle celebrants drinking too much during holiday celebrations, particularly *uisge*, giving them sufficient time before discovery of their absence. The five Spaniards agreed to meet at the parapet in a few hours, at dawn on Christmas day. They were to bring warm cloaks, knives, fishing string and hooks, food and other items they had been stowing away in a special cache since Francisco had decided that escape was their only option.

"Esteban, after we are gone and people wonder where we are," said Francisco in his final instructions, "you are to tell Mac Clancy how enthusiastically I thank him for his immense kindness and hospitality, that I shall always highly esteem him, his wife, his sons and his magnificent sister. When I return to Spain I shall ask King Philip to honor him in some way. If life's unpredictable pathways allow it, I hope to return someday to Rossclogher castle."

Dawn was leaching through the darkness as they climbed down from the parapet on ropes and launched their boat. The morning breeze blew chill across Lake Melvin. They rowed hard against the choppy waters around Promontory Point, avoiding Mac Clancy's village entirely. They were afraid of barking dogs. Francisco remained calm but being a fugitive again brought tightness to his gut. Under a sky touched with dawn's earliest gray, the five Spaniards beached their boat softly on the pebbly sand.

"Now we must walk briskly to the woods," said Francisco softly. "Mac Clancy will likely send his dogs and horsemen after us. He's a good man but one who doesn't tolerate being crossed."

They hurried to the edge of the forest where Francisco scanned the shore of Mac Clancy's village in the dim light. What he saw surprised him. They had apparently been pursued across the lake by a single oarsman. "Let's see what he's got to say."

Francisco said in a quiet voice, "*Benvenutus, amicus. Pax tibi in nomine Christi infantis.*"

"*Pax tibi, Don Francisco, Honoratissimus.*" Francisco recognized one of Alana's servants who had trained for several years for the priesthood and therefore knew Latin. "The Lady Alana wishes you well on this and future journeys. She sends this extra sack of food and a pouch of coins. To Don Francisco she gives this chain and locket as a token of her special esteem."

The man handed Francisco a beautiful old Irish chain of two heavy strands of gold twisted together, from which hung a large ruby in the shape of a heart.

"It is a most beautiful token from a most beautiful lady," said Francisco with constriction in his throat. "Our gratitude and admiration will follow her always." Further words failed him. The servant ran to his boat and rowed back towards the castle.

Pedro picked up the sack of provisions. Francisco hung his new chain around his neck and touched it fondly. They began walking rapidly to the woods. Francisco limped minimally without pain. He told them that if they could get across the River Erne into Ballyshannon they would be out of Mac Clancy and O'Rourke territories and into O'Donnell country where they would be safer.

It seemed strange to be running away from friends into regions of people with variable friendliness and potential hatred. It was known that under new pressures from English Lord Deputy William Fitzwilliam, many formerly friendly and well-intentioned Irish had been handing over Spaniards for rewards or from simple fear of reprisal.

The fugitives moved at a good clip for a mile along a wooded trail in the general direction of Ballyshannon, then slowed to a more maintainable pace. The month's respite had added dozens of pounds to their frames. Although they were dressed in Irish pants, shoes, jackets and cloaks, Francisco knew that their swarthier skin and facial appearance would give their identity away to any discerning passersby.

So far they had met no one on the cart path. It was evidently not the main road from Kinlough to Ballyshannon but, according to the location of the newly-risen sun, it was steering them in the right direction. All their senses were focused on reaching the River Erne before any horsemen of Mac Clancy could capture them. They listened for thudding of hooves and barking of dogs but only the shrill cries of ravens, the scolding of a squirrel and the sudden whir of a startled partridge had stirred the air.

In a few moments their byroad met and joined the coast road from Sligo. Francisco suddenly held up his hand signaling them to stop. He quickly lay down, put an ear against the ground, and said, "Horsemen are coming! Quick, we must hide!"

Marco and Zorco ran ahead and called back, "The river!" Francisco was amazed that their steady pace had moved them almost five miles to the River Erne. In a moment the Spaniards were on the shrubby, steep river bank. A quarter of a mile to the right they could see a waterfall and the bridge to Ballyshannon, too far to reach in time. A hundred yards to the left were eight or ten little boats lying upside down on the beach. They had to get out of sight fast. It was broad daylight and they were easily spottable by any citizen out for a stroll or a fisherman mending his nets. "Under the boats!" called Francisco. "They must be Mac Clancy's men."

They each ran down the beach and crawled under one of the boats. The Spaniards could hear the wild barking of dogs across the river and the sound of approaching hooves. The thudding became louder, louder, then suddenly stopped on the bank above them. There was urgent talking from one horseman to another. There were no cracks in the boat through which Francisco could look. He could only lie still, hoping that none of Mac Clancy's men would check under the boats.

There was complete silence for a moment, then very near a voice called up to the others in Gaelic. The emissary had evidently looked under the end boat and found nothing. Francisco's boat was next in line. He couldn't swim but had noted a small log on the shore. The current in mid-river would be strong because of winter rains but if they could get across they were in O'Donnell territory.

"Ah, hah!" cried the Irishman, lifting up the boat. Francisco seized the man's legs, toppled him and jumped up, shouting to his comrades to head for the river. He seized the man's battle-axe and knocked him out with the flat of the blade. He certainly didn't want to kill one of Mac Clancy's men. He raced for the river, grabbed the log and jumped in. The three Irishmen on the bluff dismounted and rushed down to the river, the second largest in Ireland.

Francisco and his companions headed across the river, straining to make the opposite shore a hundred and fifty feet away. Francisco pushed the log ahead of him and kicked his legs. The first smooth water portion of the river was easy but now he was approaching the stronger current in the center. It was his strength against the river's power as he was swept diagonally downstream. He slowly gained against the swift current and the shore came nearer.

Francisco could hear shouts from the shore. He put his final ounces of strength into the effort and lay gasping on the beach, his mouth open like a dying fish. He turned and saw that no one was swimming after them since it was all O'Donnell territory from the river's mid-line.

It was only now that Francisco saw there were only three of them, including Marco and Zorco. What had happened? Half the answer came as his eyes scanned the far shore. Don Antonio de Ulloa apparently let fear dominate him and he hadn't run to the river. He had been hauled out from under the boat and was being marched up the bank. Poor Don Antonio! Yet he would make the most of it, Francisco felt sure, perfecting his Gaelic, studying Irish customs, fitting in as well as possible. Perhaps he would take an Irish wife and settle down. Francisco could imagine a worse fate than marrying an attractive, vibrant colleen!

After the horsemen had ridden away, the three Spaniards walked along the bank looking for Pedro. There was no sign of him. It was clear to Francisco that the River Erne was sweeping him out to Donegal Bay and the Atlantic, far from Florence which had been in his dreams for so long.

Francisco sat on the river bank with Marco and Zorco. They had discarded their cloaks before jumping into the river. Francisco asked himself, *What is the best strategy now? We have to throw ourselves on O'Donnell's mercy and pray he won't send us, haltered in ropes, to the English in Dublin. Once again we must live on hope.*

They walked up the slope and into the village of Ballyshannon. "We should try to find a priest," said Francisco. "I will be able to communicate with him in Latin and he will more likely treat us with decency and tell us how to find our way safely to the nearest port. Although I learned quite a bit of Gaelic from Alana, I don't feel very confident in my linguistic skills."

The first person they met was an old woman. "Peace to you," Francisco said in Latin to the old woman. He placed his palms together in the steeple of prayer and then crossed himself.

The woman uttered a semi-shriek and cried out "*Spainne! Spainne!*" and clumped away. People appeared from all directions. They crowded in upon the three Spaniards and began to tug at their shirts and breeches. *It's amazing how the Irish believe they have a perfect right to strip any Spaniard naked and steal his clothes,* Francisco thought. *So lovely a culture in many ways but also so primeval in others.* Francisco's coins, chain and locket were now in danger of being discovered.

"No! No!" he cried in as loud a voice as he could muster as he pushed the hands away. "Maglana! Mac Clancy! O'Donnell!" At the mention of those powerful names the crowd gave way sufficiently for the Spaniards to be free of the pawing and get some airspace. By good fortune a man with a tonsured head now appeared at the edge of the crowd.

Francisco called out to him in Latin, "*Pater! Pater!* We are Spaniards with many friends in Ireland—O'Rourke, Mac Clancy, Fingal Bhaird and others. Here as a token of his friendship is a square of green and black cloth given us by O'Rourke's father. We would beg permission of Chief O'Donnell to pass safely through his territory."

The priest came forward and questioned them. After several minutes he consented to take them to O'Donnell who was descended from the family of O'Neill or Niall of the Nine Hostages, a powerful High-King of Ireland in the early fifth century. The chief was not well pleased to be presented with yet another "Spanish problem" which had the potential of putting his clan in jeopardy with the English. He spoke emphatically, the priest translating into Latin his words:

"The Chief says that the English have decreed death to all who shelter Spaniards and they mean it. Therefore, he cannot officially help you. However, he sympathizes with your plight and says you may pass freely through his territory but please pass quickly."

Francisco put his right hand on his heart and bowed. O'Donnell gave a barely perceptible nod and walked to the stable to go on his morning ride.

"We thank you," said Francisco to the monk. "Any chance of acquiring some blankets or cloth to shield us against the cold? We are your Catholic brothers of Spain."

The monk spread his hands apart in the gesture of futility. "We, too, are poor, my brother. The Sassenachs have taken our food, our clothing, our everything. They frequently quarter their soldiers with us and eat and drink all our reserve supplies, never with any recompense. We have already sheltered dozens of Spaniards since September. We can do no more."

After a moment of silence he added, "However, come and warm yourselves by my fire. I will give you and your companions a few acorns and some hot broth of wild onion—not rich fare but perhaps temporarily adequate for simple monks and itinerant Spaniards."

CHAPTER 25

Fairy Tunnels

(December 1588)

Curious villagers stared at the Spaniards as they walked out of Ballyshannon. The three moved at a steady pace for a mile along a dirt road paralleling the river to reach the gray stone Abbey of Assaroe, founded in 1178. They were guests at the Abbey for three days to allow time for any Mac Clancy search parties to dissipate.

It was a cold night but it was time for Francisco, Marco and Zorco to set out again. There was no moon but the pale greenish glow from the shimmering Aurora Borealis added a little light. At the last moment the friendly monks brought out a warm cloak of a fellow monk. "Our brother is dead," one said, "and it has been decided, since our Order is sadly diminishing, that you may have his garment. If slit in half it could make coverings for two of you."

"Thank you, father. It is a gift greatly appreciated. We have almost nothing to stave off these chilly winds," said Francisco. "I wish we could reward you but the Lord surely will."

Francisco asked Marco to hold one end of the garment. Then, taking the sharp knife from his belt, he walked towards Marco while slitting the cloak in half. It was old, crudely woven wool soiled by drippings of many meals. Francisco gave the two pieces to his companions. His own clothes consisted only of a smock-shirt, breeches and simple leather coverings for his feet.

Figure 5. Further locations along Francisco de Cuellar's escape route in Ireland.

The monks had drawn a rough map of the road to Donegal town. For three hours the Spaniards trudged silently along the deserted road. Francisco suddenly stopped and said, "I think I hear men shouting and dogs barking. We'd better get off this trail."

The elevated pathway had been built up out of boggy land. The three Spaniards slid carefully down the ten foot slope trying to feel their slippery way. There were no piles of cut peat to hide behind, no clumps of vegetation, only low mattocks of grass.

The sounds got louder. Francisco could at last make out "Mac Swiney, *aboo, aboo!*"

"It's a foray," said Francisco. "The Mac Swineys of Donegal must be on a clan foray or else they're pursuing invaders of their own territory, O'Donnels probably. Down, men, down!"

The sounds in the road only a hundred feet away were now a loud din. Two groups were doing battle. There were sounds of clubs on metal, metal on metal, loud shouts, oaths and groans.

"Lie like boulders," said Francisco softly.

After a few minutes the loud battle noises began quieting down. There was a final outburst of yelling from the road, a galloping to the south by one group and to the north by the other. Francisco raised his head and watched in the dim glow of the Northern Lights as the last Irish warrior runners disappeared behind the galloping horses.

When it was completely quiet, Francisco, Marco and Zorco made their way mattock by mattock up to the road, then walked carefully to the battleground. Three combatants lay dead and one was groaning. Francisco bent over him and said in Latin,

"Pax pacis. Peace."

"A pox on all Spaniards and Mac Swineys," replied the dying man in good English.

He must have learned the language as a seaman in the English merchant fleet, thought Francisco. Putting his hand on the man's forehead, Francisco said in slow Gaelic, "All of us are one in the sight of our Lord, my brother. I commend you to God."

The man's stare became wider, then fixed. The O'Donnell was dead.

The Spaniards examined the bodies, took two sweaters, a jacket, one pair of gloves, one pair of shoes which fit Marco, two pairs of homespun woolen pants, two daggers and a rapier. Francisco did not regard these acquisitions as an ethical dilemma.

Francisco, Marco, and Zorco made good headway along the road to Donegal during the brief remainder of the night. As dawn brightened, they could see in the distance the clustered huts of a little village. The bogs had ended and along the road grew a number of trees.

"I think," declared Francisco, "it's time to get off the road and away from people. Let's head toward those little round hills and find a place to sleep the day away."

They looked for suitable tree branches and made walking sticks. They now approached glacially-formed ridges the Irish called "drumlins." Realizing how distinctly even in early morning light their dark silhouettes might show against the hill, they walked rapidly around the base to the other side. They noticed that the hill was terraced and that there were traces of crumbled old earth walls. From Don Antonio de Ulloa's frequent allusions to these Irish historical relics, Francisco recognized it as an ancient hill-fortress.

A frightened rabbit scurried across their path into a branch-covered hole under a hummock. Francisco stooped down to investigate. Hacking away at branches with his knife he found an opening large enough to admit a man stooping. "This might prove a good hiding place."

"What? A rabbit hole?" exclaimed Zorco. "Have we come to that?"

"It's not a rabbit hole, Zorco. It's a passageway made hundreds of years ago probably leading to the next hill. Don Antonio told me all about these ancient escape schemes. The Irish country people are frightened of these places, considering them openings into the devil's domains or, at best, into the land of the fairies from which escape may be difficult."

"I'll sleep outside, thanks!" exclaimed Zorco.

"Me, too!" echoed Marco.

Francisco smiled and continued to hack away the brambles with his knife. Finally, he bent over and started to enter. "For God's sake, don't go in," said Zorco. "You might disappear forever!"

Francisco laughed and crawled in. It was cool and dark inside, with a somewhat moldy, earthy smell which was rather appealing. He got up and stooped, walking slowly for about ten feet. Then he felt his way down three steps and discovered a circular chamber about twenty feet in diameter. The tunnel continued through an opening at the opposite end which was taller and one could now walk upright. *A fine hideaway*, thought Francisco. *Clever people, those prehistoric Celts.*

He retraced his steps. His two companions had curled themselves up in the dry grass on the southeast side of the mound away from the wind, each under his new half-cloak.

"What if a shepherd or hunter comes along?" asked Francisco.

"Everything's deserted around here," answered Zorco. "Nobody will come."

Francisco crawled back into the chamber and went to sleep. In the late afternoon he was awakened suddenly by dogs barking. He moved rapidly to the entrance and heard sounds approaching. He shook his companions awake and urged, "Quick! Quick into the hole!"

"We'll be killed down there by the Devil," replied Zorco.

"You'll be murdered up here if you don't follow me! Come quickly." Francisco grabbed Zorco and tried to drag him by his arm but he resisted. Taking his knife from his belt, Francisco said threateningly, "You can betray yourself into danger through your stupidity, Zorco, but I won't permit you to betray Marco and me!"

Terrified, Zorco and Marco crawled on hands and knees into the opening and Francisco followed, placing the briers back over the entrance. Just as Francisco was drawing the last twigs over the hole he could see three large hunting mastiffs and two hefty Irishmen holding guns. *The dogs have been tracking the rabbit,* Francisco thought, *but now they must smell us.* Francisco stood poised to slit the throat of any dog which appeared.

"You'd better go on down the tunnel," Francisco whispered to his companions. Regaining their military courage, Zorco and Marco stood with him, knives in hand. They could see the round hole of the entrance. Now one of the Irishmen kicked aside the brambles, the three dogs barking wildly. The first mastiff rushed in.

Francisco had time only to exclaim, *"Maria!"* when fanged death leaped at him. Francisco caught him in the neck with his knife, falling backwards as the beast landed upon him. The dog rolled off, whined and began breathing deeply. The injured dog lay still for a moment, then heaved itself up and began dragging himself up the steps.

"Let him go," whispered Francisco. "I have an idea. Thinking there's a tusked boar in here, the hunters may soon send in the other two mastiffs. Let's start making weird sounds like banshees in this echoing chamber. They may be scared witless and run away. It's worth a try."

The wounded dog had reached the entrance. There were exclamations, then talking. "Now!" ordered Francisco. "High and shrill. Pretend you are witches of old." He started the cacophony himself with loud eerie moaning. The other two joined in.

There was stillness outside. Then there was a man's loud shriek and yelps of dogs receding into the distance. The Spaniards had a good laugh and crawled along the tunnel to the entrance. The knifed dog had died and was lying in a pool of blood.

"It's twilight and time to head for Donegal," said Francisco, "but let's eat first." He picked up a dead rabbit which the frightened hunters had dropped. He felt in his pocket for the flint which he had brought from Mac Clancy's castle but it had been lost during the river crossing.

"Let's just eat it raw," said Zorco. Francisco's lip curled in distaste but there seemed no other way. They skinned the hare, cut it up and, like Pre-Promethean Man, began to munch it. After the first few queasy moments, the bloody meat slipped more easily down the throat but Francisco could manage only one piece. He gave the rest to his companions.

The three Spaniards now set out towards the road to Donegal, trying to strike it at a more northerly point. "It's very important," said Francisco, "that at this crossroads seaport town we find the exact road that goes northeast towards Ballybofey, the River Finn, Strabane and Derry as shown on the monks' map. Mistakes could be dangerous or even fatal."

As they walked past the dark shape of an Abbey at the edge of town they could see the faint flicker of taper light through a few of the paneless windows. Zorco wanted to stop and ask for food but Francisco thought they had taken enough hospitality from monks. They hurried along the deserted streets, encountering only a stray cat and a wobbling drunk. Padding quietly along in the cold they soon arrived at the edge of town where they found intersecting roads.

"Here we are at last," said Francisco. "To the left must be the road to Killybegs Harbor where some of our fortunate comrades got aboard De Leyva's *Girona* and are now safe in Spain. To the right is our road to Derry and the North Channel which, God willing, will lead us safely back home."

CHAPTER 26

Peace Be Unto You

(January 1589)

The three men hurried along in the darkness and crossed the Eske River bridge. When morning light came they could see the blue of Lake Eske with a beautiful castle near the banks of the river.

"We'll have fish for breakfast," declared Francisco, "and I think I'll be able to start a fire."

"I hope so," said Marco. "My stomach objected to our last meal of raw bloody rabbit."

"You're too finicky, Marco," said Zorco. "Eating is eating, however you do it."

"That's one philosophy of eating," said Francisco, "but I hope you don't choose to be a restaurant chef when you get home!"

They went down to the river where a clump of trees could conceal them.

"Luckily we have fishhooks and some line," said Marco. "What should we use for bait?"

"Let's see whether there are any bugs or grubs under stones or tree bark."

The three Spaniards made a search and finally came up with four grubs and two small crayfish. They baited their hooks but caught only one eight-inch trout. "This isn't worth cooking," said Francisco. They scraped

164

off the scales with a knife, cut the small fish into three sections and ate the segments raw, even Francisco.

"This makes me hungrier than ever," said Zorco. "I told you we should've stopped at that abbey for food. We'll die of starvation soon and it'll be your fault, Francisco!" Zorco's eyes blazed.

"Go your own way then, Zorco, if you don't trust me to lead you into the country of O'Cahan and Sorley Boy Mac Donnell. There's nothing to stop you! Nothing!"

"Who are you to lead us, anyway?" shouted Zorco. He was the son of a ship chandler of Malaga, half-Arabic and emotional. "You are a disgraced Captain who couldn't even lead your own ship! I think it's time for a change." Zorco's hand reached for his knife.

Quick as a flash Francisco's hand landed on Zorco's wrist like a blacksmith's hammer. The knife shot out of Zorco's hand. Seizing Zorco by both wrists, Francisco twisted him to the ground, laid him flat, and pinned one of his arms behind him. Francisco used his free hand to whip his own knife out from his belt. Holding it to Zorco's neck he said sternly:

"This is the one thing which will be our undoing. We are fighting for our lives against huge odds in a hostile country. If we stick together we may pull through. If the Devil divides us, we will surely perish and our bones will whiten this land of misfortune like the bones of our comrades at Streedagh Beach. We must not quarrel. There must be a leader to make decisions at critical times."

"Why you?" The body that lay beneath Francisco trembled with continuing anger.

"You decide, Marco. I resign my leadership. Shall you or Zorco lead us?"

Marco was a blander type than Zorco, older by twenty years. He had served in Don Juan of Austria's campaigns at Terceira and in many other conflicts. "You should lead us, Don Francisco. You haven't guided us home yet but you've done a good job. Zorco isn't thinking clearly."

Zorco became silent. Francisco let go of him and rose to his feet. "Come with me, Marco. We'll hunt for edible plants."

A few moments later Zorco overtook them. "Forgive me, Don Francisco. You may have a limping leg but you're a fine organizer. I'll follow you. I would be a terrible leader and I know it. My temper sometimes gets the best of me but I'll make no more trouble."

Francisco clasped his hand. "Thank you, Zorco. I forgive you for your biting words. These are difficult times which fray the nerves of all of us but please have faith. We'll make it home."

The three men looked under bushes and behind rocks as they walked along the riverbank. Finally they found a few stems of cress which they devoured but which only made them hungrier. From the road above two Irishmen stood looking down at them intently. Francisco had the quick-wittedness to make the gesture of greeting he had often seen the Irish make to one another, a quick bringing of the index and middle fingers of the right hand to the temple. He then whispered, "We're being watched. Don't look up and don't speak. Walk with me slowly."

They walked casually. Francisco even threw in a staged yawn. The two men at the top of the bank conversed for a moment, then walked away.

The time had come to find a place to hide and sleep. There were two sizable hills on either side of the road. Francisco selected the one on the right about a third of a mile from the river. It was a bare hill but there was a thicket at the base which might provide shelter. It began to rain. On close approach they found that there were a number of tall stones standing upright with cross-stones over several pairs of them—the ancient dolmens which he and Don Antonio had discussed several times.

The three crawled under the dolmens to sleep, achieving narrow shelter from the rain. It was a cold, wet early January day. Towards late afternoon the wind died down and the rain stopped. Then a repetitive clacking sound drifted into the consciousness of the sleeping Spaniards. Francisco dreamed of sheep grazing on the Segovian plain.

The sounds came nearer. There was a ba-a-a-ah almost in Francisco's ear. He awoke suddenly and stared into the white face of a ewe gazing down at him. He slowly rose on his elbows. Some twenty-five sheep had already come around from the opposite side of the hill, all large well-nourished animals with somewhat dirty wool coats that puffed out like gray clouds. The creatures kept coming through the dolmens with no dog or shepherd yet in sight.

Francisco tweaked the cloaks of his fellows. Marco and Zorco blinked and sat up. "Sh-sh-sh. Come under my dolmen where you'll be better hidden. Lie low. We may not be discovered and it may not be too bad if we are. The shepherd can't leave his flock long enough to turn in an alarm and what's one shepherd against three valiant Spaniards?"

Marco and Zorco crawled to Francisco's dolmen.

"This makes me hungry," declared Zorco. "I think I'll cut me a sheep from the flock."

"Not yet, for God's sake, Zorco. Wait until we can size up the situation, whether there are one or two shepherds and how many dogs there are. If all goes well, when they start to leave we can try to grab a sheep but have you ever tried to catch one? It's not an easy task."

"They're the stupidest animals on earth," said Zorco. "Who the hell couldn't catch one?"

Francisco laughed quietly. "I've owned a few sheep in my time and have tried more than once to catch a stupid sheep. I can assure you it isn't easy. The Devil gets into them."

Fifty or sixty sheep began to crowd around them and they listened to the sounds of chomping, bleats and the barking of a far-off dog.

At last the shepherd and his mastiff, trained to protect the flock from wolves, loomed around the hill. The shepherd could now be heard talking in lilting Gaelic to his dog. How soon would the dog scent them? It would not be pleasant to be torn to pieces by such a dog or clubbed by the husky shepherd, whose shaggy, hairy appearance and bulging muscles were formidable. The three Spaniards held their breath as man and dog moved towards them, only thirty feet away. The dog lifted his muzzle and began to sniff. All three men pulled knives from their belts.

The dog stopped, its muzzle high as if ready to plunge forward in a bound towards the dolmen. The man, too, animal-like, seemed to be sniffing the air. Then the dog suddenly turned and raced down slope towards the river, barking furiously. The three men leaned up further on their elbows and saw that the mastiff was chasing a pair of gray wolves. The shepherd began to move downhill in the same direction, poking at the lingering sheep as he went.

Now Zorco stood up knife in hand and made for the nearest ewe. With amazing alacrity, betraying the basic kinship of sheep and goat, the ewe jumped with agility and bounded away. Zorco made for another ewe which similarly escaped with ease.

"Come back, Zorco, come back!" called Francisco in a hoarse whisper.

One more try and Zorco gave up. The flock was out of reach and moving away, scuffling down the hill.

"A whole flock of sheep within hand's reach and not a morsel to eat," exclaimed Marco. "A fine provider you are, Zorco," and he laughed. "So much for the stupidity of sheep!"

Francisco smiled as he thought of life's strange ironies. Francisco de Cuellar, former Captain over three hundred men on the Armada's galleon, *San Pedro,* participant in the planned invasion of England, now completely failing to lead two armed warriors to victory in an epic battle against a flock of sheep on the soggy hills of Donegal.

As the sheep, shepherd, wolves and dog disappeared into the distance, it began to rain such a pelting downpour that any thought of continuing their northeast walk had to be abandoned. The three men huddled together under the collapsed dolmen.

"Do wolves come out to prowl in the rain?" asked Zorco. "We'd make a tidy meal."

"Best not to think about it," said Francisco. "We have our knives. Try to get some sleep.

When the rain stops we'll fish again and gather plants. We won't starve."

Francisco slept fitfully, dreaming of wolves encircling the dolmen with topaz eyes, scarlet tongues and large glistening fangs dripping saliva.

It was still raining when they awoke a few hours later. Impelled by hunger, Francisco decided that he and Marco should go down to the river to fish no matter who might come along the road. Zorco would keep general watch. It was now easy to find worms for bait.

"If you don't return with fish, I shall eat worms," proclaimed Zorco.

After two hours Francisco and Marco returned fishless with a few bunches of chicory and wild spinach which Francisco had seen Spanish gypsies eat. Finishing his share, Zorco put his hand over his belly. "Almost worse than nothing," he said. "Any worms left?"

Marco lifted an eyebrow and smiled. "Yes, I've got one here. Still clinging to my hook. Want it? *Buen apetito*!" He dangled the worm in front of Zorco.

Zorco took the worm off the hook, held it up for a second, then swallowed it.

It was growing dark. The rain stopped and the three men left their Neolithic shelter. A few stars shined through breaks in the coal-black clouds. They walked slowly down to the river, waded across and walked along the muddy road. Towards midnight they rested. Marco and Zorco dozed off but Francisco kept his vigilance. Before many minutes had passed he became aware of motion in the darkness around him. Vague shapes, almost as dark as the night, seemed to move in front of him, come to a pause and then shift position. Shadows from clouds? Stray sheep? Wild dogs? Wolves? He mustered his senses, feeling uneasy. The shadows were quiet now, unmoving. His skin began to prickle. He now became aware of a faint animal smell.

"Wake up," Francisco said in a calm voice. "We have company." No response. "Wake up," he said more loudly. "Don't panic but we are surrounded by wolves. Jump up suddenly with me and make a terrific noise. Yell loudly and have your knives ready."

"Jesu," said Zorco, "What next?"

Francisco leaped up and let out a wild roar. His companions yelled. The shadows bounded quickly into the encompassing night. "Danger is our constant companion. They were surely wolves. I could smell them."

The three started walking again, their senses acute. They could see better as the clouds scattered. Every bush or boulder seemed to represent a lurking-place for an unknown danger.

When day broke clear the three Spaniards were at the summit of Barnesmore Gap according to the map Francisco had memorized. The scene spread out before them hardly suggested an environment for misfortune. Below lay two emerald lakes—in the distance the sapphire-colored Lake Swilly, to the right the green-purple Sperrin Hills and to the left the Blue Stack Mountains. Many a brook and river threaded through the valleys. Between the two lakes could be seen the clustered huts of Ballybofey and Stranorlar.

Francisco explained the layout. "Indeed a beautiful view but I'd give every blade of grass in Ireland for a single glimpse of the golden plains of Segovia and my own oat fields."

"And I for the sweet slopes of the Pyrenees," said Marco.

"And I for the smelly docks of Malaga," said Zorco.

"We'll see them all, God willing," said Francisco. "I believe that stretch of blue far ahead is the lake that leads into the sea, Lough Swilly, where the Mac Sweeneys have castles. This should be friendly country unless there are English on the prowl."

They strode down from the Gap and reached the edge of Lake Mourne. "Fish for breakfast!" said Zorco.

They hurried ahead into the thicket on the margin of the lake and paused. In front of them was a man fishing from the shore, with his horse nearby. Marcos exclaimed:

"*Dios. Por piedad!* (Merciful God!)"

"*Ninguna causa por miedo* (No cause for fear)," replied the fisherman, looking at them over his shoulder with an amused smile. He was a handsome young fellow with well-combed black hair above narrow green eyes, aquiline nose and a merry mouth over a deep cleft chin. His blue cloak was of good cloth and the cap over his brow was tilted at a devil-may-care angle.

"Good morning, Don Irishman," replied Francisco in Spanish. "How does it happen that you speak our language so well?"

"Why not? Is it not a good language?"

"Have you been to Spain or did you deal with Spanish traders in Galway?"

The Irishman didn't answer immediately for he was in the process of playing with his long, supple willow rod a fighting fish. Landing the three-pound brown trout, he let it flop on the shore and motioned the strangers to sit down beside him.

"I learned Spanish from my father's guests. We have been sheltering Spaniards since the first galleons went down in Donegal Bay four months ago."

"You must be good at languages," said Francisco. "I wish I could speak Gaelic as well. And what may your name be?"

"I'm Rahan Mac Sweeney of Castle Rahan near Killybegs Harbor."

"Killybegs," said Francisco. "That's where our great galleass, the *Girona*, was refurbished and sailed away with a load of stranded Spaniards."

"Yes, I was there at the time. My father and I sheltered at least a hundred of them and then we helped with outfitting the *Girona* before it sailed."

"God bless you!" exclaimed Francisco, laying his hand on Rahan's shoulder. "I was to have sailed on that very ship but a most unmerciful fate crippled me so that I couldn't get to Killybegs in time. Yet it warms the heart to think of that brave shipload now back in Spain."

"They couldn't be back in Spain yet. I recently visited my Mac Sweeney cousins at dTuath Castle on Sheephaven Bay. The *Girona* had anchored there briefly five weeks ago. After a few days of emergency repairs, the *Girona* sailed out again and my cousins watched her go. They told me they didn't like the looks of her. She was listing a bit and her seams were unstable. Will you have supper with me after I catch another trout?"

Mac Sweeney caught two more brown trout, the second one weighing at least four pounds. He cleaned the fish, brought out his flint and made a fire. He then found three waterlogged sticks, sharpened them, skewered the fish and barbecued them over the fire. He pulled out a number of oat cakes from his saddlebags. The simple meal was aided by cold clear water from a nearby stream. The warm fire and lovely lakeside setting added to the peaceful atmosphere.

The talk was friendly, with tales of adventures from all four. Rahan himself had had many a narrow escape from Sassenach invaders. When the time came for leave-taking, Francisco asked Mac Sweeney's detailed advice for the rest of the journey, including drawing a map on the ground for Francisco to memorize. Rahan informed them that it was mainly friendly territory but there were undoubtedly squads of English lurking around the important harbor city of Derry. Most of Bingham's army had gone back to winter at Carrickfergus near Belfast. However, there were spies in the pay of the English all through the country. Rahan warned them to be very careful with their trust. He also confirmed that the O'Cahans in northeast Antrim were fierce English-haters and so were Sorley Boy McDonnell and his son, James.

"If anyone starts treating you in a hostile manner between here and O'Cahan's fort at Ballycastle, show them this. When you get to Ballycastle, give it to O'Cahan and ask him to send it back to me in his own good time." From a small leather bag that was sewed under the left armpit of his jacket he drew out a ring with the shape of a wild boar carved in black against Connemara greenstone. "It's the Mac Sweeney device," he said. "Everyone knows it well."

"If I lose it or am killed along the way, you'll never get it back. Dare you trust it to me?"

"It would be found and returned. Respect and strength carry weight in these parts."

"A hundred thanks for your kindness. You consider it safe for us to travel now by day?"

"Life is never safe but danger adds spice to the stew of life!" Rahan's green eyes twinkled. He rose, shook hands with all three, wished them luck on their journey, unhitched his horse, mounted, waved again and was off down the road to his castle in its scallop of Donegal Bay.

The three Spaniards felt refreshed as they set out on the road to Ballybofey. Following Rahan's advice they remained wary, trying to avoid settled places with barking dogs and inquisitive adults, any one of whom might be willing to betray them for a few shillings.

They struck through the woods before coming to Ballybofey, turned east until they found the broad River Finn and walked along it through brambles, thickets and slithery banks until in the late afternoon they came in sight of a castle. Rahan had told them this was an O'Neill castle the heir to which, Hugh O'Neill, was being educated at the Court of Queen Elizabeth.

As they stood there wondering what to do, Francisco heard a slight scuffing of stones and a pedestrian came up behind them. He was a tall, distinguished white-haired man wrapped in a dark green cloak. "From the Spanish ships?" he inquired in Latin.

"Yes. We are friends of Mac Sweeney," said Francisco producing the boar ring. "What kind of welcome would we have at this castle?"

"Not tonight, my friends. It is Epiphany and there will be a great feast, probably including self-invited English intruders. I'd keep walking and stick to the byroads. Once you are past Lough Foyle and Limavady you are safer, although Sassenachs have a way of turning up unexpectedly. Make for O'Cahan country as fast as your feet will take you."

He unfastened a small pouch from around his neck. "Here, take this." It was a Scottish gold noble. He laid it in Francisco's hand.

"*Gratias, gratias!*" exclaimed Francisco. "*Deus te benedicat.*"

The old man touched his temple with his forefinger and moved away with dignity.

"Beautiful, isn't it?" commented Francisco, looking at the coin gleaming in his palm.

"Yes, but one can't eat metal," remarked Zorco, shaking his head.

Francisco was worried about Zorco's frayed nerves and fixation on food even though they were by no means starving. He stuffed the shining coin into the pouch with the boar ring. "True but a generous spirit warms one's soul and temporarily diminishes one's hunger. Come, we must go."

"I think I smell meat roasting for the feast," declared Zorco. "I feel like dashing into the castle kitchen, snatching a lamb from the spit and rushing out again before anyone can seize me."

"More easily said than done," commented Marco. "You might find it as difficult as your quest for a stupid hilltop sheep and somewhat more hazardous!"

"How do you propose to get us food this time?" challenged Zorco.

Francisco thought quickly. "Those who aren't going to the castle will be celebrating Epiphany in their own cottages, roasting a goat or pig or duck they've been saving for the occasion. I don't see why you should be hungry so soon again but I'm willing to walk quietly with you into the next village soon after dark, go into some promising-looking house at the far end of the village from whose chimney the sweet scent of roasting meat may be rising, snatch the roast, drop the Scottish gold coin on the table and make a dash into the night. Such an adventure is far safer, Zorco, than trying to attack a castle single-handed, don't you agree?"

"Very well, Don Francisco. Where do you figure the nearest village may be?"

"In about four miles we should reach the River Mourne where there is a village called Strabane. We'd better conceal ourselves somewhere along the riverbank until night falls."

The Spaniards soon found a hideout in a thicket of shrubbery and lay down to take a nap. In late afternoon Francisco awoke, saw that the road was almost deserted and wakened the others. They reached Tyrone County's River Mourne in the afterglow of sunset with the flowing water appearing gorse-yellow. The roadway led along the south bank to Strabane and Londonderry. Marco and Zorco, wearing the monk's half-robes, drew the cloaks up to their eyes when any pedestrians passed by. Francisco walked behind them. There was no misadventure although several passersby stopped and gazed at them with sharply curious eyes.

They walked across the bridge into Strabane, quickly left the road, found a small stream and followed it through bushy entanglements for a quarter of a mile. Then Zorco reminded Francisco that it was time to search for roasting meat. They found the road again and came upon a whitewashed house with a thatched roof. There were two high window-openings at the front and a cowhide door. There was the sound of loud talking inside and from the chimney came the strong fumes of meat roasting.

"Zorco, make a footrest for me with your hands and let me take a look."

Zorco made a stirrup and Francisco looked in cautiously. "This isn't it," he whispered. "There are five burly Irishmen in there, two women and two mastiffs. It's a miracle the dogs haven't scented us. Most houses will be roasting meat to celebrate Epiphany so we should have plenty of choices. We must be patient."

The next house a hundred yards farther was small and simple, with cloth at the windows and the same enticing smell of roasting meat permeating the air. Francisco went close and listened. There was quiet talking. Francisco cautiously looked in. He turned to his companions and whispered, "This is it. There's only an old man and woman, a small dog and a middle-aged woman tending a scrumptious roasting kid. I hate to do this but I think God will forgive us if we give them the gold coin in exchange. It's worth a lot more than the goat. Men, listen carefully: no killing, no shedding of a single drop of blood, not even the dog. We can manage this easily with no hurt to anyone." He explained the details.

Marco and Zorco dropped their cloaks in front of the door. Zorco moved to the left-hand window, the other two to the right. At Francisco's signal Zorco pushed his window open, Francisco and Marco the other, and all three climbed into the room with knives in their hands. The two women screamed, the dog barked and the man reached with one hand for his belt-knife and with the other for a cow-horn that hung over the mantel. Francisco cried out in Spanish to Marco: "Seize the horn while I disarm him."

The horn was quickly snatched away but Francisco had to battle mightily for the knife with the staunch old Irishman and it took Zorco's help to get it out of the old man's grasp. The dog was yapping furiously. Zorco leaned down and hit the dog's head with the butt of his knife.

Francisco said in Gaelic, "We do not intend to harm you. We are very hungry, that is all."

"Could you not," asked the old man with dignity, "have asked for our hospitality? We have made it our policy to welcome strangers, even Spaniards who are living in such constant danger."

Francisco, strangely moved, answered, "We were told this region was hostile to Spaniards. We have faced death many times recently and have learned it is safer to be very careful." He speared the roast kid with his knife, lifted it off the spit and threw the Scottish gold coin upon the table. "We thank you and apologize for the intrusion on this holiday. Come, *amigos*."

All three rushed out, Marco and Zorco stopping to retrieve their half-cloaks.

"*Pax vobiscum*," said the old Irishman as they plunged into the night. There was no alarm from the cow-horn and no shouts of alarm from the house. They ran for a short while before turning along a thicket next to a stream. There was a log at the stream's edge. "We'll use this as our table," said Francisco, depositing the roast kid upon it.

As they ate the meat with gusto Francisco's conscience troubled him. "Little did I think I would ever become a thief. Is hunger a satisfactory excuse for behaving like a criminal? Does paying with a gold coin of far greater value justify our deed?"

"Thieving is less than killing," put in Marco.

"In a way, when you rob you kill," went on Francisco, thinking aloud. "You kill justice and you kill fair play."

"Don't sermonize, Don Francisco. They seemed content with our coin. Now we can enjoy our own Epiphany feast," said Zorco, biting into a tasty brown thigh.

"Yes, we need this food more than they do," said Marco. "There were a few potatoes roasting in the fire and a jug of something on the table, so they won't be starving."

Francisco replied, "But could *you* say to someone who entered your home and stole your holiday dinner, 'Peace be unto you,' as that old man did?"

"No way," said Marco.

"Not I," concurred Zorco.

Francisco added, "That old man almost welcomed us to his table with Christian charity despite our barging in on them with knives drawn. Curious people, these Irish. Just when I am convinced they are savages, they become civilized and we become the savages."

CHAPTER 27

Most Wanted

(January 1589)

The three Spaniards were so full of roast goat that all they could do was lie down and go to sleep. Before dawn they were back on the road. The first hint of gray was in the sky when two approaching figures became discernible. Francisco and his companions tried to slip past but one of the men asked in Gaelic, "Who are you?"

Francisco replied in Gaelic, "The blessing of God be upon you. We are three travelers going to Derry. And who are you?"

There was silence. Then one of the men said to the other in English, "I don't like the way he speaks Gaelic. They look Spanish to me."

Francisco recognized the English tongue and caught the reference to Spaniards. They weren't dressed in military outfits but each wore a sword on one side and a knife on the other. He quickly thought, *They must be part of Bingham's occupying military force who wear civilian clothes with weapons.* He immediately cried out to his companions, "Run for it." Then he drew his knife and plunged it into the chest of the Englishman nearest him, then pulled the blade and turned to take on the other soldier. But Marco, who had not run, had already stabbed the Sassenach in the neck. Both lay in the road, one quiet, one who moaned for a minute, then became silent.

"This finishes us for the road to Derry," said Francisco. "We must make for the sea, heading cross-country. Come, it's getting light. Let's lift the bodies off the road without dragging them. Then let's get out of here."

They left the road and walked rapidly across rocky fields towards a ridge of land. Spiky gorse tore at their travel-thinned leather shoes and scratched their legs but they hurried on. Calculating their direction by the rising sun, the three Spaniards headed northeast straight over the ridge. As they neared the top they went into a crouch to minimize their silhouettes. On the summit there was a cluster of six ancient pillar stones.

"Get down on your hands and knees," directed Francisco. "Look at that crowd of Sassenachs already gathered where we left the bodies."

"They'll come quickly after us," exclaimed Marco. "Soon we'll be hearing the howling of bloodhounds."

Francisco had forgotten about bloodhounds, of which there were many in Ireland. His right leg was beginning to ache. They crawled on hands and knees until out of sight of the Sassenachs. Francisco studied the landscape. Directly below them a small stream ran into a river. The valley was about three miles wide. There was only one small cluster of cottages in the middle of it with low hills beyond.

To walk northeast across these hills might be safer but it would make a far longer journey than walking along the smooth road past several villages to O'Cahan's Ballycastle. Now that they had killed two English soldiers, their primary concern was successful flight from English justice which they knew would take the form of hangmen's nooses or prompt decapitation.

"Come, friends," said Francisco. "Since we've now been able to catch our breath, let's head down the stony slopes and into the cold streams below so the bloodhounds can't follow us."

The three scrambled down the rocky hill. The stream was easy to cross but the larger river was another matter. "We can't cross it here," declared Francisco. "We'll have to follow it upstream, in our desired direction, until it narrows." He looked back up the hill to see whether any human figures had reached the summit but the ridge was bare without any sound of bloodhounds.

They had proceeded for only a mile when Francisco, dropping suddenly to the ground, cried out calmly, "Down, get down. There are men on the ridge." They watched as the pygmy figures hesitated for a few minutes, then disappeared back over the crest.

For the next few days, the Spaniards were busy hiking the northern foothills of the Sperrin Mountains. Berries, plants and roots provided the energy for their steady pace but progress was slow because of heavy rain, mud and slippery rocks. As the January cold penetrated through wet clothes into his marrow, Francisco pondered the implications of now being a fugitive near or at the very top of the English "Most Wanted" list.

CHAPTER 28

All That Glitters Is Not Gold

(January 1589)

It took the Spaniards three days to make the journey through the glen of Dungiven and the hills of northeast County Derry to Sconce Hill, four miles from the northern ocean. To get their bearings, they climbed the tall hill as the sun came up. From its summit they could see the wide blue expanse of Lough Foyle with its opening into the sea, the River Bann to the northeast, peat-smoke from the many little chimneys of Coleraine and a great castle standing on a high cliff over the sea to the east.

"That must be Sorley Boy Mac Donnell's castle, the one I was told he captured in battle in 1565 from the McQuillan Clan who had owned it since the 13th Century," said Francisco. "We should head straight for it. Then, perhaps, we'll have temporary safety."

"Who knows what misfortunes lie in wait for us between here and there," said Zorco.

Francisco replied, "It's well, I think, to thank God for bringing us this far and to hope and pray that He will guide us home. Our brothers on the *Girona* must now be back in Spain and many other Armada ships surely have safely reached home. I judge the castle to be about ten miles distant but the roads along the sea are doubtless thick with English spies. Let's head directly for the castle when night comes but we'll have to keep close vigil for adversaries." The others agreed.

They went to sleep, awakening in the early evening. They set out along a wide cart path which soon merged into a road. People were passing to and fro across the bridge over the River Bann at Coleraine but in darkness no one accosted the three Spaniards.

When they encountered a path leading northeast, Francisco said, "This looks like the right direction but it's hard to tell without moonlight." The way led through woodland. After about a mile they saw a gleam of light and heard a barking dog. A few steps brought them to a small clearing and two huts. Francisco pushed aside the edge of a cloth window sufficiently to see the room's interior. The usual peat fire was flickering brightly. Around it were two middle-aged men, two women and a mastiff. Both men had risen and one of them was holding the dog by the collar. Francisco whispered a report of what he saw to his companions and added, "I think I'll chance knocking but I don't like the looks of the dog. Keep your hands on your knives."

Francisco knocked gently on the door and then gave a Gaelic greeting. The door opened and he repeated the greeting. The Irishman at the door looked at the three strangers with narrowed eyes, then exclaimed, "*Spainne.*"

"Yes, Spanish," answered Francisco in Gaelic. Now he put his hand under his mantle and shirt and brought out the boar-ring which Rahan Mac Sweeney had given him, adding in Latin, "*Amicus meus*, Mac Sweeney. *Amicus.*"

"Ah-h-h-h." The Irishman fingered the ring, turned it over, held it up, evidently found it authentic and handed it to his companions for appraisal. They made a comment in Gaelic and the Irishman opened the door wide and bade them welcome. The dog stopped barking.

Places were made at the fireside benches for the travelers. One of the women went outside and, returning with a crock of buttermilk, took seven wooden mugs from a shelf and filled them. The Spaniards drank heartily. When the mugs were empty, the same hostess looked intently at the three Spaniards, rubbed her belly with a round-and-round motion of one hand, made a zero with thumb and forefinger of the other and made the humming sound of query.

Zorco understood and replied emphatically in his own language: "Ah, *si, si. Nada en el estomago! Nada. Mucho hambrientos.*"

Francisco, laughing, translated Zorco's sentiments into halting Gaelic. The hostess brought bread, cheese and honey and the three men ate eagerly with interspersed thanks. Conversation proceeded bit by bit with Francisco's oddments of Gaelic, a little Latin and hand signs. The host informed them that he was Shaemus Mac Rae and that his friend was Padraic Magarry.

The three Spaniards stopped eating and put out their hands to shake. It was apparently not thought necessary by the Irishmen to name and present their women but the gallantry of the Spanish prevailed. Francisco indicated the two women with a query and they were introduced. Then Francisco presented himself and his companions by name. Now Mac Rae asked:

"*Barca? Galleas? Galleone? Nomen?*"

Francisco named the *Falcon Blanco* and *San Marcos*, made the shape of the prow of a ship with the fingers of both palms tipped together and plunged the prow down. "*En el mar.*"

"*Naufragi, San Marcos . . . San Marcos . . .*" repeated Mac Rae, knitting his brows as if trying to remember something. Francisco was able to make out just enough to understand that Mac Rae had heard of the ship from a Spaniard who had been on it. The Spaniard had stayed here in this very house, an unforgettable young man, so charming, so impudent, so daring.

"What was his name?" asked Francisco.

"It was Sebastian," put in Mac Rae's wife.

Francisco's emotions so choked him that he had to pause. "His last name?"

"He never told us."

When and how did you see this Sebastian? What did he look like? Very dark?"

"Yes, darker than the Irish."

"Tell us how he came here," said Francisco.

Mac Rae told the story, Francisco often interrupting to ask a question in Gaelic or Latin.

Mac Rae spoke slowly, "Big ship, galleass . . . storm . . . rocks . . . wreck."

"Yes, yes, we know all about it. Many ships went on the rocks. Sebastian de Carvajal, my best friend and I went down together in Donegal Bay."

"Not Donegal Bay. Here, here, on the Rock of Bunbois."

"No ship was lost here. We lost one up at Fair Isle, none along this coast."

"*Señor*, I am speaking of recent days. A great Spanish galleass was wrecked under Castle Dunluce only a few miles from here three and a half weeks ago, smashed into pieces on jutting rocks during a sudden violent storm."

"What ship?"

"The *Girona*."

There was a terrible stillness. Francisco covered his head with both hands and cried out that ancient futile disbelief against the irreversible tragedies of life: "No! It cannot be! My God, no."

To Francisco the *Girona* had become a symbol of salvation, a singular triumph out of the disaster of the Armada's unwise adventurism. Some of Spain's finest leaders had sailed away on the *Girona* including Don Alonso de Leyva, son of King Philip and a beloved commander who had survived the shipwreck of his first ship, *La Rata Santa Maria Encoronada*. Also Don Tomas de Granvela, a favorite of the king, and many other great men as well as the group that Francisco had met at O'Rourke's Castle.

Could Sebastian have survived the leap from Staad Abbey to the cliffs below? Had he really reached the Girona, *the ship which I myself had so longed to sail away upon?* "How many survived this wreck," Francisco asked at last.

"Nine men, they say, came out alive. About thirteen hundred dead."

"My God! And Sebastian? Where is he now?"

"James Mac Donnell, Sorley Boy's son, sent him to me for protection. I hid him here for two weeks until the English spies stopped hunting for survivors. Then he went off three days ago to find a ship bound for Scotland. A fine man. God saved him but he does not believe in God."

"I think he believes in God," asserted Francisco, "but he calls Him by another name."

Mac Rae got up from his bench and went to a corner of the room. He dragged over an old sack, lifted it up and dumped the items on the table. There was a black velvet cape lined with red silk. The silk was torn and the velvet was water-stiffened but the red was still brilliant. Francisco wondered whether Don Tomas de Granvela had been its noble owner.

"Gown for my wife," suggested Mac Rae, smiling. There was a velvet cap with a bedraggled green plume. Magarry set it jauntily on his own head. Francisco fell silent as he thought of the drowned Spanish owners. There was a piece of torn Spanish lace from an altar-cloth and a pair of leather boots. Mac Rae turned a stocking inside out and released a medal, half a dozen golden ducats and three gold doubloons.

Francisco picked up the medal. It was the beautiful Order of the Golden Fleece, the shining sheepskin hanging from a sun-rayed blue and gold enameled stone. It was only bestowed upon royalty or high nobility. Francisco realized that it could only have belonged, even in that noble boatload, to the King's bastard son, Don Alonso de Leyva.

"The King of Spain would pay you much money for this," said Francisco slowly in his awkward Gaelic, then repeated it in Latin. "It belonged to the Spanish Commander, Don Alonso de Leyva, son of the King of Spain. Hide it. Show it to no one. If I get back to Spain I will tell our King about it. He will surely send an emissary to buy it from you for a good sum of money."

Mac Rae asked, "This medal is worth more than these golden coins?"

"Much more in itself and for its great sentimental value to the King of Spain. He loved Don Alonso with great pride and love."

"What, then, are these coins worth?"

"These little ones are ducats worth about nine of your shillings. The larger ones are doubloons worth much more."

"Ah-h-h-h, so I am rich, no? I must make sure the Sassenachs don't find out about them."

Francisco, with Alana's heart-chain still around his neck and the coins she had given him still in a pouch at his belt, knew well the irony of coins and valuable possessions in the face of starvation and thirst. Riches were relative, indeed. Looking at the gold coins, he then looked up at the two Irish couples and commented, "You know you have gold, much gold that is not gold."

"Gold that is not gold? What do you mean, *Señor?*"

"You have buttermilk, cool water, bread, honey, oatmeal and edible green plants. You live in a land of great beauty. You have love, family happiness and friendship. Yes, that is gold in a different form."

The four Irish smiled and nodded their heads. "We see what you mean," said Mac Rae.

"Yes," put in Magarry's wife, dribbling the doubloons through her fingers, "but those other things you mention do not shine like this gold."

Mac Rae's wife commented, "Our simple lives do shine. I am content. We do not need golden coins. Perhaps they bring more trouble than happiness."

"Ah, but wouldn't you like to be swaggering in a red silk skirt, red velvet cape and plumed hat like my Lady O'Neill strutting at Derry?" asked Magarry.

"Would I be happier?" asked Erna. "Would the birds sing lovelier to me than in this glen? Would the stars shine brighter? Would Mac Rae love me better? Now, would you, Mac Rae? For then, only then, would I wear expensive clothes."

Mac Rae clapped his hard-worked hand over hers affectionately. "I couldn't love you better, lass." He added to Francisco in Latin, "She's a good girl but sometimes not very practical."

"I advise you to put away the money and the medal. Hide them well. Wait until our King's messenger comes or such time as the Saxon devils are driven out of Ireland and Spanish ships come trading again to Galway and no one is afraid any more."

"May that blessed day may soon come!" said Erna Mac Rae.

"I think God will take care of it eventually," said Francisco. "Entrenched evil is difficult to uproot but ultimately it gets eliminated by the forces of good."

CHAPTER 29

Brief Haven

(January 1589)

For breakfast Erna Mac Rae set down a pitcher of cold spring water, a few heated acorns and three fried eggs for her Spanish guests. It was simple fare but offered with smiling grace. Mac Rae drew a map with his knife on a piece of dried peat indicating the short mile and a half route to Dunluce Castle of which Sorley Boy Mac Donnell's son, James, was now Constable. Sorley Boy himself was over eighty and had moved into a small home nearby with a housekeeper.

James had helped rescue the nine *Girona* survivors and had housed many other Spaniards trekking through the area. Now, however, English General Richard Bingham was intensifying his warnings that any Irishmen who aided Armada survivors would receive harsh reprisal.

Francisco's leg was tender and aching but he limped away with his friends after giving Mac Rae and his wife warm handclasps. They walked the woodsy trail towards Dunluce Castle. Where the trail joined the road below the castle, Francisco went on alone. A single horseman came galloping down from Dunluce. Francisco wondered, *Would this be a castle of destruction or salvation? How easy it would be for that horseman to lop off my head with his sword as he rides by, like a boy flicking off the heads of flowers with a stick.* The horseman said something friendly as he rode harmlessly past.

Francisco continued up a stony path to the castle gate. The entrance was well guarded by twelve soldiers. Francisco gave his greeting in Gaelic, then showed Mac Sweeney's ring and requested an audience with Mac Donnell. The gate guards sent a messenger inside. In his halting Gaelic, which often moved the guards to laughter, Francisco answered their questions while waiting for thirty minutes.

The messenger finally returned saying that James Mac Donnell was waiting at the upper gateway. He was tall and fair-haired with obvious Viking blood. He bade Francisco welcome in fair Spanish and led him up to the main hall. The castle was built on an outjutting rock promontory so windows of this splendid room overlooked sea and shore from three sides.

Francisco began by asking, "The *Girona*, where did she go down?"

Mac Donnell pointed out a shore edged with tall basaltic cliffs. "She foundered against those unusual cubed rocks. Most of the flotsam came to rest along that sandy beach. It was one mass of timbers, rigging, barrels, chests and corpses."

"How did the *Girona* get so far off course? Wasn't she trying to sail directly south to Spain after getting repaired at Killybegs?"

"I heard from those we saved that a day after leaving Killybegs the *Girona* was hit by a strong storm from the south. The ship was heavily overloaded with 800 survivors from the *Rata Encoronada* and *Duquesa Santa Ana*. It was leaking more and more from its seams and the rudder repaired at Killybegs was damaged again. They were being pushed steadily backwards so Commander Don Alonso de Leyva turned her around and headed for the safety of Scotland."

"In the opposite direction from Spain?"

"They really had no other choice," said Mac Donnell. "The leaks continued to worsen so they had to anchor for several days in Sheephaven Bay in County Donegal for emergency repairs. Then they made a run for it and got more than half-way to Scotland when another powerful gale pushed them inexorably closer to our shore. The ship finally grounded on the jutting rocks of Giant's Causeway and was smashed to bits near our castle killing 1300 men, including de Leyva."

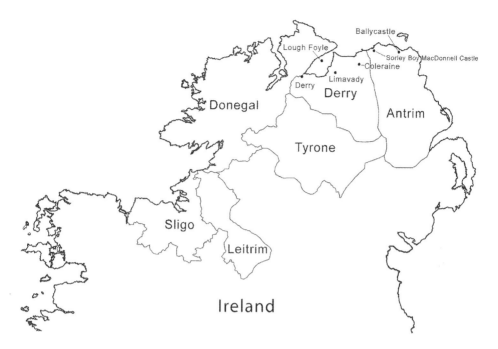

Figure 6. Locations relevant to Francisco's adventures in the north of Ireland.

"My God, what a tragic tale," exclaimed Francisco. *"La Girona"* didn't have a chance. They needed a miracle and God didn't grant it."

"It was a dreadful disaster. We looked everywhere but found only nine survivors although the ship wrecked close to the shoreline. The tempest was a monster which even Finn McCool, our legendary giant, would've had a difficult time surviving."

"On another subject," said Francisco, "I had a dear friend on that ship, Sebastian de Carvajal who may have been one of the survivors. I'd give the world to know if he is the Sebastian you rescued and sheltered."

"He is, Don Francisco, he is. A very likable chap indeed. He has survived incredible misadventures since his first shipwreck on Streedagh beach. It's the Devil who protects him, he says. Having heard his stories, I'm almost inclined to agree!"

Francisco laughed. "Where do you recommend that I and my companions go now?"

"To Limavady in Rory O'Cahan's territory. Rory has a fleet of fishing boats out of Lough Foyle. He's usually willing to run Spaniards over to

Kintyre, Scotland where he has connections. Bring your friends here to recuperate before you head to Limavady."

"Thank you, again, Chief Mac Donnell. We'll accept your hospitality for a day or two."

"You should spend at least three days here. It's hard to imagine what you're going through. You must have had a few adventures yourself, Francisco. You must tell me about them."

"Yes, I may be able to conjure up a few. They won't require much embellishment."

For three days James Mac Donnell fed the Spaniards and fed them well. James declared it was an even draw between Francisco and Sebastian as to the drama of their adventures and the quality of the telling. Mac Donnell promised to return the boar ring to Rahan Mac Sweeney, gave each Spaniard a new cloak, a small bag of victuals and a pouch of shillings. He loaned them three horses and sent them off at night with a mounted escort to Coleraine.

CHAPTER 30

Hilltop Medical Clinic

(January 1589)

The three Spaniards and their armed escorts had already joined the main road to Coleraine when two horsemen came trotting up the highway with a message from O'Cahan that Coleraine was free of Sassenachs. O'Cahan was sending a special ketch to Scotland in the regular fleet of fishing boats leaving at sunset the next day and had room for them.

Hearing the news, army cavalrymen Marco and Zorco immediately put their horses into a gallop. The escorts went after them to bring them back. As Francisco rode on alone, absorbed in the selfish behavior of his comrades, he failed to see a jutting tree branch in the dim light, was struck across the chest and thrown off his horse. He landed with his right leg striking the road's hard rocky surface.

Francisco breathed a sign of relief when he found no evidence of broken bones. His right lower leg wound, however, had opened for a couple of inches and was briskly bleeding. He bound it tightly with his shirt and cursed the desertion by his comrades and the bad luck it brought.

The escorts returned a few minutes later with Marco and Zorco who apologized and helped Francisco mount his horse. They all started off more slowly. The escorts accompanied them to the west edge of Coleraine and then departed, taking the horses with them.

The Spaniards started walking through the hills with Francisco trailing behind and limping badly. Finally he urged them to go on ahead. "The Captain knows we are coming and will put you aboard."

"You think you can make it, Don Francisco?" asked Marco.

"Yes, but only if I go at my own pace. *Adios*, comrades. May God be with you." Francisco watched their shadowy figures disappear into the darkness. He found a stick for support and walked slowly. When pain pulled him to a virtual stop on a particularly steep slope, he decided to rest. He lay down, put his head on a boulder and fell asleep.

Later, through the lattice of sleep, Francisco heard a woman's compassionate voice in Gaelic say "Poor Spaniard." He opened his eyes to a clear cold morning with an elderly Irish woman looking down at him. Francisco spoke the Gaelic words of greeting, "*Bail ó Dhia ort,*" "God bless you." The woman returned the greeting. Her gray hair escaped slightly from under her dark hooded cloak. Her blue eyes were full of kindly understanding.

Francisco pointed to his leg but indicated that he could walk. The woman looked at the leg wound, shook her head and said, "You understand my Gaelic? My name is Gleanna. You must wait for me here. You understand? I will return soon."

"Thank you," he replied in Gaelic. I understand."

Francisco looked down over the sunshine-brightened landscape. He could see the River Bann and the houses of Coleraine with the smoke of peat-fires rising gently from chimneys.

Before long he could hear voices approaching. What if the old lady's menfolk did not share her compassion and would use their shillelaghs instead?

An elderly Irishman with a grinning face appeared and then the slim figure of a woman of about thirty with dark hair, blue eyes and a very pretty face. She smiled at him broadly and said, "Good morning!" in Gaelic.

"Welcome to Formoyle Hill," said the man, "I'm Finian Formoyle that be descended from King Finian of a thousand years ago. But you'd never guess it," he added with a laugh. "We don't live in a palace but you're welcome to our little home in the hills. Gleanna says you mustn't walk anymore so we will carry you up."

Francisco argued the point but Gleanna shook her head firmly. With the father in front and the two women on either side lifting his legs above the knees, they proceeded slowly, with many stops, to carry him up the west slope of Formoyle Hill. It was mid-morning when they decided to rest near the summit. There was a view to the west over the River Roe, Lough Foyle and beyond to the promontory of Inishowen Head. Gleanna pointed out the landmarks to Francisco.

"Do you think I'll ever make it to Scotland?" asked Francisco.

"Never despair," counseled Finian. "Despair is the enemy of God. We Irish have learned that lesson through a thousand years of troubles. A way may come but first you must get well. You are in good hands. My wife and both of my daughters know the deepest secrets of the herbs."

"Tara," Finian continued, "I think it would be better if our guest moved in with you and Keanna while you two provide the care. Your mother and I will take care of meals and firewood."

When Finian and Gleanna had walked away, Tara came close, began to stroke Francisco's face and spoke to him in slow Gaelic. "As you heard, my name is Tara and I am the older daughter. I am twenty-nine and a widow with no children. My younger sister, Keanna, is twenty-two and not yet married. What is your name, my new Spanish friend?"

"Francisco. Thank you for your offer of help."

"We don't often have visitors up here and we regard it as a great privilege to aid you. We have been well trained by our mother who is the best in northern Ireland in the use of herbs. Our healing practices are a family tradition passed down through the women of several generations."

"God clearly wants me here with you. I feel very fortunate."

"All the necessary curative plants are here on the mountain or along nearby streams in the valley. Be confidant in our traditional knowledge. We are in harmony with Nature."

Finian and Gleanna came back with Keanna, a diminutive five-footer with immense charm. She was slim with a very large bust and a face like a lovely porcelain doll. She had the same blue eyes and black hair of Tara, to whom she deferred most conversation. Her timid reticence and beauty were most appealing.

Francisco now insisted on walking, resisting all attempts to persuade him otherwise. With Tara holding one arm and Kara the other, he limped slowly on a path through a thicket of shrubs and small trees. After half a mile they came to a clearing in which was a medium-sized, rustic square house made of wood and clay with a single large stone chimney.

A hundred feet beyond was a small round house made with mud and sticks, with two windows. Inside was a central fire-pit, a table, two wooden benches, a wooden tub and a supply of firewood. A large iron kettle was warming water. It was held over the fire by a large hook hanging by a chain from a ceiling beam. Soft rushes were stacked along the wall next to a pile of woolen blankets. Francisco knew that the round shape of the house, like a bread oven, made it easy to heat with only one or two slowly-burning logs.

"We believe in a simple life up here," said Finian. "It's human relationships and love of nature which provide richness to life."

"But how do you live? How do you manage to eat?" asked Francisco.

"My wife and daughters range the fields and woods for edible plants, roots and fruit. Now and again someone from the valley gives my wife a coin or two for her medicining. We have a few sheep, chickens, pigs and cows, keeping most of them hidden from those who are covetous. When enemies are nearby we lead our animals into an underground chamber built long ago by gods and fairies. Our sons bring home plenty of fish and supplies. We are content and never think of ourselves as poor."

"We are very happy here," repeated Tara, "especially when we are lucky enough to have guests." She put her hand softly on Francisco's shoulder.

Now Finian said, "You will need at least two meals a day to get well, which Gleanna and I will provide. When you have improved, you will eat with us at our home. Tara's and Keanna's herbs and poultices will get you well but it may take awhile."

After the parents had left, Keanna added more firewood and moved the empty tub next to Francisco which she filled with hot kettle water, adjusting the temperature with cool water from buckets. Tara put reassuring hands on his chest. "Trust us and our ways, Francisco."

Tara and Keanna slowly removed all his clothes and gently bathed him, handing him the soapy cloth to wash his private areas. They examined his wounds carefully. "Did you injure this leg in the shipwreck?" asked Tara. Francisco gave detailed descriptions of his wounds including the initial powerful crush injury followed by the knifing and subsequent fall from the horse.

The two young ladies heated flax, nettle and mistletoe plants next to the fire and mixed them onto a piece of white cloth they had boiled. While Tara wrapped the herb bandage around his leg and tied it on with strips of hide, Keanna chanted a brief incantation in Gaelic:

"In the name of our sun's ancient healing powers and those of our moon woman, may the wisdom of nature cure you."

Putting a blanket over him, Tara said, "There is a good deal of crushed muscle tissue, some of it deep and some of it infected, next to the large bone in the front of your lower leg. It is not a simple case of lacerated skin. Fortunately, the bone itself doesn't appear to be infected. We must prevent that at all costs or you could be crippled for life. You must be prepared to stay with us for some weeks. Rest, herbs and our care can heal you if you are willing to give Nature a chance."

CHAPTER 31

Colleen Healing Power

(February 1589)

Every day, Francisco received a slow total body bath by Tara and Keanna, which he found quite enjoyable. When he became excited, Tara told him that nothing about life should be embarrassing and just to enjoy the bathing process. At those times, she often turned over the bathing duties to Keanna who seemed very fascinated and, at times, got quite creative.

After changing the right lower leg bandage and removing small bits of dead muscle tissue, Tara or Keanna added new herbs and assured him they were pleased with his progress. Sitting around the fire, they spent several hours every afternoon and evening discussing their life experiences, good and bad. The only item Francisco held back was his glade-time with Alana.

Tara had short, curly black hair, brown eyes and a very attractive face with a smile and twinkle in her eye which added allure and charisma. She was tall, trim, an easy conversationalist and enthusiastic about life. She described how she had waited to be married until twenty-three. She then married her sweetheart of five years, a local fisherman with whom she became immensely close— "as one." Their love life was excellent, often with intimacy twice a day. He and his boat disappeared in a storm four years later. She had been celibate for three years, not desiring any interactions with men. She had resisted the few opportunities for marriage, all from older men.

Keanna, more beautiful and more shy, said that she had spent minimal time with men and had refused several offers of marriage. The best men were already married and she had few opportunities to meet any new men unless she moved to town and engaged in a lifestyle which didn't appeal to her.

"All the young men drink too much and don't treat women with respect. They talk to you briefly, then want to hop into bed. My friends tell me that once they have sex with you, they expect it every time they see you and tell all their friends how easy it is to get you into bed. And they constantly reek of beer. No thanks."

Keanna admitted to kissing "two or three men" but only out of duty and without enjoyment. She was a virgin but was beginning to be overwhelmed by feelings of yearning. When Francisco asked her about the daily bathing process she admitted that touching him every day, sometimes intimately, was stirring forth new feelings which she was finding difficult to control. At which Tara smiled broadly and said, "Amen!" All three laughed loudly.

That evening, Tara gave wooden cups to Francisco and Keanna and filled each with home-made *uisge* given to them by friends. Keanna added a couple of logs to the fire and they talked for two hours, refilling the cups twice. As the logs burned down, Tara sipped her *uisge* and said: "Francisco, may we talk freely with you without any barriers?"

"Of course, especially if you refill my cup one more time!" She did.

"Our first four days have gone well but we must now move into a different phase. We know that you won't get well properly unless your mind heals at the same time as your body. There is clearly disharmony within you. You have been apart from your wife for a year and are trying hard to remain true to her but your body is paying a price. Your systems are out of synchrony and this is holding back your leg's healing."

"You may be right," said Francisco. "Inside I am not at peace with myself."

"Keanna and I are both out of harmony also," continued Tara. "I became used to intense, immensely satisfying romancing for four years with my husband. Now I have done without love for three years and I am beside myself with missing it. Keanna has never experienced passion but knows from me what it is like. After being with your naked body for several days she doesn't want to wait any longer, nor do I."

"Tara is right, Francisco," said Keanna." I have been shy far too long. If you approve, I want to make love with you very soon. I feel ready to burst!"

The room filled with silence until Francisco said, "Perhaps we can all think it over tonight and discuss it further tomorrow. I would like to remain true to my wife but I am conflicted."

"Raise your cups," said Tara. "Here's to the three of us and may we all become harmonious in body and mind. We will lie close to you tonight, Francisco. Let's all feel free to wander but we will withhold complete intimacy until we make our mutual decision tomorrow."

Tara and Keanna then took off Francisco's clothes and their own and lay on either side of him under overlapping woolen blankets. They kissed him, their hands meandered and their legs moved restlessly but final barriers were not passed before they drifted off to *uisge*-enhanced sleep.

The next morning after a breakfast of oat cakes grilled on a hot flat stone, served with honey and buttermilk, Francisco spoke to Tara. "Tell me more about your treatment methods."

"Thank you for asking, Francisco. Beginning at the age of ten, my mother learned about herbs from her mother. They would go on walks and Gleanna not only learned how to identify plants but also was taught their medicinal uses passed down for many centuries by our Celtic ancestors. We have been applying several plants to your wounds. After initial treatment we shifted to chamomile, crushed elderberries and dried elder flowers for your muscle infection and we removed pieces of dead muscle tissue which were making the infection worse. Muscles are usually resistant to infection but your wound was untended for too long. If it hadn't promptly started to improve, we were thinking of pouring *uisge* into it, which Keanna and I, on our own, have found useful in several patients. We are now beginning to add St. John's wort, flax and lavendar oil to increase the speed of healing . . . but you are beginning to look skeptical."

"No," answered Francisco, "but in Spain we seem to concentrate on instruments and bleeding. The art of plant usage seems to have disappeared long ago except among the Basques."

"That's unfortunate," commented Tara. "Plants have wonderful curative powers and represent the accumulated knowledge of millennia. For instance, dandelions and tea made from willow bark do wonders for fevers. Foxglove is very effective in treating heart weakness. Wild strawberry is useful for coughing and sore throats."

"But the diagnosis obviously has to be right."

"Of course," said Tara. "That's not only a special gift but takes long experience and training. Gleanna is exceptional; Keanna and I are still learning. Gleanna is also unusual because she has tried to expand her traditional knowledge by experimenting with new combinations of old plants. She also tries new plants. If a person has two wounds, for instance, from battle or animal attack, she will try a different herbal treatment on each wound to see which heals faster. Thus she is constantly improving her range of treatment options. Her reputation has spread far and wide. People now come long distances to see her in our mountain retreat."

"How about the mental side of healing which you have also emphasized?"

"One doesn't have to be a trained healer to know that a patient with a peaceful mind and harmony of soul heals faster than one with troubles and worries. You agree, don't you?"

"I never thought about it because I have always been healthy," answered Francisco.

"You seem happy here but your body is tense because of your bad experiences in Ireland and your inner tensions because of long absence from your wife. You not only feel comfortable with Keanna and me but you also like us, don't you?"

"I certainly do. You are both most attractive and appealing, not only beautiful but so full of the joy of life. Do you both really need me to relieve your inner tensions?"

"Yes, Francisco, we do. We are both very romantically frustrated women who need intimacy badly to restore us to internal harmony. We both like you very much and we love your body. We crave to become part of you. You have tried to resist the urges we bring out in you but we are your healers. We insist that to get well soon and get out of Ireland alive you must follow our advice to cure your mind and your body at the same time. We are a vital part of that process and all three of us will benefit. We will give you a few more hours to think it over."

That evening after dinner, after more *uisge* around the fire, Tara said to Francisco that, to make his decision easier, she and Keanna had made it for him. For him to heal properly and for all three of them to achieve inner harmony they would make love with him every night. Tara would be his only lover for the first two nights while they learned what pleased him. Keanna would watch by firelight. Tara reminded him that for his leg to heal, he must remain lying on his back. His main job was to work on rebuilding his endurance to prolong their interaction. Tara said she knew several tricks and would be a good teacher.

Keanna would then have him to herself for three nights since she had a lot to learn. After that, one of them would spend intimate time with him in the evening and one in the morning. Tara insisted that every fourth day over breakfast the three of them would participate in an uninhibited discussion of their interactions, including negatives and positives. She said she and her husband did that throughout their marriage and it had played a vital role in their achieving such a happy romantic life. She knew many couples who had never discussed intimacy in their entire married lives and their relationships had suffered.

After the first week Keanna said that she was benefiting markedly not only from the intimacy but also from the discussions. She was beginning to change from a reserved and passive participant to an active and enthusiastic one. She had just begun to experience repetitive responsiveness which amazed her and she wanted more. Francisco assured Keanna that he felt privileged to witness her rapid flowering and that he was also rather astounded with his own abilities with such beautiful and talented women who never seemed to tire of him. Both girls patted him on his shoulders and smiled broadly.

Keanna then expressed her worry that she would never again find a man who showed such genuine concern over her happiness. She dreaded marrying someone who would just use her body without ever paying attention to her own personal needs and would then roll over and go to sleep.

Gleanna checked Francisco's right leg wound every three days and said she had never seen such rapid healing. She told Tara and Keanna that whatever they were doing, to keep doing it. After two weeks, Gleanna insisted that the three of them walk over to the parents' house for meals.

She also encouraged Tara and Keanna to initiate rehabilitation. She told Francisco to begin walking slowly with help from the girls, not yet putting full weight on his right leg.

The girls took turns strolling with him on longer and longer walks each day despite frequent rain. They also started him on a program of lifting and doing slow squat exercises with heavier and heavier stones in his arms. Francisco also insisted that he no longer be restricted in any manner in their nighttime positionings and creativities. The hilltop colleens concurred, agreeing that this would broaden and improve his rehabilitation and enhance the final stages of healing.

Sometimes Francisco felt guilty when thinking about Zabella but he thought about her less and less, realizing how little he really knew her. He now doubted that he had ever loved her at all. He knew that he truly loved Alana. His rapport with Tara and Keanna should be regarded as special bonding outside of the definition of love—a unique, imaginative, Irish type of therapist-patient relationship fueled only by a mutual desire to enhance healing.

Francisco often shook his head in amazement at Life's unexpected twists and turns. At such times he usually found himself smiling.

CHAPTER 32

On the Run Again

(February-March 1589)

Towards the end of February 1589, waves of strength began to course through Francisco such as he had not known since he had left Cuellar in full vigor to join the Armada in April of 1588, almost a year before. After three weeks, Tara and Keanna kept him without poultices during the day but applied bandages at night with new combinations of herbs. His skilled practitioners continued to bathe him daily.

He was impressed with his rate of healing and his level of happiness in this remote hilltop retreat so far from the pressures and hostile interventions of civilization. Why didn't physicians in cities pay more attention to the role of the mind in healing? Francisco loved the simple, warm, cozy home without any luxuries. He particularly enjoyed the nocturnal lamentation of the winds which he playfully interpreted as Irish fairies pretending to be wolves. Once in the middle of a full-moon night when he was outside for reasons of bodily needs, he saw several wolves sitting on a nearby outcropping, howling plaintively while silhouetted against the moon.

Francisco found great pleasure and satisfaction in his daily intimacies with each girl—so genuine, frolicsome, natural, experimental and just plain fun without any hang-ups or reticence. He himself had never experienced so much mutual joy in physical romancing. Their interactions got better and better without any pressure to fall in love. All three were acutely aware of the time-limitations and were determined to maximize their mutual pleasure.

One afternoon Francisco noted a sense of restlessness in the household and asked Finian about it. Finian told him, "After being held up by foul weather for almost three weeks, the fishing fleet is finally going out, including the boat with the Spaniards. We're going to walk to the ridge and watch them for a time. Our three sons, as I told you, are aboard."

"Would you let me walk with you to the ridge? I'm supposed to be on that boat."

"We agree," said Tara. "Get up and start walking slowly by yourself with your walking stick. It is time for you to begin taking longer walks by yourself."

"God bless you!" he said as he stood up broadly smiling. There was a now a hint of spring in the air. When they reached the ridge they could see the fleet of twenty tiny fishing ketches in the distant sea, due west. The light of the sun caught the sails, some of which were red.

Once again, as at Bundoran, Francisco felt the gut-ache of the stranded mariner who sees the rescue ship sail past his remote island. He was happy, however, that Marco and Zorco should be on that vessel along with five other Spaniards. "God guide them home!" he said aloud.

The fishing fleet now made a wide curve to the northeast past Inishowen Head and into the North Atlantic. Leading it like a scarlet ibis was the carmine-sailed, sunset-hued ketch of Turlough Formoyle and his Spanish guests.

Nine days later the tall sons strode into the hilltop Formoyle home with their cloth bags full of salted fish. They also brought a sack of French wines picked up at the port of Ayr in the Firth of Clyde. The sons were very impressed with how well Francisco looked. They congratulated their sisters, including smiles and pats on the back.

Francisco quickly asked, "Did my two travel friends, Marco and Zorco, get aboard?"

Turlough confirmed their presence and said that the escape had been singularly uneventful. No one gave chase. The winds blew fair and the ship reached Ayr, a hundred miles distant, in the mists of the second morning. There was some haggling over the seven Spaniards but a little money to port authorities overcame the obstacle. Turlough and his boat then rejoined the other ketches at the fishing grounds with good results. No use squandering time in Scotland. "It's a dour country, all stony gray. Not green like Ireland with a heart as soft as moss."

"And how are the girls?" asked Tara.

"Not our kind, either. They look at you with aloof eyes and hardly a twinkle. Not full in the face, laughing, like our colleens and their breasts are flabby, as if they rarely eat."

There was laughter and a filling of mugs with wine. Francisco felt totally comfortable with the Formoyles. He wondered how many were aware of the nature of Tara's and Keanna's comprehensive body and mind treatment program but after awhile their knowing winks gave them away. *I don't care. I am getting well in a hurry and everyone is happy. There is too much secret-keeping in civilized societies. The Irish, with their simple, fun-loving, straightforward ways know how to be joyful and laughterful despite meager worldly goods.*

Francisco looked towards Tara and Keanna. Both had their eyes fixed on him and were grinning as if they knew exactly what he was thinking and in a short time they would confirm it.

Francisco had been working intently on his Gaelic language skills with the help of Tara and Keanna. The brothers were impressed with his improvement. At dinner one night Francisco asked whether there were any other known Spaniards hiding out in the district.

A handful of Spaniards, said Shawn, had just been captured at Derry. There was among them a certain important Don Alonzo de Lucon who would, rumor had it, be held for ransom. What would happen to the other poor fellows, God only knew.

"And yes," Shawn went on. "There are still a few Spaniards holding out in the hills between Limavady and Derry, a shrewd group whom the Sassenachs find impossible to locate."

That sounds more like Sebastian, thought Francisco.

"But the hell of it is," declared Shawn, "that with the English soldiers and spies passing continually along the coast between Derry and Coleraine, O'Cahan has finally declared this business of shipping Spaniards has too much death in it. 'I'm not going to run any further danger of turning carcass for anybody,' says he. However, he's your best chance. When you're ready to go, I'll escort you down to his castle in Limavady and have a word with him. He's been known to change his mind." Gleanna told her sons that Francisco should be ready to leave in about a week.

As the time of departure approached, Francisco and the two sisters became more quiet and reflective during their morning and afternoon walks. Their interactions at night and in the morning were even more intense, as if they couldn't get enough of each other. Their eyes never misted up. Francisco was all smiles, knowing that he would always look back upon their time together as unusually harmonious and happy, to be tasted frequently in the recollection.

A few days later, Francisco told everyone that he felt ready to travel. Gleanna agreed. He kissed Tara and Keanna fervently, telling them, "You will be close to my heart forever. I will remember you fondly 'til my dying day."

The incredible openness, honesty and unrestrained sharing with Tara and Keanna made his brief relationship with Zabella seem shallow and almost completely uncommunicative. Francisco wondered, *Are these natural, expected doubts between two people who have been apart for so long or am I exaggerating them? Had Zabella herself been right all along that I was just infatuated with her, like a college student's first romance? Regardless, she is my wife and I must return to her and work on any problems which become evident after our reunion.*

He thanked Finian and Gleanna profusely and hugged them fondly, telling them that they had given new meaning to his life. Over their objections he gave them the leather pouch of coins from Alana which he had been saving for a special occasion.

He and the three brothers started off down the hill, Francisco noting with relief that he could keep pace with the long-loping Irishmen without any pain. His legs felt sturdy, strong and normal. Instead of praising God, he praised the remarkable skills of the three Formoyle ladies. The ten miles to O'Cahan's castle were easily accomplished. He was no longer a naked outcast. He looked well-fed and even somewhat well-groomed, for Gleanna had washed his outfit and woven him a blue cap and blue woolen scarf.

Francisco and the three brothers came to O'Cahan's town of Limavady just before twilight. A number of women and girls were sitting in the doorways of their homes, knitting or making lace. They all looked up and greeted the Formoyles who were well known in the district. There were smiles and eye-flashes for Francisco, too, which meant that he must finally look healthy.

"What chance is there to see O'Cahan, Mistress Tully?" asked Shawn of a woman seated at a cottage door with her two daughters. "Is he at the castle?"

"Yes, but they're gathering and preparing for a foray tonight."

"I'd appreciate a word with him," said Shawn. "He knows me well. You stay here, Francisco. Mrs. Tully's a good woman to stay with and so are Ethne and Eileen," he added with a wink and a laugh as he strode away, his brothers following after.

Francisco got along well with the two friendly daughters who were much surprised by his Gaelic. His facility was such that he was now working on the lilt and rhythm of the language, so different from Spanish. He could now understand much of what was said around him although his vocabulary was still very limited.

In an hour Shawn returned to say that O'Cahan stoutly refused to talk with Francisco. He was through with Spaniards. The danger had become too great and he would no longer put his career, his life and the life of his clan in jeopardy. Let all Spaniards leave his territory with his and God's blessings but the sooner the better.

The Formoyles had all decided to go on the night's foray. "Goodbye, Francisco, from all the Formoyles," said Patrick, the youngest brother. "Luck be with you!"

Mrs. Tully said, "Never have a worry, *Señor Francisco*. From our perspective, God sent you to us. You can roll up beside our fire as long as you find necessary. Step inside now. When O'Cahan and the boys come along, it's best you not be seen. I already hear them."

In a moment O'Cahan and some twenty others came riding by. Behind them ran the usual twenty or thirty swift-running Irishmen who carried pikes, battle-axes, swords, knives or peat-cutters. Some even carried bows and arrows or even slingshots. It was as motley a crew as one could imagine, knit together by clan loyalty, a sense of adventure and opportunities for pillaging. As they went by, they shouted for the benefit of the women left behind in the village, "*Farrah! Farrah! Aboo, O'Cahan, aboo!*"

In honor of Francisco, Mrs. Tully wrung the neck of a chicken, roasted it over the fire and offered it with fresh buttermilk and hazelnuts. It was a laughing meal. Ethne and Eileen flashed their come-on blue-green eyes at him. Francisco was gallant but did not respond to their ocular invitations. He felt it was time for a break from colleen charms and insistences.

After two rounds of very strong *uisge*, everyone felt ready for sleep. Francisco undressed, pulled a woolen blanket over himself near the fire, closed his eyes and was asleep immediately. He dreamed that a well-formed, naked Irish girl lifted his blanket, moved alongside him, got him excited and caressed him intimately in several ways during the night and did something else which he couldn't remember but he awoke in the morning with a relaxed smile.

The family was up with the dawn and the chickens. Mother Tully stirred the fire to prepare a pot of porridge. The girls set out wooden bowls on the table. Eileen fetched a ceramic container of buttermilk which was cooling at the spring. As she filled Francisco's glass, she gently touched his shoulder and kissed his forehead.

Then they all heard the thudding sound of hooves as Eileen's voice rose high with the melody of "Dark Rosaleen":

> Oh, my dark Rosaleen,
> Do not sigh, do not weep . . .
> There's wine from the royal Pope
> Upon the ocean green;
> And Spanish ale shall give you hope,
> My dark Rosaleen . . .

"That song with our original words is a signal that the Sassenachs are coming," explained Mrs. Tully. "Here, Don Francisco! No time for escape! Quick! Sit on this stool facing the fire and don't turn around." Mrs. Tully pushed the table far away from the fire and moved the bench up to it. Francisco did as he was told, wondering what this new crisis would bring.

Two English soldiers rode up and got off their horses. Eileen was waiting at the door. They chucked her under the chin and, without knocking, pushed past her. Mrs. Tully gave the Gaelic greeting. She had already set down two bowls of porridge and motioned the Englishmen to sit down with their backs to the fire and eat. As the English sergeant came to the table, he put an arm around Ethne, looked over her shoulder and saw the sitting figure of Francisco.

"Good evening," he said in English, spinning Francisco around by his shoulder.

Francisco, every nerve alert, saw that they were both young, the plain soldier beardless, fair-haired and handsome, the sergeant slightly older, black-mustached, with a small chin-beard and sharp black eyes. They wore light metal breastplates over their uniforms, leather head-pieces and carried pistols and swords.

"Good-evening!" answered Francisco in Gaelic.

The sergeant gave him a piercing look. "Spanish," he said.

Francisco's thoughts were racing. He remembered what Shawn had told him of a group of Spaniards that had recently surrendered at Derry. He summoned what English he could:

"Yes. Spanish. I am a soldier of Don Alonzo de Lucon. I could not keep up with the company that surrendered at Derry. I have been badly hurt and not able to walk." He pointed down the length of his recently healed right leg.

"We will get a horse for you and take you all the way to Dublin but first we must gather up a few more Spaniards who are hiding in the hills. There's a Sebastian Something-or-Other who's been causing us a lot of trouble and a Don Francisco de Cuellar. You wouldn't have heard of either of them, I suppose?" The Sergeant looked at him malignantly.

At that point, Mrs. Tully repeated her invitation to eat, pointing to the bowls of porridge. They sat down facing the fire. "You sit here, Don Pedro," said Mrs. Tully to Francisco in Gaelic, indicating a place at the end of the table. "And you, Ethne and Eileen, sit close to the Englishmen and be nice to them."

Mrs. Tully brought two large wooden mugs filled with beer and set them in front of the Sassenachs. Francisco was thinking tactically. If he were taken to Dublin, there was small hope for him. He felt a small kick on his left shin by Mrs. Tully and looked up.

The Englishmen were drinking beer at a great rate, with Mrs. Tully constantly filling their mugs. They wiped the froth and porridge from their mouths and began to put their arms around the girls. The girls looked at their mother who urged them on with affirmative motions of her head.

The girls leaned over and began kissing the men. Mrs. Tully gave Francisco a vigorous nod.

Francisco waited for a particularly strong embrace by the girls and carefully but quickly made for the door. He decided that stealing one of the horses would commit him to larger paths and roads which would be unwise. Once outside, Francisco ran through the village. The local women watched him and one called out, "Run, Spaniard, run, and God go with you!"

Knowing that Sassenach riders would soon come galloping after him, he plunged into the forest glens that surrounded O'Cahan's castle. Francisco moved at a rapid walking pace up and down steep slopes, stopping only briefly at streams to take a quick drink.

How brief a respite from the often-malevolent fortunes of Providence, he thought. *It's the old unending flight from forces of potential harm and death.* As he walked through the whitethorn and blackthorn bushes, he wondered again whether he was doomed to roam forever, eternally seeing the sails of rescue ships disappearing into the sunset. *Wandering Odysseus. Wandering Aristeas. Wandering Francisco de Cuellar.*

CHAPTER 33

Salamanca Class Reunion

(March 1589)

Francisco walked over hills and through dim glens in the late afternoon. Trees and shrubbery began to thin and newly-green meadows opened up. He was not enamored of Ireland's rainfall but he did like the smell of wet grass which Donel had been able to identify while the ship was twenty miles offshore.

Francisco now felt temporarily safe from pursuit. He identified due west from the setting sun peeking behind orange and pink clouds. He must now once again hide by day and walk by night while looking for the rumored group of hiding Spaniards, hopefully including Sebastian. He could see no huts, cottages, roads or trails. He went back into the woods and hunted for nuts and watercress. He only found some bitter green sprouts.

He sat down next to a stream and watched a fox scamper out of the woods. He lay down, drew his cloak over his tired scratched body and went to sleep. In two hours began that gentle Irish sprinkle which is half mist and not acknowledged as rain. At about midnight he awoke and knew he must get moving again. Clouds in the north began to shred and the Big Bear put his paws through.

In the early light of morning he saw a body of water before him. He had to wade through a waist-high river to get to it. As he worked his way along the lake, he saw a herd of cows being led down to the water by two drovers. Hoping they were too young to have malice towards Spaniards, he approached and gave them a Gaelic greeting.

"Where do you come from?" asked the older boy, a good-looking fellow with a quick smile.

"Just now from O'Cahan's town," said Francisco.

"And before that, Spain, perhaps?"

"Yes, a long time ago. I'm thoroughly Irish now!" The boys laughed and seemed friendly.

The older one spoke again. "I'm driving these cattle to O'Cahan's castle. The Chief's coming back from a foray with a big feast scheduled for tonight. He told me to bring him a couple of animals in case the foray wasn't successful. What are you doing in these parts?"

"Trying to escape from Sassenachs. When you're at the village near the castle would you mind finding out what became of the two English soldiers from whom I escaped? And if you see Mrs. Tully, please thank her for saving my life."

"Of course. Good excuse to get to know her daughters better!"

"What's your name, lad?"

"I'm Michael Campsey and this is my cousin, Clandy. And what may your name be?"

"It's Don Odysseus. How about letting me have a squirt of fresh milk? I'm ravenous."

"All right but I haven't any jug. You'll have to drink while lying on your back."

Francisco lay down near the cow that Campsey pointed to. With expertise the young herdsman squirted warm milk into Francisco's mouth. When the milk splashed over his face, they all had a good laugh. When the stream of milk came to a stop in a few minutes, Francisco clapped his benefactor on the shoulder and thanked him for his local brand of *uisge*. They all smiled.

"Where are you heading for now?" asked Michael.

"Lough Foyle, to look for a boat heading for Scotland."

"Risky business. A lot of spies and Sassenachs in these parts. Better go up the hill and talk to my father. He knows a fellow who has helped a lot of Spaniards."

Francisco couldn't believe his luck. "I would love to do just that."

"Clandy will take you to him when he herds the cows home this afternoon. Our families have been hiding out from the English for two years." Michael cut two steers out of the herd, said good-bye and headed off.

Clandy then said, "How about climbing to that fairy mound over there and standing watch for me? I've got a girlfriend near here who is always happy to see me. It may take me a few hours to say hello."

Francisco enjoyed a quiet day looking down at the silvery lake and emerald grassland. As the yellow of late afternoon came into the sky, Clandy returned looking flushed and happy. He led Francisco two miles across the grasslands and up a hill to two well-concealed huts. Francisco was warmly welcomed by Michael Campsey's extended family and shared the usual simple Irish supper. They talked about rural Irish life and the negative impact of ever-present Sassenach troops.

Francisco finally asked about the Spaniards hiding out in the hills and who was leading them. "It's a bishop named Redmond O'Gallagher," said Campsey, "crafty as the Devil. He was so hounded by the British that he felt forced to put away his frock and take to the hills a year ago. He's sheltering all Spaniards who come his way. He's been very clever in eluding the Sassenachs and in getting small groups of Spaniards aboard fishing boats headed for Scotland."

"How is he so successful?" asked Francisco.

"He keeps moving from place to place in the Sperrin Mountains along the line between Derry and Tyrone counties. The local folk will direct you to his current location and give you any news of Sassenach activities. In order to survive, we have a pretty good spy system up here."

The next night after supper the family was sitting around the fire when Michael plunged in out of the rain, took off his cloak, shook it, hung it on a peg and sat down at the table announcing with a smile, "I'm so hungry I could eat cow patties. Bring on the banquet, mother o' mine!"

They let him finish his meal, knowing that if he had news from his visit to O'Cahan's castle, the story had to be nourished with food and time. When he had packed himself with oatcakes and buttermilk, he wiped his mouth with the back of his hand and with a slow smile said, "They were like the squeaking monkeys at the fair at Berry! They were like the mad dog that chased its own hind-quarters 'round the hill! They . . ."

"Who were, lad, who?"

"Ah, be patient, grand ole Father o' mine. "They were like the wood mice that dance in a circle in the moonlight . . . they cursed and went round and round, ferreting and beating on doors with their pistols . . ."

"The Sassenachs!" exclaimed his father and mother together.

"Yes. The Sassenachs," said Michael. "It seems they'd caught a Spaniard at the Tullys'."

"No harm to the Tullys?" asked Francisco.

"No. The girls are quite popular with the English, always able to provide their needs. Seems Mrs. Tully plied the Sassenachs with beer and got her girls to distract them, at which time the Spaniard gave them the slip. They didn't even notice he was gone for several minutes. They caught hell from their commander because the man was one of the two most wanted Spaniards in all Ireland. His name would be . . ." and Michael let his eyes rest full on Francisco, "Don Francisco de Cuellar, Captain of the *San Pedro* which wrecked on Streedagh Strand in September. He's been a wanderer for six months, slippery as an eel. Now you wouldn't by any chance have heard of him, would you, Don Odysseus?" They all looked at Francisco.

"I know him well," said Francisco, "though I've never in my life looked him in the face. He seems to have the luck o' the Irish. I've heard he's a marvelous fellow, well worth knowing, his only weakness being a fondness for warm milk taken straight from cows' teats."

Francisco knew that if the local Sassenach armed forces were as angry as Michael described, they would soon be combing the whole region for him. He wondered whether the militia would include any of the humiliated attackers of Mac Clancy's island castle. He must find Bishop O'Gallagher and warn him of the increased danger. The locals told him the Bishop was hiding in the Sperrin Mountains ten miles to the south but that he would soon move north to ship out a new crop of Spaniards.

The elder Campsey and Clandy described nearby landmarks and suggested that Francisco, in trying to find the Bishop's group, head south along the Faughan River, climb the hills above and inquire of wayfarers any news of strangers in the hills.

"It's not unlikely," put in Campsey, "that the Bishop may be in the vicinity of Slievekirk, the twelve-hundred foot mountain seven miles south of here."

"Many thanks for your excellent hospitality and advice," said Francisco.

"I've got a present for you," said Michael as he handed Francisco a flask. "It's milk from your favorite cow, Branna, who seems to have taken quite a liquid shine to you!"

Francisco laughed and left, slogging downhill into the wet night. Far off he could make out the lights of Derry which looked like phosphorescence on a damp forest log. The town was founded on the River Foyle which empties into Lough Foyle a few miles north. Francisco squished through mud and damp thickets, then leaned against a tree, appreciating for a moment the rising and falling inflection of river sounds. He smiled as he once again concluded, *That river is speaking Gaelic! No wonder the Irish speak as if they were singing. For millennia they have listened to the lyrical tunes of rain, rivers, streams and tiny brooks and have harmonized their language with Nature.*

He moved closer to the river and came upon a small path. Feeling his way with his hands to give warning of tree trunks and thorn bushes, he moved slowly through the rain. The early spring-roused tree toads were beginning to make themselves known. Now and then their clacks broke through the night, reminding him of dancing gypsies with Spanish castanets. *Oh, beautiful sun-drenched Spain! Will I ever get out of this muddy morass, this Irish quagmire of danger and charm?*

When morning broke, Francisco was soaked through. He had walked slowly and carefully, making not more than four miles downriver during the night. He sat on a log and ate his soggy oat cakes. Then he lay down next to the log, pretended to shake himself like a drenched dog, smiled, pulled his wet cloak around him and slept.

When he awoke, it was evening and time to be on the move again. He walked without pain.

He followed the river until he came across a large meadow gleaming in the light of a three-quarter moon. He decided to cut across it towards Mount Slievekirk, sure that the vagrants would hide on a mountain rather than in a valley. As he ascended the increasingly steep hill, he wondered whether Sebastian was in the vicinity. Could it be possible?

The rain stopped and he surveyed the country. To the northeast he could make out the dark glens of Limavady. He looked towards the bare outlines of Slievekirk Mountain. At the summit or in some nearby cave might be Bishop O'Gallagher and his latest collection of motley Spaniards. Stars were out, looming so near that they seemed to brush the hilltop. He recognized white Castor and golden Pollux, dear to men of the sea, directly above the mountain.

A cold wind from the north blew Francisco along his climbing path. He paused frequently to use all five senses and the sixth that the gypsies found he possessed and had taught him to enhance. At last he became vaguely aware that a small star, far below Castor and Pollux, seemed to become larger as he moved towards it. He walked carefully. The light just below the ridge grew slowly larger and more yellow. Intermittently it snuffed into darkness, as if figures were moving in front of it. Because of wind blowing past his ears, he could hear no human sounds.

As he moved cautiously closer, was he now smelling meat roasting? The odor intensified and it was more enticing to him than his favorite smell of freshly-baked bread. In a moment he saw a fire underneath an overhanging cliff protrusion, what the French called an *abri*. Such shelters had been used as living quarters in Europe for hundreds of thousands of years by prehistoric ancestors when they couldn't find an actual cave. Friend or foe? He must be careful. Perhaps they were not the Bishop's group but Irish renegades who might gladly turn him in for an English reward or bash his head just for the sheer hell of it. They might even be Sassenachs. He crouched down but his movement scuffed a rock underneath his foot.

"Who goes?" called out a guard in Gaelic. Francisco thought he detected, even in the two words, a Spanish accent. He chanced his life on the surmise and answered loudly in Spanish:

"A Spaniard from the *San Marcos* that went down off Donegal Bay. Greetings, *amigo*!"

There was a rush of people toward the greeting and suddenly a voice rang out, "Francisco, you old bastard. I thought I had finally gotten rid of you!"

"Likewise, you Salamanca son-of-a-bitch!" answered Francisco. "You deserted me just because of a minor shipwreck! What kind of classmate are you?"

Sebastian de Carvajal and Francisco grabbed each other in a tight embrace. "Oh, Sebastian, I can't believe it's really you."

When the bear-hug finally ended, Sebastian said loudly:

213

"Gentlemen. This is the esteemed Armada captain, Don Francisco de Cuellar. He was a guest on the *San Marcos* when we shipwrecked on the rocks near Streedagh beach. Seeking fame, he abandoned me to my fate so he could experience his own adventures for future embellishment. His major fault is that he doesn't believe in the Devil!"

There now came forward a tall white-haired man dressed in a ragged cloak. His eyes were deep-recessed, his chin narrow, his lips thin. Francisco knelt and kissed the bishop's hand.

"Rise, Captain. God bless you and welcome. We're all equal fugitives here, all fourteen of us, and we'll have no kneeling. We still have a few ribs from the injured doe which Sebastian found under a bush this morning but claimed he shot with his arrow. Sit down and eat, then tell us tales of your growing love for Sassenachs."

It was incredible to Francisco that he and Sebastian were together again after all they had been through. His friend seemed unchanged, ever the same happy cynical character. It was a bit bewildering because Francisco knew that he, himself, had changed significantly.

Bishop O'Gallagher left the retreat to make departure arrangements at the Fiord of Foyle. Francisco and Sebastian sat on the edge of the *abri*, looking out over the valley. The Bishop had chosen the location on the south side of Mount Slievekirk, away from Sassenach eyes. The view was beautiful, commanding the far windings of the Mourne River and the lavender folds of the Sperrin Mountains.

The two old friends summarized to each other their many perilous adventures, escapes and wanderings. "At times," said Francisco, "I wonder if we ever *will* get home but I still have strong faith in my religion's teachings. If God dooms me to wander the green hills of Ireland forever, I think I can come to accept it."

"You're God's fool, then. You used to be a man of spirit. Now life's adversities have beaten you down into a spongy pulp of passivity. I have no use for such spineless acquiescence." Sebastian hesitated, then laughed and said "I shock you more than ever, don't I, *amigo*?"

"Yes, sometimes you do, Sebastian, just as in our university days. It seems remarkable that you've faced death so many times recently, leaping down cliffs, surviving the *Girona* shipwreck, escaping from wolves, mastiffs, shillelaghs, bullets and savage behavior and yet remain unaltered. Did death never speak to you with the voice of God?"

"You take death too seriously, my friend. Why are you religious people with all your salvations and redemptions, saints, angels and immortalities so much more afraid of death than we are who believe only in the beautiful nothingness? I like what old Seneca said, '*Post mortem nihil est*' (After death there is nothing). I love life and rejoice in every minute of it. I simply don't fear the termination at which all living things must arrive."

"All I want is to go home to Zabella and beget six sons starting immediately! I, too, love life, *amigo*! Brushing death so often recently has given me a passion for living."

"*Bravo! Bravo*, Francisco. Life is far too serious to be taken so seriously. It has to be treated as a comedy. Only then can one be happy. If life plays a joke on us we must go along with the joke. Breathe the moment, Francisco; ride the billows, ride the currents."

"Which is exactly what we've been doing for many months, my friend. Let's agree that Life is both a comedy and a tragedy but let's try to attenuate the scenes of suffering and infuse more acts of pleasantry into our current life drama."

They continued their discussion of religion and the meaning of life and death for another half hour until a linnet, returning early from its tropical winter, landed on a nearby tuft of heather to trace its melodious song of rapid trills and twitters across the pale blue air. Francisco commented, "That lovely linnet, with its handsome crimson forehead and chest, is telling us that our thoughtful discussion is becoming tedious."

"Ah, Francisco," said Sebastian, laying an arm over his friend's shoulder. "You still seem to have your sense of humor although your sightseeing tour of Ireland has made you think too much. You are still my best friend in spite of your cognitive faults and I still might even save you in an emergency. I agree, however, that it's time to stop fracturing these trees with our earth-shattering philosophical insights. Let's grab bows and arrows and go hunting for game which I'm sure we can agree upon—wild deer and wild mountain women."

CHAPTER 34

Turbulent *Déja Vue*

(March-April 1589)

The Bishop returned in four days stating that all arrangements had been made with Owen Campsey, the pinnace owner and older brother of Michael. The weather was good and the boat would depart in two days, on April first. Owen would land them in Argyleshire near the castle of Niall Mac Sweeney who was friendly to Armada survivors.

The group had to start walking towards Derry this very evening and there was much to do. Food must be packed and the rock shelter vacated and meticulously cleaned so the English wouldn't identify it as a hiding place. Francisco and Sebastian had killed a red deer stag and doe so no further meat was needed. Red deer were large animals of the elk family and their meat was superb, preferred by most Irish over beef. By late afternoon the party of fourteen, the Bishop leading, started down the mountain.

"Ah, the last lap to home!" exclaimed Sebastian.

"I seem to have heard that before," replied Francisco. "I wonder what happy catastrophes your scheming Devil has conjured up for us this time."

During the night the Northern Lights glimmered as if they were St. Elmo's fire on the great mast of the world. By morning the group had reached the village of Drumahoe near Derry. They hid in a forest, roasted some elk haunches, ate and went to sleep.

They became so talkative during the second night as they moved along the Faughan River that the Bishop had to shush them several times when they passed close to settlements. On the morning of March thirty-first they began to whiff the kelpy, clammy smell of Lough Foyle which was connected to the sea. They became swallowed up by thick fog and had to walk slowly.

Before dawn the bishop began giving low intensity dove calls. At last the boatman returned the call. In a few minutes they could hear the lapping of water against the pinnace and see the fuzzy glow of the ship's lanterns.

"Who goes?" called out Owen Campsey gently in Gaelic.

"Scottish fishermen," answered Bishop O'Gallagher in quietly-voiced Gaelic.

Owen stood on the small dock next to his boat. The bishop asked the men to kneel, said a brief mass and added a prayer of his own for their safe passage over the sea. The thirteen grateful Spaniards thanked the Bishop enthusiastically and were hustled aboard.

Campsey released the ship's rope from the snubbing post and they paddled away from the dock before hoisting sails. For three hours there was fair going as the small but seaworthy fishing vessel progressed out of the Fiord of Foyle and sailed into the open sea. It seemed unreal to Francisco finally to be on board a boat actually leaving the shores of Ireland.

The gray dawn transitioned into dark yellow-black mistiness which often meant bad weather. The wind picked up in intensity with sudden changes in direction. The men began to get concerned because it was just such dark yellow skies and crescendo gusts that had hurled these men and their ships into Irish coastal rocks seven months previously.

The wind changed suddenly and charged up strongly from the southeast. Owen shifted sail. Soon the wind hit them from the south. Owen again re-oriented his sails, crying out, "It's too strong for tacking. Nothing to do now but run before the wind wherever it takes us."

The pinnace began taking on water from higher waves. The fishing boat was like a cockle shell compared to the size of a large galleon. Wind blasted, waves mounted, the boat rising and plunging. Francisco remained calm but wondered why God was putting them through such a turbulent *déja vue*. He recalled Tara's vivid description of her young husband's disappearance in a storm, ending their brief idyllic marriage so pitilessly.

"Where are we heading?" shouted Sebastian at Campsey who stood at the helm steering the ship through the increasingly tumultuous seas. There was a touch of magnificence about the way he stood, head and shoulders thrown back, seeming to defy wind, waves and peril like a Viking navigator expertly guiding his longship through a storm.

"To the Hebrides, I hope!" Campsey shouted back.

Two of the Spanish soldiers became seasick and lay down on the deck with water slopping over them. Francisco, Sebastian and three others bailed water, taking turns with two pails.

Now rain began to pour. It was always when Francisco was coldest and wettest that his thoughts began to wander and the sunlit picture of home came back to him most vividly. *Being early April, it is just getting warm now in Cuellar—almond, cherry and apricot trees may even be beginning to blossom early, little buds appearing on the grapevines, red earth lying in crimson furrows awaiting seeds of wheat, oats, onions and beets. Olive groves are pale silver with mustard and daisy blossoms brightening the earth beneath them. How I miss my home!*

At Castle Cuellar there would be a stir of spring activities. Mother and wife would be supervising cleaning of the castle, polishing of ancient family armor in the hall, planting of kitchen gardens and flowers. He wondered whether they thought him dead or whether they were saying, "We must get everything spic and span for Francisco's imminent return." Would Zabella then sing "The Song of *Conde Claros*," thinking of Francisco with affection and longing: *Conde Claros con amores, No podía reposar.*

A bolt of lightning struck the sea only a few meters ahead, jolting Francisco into immediacy. "Thy will be done," he spoke quietly. Sebastian read his lips and lifted his arms outward, shrugging his shoulders and mouthing for Francisco's benefit, "Come what may, the Devil will have his say!"

Francisco, in reply, looked into Sebastian's eyes and made a large sign of the cross over his chest. As he resumed bailing they both smiled. They greatly enjoyed their repartee even though neither had changed his religious thinking one iota during their ten years of friendship.

The storm roared and gusted all afternoon. Toward evening the rain and wind eased off. It was still impossible to sail anywhere except due north, before the wind. The Spaniards, all except the two who still lay on deck, were propped up against benches and had roped themselves to the boat. They now ate some bread and salted fish, wringing out their shirts for fresh water.

By nightfall, moonlight shone between scudding clouds as the wind tapered and the sea began to calm. Campsey told them he wasn't sure how far off-course they had been blown. They needed to lay up for a day to check the boat and let the passengers recover. When the wind favored, they would make the final run to the Fiord of Sween on the west coast of Argyll, Scotland.

Dawn presented a gorgeous panorama of pink, red and orange scattered clouds. Faint gray-lavender hills showed to the east. In the clearing light Campsey found that they had been blown much further north than he thought and they were now in the lowest group of islands of the Outer Hebrides. He sailed past the Island of Vatersay, then past Kisimul Castle of Clan Mac Neil built on a small island in the bay. He brought the pinnace to dock in Castlebay on the Isle of Barra.

Francisco and his small group of Armada vagrants were safely in Scotland, finally untethered from the endless life-threatening hazards of Ireland.

CHAPTER 35

Bony Scarecrows

(Spring, summer and early fall 1589)

Campsey and his boatload were hospitably welcomed at Kisimul Castle by Walter Mac Nell, a good Catholic Scot. He fed them well for two days and gave warm cloaks to three of them. On the third day they sailed south toward their intended destination closer to Edinburgh, capital of Scotland. A fair wind was blowing from the south and the ketch slanted southeast into it, sailing without misfortune between the islands of Coll and Tiree towards Jura in Scotland's inner Hebrides.

A day later they sailed into the opening of Loch Sween and anchored in the lagoon near the square-towered, 12th Century Castle Sween of Edmond Mac Sweeney. This Scottish cousin of the Mac Sweeneys of Donegal and Connaught was, like most of his relatives, hospitable to Spaniards.

Francisco, Sebastian and their group basked in the friendly welcome, comfort, good food and welcome heat of the great fireplace. Views of the fiord, ocean and islands of Jura and Islay were beautiful and peaceful. Could all their troubles be over?

On the seventh of April they watched Campsey unfurl his sails in the lagoon below. The fishing boat butterflied down the southern reaches of the fiord towards the island cluster at its mouth. The Spaniards' last human link to Ireland then disappeared into the ocean vastness.

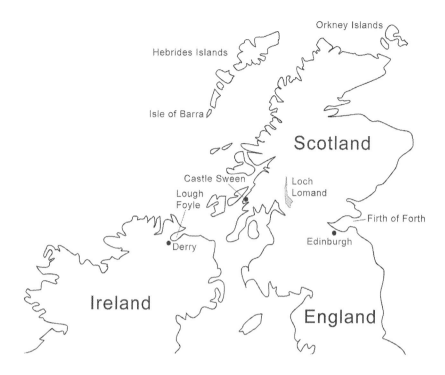

Figure 7. Locations relevant to Francisco's journey
from the north coast of Ireland to Edinburgh.

"God lead us home!" exclaimed Francisco.

"May the Devil allow it!" said Sebastian. They both laughed.

Preparations were now made for the trek to Edinburgh and the vital question: would a chronically weak and vacillating King James give them permission to exit Scotland and head home? He had been brought up a Catholic by his mother, Mary Stuart, Queen of Scots but now was King of a Protestant country.

Francisco knew that James had been taught since childhood that his main goal in life should be to become King of England and unite the realms of England and Scotland. Therefore he obviously had to base all of his policy decisions on what the English Queen would think of them. Francisco wondered how James could possibly get approval from Queen Elizabeth to be kind to Armada survivors who had just tried to invade and conquer England and destroy her Tudor Monarchy. Thus their very lives

221

depended on the collusion and whims of two absolute monarchs—not a comforting conclusion.

Mac Sweeney wrote letters for them to King James and three powerful nobles he knew personally at the Royal Court in Edinburgh—the Catholic Earl of Huntlay; the Fifth Earl Marischal, George Keith; and Lord Maxwell. Mac Sweeney drew a map of the highway route to Edinburgh. He had a mule loaded with supplies and provided a guide as far as Loch Lomond.

They set off from Castle Sween with high hopes for a safe trip among friendly Scots but the hundred-mile journey to Edinburgh was a disappointing trek. Despite being Catholic until recently, the Scottish Lowlanders were almost as hostile as many of the Irish—villagers derided them, children threw stones, and any stragglers had their clothes stolen. Francisco forbade any use of pistols or other weapons. In order to survive they had to continue their journey as helpless beggars rather than proud men of the Armada who had tried to carry out the will of God as interpreted by their King.

On a tiny scale, it was reminiscent of the hazardous retreat of the ten thousand Greeks from Babylonia to the Black Sea in 401 BC. It was Odysseus returning from the Trojan war and having to cope with the formidable barriers and antipathy of Cyclops, Circe, Scylla and Charybdis.

At the outskirts of Ardlin at the head of Loch Lomond they unpacked the mule's load of food supplies which were now distributed among the thirteen. Unfortunately, local ruffians were watching and went after the Spaniards with clubs and fists and stole much of the food.

Francisco tried to be encouraging. "Be of good cheer, shipmates. Our troubles will soon be over. God will punish our foes and guide us home safely."

One Spanish soldier was heard to say, "Like hell He will. He's completely forgotten us."

Francisco figured that Edinburgh must now be about seventy-five miles southeast, a trip of five nights. Under the joint leadership of Francisco and Sebastian, the group moved slowly but steadily each night, hiding out in daytime. On the fourth evening they moved along the Firth of Forth, meeting only a few elderly couples out for a beach stroll who were either friendly or diffident.

The Spaniards arrived at Edinburgh's large hill castle tired, hungry and tattered, looking like the homeless stragglers they were. An unfriendly guard at the gate grabbed the handful of letters of reference which Francisco handed him, saying, "For God's sake, why did you warriors leave Spain in the first place? Why should we help you? You would've invaded us next since we're Protestants now!"

After two long hours the guard returned with word that the King as well as the Lords of Huntley and Maxwell were all busy with weighty matters of State and could not see them. George Keith was in Denmark. His hereditary job as Earl Marischal of Scotland was to protect the King when he attended Parliament, serve as custodian of Royal Regalia and carry out personal missions for the King, in this case to make marriage arrangements with Princess Anne of Denmark.

"What are we to do now?" Francisco asked. "We are in dire need, looking like vagabonds but we are officers and men of the Armada of His Illustrious Majesty, King Philip of Spain."

A smile, feathered with scorn, twitched at the bearded lips of the gatekeeper. "Perhaps your King should help you dredge up your sunken galleons from the bottom of the sea. Our King had nothing to do with your current troubles. Wait patiently and be silent is my advice."

"Our letters of introduction, where are they?" asked Francisco.

"With a clerk of one of the Chamberlain's undersecretaries."

"Sounds like a bottomless pit to me," scoffed Sebastian in Spanish. "The 'undersecretary' is probably a complete fabrication by the guard."

"Have faith, Sebastian," said Francisco.

"In whom, in what? All we can possibly trust in this world is ourselves, a friend or two and his Most Excellent Majesty, the Devil! Apparently we must learn how to play the waiting game while King James and his government puppeteers decide our fate as we dangle on their marionette strings." He laughed loudly and walked away singing his favorite Spanish song, *Qualbi qualb a'rabi, qualb Arab*! My heart is the heart of an Arab!

Many of the Spaniards crossed themselves as protection against possible heavenly retribution. Only a few were amused this time though they usually delighted in Sebastian's unquenchable, often devilishly-tinted humor.

"Trust in whom you will, Sebastian, but the rest of us prefer to trust in God," said Francisco. "Come, friends, let's head southwest out of

Edinburgh, away from people. We'll find the Water of Leith and make our homeless home on the river bank."

Two days later, Francisco raised himself uncomfortably from the river bank of the Water of Leith and leaned on his elbows. He gazed across the twenty-foot wide river and watched a large gray heron walking slowly upstream next to the opposite bank. Suddenly the heron darted his beak downward into short grasses, lifted a very surprised struggling frog, flipped it in the air and swallowed it headfirst. Reminded how hungry he was, Francisco's stomach began to ache. He looked at his best friend who had just awakened nearby, was struck by his tattered clothes, skinny arms and protruding ribs and said:

"My God, Sebastian! We're barely more than starved bony scarecrows!"

"Once again, you ugly ex-Captain, you are blunt but truthful. What a contrast with our appearance and pride last year in being Spaniards when our invincible Armada gathered on the Tagus. Remember when we attended church services in the lovely *Igreja do Carmo* in Lisbon with its gray-gold interior lit by hundreds of tapers and with brightly-colored ship banners hanging gloriously from the walls?"

"Yes, how stunning we all looked," replied Francisco, "with our supremely confident militiamen strutting in their shining helmets, wearing coats of mail and gleaming swords, proudly bearing their embroidered silk standards flapping gently in the breeze. The accompanying gentlemen adventurers added a colorful panorama of scarlet and canary cloaks, gold-braided doublets and breeches, velvet caps with diamond and ruby brooches—a marching rainbow with all Armada participants convinced that we were launching a regal, God-inspired mission."

"I wonder what's taking so long for King James and his government ministers to make arrangements to get us back to the coast of Europe?" said Sebastian. "We left our papers and request for boat passage weeks ago."

Francisco and Sebastian had returned to the Royal Castle in Edinburgh once a week to request audience with the King or his counselors but got no response. Two months after their arrival, the King and his Court came riding out of the gate. Observing a courtier with a large silver cross shining from a silver-beaded rosary against his black velvet coat, they ran beside his horse.

"Your Grace, we are officers of King Philip's Armada," Francisco cried out in Latin. "There are eleven other men with us who escaped from shipwrecks. We have wandered for many months and barely escaped death many times. Two months ago we transmitted referral letters to the King and to Lords Huntley, Maxwell and Marischal from Edmond Mac Sweeney of Argyleshlre. We have petitioned weekly since then without any response. We earnestly request an audience."

"I have not heard of you."

"Our petitions never reached the Court?"

"I fear not but there are many more than thirteen of you. There are several hundred scattered all around Scotland. They are all hoping for passage to the continent. It is a great problem for us but we are working on it. A way will be found. Frankly," and there was a smile under his black beard as he said it, "we would rather have you go than stay."

"You won't turn us over to Queen Jezebel, will you?" asked Sebastian.

"I doubt it but you mustn't forget that she is kin to our King and there are many complex political considerations. As an aside, there are many Protestants here now and it would be wise not to allude to her as Queen Jezebel."

The cavalcade had moved ahead. The friendly nobleman took a pouch of coins from his belt and tossed it down to the two Spaniards.

"God's blessings on you, my Lord!" cried Francisco as the courtier spurred his horse forward. The Scot looked over his shoulder and waved his riding-crop.

Francisco hurried back to the gate. "Who was that noble Lord?" he asked the gatekeeper.

"The Earl of Maxwell."

"Our messages never reached these high-ranking earls?" Francisco asked the gatekeeper.

"So? We've been busy. We can't do everything requested of us."

Francisco decided to move the group into the Pentland Hills, farther from the animosity of local Protestant Scots. Soon they were joined by thirty other disheveled Spaniards wandering the hills. The generous pouchful of money from the Earl of Maxwell kept the group of forty-three men in simple food for almost a month, purchased from fishermen and purveyors in Edinburgh. After that, they tried to gather plants, catch fish and hunt wild game as best they could. It was scant fare.

Three weeks later, Francisco sent the Earl of Maxwell a message asking whether any progress was being made in shipping the Spaniards out of the country. The next day the messenger brought a small pouch of money and a brief note, "Be patient. There are many issues involved."

The summer of 1589 passed. Rumors were rife. Francisco and Sebastian tried hard to elevate group morale by assigning tasks and encouraging the men to seek summer work at local farms. Raiding, poaching or bothering the local herdsmen or farmers were absolutely forbidden. Their very lives, they were told over and over by Francisco, depended on decent behavior.

From the highest points of the Pentland Hills they could see the North Sea, so cruel to them during the stormy year before. It was now almost September 1589 and Francisco had said good-bye to Zabella sixteen months ago. *A long time for a fervent young bride,* he thought.

September opened badly. A group of hunters came up into the hills and began discharging their guns all around them, not to hit them but to drive them out of their hunting area by threat alone. The Spaniards moved into a more remote area. The rains began. Cold winds blew across the hills. Their garments were so tattered that Francisco taught them how to make coverings out of ferns. Feelings of pessimism once again became pervasive.

One afternoon in mid-September, two couriers on horseback rode up the hill as the Spaniards were preparing their supper. "Here comes our death warrant, in one form or another," exclaimed Sebastian as they all rose to greet the emissaries. Francisco went forward.

"Captain Don Francisco de Cuellar?"

"I am he."

"This message is for you." The courier placed a small rolled parchment in Francisco's hands. He opened it, saw the King's seal and signature, gathered his men and read aloud:

> His Royal Highness, James VI of Scotland, is pleased to advise Captain Don Francisco de Cuellar that arrangements have been made with the Duke of Parma to transport the officers and men of the Spanish Armada yet remaining in Scotland to the coast of Flanders. A merchant of Flanders will have his four vessels anchored in the roadstead of Leith on the twentieth day of September.

You are hereby enjoined to gather together as many of your compatriots as possible from the Pentland Hills and the County of Midlothian and direct them to be ready at the place and date above designated. Similar directives are being sent throughout my kingdom wherever survivors of the Spanish Armada are known to be.

We wish you a prosperous return to your King and country.

Francisco lifted his eyes from the parchment and gave his answer to the couriers. "We thank His Majesty for his magnificent efforts on our behalf. Assure him that we will do his bidding and be ready to take advantage of this great opportunity of going home."

As the two couriers rode down the hill, some of the Spaniards were weeping. Sebastian shook his head and asked, "Could this be a trap? Can we be sure that Queen Jezebel's warships will not be waiting for us off England's coast to demolish us?"

Doubts were dispelled the next day when another courier arrived with a letter from the Earl of Marischal, recently returned from long but successful marriage negotiations in Denmark. He emphasized that Queen Elizabeth had promised not to send her warships to attack the four Flemish vessels containing the Armada survivors.

Sebastian remained skeptical of Queen Elizabeth's intentions and those of her weak and spineless cousin, King James VI of Scotland. "Beware of the unrestrained fury of the English Queen whose shores we tried to breach and whose monarchy we tried to overthrow," he said more than once in the ensuing days. "She is an Absolute Monarch who claims she rules by Divine Right. No matter how often our King tries to preempt God for his own purposes, the Queen is equally sure that God will approve any scheme of hers. Beware, take heed."

"You are so cynical and distrustful, my friend," replied Francisco. "King James not only pities us but wants us off Scottish soil. Remember that Queen Elizabeth treacherously chopped off the head of James' mother, Mary, Queen of Scots. Surely he won't renege on his promise to get us safely to Spanish-held Flanders."

The men who came down from the Pentland hills four days later toward the Firth of Forth were clad in cloaks which hung in strips, shirts worn to shreds, ferns and fragmentary shoes or none at all. This time the local Scottish townspeople kept their silence as they watched the pitiful vagrants hobble slowly towards their ships of freedom.

CHAPTER 36

Shadows in the Fog

(September 21 to October 4, 1589)

Most of the hundreds of Spanish Armada survivors expected storm and shipwreck on their voyage. Since the tempestuous disasters at sea the previous year, it seemed inevitable that the ocean would never be smooth for them again. However, the five-day journey from the Firth of Forth to the coast of Flanders, while full of lightly veering winds, was neither difficult nor dangered.

On the morning of September 25, 1589, a thin fog hung over the sea. A cheer went up from the Spanish when, through the haze, there began to appear faint shadows of the dunes of Dunkirk, a Spanish possession. Here was a totally friendly land close to home at last, after the savage seas and hostile shores of the north.

Suddenly out of the mist, moving shadows darker than the dunes began to emerge. Orders quickly came from the captain of Francisco's ship, shifting sails immediately to a new course. The captain shouted that the moving shadows were enemy vessels of Protestant Netherlands seeking to destroy them. The Netherlands had been at war with King Philip's army since 1567 trying to preserve their independence from Spanish invaders.

"Good God!" said Francisco. "You were right, Sebastian! King James and Queen Elizabeth have colluded to kill us just before we land safely in Dunkirk!"

Their ship and the one adjacent made a dash for the harbor through the widest space between enemy warships. The entrance was narrow and shallow and known to their captains but, in their haste, they came in at a slant and both ships grounded on a reef fifty yards to the left of the safe channel. The sea beat roughly against the two tilted ships. Francisco moved along the deck shouting to his companions:

"Lay hold of barrels, chairs, benches, planks, anything that floats. Be ready to throw them in and jump after them unless rescue boats come out very soon."

The decision was quickly made for them. A Dutch frigate came gliding out of the fog and began to bombard both ships. Men jumped overboard, many in their fear failing to carry wooden objects. The air was filled with desperate shouts and screams, booming cannons and splintering of the stricken ships.

Francisco stripped off his cloak, threw an empty barrel into the sea and leaped in. Pushing the barrel in front of him and using his legs, he rode in on the waves. With great effort, being a non-swimmer, he came abreast of the harbor entrance. As he came up on the crest of a wave, he looked back for Sebastian but it was impossible to distinguish one bobbing head from another. A long wave rode him towards steps cut into the inner stone wall of the harbor. Three men were kneeling on the steps, arms outstretched.

"Ah, brave warrior," cried one in Spanish. "Give us your hands!" Francisco reached out and was lifted onto a slimy green step. The mist had lifted and he could see the gruesome drama. The other two Flemish merchant vessels had also tried to run the gauntlet and enter the harbor directly but had been cut off and surrounded by Dutch warships. Now they were being boarded by militia with drawn swords and daggers. Helpless Armada men toppled to the deck or fell overboard.

No mercy was shown by the Dutch who had been slaughtered for twenty-two years by invading Spanish armies in the Netherlands now commanded by the Duke of Parma. The only Dutch crime had been to reject the Catholic faith and switch to Protestantism—which King Phillip considered an unforgivable transgression.

Within the harbor, small boats put out from the docks of Dunkirk to rescue any survivors. Francisco, filled with horror at what he saw, put his head in his hands and thought, *For God's sake, stop the killing! Haven't we suffered enough?* He could see there would be few survivors.

It was now obvious that King James and Queen Elizabeth had planned this treacherous betrayal of the Armada shipwreck survivors, most of whom were weaponless soldiers and sailors. Thus would King Philip be warned once more not to try invading England ever again.

As Francisco looked at the tragic scene, he saw Sebastian swimming towards the same set of slippery stone stairs. With blood streaming down his face, he was clutching a wooden plank. Francisco helped him up and the two friends walked silently into town as the one-sided slaughter continued.

Nine days later, on October fourth, 1589, Francisco sat in his room on the second floor of Antwerp's Scheldt Inn overlooking the broad, shallow River Scheldt. Sheets of parchment and several quill pens were on the table in front of him.

Antwerp had been conquered four years before by the Duke of Parma and was now part of the Spanish Empire. The Duke had allowed the city's non-Catholic citizens to emigrate safely into Protestant Netherlands so the city was now, as it should be, completely Catholic.

Sebastian spoke from Francisco's open doorway. "Write your narrative diligently to your cousin, old fellow. We're off for home in three weeks or so." Most of their small Spanish group were eager to return to Spain but weren't yet strong enough and didn't want to appear as gaunt skeletons to their relatives and friends.

"I shall," replied Francisco. "The true Armada saga should be recorded while details are still fresh. I need to write without a break. I plan to make a summary for the King since I'm sure he has heard many fabrications from lying high-ranking officers afraid of damage to their future careers."

"Yes, I hear ridiculous gossip every day. Sorry you can't join us as we explore the taverns of Antwerp. You would enjoy the Dutch women, who are proving to be tastier and more quenching than Dutch beer!" Sebastian left and walked towards the center of town.

Francisco had already heard of Philip's responses to the leading officers of his shattered Armada. General Bovadilla had been summoned before the King and had tried to defend himself by declaring that he and Duke Sidonia had conscientiously followed orders. The King had replied: "I did not give orders to you or the Duke to engage the English navy or to retreat as fast as possible at the first hint of misfortune!" After that strong rebuke, Bovadilla had gone home knowing his career was over. He shut himself in his room refusing to eat and died ten days later.

Medina Sidonia, on the other hand, in a letter to King Philip took personal responsibility for the Armada's defeat, admitting that he had failed his King and his country. He begged leave to go home to manage his long-neglected agricultural estates. His brief message was so truthful and his assumption of blame so open and honest that the King granted his request.

Francisco looked out at Antwerp's gabled red brick houses. White clouds drifted through a clear blue sky. The serenity was hard to believe after so much tumult and tragedy. He and Sebastian had been given enthusiastic welcomes by Antwerp's officials and citizens, who also donated clothes and hotel rooms. The Duke of Parma's gifts of money and fresh horses were beyond expectation.

Francisco wondered again why King Philip thought it necessary to invade every country that had left the Catholic Church. *Why couldn't Spain leave people alone and let them choose their God and their religious services? Was Philip really trying to save the world or was he actually striving to enlarge his Empire for his own glory and personal treasure? He was certainly bankrupting Spain in one military misadventure after another.*

Francisco's thoughts drifted back to home where his devoted wife and beloved mother awaited him. *What a great rejoicing there will be when I finally appear on that golden hill! I won't send any message ahead. I want to savor fully the glory of my surprise return to Cuellar.*

Francisco considered it vitally important for an unbiased person to record the truth, not only for the reputations of those involved but for historical accuracy. He shook his head in wonderment that his adventures had actually happened and that he had survived against such formidable odds. He set his quill to paper and began writing the letter to his cousin:

Most Esteemed Cousin Eduardo,

I believe you will be astonished at seeing this letter on account of the slight possibility that I could return alive. I should have died many times because of the great hardships and misfortunes I have experienced since the Armada sailed from Lisbon for England from which our Lord, in his Infinite good pleasure, has finally delivered me.

God has brought me safely to these States of Flanders where I arrived in late September with the Spaniards who survived the Armada shipwrecks in Ireland and the Shetland Islands. We were fortunate enough to escape the final treachery of Queen Elizabeth and King James who arranged for us to be slaughtered by the Dutch only a few yards from safety in Dunkirk harbor.

God seemed to desert our King's armada in its noble mission to punish the English Protestant heretics. Why He cast his grace upon me and a sparse few others, allowing us to survive the many hostilities hurled against us, remains a mystery.

It occurred to me that perhaps He wanted me to describe, in accurate and unembellished prose, the saga of our Armada from the time we began to encounter foul weather after leaving Lisbon, to the disaster of our ships trying to fight the superior navy of England, to our shipwrecks on the hazardous Irish coast and the ensuing endless battle for life against the hostile forces of Nature and Man in Ireland, to the time a precious few of us were able to land safely on the continent of Europe.

Honorable Cousin: In order to counteract false, misleading reports of our Armada's sad fate, I have decided to set down and publish, as soon as possible, an accurate account of our remarkable misfortunes, fulfilling my final duty to history. Therefore, please forgive me if I attach to this letter a third-person narrative of my truthful chronicle which I hope to publish if the opportunity is afforded me. Please hold it until I am able to pick it up in person from you in Spain—soon, I hope.

The current title of my manuscript is: "True Narrative of the Spanish Armada by One Who Survived Tempestuous Weather, Shipwreck in Ireland, Hostile Adversaries and Severe Misfortune."

From the City of Antwerp, 4th October, 1589.

Fond salutations from your cousin,

Francisco de Cuellar

CHAPTER 37

Captain and King

(October 1589 to January 1590)

Most of the Spaniards who trudged down from the Pentland Hills and left Scotland with such high hopes did not survive the sudden Dutch attack at the harbor entrance to Dunkirk. Of the two hundred seventy Spaniards on Francisco's boat, there were only three survivors, including Francisco and Sebastian. Most soldiers and even sailors were unable to swim. From the other three ships only thirty-one reached shore safely out of many hundreds.

A few survivors chose to stay in the Netherlands and join the Duke of Parma's army in King Philip's long quest to force the Dutch to reestablish Catholicism. Some decided to run the gauntlet of the English Channel and return to Spain by sea. A few were placed in hospitals in Dunkirk, Bruges and Antwerp, subject to bloodletting and the high mortality rates of European medical care.

While Francisco spent his days and nights writing his journal, it was primarily Sebastian, with help from the Duke of Parma, who planned the cavalcade of twelve Spanish survivors to go in gradual stages on horseback to Paris, then to Orleans, Bordeaux and Bayonne, entering Spain at San Sebastian, a journey of some seven hundred miles.

Before returning home to Cuellar, Francisco considered it important to discuss several matters in person with the King, including his illegal removal as Captain of the *San Pedro* by General Bovadilla and clearing the name of Don Cristobal de Avila, so treacherously hanged by Bovadilla. Sebastian, like the good friend he was, insisted upon accompanying Francisco to Madrid. He had no parents, wife, or sweetheart. A brother and sister lived in Corunna and he would visit them but he wasn't in a hurry.

There were delays on the trip occasioned by border patrols, illness, passport problems and injury to horses. It was mid-December before Francisco and Sebastian rode over the snowy passes of the *Sierra de Guadarrama* into the basin of the Manzanares River and onwards to the plateau of Madrid where King Philip was currently holding Court.

The two Armada survivors put up at the *Posada de los Conquistadores*, a name which caused them both to laugh. They certainly didn't feel like conquerors. Francisco immediately sent a message to the Court with a request for an interview with the King to give his version of Armada battles and the aftermath. He also enclosed a summary of his long narrative written in Antwerp.

Three days later a messenger brought a reply from the King. His Majesty thanked Don Francisco for his transmitted material. He needed time to study the document and for his consultants to verify the specifics. Would he kindly await the King's pleasure, remaining at his inn on *Paseo de San Vicente* until summoned to Court?

Although Francisco begged Sebastian to use the time to visit his relatives in Corunna, his friend not only wished to stand by him but also was having a very good time with the alluring *señoritas* of Madrid.

Christmas came and went. Francisco was getting tired of waiting. Had King Phillip forgotten him or was the investigation into his truthfulness really taking that long? It was a cold, windy day in mid-January when Francisco at last received his summons to audience with the King. Sebastian went with him and, somewhat to his surprise after some detailed questionings by the Chamberlain, he was admitted along with Francisco. King Philip welcomed them:

"We are pleased to greet two of the participants in our great Armada, two whom God and Our Lady seemed especially desirous of bringing home through many trials and misadventures. We acknowledge the special honor of greeting the son of our late Lord Treasurer, Don Francisco Gutierrez de Cuellar and great grandson of Don Cristobal de Cuellar, Treasurer of Cuba. With pleasure we also greet Don Sebastian de Carvajal, son of Don Tomas de Carvajal who acquitted himself so well under our brother, Don Juan, at Lepanto.

"We have checked your story at every point, Don Francisco, not that we had cause to disbelieve you but such travails often skew memory and judgment. We were able to corroborate almost every point, thereby confuting several false tales which had reached my ears. After you were thrown upon the coasts of Ireland, there are few available witnesses. We find, however, that your account tallies well with our other reports and the rest is quite plausible by detail and tone.

"We are pleased, therefore, to vouchsafe you and Don Cristobal de Avila, for whom you seemed to show as much concern as for yourself, a clean record. I am restoring your Captaincies as if they had never been withdrawn."

Francisco knelt before King Philip with bowed head and thanked him as he received the two parchments of exoneration.

"Rise, Captain Cuellar . . . and now, what are your plans for the future?"

"Sire, I would hope to be placed in the reserve and be permitted to return to Cuellar to repair my castle, restore my herds, my crops and my vineyards and raise a fine family of sons to serve Spain in the future. I have a very attractive wife, Your Majesty, and I would like to make up for lost time with her and with my beloved mother, Maria Velasquez de Cuellar. It goes without saying that I would always be ready to serve Spain whenever you deem my services needed."

"You somewhat disappoint me, Captain. I had hoped to give you a commission soon after your family reunion. Your credentials and honorable conduct in peace and war are impeccable. I find that many of your kinsmen have been active in the New World, especially Mexico and Cuba. Your brother, Don Cristobal, serves me in Havana as warden of the forts. Your great uncle, Diego Velasquez, went to Cuba with Cristoforo Colombo in 1493 and later founded the city of Santiago de Cuba. I had hoped to appoint you Commander of all our ships patrolling the waters of Cuba."

"Sire, I am deeply moved . . ."

"I see that you hesitate, Captain. After all your trials, your longing for wife and home is only natural but perhaps it will prove transitory. I will give you four months to think it over. Perhaps you will decide to do something different with your life and will wish to relocate your family to Cuba."

"Thank you, Your Majesty. I respect your wisdom and I shall use the four months wisely to rehabilitate my farm and contemplate my future. May I now change the subject? The last part of my letter concerned possible rewards for certain Irish friends of Spain. There are a number who warrant special consideration—young Morven Mac Carthy who deserves to be brought to study at Salamanca; Sir Brian O'Rourke, fearless in his friendship for Spain; the Mac Sweeneys of Connaught and Donegal who were hospitable to so many Spaniards; Chief Murtagh Mac Clancy who was such a kind and generous host when we were in desperate straights but who now holds Don Antonio de Ulloa against his will; and Mac Clancy's beautiful sister, Alana, who helped me in one of my escapes. A gold necklace for her, perhaps, when you send the release money for Don Antonio?"

"I shall arrange rewards for all of these helpful Irish in good time."

"Thank you, Sire. There is also, I had almost forgotten, an attractive girl near the coast where my ship was wrecked to whom I promised a red velvet gown. She saved my life twice."

The solemn earnest King who rarely smiled and almost never laughed, smiled now. "I shall so instruct our Court's *modista* to fashion such a gown. It shall be sent in due course. It seems you owe your life to fair ladies! How do Irish girls compare with our Spanish maidens?"

"I found them bright, charming and often beautiful in the extreme. They would grace any Court in the world. Some are also rather mischievous, Sire, and perhaps even tend to enjoy life a bit too much, a behavior to which, over time, even a recalcitrant Spaniard can adapt."

The King laughed.

"There is one more matter, your Majesty, which concerns you closely. I am told that you already know about the loss of the great ship, *La Girona*, on the Rock of Bunbols in Antrim."

A visible cloud of darkness came over the King's face.

"I am sorry to mention this grievous subject but in a little hut near Coleraine I saw, in the hands of Shaemus Mac Rae, the medallion of the Order of the Golden Fleece."

The King tightened his grip on his chair. "I would give half my kingdom to have Don Alonso back again and I value that medallion of memory very highly. Do you think you could give me directions as to how Mac Rae might be located? I shall arrange a large reward in exchange for that medallion." The King sank back in his chair.

"Yes, Sire. I will make a careful map tonight and send it to the palace tomorrow morning."

"Your Majesty, may I speak?" asked Sebastian.

"Proceed."

"Is there not something for me also to do in Cuba? I am ready, Sire. I am one of your soldiers and I crave to serve you further."

"You, then, are still eager for more adventure after all of your remarkable months in Ireland? No home ties? No beautiful wife? No vineyards?"

"No, Sire. I have no wife or parents, only a brother and sister at Corunna. I would like a short holiday with them and then I am as free as a *señorita* on Saturday night in Salamanca."

The King smiled again. It was getting to be almost a habit. "I think I can find you a military commission in Cuba. You are a sergeant?"

"I am now a sergeant, Sire, but I think I would make a very good general."

King Philip laughed for the second time, his advisors again looking astonished at this monkish monarch whose somber demeanor had been accentuated for months by the cascading details of his Armada's disastrous defeat. "Although I am not a comedian myself, Sebastian, I do appreciate a sense of humor, especially after all you've been through. I am aware of your degree from Salamanca, your postgraduate studies and your excellent, albeit brief, record in our army. But could we compromise and make you a mere Major? Would that suffice?"

"Indeed, Sire, I would try to adjust to that lesser status although I believe I could roust up a bevy of beautiful women to testify to you that my qualifications and skills justify a higher rank."

The King smiled again. "You have undoubtedly matured during your Armada adversities and hazardous experiences in Ireland and are ready for a significant promotion. Perhaps we need more senses of humor and newer viewpoints in our military. Mistakes have been made recently which require reevaluation. There are several great Spanish forts in Havana.

Perhaps you might like to command one or more of them. Let me think about it. It so happens that two of my ships are going out from Corunna to Cuba in late April. You can see your family and sail from your home port. Perhaps you, Captain Cuellar, will wish to join your friend."

"Thank you, Sire," replied Francisco. "I will give it serious thought."

Francisco knew in his heart, however, that his sole wish was to live in his castle, tend his fields, make love to Zabella and raise a bevy of children in peace, far from any potential adversaries on land or sea.

CHAPTER 38

Home At Last

(January 1590)

The cold wind and snow flurries did not dampen Francisco's mood as he rode with Sebastian through the pass in the Guadarrama mountains on the way from Madrid to Segovia. He was happy and exuberant. He had survived and now, at last, he could reunite with his family and begin a normal life in Cuellar, far from the horrors of Ireland.

Francisco's heart sang for joy. He was nearing home at last! He and Sebastian intermittently burst into songs such as "My Heart Is the Heart of An Arab" and *"Viva la Alegria, Viva l'Amor!"*

Every landscape was appealing to Francisco—evergreen forests crystalled with snow, jubilant waterfalls, wood-choppers' huts with sea-blue smoke rising to the sky and, at last, the first glimpse of towered Segovia. In the haze of distance to the north would be Cuellar. Francisco said a brief prayer to himself, not wanting to trigger any more tree-fracturing debates with Sebastian.

In the valley, ancient church towers and white houses with red-tiled roofs shone brightly in the sun. The red earth lay fertile and dormant in anticipation of spring plowing. "How attractive Spain is," exclaimed Francisco. "So beautiful and peaceful."

"It's a good land," said Sebastian. "I may come back and settle near you in my old age, Francisco. Meanwhile, an exposure to Cuba sounds exciting. I still have a taste for the world and my spies tell me that Cuban *señoritas* are as torrid as the climate."

Francisco could only reply, "God has led us home."

"Or my good friend the Devil!"

"Ah, Sebastian, you are still full of mischief. You enjoy playing the devil's advocate just to bait me. No matter how hard you try to fight it, I've noticed that you've grown kindlier during our Armada experience. Perhaps your faith has strengthened in spite of yourself."

"Well, we both seem happy so what does it matter? Continue to worship your God and I will keep on worshipping the only two verities on this planet—the indubitable beauty of Earth and the enchantment and fickleness of women." With a laugh Sebastian spurred his horse down the snowy forest path towards the Eresma River valley.

They circled the great hill on the western side of Segovia and struck straight north on compacted red earth roads across the golden plain towards Cuellar. Ravens rose from the misty morning fields. Countrymen on burros greeted them with *Buenos dias! Hola,* or *Como le va?"* As the hilltop town of Cuellar began to appear, Francisco quietly said, "Oh, Sebastian, is there ever such joy as coming home after a long absence? It seems as if every hardship we faced has but whetted the pristine bliss of returning."

Sebastian thought for a moment, then rode up close beside Francisco. "My friend, beware of putting too much faith in anything, even a homecoming. Has it occurred to you that you have been gone almost two years? That is a long time, *amigo*." Sebastian looked intently at Francisco.

"What would you mean by that?"

"I mean that time often deals unkindly with life and leaves expectations unfulfilled. Things, important things, can change in two years."

Francisco threw a reproachful look at Sebastian and said, "True but not with my family." He wondered why Sebastian had emphasized their long time away.

By mid-afternoon the hill of Cuellar loomed and Francisco could make out his castle clearly. He strained to see whether there might be any figures standing on the parapet of its square tower. There were none. Often during past months he had pictured Zabella and his mother watching daily for his return. He spurred his horse and the dust rose behind him as he galloped towards the hill. It was the hour between mid-afternoon and sunset when the sun adds golden color to the empty winter fields.

When he reached the spot where he had waved goodbye to his mother and Zabella twenty-one months before, he drew rein for a moment, overwhelmed with emotion. *Have I really managed to survive the Armada disaster and all of its subsequent calamities?* He thought about the thousands of his comrades who had died, so often experiencing terrible and ignominious last moments. *How fortunate I am to be returning home safe and sound to an enthusiastic and loving wife and mother.*

He passed his vineyards and fields at the foot of the hill. They had an unkempt appearance. *Yes,* he thought, *there will be much hard work to do but it is fruitful toil in my own sweet fields with no one to threaten my very existence.*

They approached the gate of San Basilio, the old Arabic gate in the southwest part of town. In the open space outside the gate a dozen children and older boys were playing. Like a herd of colts they rushed to inspect the travelers and hurl a volley of questions.

"Who are you?"

"Where do you come from?"

"Where are you going?"

Before Francisco could answer, one boy recognized him. "It's Don Francisco!" "Don Francisco of the drowned Armada!" cried a second boy. "Couldn't keep his boat afloat," shouted another.

The boys crowded around Francisco's horse. Some boys were friendly but others made tasteless jokes. Sebastian wheeled his horse close and the boys moved aside. More children joined the encirclement, children whom Francisco recognized as friends of previous days to whom he had told stories and sung songs. One older boy said, "Better not go home, Armada-man."

Sebastian drew his horse close to Francisco's and quietly said, "Courage, friend, courage. Don't respond to them. They don't understand their cruelty."

A faint shiver ran through Francisco. *How can children be so unkind? I must forgive them but I hope these taunters won't accompany me all the way to the castle.*

The boys gradually ran off as Francisco turned his horse uphill, branching away from the plaza of San Miguel Church. Francisco noticed that a number of older people he knew stood at their doors looking at him as if dumbfounded, despite his waving to them. Sometimes they made incredulous gestures of their hands or shook their heads. *Have I been reported dead? What does this odd behavior mean?*

Sebastian came close alongside again and gave Francisco's knee an affectionate pat. "As we both know only too well, life is full of vicissitudes despite our highest hopes. Two years is indeed a long time, Francisco. Steel yourself. It is clear that something is not right."

Francisco was confused. *Am I not coming home after risking my life for my country? Isn't home one of the few places in a perilous world where one can feel safe? Am I not within a few hundred feet of my family castle, only a few minutes from my wife, mother, home and love?"*

Now he could hear a man's voice calling. "Don Francisco, Don Francisco! Wait, I beg of you. Wait."

He turned in his saddle and saw Dom Pedro, the priest, in black cassock and hat, hurrying towards him. Several villagers were following him. Francisco and Sebastian halted and dismounted. Francisco looked at the beautiful, wide-sweeping view of the red-gold plain capped in the distance by snow-capped mountains, a view about which he had thought so many times in Ireland.

Before catching up with Francisco, Dom Pedro turned and, sweeping his arms back and forth, called out to the people along the street, some of whom were now surrounding Francisco.

"Go home, please. Respect this brave officer of His Majesty, the King. May God preserve you from all the disasters he may have lived through during the past two years. All of you, go back to your houses. I will explain to Don Francisco, without your help, what has befallen."

Sebastian took hold of Francisco's arm as Francisco looked into the priest's eyes and asked, "What, Father, has befallen?"

The priest took him by the other arm and, with Sebastian, led him to a low wall and seated him on it. Taking his place beside him, Dom Pedro said, "My son, you have been brave, I know, these many months past in the King's service. You have been gone a long time. As details of the Armada disaster drifted in, you were presumed dead. It is God's miracle that you have returned." He put an arm around Francisco's shoulder.

"Yes, Father, but for God's sake tell me what has befallen."

"If you have been brave before, my son, you must be brave again. The Lord asks it of you."

Francisco felt a perfusion of strength from an inner well dug deep by his long ordeal. He knew he had the ability to remain calm in an emergency and he would be so now.

"I am ready to hear," said Francisco in a quiet voice.

"Very well. Let me tell it, little by little, my son. The remnants of the Armada began to return in September and October, a year and a half ago. They straggled in for several months. There was no sign of you. There was only the word that there had been some disobedience at sea and that you had been deprived of your Captaincy.

"Then came a few survivors by way of Scotland and France and with them came the word that you had drowned off the west coast of Ireland. Your blessed mother survived this news by only three weeks, my son. She died ten months ago, on the eleventh of March."

Francisco could not speak. His beloved mother. There was a long silence. Then Dom Pedro continued in a low voice.

"That is not all, my son. In the month of May, a certain merchant from Rome was returning from doing business in Salamanca and stopped here to rest for a few days. During that time, Don Francisco, I deeply regret to say, this man met and fell in love with Zabella."

"But she is my wife . . ."

"I also deeply regret to tell you that she was equally infatuated. They came to me begging me to perform a marriage ceremony since it seemed obvious that you were dead. I am glad to say, Don Francisco, that I refused to do so. The twelve months since your departure seemed an unseemly short time and the news of your death might have been only a rumor. I did promise them that I would consent to marry them if they waited another year."

Francisco took the priest's hand suddenly in his and gripped it tightly. "Thank you, dear Padre. Then I must rush to see my wife and convince her that I am indeed alive!"

"Alas, Don Francisco, the castle is empty. When the man from Rome rode out of Cuellar on a moonlight night towards the end of May, there were two people on the saddle."

There was stunned silence. Francisco plunged down, down, down into the blue-black waters of Donegal Bay once more. "Where is she, then?"

"In Rome probably. And your castle is under litigation. Your cousins of Velasquez and Albuquerque are contesting ownership in the courts of Madrid."

Francisco asked, "Did she not consider me at all when deciding these matters? Did she not grieve when word came of my death? Did she not hesitate at all in giving her love to this man?"

"I am sorry to tell you, Don Francisco, that while you were away she gave her love along with herself to a number of men both in Segovia and here in Cuellar. I think it was this behavior which helped undermine the strength of your mother before the news of your death reached her. She tried but was unable to change Zabella's behavior."

Francisco was shocked into silence. He looked out at the distant mountains and shook his head in disbelief. "It is almost impossible to believe, Father. In my mind, through the trials of many severe hardships, I made of her an image of angelic beauty. When the image falls it crashes hard, Father, and leaves a hollow as deep as Hell. She betrayed me and my mother and contributed to my mother's death. Can one learn to forgive such behavior?"

"I have reason to believe, Francisco, that her pattern of behavior was merely a continuation of years of similar behavior in Salamanca. That was the word I got from friends of mine there."

"My God, what a complete fool I have been! Perhaps I am lucky to be rid of her at this early date. I have no child, then, no son born while I was away?

"No, there was no child."

Francisco at last broke down and unashamedly wept. Dom Pedro signaled to Sebastian to let him weep himself out. After a few minutes, Dom Pedro said:

"Remember that she is still legally your wife, no matter how errant she has been, until one or the other of you dies or the marriage is annulled. I can arrange an annulment without difficulty or you can try to find her in Rome. Think over your problem carefully from a long-range viewpoint."

Dom Pedro laid a gentle hand on Francisco's head, blessed him, shook hands with Sebastian and walked back towards the church. The streets were deserted. The gold-edged shadows had deepened. Francisco took his horse by the halter and led it up the street, its hooves on the cobbles making a hollow sound as if the stones underneath were empty, as if the whole world were empty.

In a few minutes, he and Sebastian were at the castle gateway. They left their horses to graze outside. The gate was ajar. They pushed through and entered the courtyard. The galleries of arches and granite columns were as stately as ever. The elegant stairway was dusty but intact. The flower gardens created by his mother on the southern side of the enclosure had already yielded to weeds. Francisco, his heart hurting, moved across the courtyard. Several feral cats ran quickly away at his approach. The little vegetable garden was overgrown with small prickly-pear cactus and thistles. It was indeed a place of thorns.

Several sticks of the arbor had been loosened by wind and weather and now protruded like broken bones. The arbor grapevines sagged. The chair of Doña Maria Velasquez de Cuellar leaned at a stricken angle against the weather-beaten table. Francisco found himself gently stroking the back of the chair. There was a second chair which had fallen backwards onto the flagstones. A crow croaked raucously from a tower merlon.

Francisco put his right hand to his forehead. "Oh, Sebastian, this is not as I dreamed! I never fully realized that places in themselves are nothing. Places are people."

"My poor Francisco, there are risks in giving too much trust and too much love."

"Except to God, Sebastian. Strangely, He seems very close to me now."

Francisco put his arm around his friend's shoulders and began to walk around the courtyard. They came to the place under the gallery where the beautifier of the castle, his great-grandfather, had placed his carved stone shield more than a hundred years before. "*Agro Dolce*" read the device upon the shield, "Bitter sweet."

"A good definition of life," said Sebastian.

"*Agro dolce*," said Francisco softly. "*Agro dolce.*"

CHAPTER 39

Contemplating the Future

(February 1590)

While Sebastian visited his relatives for two weeks in Corunna, Francisco made basic repairs to his property and hired a full-time farm manager from Segovia to oversee all agricultural activities. Putting together herds of cattle and sheep would begin later. Many months of work would be necessary to restore his neglected agricultural estate to viability

After Sebastian had returned, they were sitting in chairs on top of the castle tower drinking *jerez* one late afternoon and admiring the Segovian plain with its mountain backdrop. "This view has immense charm, Francisco. No wonder you love it so."

"As I said before, Sebastian, and as I'm sure Stone Age Man used to say in his caves, places are people. I don't love it here any more. It now gives me a harsh, sour taste like wine with too much acid. I think I'll sell it to my Velasquez cousins with whom I have been corresponding. They used to spend summers here and we grew up together. They are good people who already love it and will take good care of it. They are affluent enough to give me a down payment and provide me with annual payments for the next ten years, allowing me to start afresh somewhere else. Emotionally, I just don't think I want to continue life here in Cuellar. That would require inspiration and *joie de vivre*, both of which have been crushed and driven from my soul." There was a break in his voice and he looked down at the ground.

"You'll be going away, then, to Rome, perhaps, to hunt for Zabella? The church says she's your wife 'til Doomsday."

"Never! She has made her choice. Let her have that Roman lover or any other man she desires and I suspect there will be many. I shall never look upon her face again in this life or the next. She helped kill my mother and has wounded me severely, making me feel like an absolute fool, which I was."

A silence fell between the two friends. Francisco filled their glasses. Finally Sebastian said, "You won't, I hope, enter a monastery?"

"Certainly not! The only benefit of that would be to garner more ammunition for our debates! Sebastian, you and your Devil have strongly won this round with the help of an experienced temptress, Zabella. I must now concentrate on what I have learned from the Armada disaster, our perilous peregrinations in Ireland and Zabella's foul contamination of my future aspirations here in Cuellar. I must make something good happen."

"Yes. I, also. That is clearly the best way to handle severe adversity."

"I must do something so life-changing that I will always be grateful to Zabella for impelling me into an entirely new lifestyle which I never would have done without her abysmal intrusion into my life."

"I am beginning to feel a new zest within you, Francisco. You are gradually becoming eligible to deserve my rare plaudits. What are you thinking of?"

"My lifelong dreams have been defeated by the bludgeons of your cagey Devil, Sebastian. I've lost everything I ever loved except you and my older brother in Cuba whom I haven't seen since I was a boy." There was a pause before he added, "From a letter I have learned that he now has six children, quite enough to fill the world with Cuellars but I would like to add a few myself."

The first red from the setting sun had begun to color the snowy flanks of the *Sierra de Guadarrama*. "God has thought it wise to take all this from me," said Francisco somberly," which I have loved all of my life—the town of Cuellar, my family castle, my thriving agricultural enterprises and the wonderful way of life here which my family has enjoyed for 250 years. I must confess that He puzzles me but I have decided to forget about God for awhile and begin making choices for myself alone."

"*Bravo!* You think of yourself much too rarely. It is time to ask Dom Pedro to annul your marriage so you can start completely afresh. You're only twenty-nine and the world is at your fingertips!"

"I concur! While you were away I asked him to start the annulment process immediately. I want to cut the cable of that scandalous and dishonorable anchor as quickly as possible."

"What are your plans while awaiting the annulment?"

"I may already have decided my future but first I must ride to Avila to tell Don Cristobal's family the terrible injustice General Bovadilla did to him, how very gallantly he died and to give them his Parchment of Exoneration from King Philip. I must also go to Saragossa to tell the wife of Judge Don Martin de Aranda of his drowning and of his last words of great love for her.

"I must also meet my Velasquez and Albuquerque cousins in Madrid to discuss the future of Cuellar Castle and its lands. I favor those from Velasquez whom I know better, especially Cousin Eduardo to whom I sent my book manuscript. We are all good friends. Now that I have returned alive it is my decision alone, not the court's. It is very gratifying that my relatives, who are very *simpático*, all want to continue the family tradition here in Cuellar. If a compromise is available which they all favor, that is fine with me. My price is a generous one and I would like to encourage family harmony. If there is disharmony, I will sell it to Eduardo."

"Any remaining business in Madrid?" asked Sebastian.

"I do want to stop by the King's Court, either at Madrid or the Escorial, to make sure that messengers and gifts go out to my friends in Ireland—to Donel's father, to Morven Mac Carthy, and to Sir Brian O'Rourke. Also to the Mac Sweeneys, Mac Donnell, Mac Clancy and the girl to whom I promised the red velvet dress despite her stealing my coins and my rosary! Also, I do want Alana to have a beautiful necklace from the King to match the lovely rubied heart she gave me."

"Why, in the name of Heaven, can't you take that gift to her yourself or send for her to come here? You told me you saw disaster coming for Alana's brother when you did the palm readings of his wife. They might be in danger already."

Francisco responded with reflective silence for a few moments, then said, "That is exactly what I intend to do, Sebastian. I have made up my mind."

"*Bravo, amigo!* After more than ten years of friendship, at last you are beginning to think like me! Makes a grown man want to weep. Fill our glasses and tell me more of your plans."

There was another long pause during which the rose color deepened over the plains of Segovia. "Within the month, Sebastian, I am leaving for Ireland to try to convince the lovely and enchanting Alana to join me for the rest of life's journey."

"Wow! Count me in! By what route will we travel?"

"It's not easy to get rid of you, is it, my friend? By land to Brittany, then hire an experienced boat captain to take me to Sligo and fetch me a bride. You must not go with me, Sebastian. You should accept the King's job offer and head for Cuba. You will soon be a General in charge of Deviltry, Laughter and Love in the Caribbean!"

"The King has delayed my life sufficiently that he can wait a few more weeks. I will inform him of your noble purpose to rescue a Celtic Colleen from the Curse of Spinsterhood. How can King Philip disagree? He did the same for Queen Mary of England many years ago, marrying her and briefly becoming King of England!"

"Too bad she died prematurely, requiring him to invade England to get his Kingship back!"

"I wouldn't miss your trip back to Ireland for anything. When you return with your bride, do you think you will accept the King's offer to become Commander of all Spanish ships patrolling the waters of Cuba?"

"That job certainly fits well with my training and experience but the Armada tragedy compels me to make a complete break with Spain's military adventurism. It has scarred my heart and soul forever. I want no part of war or killing ever again. I want to start my life over truly afresh. Cuba is bursting with new opportunities. Perhaps I will go into the import-export business and use my castle funds to build a lovely home in the hills of Havana. No more long absences from home! I want to spend my life with Alana and a growing family, not alone at sea on a warship."

"Amen. For the first time since we met as students at Salamanca, you are making complete sense."

"So be it, Sebastian. The Lord and the Devil work in mysterious ways."

CHAPTER 40

Tir Na nOg
(May 1590 to September 1591)

Three months later Francisco and Sebastian returned from Ireland to Cuellar. They had landed in the trading town of Sligo and kept a low profile. Francisco's knowledge of basic Gaelic helped ease their tactics. They learned that the hated English Governor of Connacht, Richard Bingham, had lured Chief Mac Clancy into a trap, captured him and beheaded him without trial. Most of his clan escaped into the mountains, including Alana.

Francisco got a message to her that Zabella had run off with another man. Francisco was annulling the marriage. He told Alana that he loved her beyond bounds, missed her terribly and would she come with him to Spain to marry him? They could then plan their *vida nueva*. A week later she got a message to him imploring him not to search for her. Sassenach spies and troops were everywhere. She loved him dearly and was excited by his proposal but needed time to think about such a complete change in her life course. Please give her two weeks.

A fortnight later, Francisco received her answer:

> My Dearest Love,
>   Yes, I want to marry you but please leave and don't try to locate me. I will eventually get to Ireland's southern

coast, hire a boat to take me to France and wend my way to Cuellar.

Your name tops the list of hated enemies of the English. If they catch you they will kill you quickly, as they did my noble brother. Let me come to you, my Darling. It could take many months but I will be successful.

I love you,
Alana

Francisco was frustrated by the absence of alternatives. His logical mind craved options. After long discussions with Sebastian, however, Francisco wrote her that he was thrilled with her acceptance and would follow her wishes. He would depart Ireland immediately and wait for her in Cuellar with overflowing love in his heart.

Sixteen months later, in September of 1591, Francisco was playing his *vihuela* and singing Spanish and gypsy songs while sitting on the wall next to the towered gate of San Basilio. He was facing uphill towards his renovated castle, his back to his reconstituted fields of wheat, oats, beets, onions and grapes in the plain below. As was his habit, he had walked down from the castle singing his favorite songs. Fifteen children of all ages were seated in a semicircle around him on the cobblestones, facing out the gate, sometimes singing with him, sometimes clapping in unison.

As he was singing *"Jelem,"* a haunting Romany song about love and nomadic gypsies, a cute little boy about two years old walked through the gate and sat down at Francisco's feet. He had curly bright orange hair, green eyes and an engaging smile. As if spellbound by the music, he swayed gently from side to side, gazing up at Francisco, who wondered why he had never seen the boy before.

When the song ended, Francisco, without thinking, spontaneously began to play and sing an ancient Gaelic song, "One Day When I Was On the Misty Mountain." The boy stood up and began to clap his hands in glee. Francisco looked into the boy's eyes and was captivated by his joyful enthusiasm. Francisco kept singing but put down his *vihuela*. He picked up the boy and put him on his left knee, patting his own right knee in rhythm. When the song was finished, Francisco softly touched the boy's hair and studied his strangely familiar face.

Suddenly, he was struck by a thunderbolt of recognition. He quickly picked up the boy in his arms, turned around and there was the enchanting Alana with her orange hair streaming over her shoulders onto a green-embroidered, white Spanish blouse. Her long black skirt was hemmed with red and green flowered designs. Francisco was transfixed by her flashing emerald eyes and the broadest, most encompassing Celtic smile ever to grace the gates of Cuellar.

While still holding the boy, he embraced Alana tightly. Tears formed in his eyes as he said, "You are the loveliest apparition I have ever beheld, my darling, and I am the most fortunate man in the whole world." He kissed her fervently.

The children stood up and clustered around the threesome. Alana, Francisco and the boy looked out upon the Segovian plain which was highlighted by brilliant gold and pink clouds and a fiery red sun just beginning to be indented by the purple-shadowed Guadarrama mountain peaks.

Stunned by the emotional drama and pervasive beauty of the scene, Francisco remained silent for a few seconds, then said in a quiet voice:

"Welcome, Alana, to our new life together, which will be forever cemented by our mutual love and devotion. May I assume that this captivating boy is your son? Will you introduce us?"

"Clancy, this is your father. Give him a nice kiss on the cheek." Then, putting her hand gently on Francisco's shoulder, she said, "His full name is Francisco Mac Clancy Cuellar but he loves his nickname, Clancy. I almost named him 'Miraculous Child of the Glen!'"

As tears rolled down his cheek, Francisco embraced his son. "God does work in mysterious ways, Alana. What an incredible gift from Him after all we've been through. He is indeed a miracle."

Holding hands, they gazed silently at the sun as it disappeared over the snow-capped mountains. Francisco continued, "What do you think of spending a few weeks here midst the beautiful fall colors, participating in our grape harvest and then beginning our journey to a new life in Cuba? I now have my annulment and we will be married before we leave. By the way, your Spanish has become excellent!"

"Thanks to Don Antonio de Alloa. I kept him busy every day after he was brought back from his capture at the river. My darling, you are the one true love you foretold for me when you read my palm at Castle Mac Clancy. You saw us uniting beyond the borders of Ireland in a place looking out on golden sunsets. Here we are! You predicted we would start our new life together in a distant land across the ocean. That sounded wonderful to me then and it sounds even more wonderful to me now."

A hedge sparrow was listening attentively and responded with his high trilling notes from the top of the town gate.

Alana switched to Gaelic. "We are going to *Tir Na nOg*! That is my favorite mythical place of the Celts, located far to the west on an island of eternal youth and beauty where sickness, aging and death do not exist. Food and flowers are always in abundance in that enchanted land and happiness lasts forever." She squeezed Francisco's hand and kissed him softly on the lips.

Francisco smiled and asked, "What if the magic doesn't work for me and I begin to age?"

"I think I would laugh heartily," answered Alana. "We Celts love to laugh, especially when we have triumphed over a life fraught with hazard."

Francisco and Alana each held one of Clancy's hands and started walking slowly up the cobblestone road towards the castle, swinging him gently in the air between them, all three laughing.

AFTERWORD

Julia Cooley Altrocchi's unpublished book manuscript of 1962 which I inherited was entitled *Captain Cuellar of the Spanish Armada and His Amazing Adventures in Ireland*. In the past century, abundant historical research has confirmed the truth of Francisco de Cuellar's personal summary of his adventures which he began writing on October 4, 1589. The document was written from the lodgment of his Inn at Antwerp after his many escapes from deadly peril.

The letter and historical synopsis were discovered and first published in Spanish by Cesareo Fernando Duro in 1885 in Madrid, followed by the English translation in 1897. It describes the tragedy of the Spanish Armada from its sailing from Lisbon through very stormy seas to its defeat in the English Channel by a clearly superior English navy. He records the Armada's tormented journey north around Scotland and the Orkneys until multiple ships sank or were wrecked en route home, mainly on the rocky coast of Ireland by the worst weather in more than fifty years.

Francisco gives extraordinary details of his remarkable struggles for life against the hostile forces and almost overwhelming odds encountered in Ireland. His survival was possible only because of his remarkable tenacity, fortitude and ingenuity combined with the help of a few Irish natives, including several women whom he describes as "most beautiful in the extreme."

Books which authenticate the veracity of Captain Cuellar's document and add accurate historical material include the following:

1. Allingham, Hugh. *Captain Cuellar's Adventures in Connacht & Ulster, A.D. 1588*. Elliot Stock, London, 1897.
2. Hanson, Neil. *The Confident Hope of a Miracle*. Doubleday, London, 2003.
3. Hardy, Evelyn. *Survivors of the Armada*, Constable and Co., Limited, London, 1966.
4. Howarth, David. *The Voyage of the Armada. The Spanish Story.* Collins, London, 1981.
5. Gallagher, P. & Cruickshank, D.W. *God's Obvious Design. Papers for the Spanish Armada Symposium, Sligo, 1988*. Tamesis Books, Ltd., London, 1990.
6. Mattingly, Garrett. *Defeat of the Spanish Armada*. Houghton Mifflin Co., Boston, 1959.

The basic story and incidents of *Fraught With Hazard* remain true to Captain Cuellar's chronicle of 1589. Although I have made many changes in the inherited manuscript and have added much new material, including the maps, the book still represents primarily the creative concept and vision of Julia Cooley Altrocchi.

Very little has been discovered in the past 400 years about Francisco de Cuellar himself. Like many famous historical heroes, details of his life after his dramatic adventurings remain obscured by the intervening centuries. Perhaps this is as it should be, adding enticing luster and mystery to his courageous tale.

Captain Cuellar through his bravery, resilience and ultimate deliverance deserves to take his place among the dragon-slayers and magnificent wanderers of history such as Jason, seeker of the Golden Fleece, Sigurd the legendary hero of Norse mythology and Odysseus of Homer's epic poem.

> There is a tide in the affairs of men
> Which, taken at the flood, leads on to fortune;
> Omitted, all the voyage of their life

Is bound in shallows and in miseries.
On such a full sea are we now afloat,
And we must take the current when it serves . . .

- Shakespeare, *Julius Caesar* IV, ii, 270-275

Printed in the United States
By Bookmasters